THE HERETIC'S TREASURE

Scott Mariani grew up in St Andrews, Scotland. He studied Modern Languages at Oxford and went on to work as a translator, a professional musician, a pistol shooting instructor and a free lance journalist before becoming a full-time writer. After spending several years in Italy and France, Scott discovered his secluded writer's haven in the wilds of west Wales, an 1830s country house complete with rambling woodland and a secret passage. When he isn't writing, Scott enjoys jazz, movies, classic motorcycles and astronomy. The Ben Hope novels have sold across the world.

To find out more about Scott Mariani go to www.scottmariani.com

Visit www.AuthorTracker.co.uk for exclusive updates on Scott Mariani.

By the same author:

The Alchemist's Secret
The Mozart Conspiracy
The Doomsday Prophecy

SCOTT MARIANI

The Heretic's Treasure

AVON

AVON

A division of HarperCollins*Publishers*
77–85 Fulham Palace Road,
London W6 8JB

www.harpercollins.co.uk

A Paperback Original 2009

2

Copyright © Scott Mariani 2009

Scott Mariani asserts the moral right to
be identified as the author of this work

A catalogue record for this book is
available from the British Library

ISBN-13: 978-1-84756-082-7

Set in Minion by Palimpsest Book Production Limited
Grangemouth, Stirlingshire

Printed and bound in Great Britain by
Clays Ltd, St lves plc

Acknowledgements

As ever, I'm indebted to the team of people who have helped make this book possible:

A big thank you to 'D', the real Ben Hope, and all at Prometheus Medical for advice and information. I'm also grateful to Elizabeth O'Connell at the British Museum for kind help in translating hieroglyphics.

To Broo and Robin of the Wade & Doherty Literary Agency: thanks again for your wisdom and support (and champagne, too!). And last but by no means least, I'd like to specially acknowledge all the team at Avon, whose energy, dedication and enthusiasm are an ongoing inspiration.

This one is for Malu Pothi,
a very special Bengal tigress

You are in my heart and none other knows thee
But your son 'Akhenaten'.
You have given him understanding of your designs and
your power.
The people of the world are in your hand . . .

From 'Hymn to the Sun'
The Pharaoh Akhenaten

Chapter One

The Western Desert, Egypt
Late September 2008

Nobody knew how many centuries the desolate Bedouin fort had been standing out here among the oceans of sand, its crumbling walls abandoned long ago.

Perched up high on a ruined tower, a vulture cocked its head and peered down at the line of dusty 4x4 vehicles that passed through the gateway and pulled up in the courtyard.

The passenger door of the lead vehicle swung open. A combat boot crunched down into the sand and a man stepped out of the car, stretching his cramped muscles after the long trek westwards and shielding his eyes from the sun's white glare. There was no wind. The air was a furnace.

The man's name was Khaled Kamal, and he was one of Egypt's most wanted terrorists. The man without a face, the one they could never catch.

The rest of the group climbed down from the

vehicles. Eleven men, all watching their leader. Nobody spoke. They wore a mixture of military combat fatigues, T-shirts and jeans. Six of them had stubby AKS-74 assault weapons slung over their shoulders. There were a lot more guns in the vehicles, the smell of cordite still on them.

Kamal scanned the empty ruin. He scratched the three-day-old stubble on his chin and thought about the events of the last thirty-six hours.

The diversion had worked well. If the choppers had been mobilised after the attack, then the anti-terrorist forces were hunting in the wrong place. Nobody would be looking for them out here in the middle of nowhere, hundreds of miles west across the desert from the Aswan to Cairo railroad where Kamal and his gunmen had opened fire on a northbound tourist train.

He smiled to himself as he replayed the fresh images in his mind. The passengers had been sitting ducks. Six carriages ripped to shreds by automatic fire. Blood on the tracks and on the sand. Another successful job.

But, after more than a decade, Kamal was getting bored with taking potshots at Westerners. Back in 1997, when the radical Gama'a al-Islamaya group had massacred more than sixty tourists at Hatshepsut's Temple near Luxor, Kamal had been the only one who got away from the anti-terrorist commandos. Since then he'd been involved in dozens of bus ambushes, tourist resort bombings, gun attacks on Nile river cruisers, assassinations of US business travellers. Kamal had personally packed the nails into the motorcycle suicide bomb that had caused carnage at the Khan al-Khalihi bazaar in 2005.

All small stuff. He had his sights on something bigger, much bigger. He had the talent, the will and the manpower. And, most importantly, he had links to networks all across North Africa, the Middle East and beyond. All he lacked was funding, and for the kind of plan that had been forming in his mind he knew he'd need a lot of it. A hell of a lot.

But all that was for the future. Now the dozen men needed to escape the murderous desert heat for a while. It would be cool later, but the sun was hot enough to cook a man in his boots. The ruined fort offered shade – as well as something more valuable. Kamal unscrewed the top of his canteen and poured the last drops of water into his parched throat. He tossed the empty container into his black Nissan Patrol and wiped his mouth with his sleeve.

Hani, the youngest of the crew, was gesticulating and grinning. 'See, didn't I tell you?' he laughed, pointing at the round stone well in the middle of the courtyard.

Kamal shot him a look. He hadn't stayed alive this long by trusting people, and he was about to find out whether he could trust this one.

They leaned over the edge of the well and peered down. The shaft was deep, disappearing into darkness. Kamal picked up a loose piece of stone and dropped it in the hole. He listened for the splash. Nothing.

'You said there would be water here,' he said. He slapped away a sandfly.

Hani said nothing, just made a face and shrugged.

Youssef joined them at the edge. His bald scalp was glistening with sweat. He wiped it and replaced the tattered green baseball cap that he always wore. 'We should have headed for the Farafra oasis instead.'

Kamal shook his head. The oasis area was only thirty miles to the south, and its inhabitants were mostly Bedouin. It should have been a safe haven for them – but you never knew when a police informant might be watching. The train attack would have been on radio and TV by now, the news spreading far and wide. He couldn't afford mistakes.

'Get down there,' he ordered Hani.

Hani thought about protesting, but Kamal wasn't someone you protested against.

The plump, bearded Mostafa and Tarek, the gaunt-looking eldest of the gang, fetched a rope from one of the 4x4s and fastened one end to its bull bars. They looped the other end around Hani's waist. The young man's eyes were bright with fear but he obeyed. He clambered up onto the stone mouth of the well and three of the men grabbed the rope to lower him.

It was a long way down. Hani's boots finally connected with the dirt at the bottom. He crouched in the darkness, scraped with his fingers in the dry sandy earth, then craned his neck upwards at the distant mouth of the well, up to the small blue circle of sky and the faces peering down at him. 'The well is dry,' he called up to them. His voice echoed in the shaft.

Then something dropped down the well, making him flinch. It hit him a glancing blow to the head and, for a second, he stood there dazed, unsteady on his feet. He put his fingers to his brow and felt blood. He groped at his feet and found the object that had been thrown down the well at him. It was a small folding shovel.

'You brought us here, you shit-headed little moron,' Kamal's voice shouted down at him. 'You can dig for the water.'

'Son of a whore,' Hani muttered.

He hadn't meant for the curse to reach their ears, but Kamal heard it echo up the well shaft and reacted instantly. The others watched as their leader stormed over to his Nissan and grabbed the massive M60 light machine gun from the back seat. He racked the cocking bolt. Strode back over to the well. Jabbed the long muzzle in the hole.

'Shine a torch on that bastard.'

Youssef grimaced. 'Kamal—'

Kamal's eyes blazed. '*Shine the fucking torch.*'

Youssef sighed. He knew it wasn't a good idea to clash with Kamal. They might have been friends for twenty years, but he could see when the man's blood was up. Which was most of the time. He pointed his Maglite down the hole.

Hani's face blinked sheepishly up at them.

Kamal didn't hesitate. He braced the M60 to his shoulder and let off a sustained blast of gunfire that exploded the desert silence.

There was nowhere for Hani to run. He tried to clamber up the wall, scrabbling at the clay in desperation. Kamal swivelled the weapon after him, the shots churning up the wall of the well. Spent cases showered the sand at his feet. Youssef held the torch steady. The other men backed away, covering their ears.

Above them, the lone vulture flapped away on broad, tawny wings.

Kamal stopped firing, and the M60 hung loose in his hands. He flashed a dangerous look at Youssef. 'Don't ever question me again, old friend.'

'I'm sorry.'

Kamal propped the gun against the side of the well. 'I never liked him anyway.' Grabbing the Maglite from Youssef's hand, he shone it down the hole and gazed impassively at the broken, mutilated corpse at the bottom, half covered in loose clay and dirt.

'We should move on,' Youssef said, averting his eyes.

But something else had caught Kamal's attention, and he swept the torch beam upwards. The raking gunfire had collapsed a section of the shaft wall about halfway up.

And there was something really strange down there.

It wasn't natural rock he could see behind the clay. It was smooth, worked stone, and he could make out odd markings on its surface. Rows and columns of them, man-made and ancient-looking. He narrowed his eyes. *What the hell?*

'What are you looking at?' Youssef said.

Kamal didn't reply, just pocketed the torch and tugged on the rope. It was loose, severed by the bullets and he pulled it up. It was spattered with Hani's blood, but Kamal didn't care about that. He looped it around his own waist. 'Lower me down,' he commanded.

With his legs and back braced against the shaft wall he held the torch with his left hand and used his combat knife to hack away at more of the clay, bits raining down to bury Hani's corpse below.

Digging furiously, Kamal could see this was no ordinary stone slab. It had corners that extended deep into the sandy earth. The more he dug, the more he realised that it was a chamber of some kind, buried far underground. And it had been there a very long time.

In the torchlight he studied the strange markings in the rock, and realised what he was seeing. These were hieroglyphs, and they had to be thousands of years old. They meant nothing to him, but he was smart enough to know there was something behind here. Something inside.

But what? He had to know.

He yelled for someone to toss down his bag and moments later the small military knapsack was tumbling down the hole. He caught it, slung the strap around his neck and reached inside for one of his plastic explosive shape charges.

As he emerged from the hole, the others were firing inquisitive looks at him. 'What is it?' Youssef asked, frowning. Kamal was already reaching for the remote detonator, gesturing at them to follow him.

Behind the cover of the trucks, he activated the charge.

Fire and smoke blasted from the hole. Flying debris showered down and rattled off the vehicles as the men shielded their faces. Smoke drifted across the sand.

Before the dust had even settled, Kamal was on his

feet and striding back towards the shattered well. He grabbed the rope and slithered over the edge, his torchbeam cutting through the vortex of smoke and dust.

The blast had crumbled away a large part of the shaft wall. Hani was now completely buried under a ton of dirt. But Kamal had forgotten all about the dead man.

His instincts had been right. There was some kind of hollow chamber here. His heart beat fast as the torchbeam settled on the long, ragged split in the stonework. The shape charge would have cut a neat square in a modern block wall, but this was solid stone and two-foot thick. Kamal used the shaft of the torch to knock away loose pieces of masonry, and stuck his hand through the hole. Cool air on his fingers.

He pulled out his hand, poked the head of the torch through the split and peered in after the beam.

And his breath left him when he saw what was inside.

Chapter Two

Near Valognes, Normandy, France
Seven months later

Except for the light rain that pattered off the roof of the little house in the woods, everything was still.

At the edge of the clearing, a twig snapped. A startled rabbit looked to the source of the sound and darted for cover.

The six men who emerged from the bushes were all wearing green camo fatigues. They kept their heads low as they stalked out from the foliage, eyes darting cautiously this way and that, moving towards the house with their weapons cocked and ready.

They knew the children were inside, and they also knew that it was going to be difficult to get in there.

The team leader was the first to reach the old peeling door. It was locked, but he'd expected that. He backed off two steps and covered the entrance with his pistol while the guy to his left flipped the safety off his cutdown Remington shotgun and blasted the lock apart. The deafening gunshot was absorbed by the electronic earpieces the men were all wearing. The shattered door crashed inwards.

The team leader went through first. As the entry man, he'd been taught that he could expect to take a hit, or at least get shot at, as he went in. He'd also been taught that, in the heat of the surprise assault, the kidnappers' fire would be rushed and inaccurate. He trusted his body armour to take the hits while he returned fire and took the shooters down.

But there was nothing. The hallway was empty, apart from the ragged splinters of door that the shotgun blast had blown across the floor. The team split into pairs, covering each other at every turn through the bare corridors. They moved slickly, weapons poised.

A door suddenly crashed open to the left and the team leader whipped around to see a man lumber out of the doorway. There was a stubby shotgun in his hands, the muzzle slung low at his hip. He worked the slide with a sharp *snick-snack*.

The team leader reacted instantly. He brought his Glock 9mm around to bear, relying on instinct and muscle memory more than a conscious aim. He fired twice. The kidnapper fell back, dropping the shotgun and clutching his chest.

The team moved on. At the end of the corridor was another door. The team leader booted it in as the others covered him. He burst into the room and the first thing his eyes locked onto was the old armchair in one corner with the stuffing hanging out of it. He glanced around him, adrenaline screaming through his veins.

In the other corner of the half-lit room was a dingy mattress, and on it were the two children.

The little boy and girl were strapped together, back to back. There were hoods over their heads, the girl's long blonde hair sticking out from under the rough sacking cloth. Their clothes were torn and grimy.

The six men quickly covered the room with their weapons. There was no sign of the rest of the kidnappers. The silence in the place was total. Just the wind in the naked branches outside, and the cawing of a crow in the distance.

The team leader strode up to the children, holstering his weapon.

He was just three steps away from them when he saw it. By the time his brain had registered the device attached to the girl, it was too late.

The flash was blinding. The team members instinctively covered their faces, mouths dropping open in shock.

The incendiary device was small but potent. The children burst alight, their bodies twisting and tumbling, the flames curling around them, melting their clothes. Beneath the flaming hoods, their hair burned and shrivelled. The sackcloth dropped away to show the white, staring eyes in the blackening faces.

The room was filled with smoke and the acrid stench of melting plastic as the burning mannequins collapsed onto the mattress. Fire pooled all around them.

A door flew open, and a blond-haired man walked into the room. He was tall, just under six feet, dressed in black combat trousers and a black T-shirt with the word 'INSTRUCTOR' spelt out in white lettering across his chest.

His name was Ben Hope. He'd been watching the trainee hostage rescue team on a monitor as they'd approached the purpose-built killing house he used for tactical exercises.

The team lowered their weapons and instinctively flipped on their safety catches, even though every pistol in the room was loaded with blanks. One of the men stifled a cough.

Behind Ben, another man came into the smoky room carrying a fire extinguisher. He was the simulated kidnapper the team leader had shot earlier. His name was Jeff Dekker, and he'd been a captain with the Special Boat Service regiment of the British Army before coming to work as Ben's assistant at the tactical training facility.

Jeff walked over to the burning mattress and the two half-melted dummies and doused the flames with a hissing jet of white foam. He looked up and grinned at Ben.

'Thanks, Jeff.' Ben reached into the pocket of his combat trousers and took out a crumpled pack of Gauloises and his battered old Zippo lighter. He flipped the lighter open, thumbed the wheel. Lit a cigarette and clanged the lighter shut.

Then he turned to the team. 'Now let me show you where you went wrong.'

Chapter Three

Two hours later the session was over and the weary trainees filed back along the dirt track through the woods to the main buildings. The rain had stopped, and the sun was coming out.

Ben glanced at his watch. 'I'd better get moving. Brooke's plane will be coming in.' It was a twenty-minute drive to the airport. He reached for the Land Rover key in his pocket.

'I can go pick her up, if you want,' Jeff offered.

'Thanks. But I've got to go and fetch some crates of wine on the way back. We're getting low.'

Jeff grinned. 'And we can't be having that.'

As the trainees wandered off to get a shower and a change of clothes, Ben left Jeff at the squat block-built office and walked across the cobbled yard to the battered green Land Rover. Storm, his favourite of the guard dogs, came running over from his kennel. Ben opened the back for him, and the big German Shepherd leaped inside, claws scrabbling on the metal floor. Then Ben swung up inside the cab, fired up the engine and steered the Land Rover off down the bumpy track through the gates, turning out onto the main road.

As he drove down the winding country lanes, he thought about the last few months, and how much they'd changed his life.

He could barely remember the young man he'd once been, the youth who'd given up his theology studies to join the British army at the age of twenty. He'd had the devil in him in those days. His relentless pursuit of perfect physical and mental fitness, his torturous determination, had seen him qualify for the super-elite 22 SAS regiment while still in his early twenties. He'd seen bloody conflict in theatres of war around the globe. Over the eight years that followed, he'd battled, sweated and bled his way up to the rank of Major.

But by then he already knew that his time fighting dirty wars for the benefit of shadowy figures in the corridors of power was over. When he'd finally run out of illusions, he walked away from the regiment forever and turned his skills to a higher purpose.

Crisis response consultant. That was a neat euphemism for the freelance work he'd become involved in for the next few years. The type of crisis he responded to was the havoc caused by a criminal industry that continued to grow worldwide at an alarming rate. From South America to Eastern Europe, Africa and Asia – wherever there were people and money, the kidnap and ransom business was booming more than ever before.

Ben hated it. He loathed nothing more than the

kind of men who exploited the emotional bonds between innocent people to create suffering and hard cash. He knew their ways and how they thought. He understood the hardness of their hearts, that they regarded human lives as nothing more than a commodity to be traded on.

And in the modern world, everyone was at risk. The predators out there had their pick, and you didn't have to be rich and privileged to get the call informing you that your loved one had been taken. The trade was so lucrative and so easy to operate that in many countries it had become bigger than drugs. In some cities, even moderately affluent families were foolish not to take precautions to protect their children from the grasp of the kidnappers. The problem was, the payouts available from insurance companies helped only to fuel the flames. It was a situation spiralling out of control. Everyone knew it, but as long as the kidnappers and the insurance companies kept raking in the money, there was little protection for the people that really mattered – the victims.

That was where Ben came in. When people went missing and their loved ones despaired of ever getting them back – when ransoms were paid and kidnappers reneged on the deal, or when the police screwed things up as they often did – that was when those people in need had a last line of resistance they could call on. He knew he'd helped a lot of people, saved lives, brought families back together.

But it hadn't been an easy life for him. Those years had been a time of sacrifice and pain, driven by the horror of what would happen if he failed to deliver the victim home safe and sound. It had happened to him only once – and it was something he could never forget.

He'd been forced to kill, too. Every time he'd done it, it sickened him so badly he'd sworn it would be the last – but it never was. What tormented him most of all was that he was so good at it.

So many times he'd wanted out. So many times he'd sat on his little stretch of beach near his rambling home on the west coast of Ireland and prayed for a normal life.

But how could he retire from it all and still sleep at night, knowing that people out there were in need of his help? It was both a calling and a curse, and for a very long time he'd felt as though he was simply destined to sacrifice himself to it. He'd tried to walk away – but every time it would call him back, drag him back in, and his heart wouldn't let him say no. Stability, happiness, relationships, any chance of a normal existence: he'd given up everything for it.

And it had cost the life of the one person he'd loved more than anyone. His wife, Leigh, had been murdered by a man called Jack Glass. A man he should have killed. He'd failed. She'd died.

For a long, long time, that had brought Ben to his knees. For a long time, he wanted to die himself.

Then, one night in Ireland a few months ago, while sitting alone on the empty beach, he'd had the idea that changed everything. More than a brainwave, it was like a miracle vision that had kept him awake all night and seemed to breathe life into him. By the next morning, his plans were already coming together.

It was a vision of a special training school, a place dedicated to passing on the skills that he'd acquired through hard experience. There was so much he could teach. As the demand for specialised kidnap and ransom insurance for high-risk business personnel rocketed higher each year, so did the need for trained negotiators to bargain with abductors and help bring people back safely. And, as the ruthlessness and organisation of professional kidnappers soared to overtake that of even the worst of the drug lords, increasingly expert training was necessary to help law enforcement response units deal with certain contingencies that normal agencies couldn't handle. Then there was the need for bodyguards to learn special close-protection skills to protect their clients from professional kidnappers. The demand for courses in situational awareness and avoidance strategies for people at risk of kidnapping. And more. It was a long list.

So Ben had started calling on former army contacts, mostly Special Forces guys he could trust, talking to people he hadn't talked to in years. He'd known from the start that some of the courses would involve firearms training. That couldn't be done in the UK, or his home in the Irish Republic. He had to move.

After a few weeks of searching, northern France had offered the ideal location in the shape of a tumble-down rural property called Le Val. Deep in the Normandy countryside, the old farm was close enough to the international airport at Cherbourg and the town of Valognes to be practical, yet remote enough to allow him to turn the place into the kind of facility he wanted. Over sixty acres of sweeping valley and woodland, accessible only from a long, winding track. The only neighbours were farmers, and the tiny village nearby had a shop and a bar. It was perfect for him.

When the sale had gone through, he'd said a sad farewell to the old rambling house on Galway Bay where he'd lived for many years, and got on a plane.

Now he knew he'd never look back.

In the months since the move, Le Val had been transformed. The renovated stone farmhouse had a large communal room for the trainees, and a huge stone-floored kitchen with a big table where they all ate together at night. Ben himself had always had simple needs, and his private quarters consisted of a modest two-bedroom apartment upstairs.

Meanwhile, new buildings had sprouted up quickly around the large farmyard: the main office, canteen, shower and toilet facilities, a purpose-built gym. Trainees were housed in a basic dormitory building across from the farmhouse. Six small rooms, two bunks to a room, with metal lockers painted olive green. It could have been a military dorm and it was a little rough and ready for some tastes – but there'd been no complaints. People knew they were getting the best. The only concession Ben had made to the softer corporate types, the suits sent to him by insurance companies keen to train up capable kidnap and ransom negotiators, was to build a slightly more luxurious conference room and lecture theatre at the far end of the complex.

But the real focus and purpose of the place was for the more hands-on stuff – the kind of training Ben specialised in, for the kind of people who were serious about learning to deal with extreme contingencies. A number of European military and police units had already signed contracts to come and sharpen up their hostage rescue skills with someone they knew was one of the best in the world. Ben had built two outdoor shooting ranges, one short for pistol and shotgun training, the other for long-range sniper work. The semi-derelict cottage in the woods had been stripped out and equipped with plywood partitions to create a maze of corridors and rooms where teams were drilled in close-quarter battle and live-fire room entry. Some weeks, the school was getting through thousands of rounds of ammunition.

The facility had been tough to set up. Apart from the arduous building work he'd had to jump through a thousand hoops and wade through a jungle of red tape to get the clearance for live-fire weapons training. There'd been official permissions to obtain from the French and British governments, from NATO, from everybody. He'd been buried in paperwork, glued to phones and knee-deep in mud and rubble for three months. He'd never been more thankful that his SAS days had left him fluent in several languages, including French, allowing him to wrangle with the local author-ities until his voice was hoarse.

But no sooner had the authorities finally greenlit

the operation, enquiries started flooding in from every-where. The diary had filled up fast and stayed that way for the last four months. Ben was in business, and he knew it was something he should have done a long time ago.

As he drove, he overtook a tractor that was ambling down the country lane. He waved, recognising Duchamp, one of the local farmers, at the wheel. The old guy waved back. Ben got on well with him, and had spent a lot of time in his farmhouse talking over bottles of excellent homemade cider. His visits to Duchamp's place invariably ended with him loading up the Land Rover with cases of the stuff. Duchamp's brother was the local butcher who supplied the meat for Le Val, and one of his cousins, Marie-Claire, came in to cook for the trainees.

When summer came, Ben was planning to hold a massive hog-roast for all the locals. He liked these people, their straightforward philosophy of life, their total attunement to nature, and the way they didn't ask too many questions about his business. They didn't care about the secrecy, the sound of gunfire, the barbed wire or the 'KEEP OUT' signs on the high wooden gates. As far as they were concerned, the facility at Le Val was just a glorified adventure tourism place for corporate types – and if they were happy, Ben was happy.

Approaching Cherbourg, he pulled up in the airport car park and left Storm sitting inside as he walked across the tarmac towards the arrivals building.

The woman he was coming to collect was Dr Brooke Marcel, a clinical psychologist and expert in hostage psychology who had been attached to police Special Operations in London for nine years. Ben had first met her back in his SAS days, when he'd attended one of her lectures and been impressed with her sharp mind and depth of insight. She'd been one of the first people he contacted when he was starting up his centre. Every few weeks, he flew her out to France to lecture the trainees – which, being half French on her father's side, suited her perfectly. He enjoyed her company and always looked forward to her visits.

He pushed through the glass doors into the arrival lounge. The London flight had just come in, and a small crowd was trickling through towards the car park and taxi ranks.

Brooke waved as she caught sight of him. She was wearing tight black jeans and a green combat jacket, and carrying a sports holdall. Her wavy auburn hair bounced as she walked. Ben noticed a couple of guys throwing appreciative glances at her. As he approached, she smiled and kissed his cheek. 'What a surprise,' she said. 'I wasn't expecting you. Normally Jeff comes to fetch me.'

'Jeff likes you too much. I don't want him getting too distracted.'

She chuckled. 'Don't worry. Jeff's a nice guy, but he's not my type.'

'So you're not into tall, dark and handsome.'

Brooke shot him a mischievous smirk. 'I prefer tall, blond and handsome.'

He ignored that. 'Let me take your bag.' He took her holdall and they walked out to the car park.

'So how's business?' she asked as they drove.

'Business is good. How's London?'

'As ever,' she said, rolling her eyes. 'I'm getting tired of it. Been there too long. Need a change.'

'I know the feeling.'

'Speaking of which, I've taken a few days off. I needed the break. OK with you if I hang around here a few extra days?'

'No problem,' he said. 'Stay as long as you want.'

On the way back Ben made a brief detour to the local vineyard to pick up some cases of wine. With the Land Rover loaded up, they headed back to Le Val.

'My God,' Brooke exclaimed as they drove through the gates and up towards the house. 'You finished it.'

Ben glanced at where she was pointing. 'The new gym? The roof went on two days ago.'

'Every time I come here, some new building has sprung up. Don't tell me – you did it yourself.'

'Not all of it. Just the walls and the flooring. I couldn't lift the roof beams on my own.'

'You're crazy. Remember, all work and no play . . .'

'Makes Ben a dull boy?'

'Or breaks his back. You don't need to do it all, Ben. Let your hair down a bit. Enjoy yourself a little. You're not forty yet.'

He laughed as he pulled up in front of the farmhouse and killed the Land Rover's engine. 'Maybe you're right.'

'I have an idea. Didn't you tell me you had an apartment in Paris?'

The small, spartan flat had been a gift from a client years ago, after Ben had rescued his child from kidnappers. 'It's hardly an apartment, Brooke. And I've been thinking of selling it anyway. What did you have in mind?'

'Well, since tomorrow's the last day of the course, maybe when I'm done lecturing we could jump in that shiny new Mini Cooper you never seem to use and head over there. It's just a hop and a skip up the road. A couple of days in Paris will be good for you.'

He hesitated. 'I don't know.'

'Come on. Jeff *can* manage without you here, you know. It'll be fun.'

He stared at her. 'You and me together in Paris?'

A smile tugged at the corner of her mouth. 'Why not?'

'My place only has one bedroom.'

She didn't reply as Ben stepped down from the Land Rover, threw open the back door and grabbed her bag. Storm jumped out, tail wagging, and headed for the barns.

After Ben had carried her bag inside and Brooke had gone to freshen up, he went over to the office to attend to some paperwork and check with Jeff that the trainees were happy and feeling looked after.

Jeff told him that he was taking the guys out in the van that evening, for a *steak-frites* and a few beers at the village brasserie. 'You fancy coming along too?' As he said it, he was opening drawers and sifting through papers.

Ben shook his head. 'Another time. What are you looking for?'

'The bloody number for those security-fence guys.'

'4642891,' Ben said instantly.

'How do you do that?'

'Do what?'

'Remember numbers like that.'

Ben shrugged. 'I don't know. I just can. Always could.'

'Beats me,' Jeff said, picking up the phone.

Dark was falling by the time Ben and Brooke sat down to eat in the farmhouse kitchen. Dinner was a rustic beef and olive stew with rice, and a bottle of the red wine they'd picked up earlier.

'I still can't believe how quickly you've got this place up and running,' she said. 'You've done an amazing amount in such a short time.'

'I might need you to come over more often, if things keep moving at this rate. Can you make it back here again in two weeks' time?'

'Love to. I like it here. I feel at home.'

'Me too.'

She cocked her head, resting her chin on her hand, watching him. 'You know what, Hope? In all the years I've known you, I've never seen you like this. You actually look happy.'

He smiled. 'You know what? I actually think I am.'

Brooke was about to answer when the phone rang from the kitchen sideboard. Ben tutted.

'Why don't you leave it? If it's important, they'll call back.'

'Better answer it.' He stood up and went to grab the phone. 'Hello?' He glanced at Brooke, as if to say, *this won't take a minute.*

But then he heard the voice on the other end of the line. It shook him to the core, instantly transported him back.

It was a voice he hadn't heard for a long time, and hadn't expected to hear again. He took the phone into the adjoining study and shut the door behind him.

When he came out five minutes later, Brooke saw the frown on his face. 'Is everything all right, Ben?'

He made no reply, and instead went back over to the sideboard, took out a bottle and a glass, cracked the seal and poured out a large measure. He suddenly remembered Brooke and grabbed a second glass. 'Sorry,' he muttered distractedly. 'Want some?'

'Sure. Something wrong?'

For an instant it was on the tip of his tongue to tell her, but he decided against it and shook his head 'It's fine. Nothing.'

'I can see it's not nothing,' Brooke said. 'Bad news?'

'I told you. It's not important.' He handed her the Scotch. Drained his own glass in a gulp and slumped in his chair at the table. There was silence between them. He refilled his glass. She'd barely started her first.

'Hey, where did the conversation go?' she said with a laugh.

'I'm sorry,' he muttered. He looked at his watch. 'Listen, it's getting late. I'm a little tired. Maybe I'll turn in.'

'I'll take care of the dishes.'

'Leave them. I'll deal with it in the morning.' He stood up, scraping his chair over the flagstones.

'See you tomorrow, then,' she said. 'Sweet dreams.'

But he barely registered it as he walked slowly out of the kitchen and headed for the stairs to his apartment.

Chapter Four

His heart was pounding and his stomach clenched.

A swirling confusion of blurs and echoes. Sounds of chaos and pain, screams and gunfire intermingled. Everything slow motion. The strobe of muzzle flashes illuminating the jungle; shapes flitting through the trees. The heat and the blood and the pumping terror. More of them coming. Always more of them.

Then the man walking towards him out of the killing frenzy, his body silhouetted black against the roaring flames. The eyes, wild and livid with hate. The fist clenching the gun. The big wide black 'O' of the muzzle, like the mouth of a tunnel leading to oblivion.

Then the searing, reverberating blast of the gunshot that filled his head, and the world exploding into white light.

Ben sat bolt upright in the darkness, the sweat cooling on his face. For a moment he was disorientated, and his pulse raced as he struggled to understand where he was. Then he remembered he was here. Home. Safe. Far away, where the horror could never touch him.

It's nothing. Just a dream. The same dream from long ago.

He reached out for the bedside light, but in his daze he felt his arm knock the lamp off the table. It fell to the floorboards with a crash.

Brooke was leaning back in bed in the next room, going over her lecture notes for the next day, listening to the wind in the trees through her open window and enjoying the lazy tranquillity of the place after the hubbub of London.

The sudden noise next door startled her. She jumped up, scattering papers, pulled on her dressing gown and went out into the dark hallway. She could hear Ben muttering and cursing through the door. She knocked, paused and went into his room.

He was sitting up in bed, naked down to the waist, setting a fallen reading lamp back upright on his bedside table. He looked up as she walked into the room. 'Sorry if I woke you,' he said. 'I knocked the lamp over.'

'I wasn't asleep. All right if I come in?' She moved over to the bed and sat down on the edge. 'You OK? You look a little pale. What happened?'

He rubbed his face. 'Bad dream.'

'Want to talk about it?'

'You sound like a psychologist.'

'I *am* a psychologist, remember?' She laid a hand on his. 'So tell me. What were you dreaming about?'

He shrugged. 'I don't want to talk about it.'

'Are you sure?' she asked gently.

'I'm sure. It was just a stupid nightmare from years ago. I get it sometimes.'

'You should listen to your dreams.' She paused. 'I bet it had something to do with the phone call. Am I right?'

He didn't reply.

She smiled. 'Thought so. The way you changed. Like a switch. You seemed so happy before, then the minute you got that call you started acting troubled, not saying much, drinking.'

'Sounds like a good idea. Want a drink?'

'Sure, I'll go down and fetch the bottle.'

'No need.' He kicked his legs off the bed, stood up, and went over to the wardrobe dressed only in a pair of black boxer shorts. She watched him cross the room. He opened the wardrobe door, reached up to the top shelf and brought down a bottle of whisky and a glass. 'Only one glass,' he said, carrying them back to the bed.

'I don't mind sharing. You go first. You look like you need it more than I do.'

He didn't argue with her. Sitting back down on the bed, he filled the glass halfway and took a long gulp before handing it across to her.

'Cheers.' She drank and passed it back to him. 'Nice. I like a man who keeps a bottle of good malt in his wardrobe.'

He knocked back more whisky.

'You going to be OK now?' she asked him.

He chuckled. 'I'm not a kid, you know.'

She touched his arm lightly. 'I can see something's wrong.'

'I'll be OK.'

31

She nodded, stood up hesitantly, stepped towards the door and paused with her hand on the handle. 'Sure?'

'Sure. Thanks, Brooke.'

'See you in the morning, then.'

Ben shook his head. 'I'll be gone before you wake up. I have to be somewhere.'

She frowned. 'I thought you were going to be here tomorrow.'

'Not any more. Jeff will look after you.'

'It's the phone call, isn't it? Something's up.'

He nodded, but didn't elaborate.

'So where on earth are you disappearing off to all of a sudden?'

'Italy.'

She looked surprised. 'What's in Italy?'

'Colonel Harry Paxton.'

'Colonel Harry Paxton,' she echoed. 'I'm guessing that's the person who called earlier?'

Ben nodded.

'And? What am I supposed to do, guess the rest?'

'And he's got a problem. He needs me to go to him, and that's what I'm going to do.'

'What kind of problem?'

'He didn't say.'

'And he expects you to drop everything and go all the way to Italy? He couldn't just have told you on the phone? Just who *is* this guy?'

Ben finished the whisky and was quiet for a moment. Then he said, 'He's the man who saved my life.'

Chapter Five

By 9 a.m. Ben's plane had touched down at the Côte d'Azur International Airport outside Nice. He threw his worn old green military canvas bag into the back of the first taxi he saw, and less than an hour later the driver was dropping him off in the middle of the coastal town of San Remo, just across the Italian border.

He quickly found a hotel off a bustling square in La Pigna, the old part of the town, and booked a room for a single night. He guessed that would be long enough.

The hotel was pleasantly cool inside, with marble floors that echoed every footstep. Any other day, he might have stopped to appreciate the simple beauty of the old building, or taken in the spectacular view across the rooftops of the rambling city, the clusters of church spires, the hazy Alpine skyline on one horizon and the glittering blue Mediterranean seascape on the other.

But today his mind was elsewhere. He dumped his

bag on the bed and headed downstairs, back through the lobby and out into the busy piazza. The sun was warm in the clear blue sky, and even the lightweight cotton jacket he was wearing was too heavy. He took it off and carried it over his arm.

The rendezvous point Paxton had given him was Porto Vecchio, one of San Remo's two ports. The colonel had been precise. A motor launch was to pick Ben up at the westernmost jetty at 12 p.m., and would take him out to sea for the meeting on board Paxton's yacht.

That part hadn't come as a great surprise to Ben. He could remember how his old colonel had always talked a lot about sailing. In his downtime he would invariably be heading for some sunny port. Had he owned a yacht back then? Ben didn't recall, and it suddenly struck him that he'd no idea what Paxton had been doing in the ten years since quitting the army.

It had been soon after his bravery award, when an already glittering military career had reached its highest peak of glory, that he'd suddenly and unexpectedly announced he was retiring. Ben had missed him, and had regretted that he hadn't kept in touch.

He'd regretted it even more when he'd heard that Helen Paxton, Harry's wife of many years, had died suddenly of a heart attack. He'd met her only briefly, years ago at some regimental function, but he could see how happy she and Paxton were together. Ben had been in the middle of a difficult assignment in South America when she'd passed away, and by the time he'd heard the news several months had gone by and it had seemed inappropriate to call Paxton out of the blue with commiserations. He'd let it go. That had upset him.

He might have lost touch with Harry Paxton, but he'd never forgotten – could never forget until his dying day – what the man had done for him. Ben had seen a lot in his life, and he generally had few illusions about human behaviour. He didn't use the term 'hero' easily. But Harry Paxton was one man who deserved it. About that, there was no doubt in Ben's mind.

And now he was going to meet him again, just like that. He wondered whether Harry would have changed much, and what he'd been doing all this time. But, more than anything else, he was wondering what this was all about.

His watch read just after eleven. He used the map he'd bought at the airport to orientate himself, and started walking west, towards the sea.

Beyond the crumbling stone archways and huddled buildings of the old part of town, San Remo had the buzz of any Italian tourist resort beginning to wake up at the start of another hot, crazy, hectic season. Ben made his way through the maze of streets, pausing here and there to check the street signs. He was deep in thought as he walked, feeling impatient and frustrated and wishing Paxton had told him more on the phone. Brooke had been right – it was strange that he'd been so evasive. Strange and worrying. He'd sounded downcast, nervous, distressed. Unless the years had done something dramatic to the man, Harry Paxton wasn't someone too easily fazed.

Which meant that, whatever this meeting was about, it was something very serious.

Ben could tell from the tang of salt in the air that he was nearing the sea. Then, emerging from a winding little street, he found himself looking out across the harbour, the long curve of beach and the calm, glassy blue of the Mediterranean.

Waves lapped at the shoreline. Within the walls of the port, the glittering white hulls of countless moored boats and small yachts bobbed gently on the water, hundreds of swaying masts pointing skywards. Ben counted ten or more long white jetties stretching out towards the sea. His eye picked out a path that would take him across the shingle beach to the westernmost jetty where Paxton's motor launch was due to collect him.

Some pitted stone steps led him down from the street. His shoes crunched on the pebbles as he made his way across the beach. The place was deserted, though he knew that would change pretty soon when the tourist season began in earnest. He could feel the warmth of the late morning sun on his face, the whispering sea breeze ruffling his hair. It was a world away from the bleaker Normandy climate.

He checked his watch again and glanced back at the harbour. He could see one or two people around, but the western jetty, his RV point, was empty. No sign of Paxton's launch. He walked a little further, to where the shingle butted up against the nearside edge of the harbour wall and another flight of stone steps led up to a walkway that connected to the dock.

Lingering a moment on the beach, he gazed out to

sea and thought sadly about what he'd left behind in Ireland. The house had been right on the Atlantic Ocean, and he'd loved to spend time alone on the rocky shore, just thinking and watching the waves and the gulls. He missed it. Knew he always would.

Just like he missed a lot of things.

He walked down towards the whispering surf, dropped down into a crouch and picked up a small, flat stone. He whipped his arm back and skimmed the stone at the water; watched it hit with a white puff of spray and bounce, splash, bounce and then disappear.

What did Paxton want? What was wrong?

As he bent down for another stone, something caught his eye, a distant sparkle of reflected sunlight out at sea. A small motor launch was tracking in across the water towards the harbour mouth. It looked as though he was about to find out the answers to his questions.

He dropped the stone, trotted up the steps to the walkway and started making his way towards the jetty.

That was when he heard the scream.

Chapter Six

It was the sound of a woman in trouble, her voice shrill and frightened. He froze, snapping his head around to look.

Fifty yards away, a woman in Bermuda shorts and a light denim shirt was running across the beach, clutching a bag on a strap around her shoulder, her long dark hair streaming out in the wind.

Close behind her were two guys. One was big and heavily built, the other slight and wiry, both wearing T-shirts and jeans. They looked serious. And they were faster than her, and gaining. Even at this distance, the look of terror on her face was enough to tell Ben that these weren't friends messing about.

As he watched, the men caught up with her. The slightly-built guy was two strides ahead of the other. He lashed out with his arm and his fist closed around the strap of her bag, yanking it towards him. She stumbled, kicking up a shower of pebbles. Screamed again. The guy yanked harder on the strap, and she went down. Then the bigger guy was on her, using his weight to crush her. A knee pressed into her stomach, a hand to her throat. She kicked out wildly, struggling like an animal. The smaller one tore the bag away, snapping the strap, and started rifling through it.

There was nobody about. Nobody was going to do anything, or raise the alarm. A woman was being robbed, or worse, right here in broad daylight.

Ben was already running. He dropped his jacket. Sprinted back along the walkway and bounded down the stone steps to the beach.

The smaller guy was tearing through the woman's bag while his burly friend held her to the ground. He had both her arms pinned down in one big fist and was slapping her around and tearing at the neck of her denim shirt with the other. Her hair was plastered over her face, head shaking violently from side to side as she screamed and thrashed. He was snarling and spitting in her face. Then the free hand went to his belt and out came the knife.

Neither of the men saw Ben coming until he was nearly upon them. The first to freeze and stare was the one with the bag in his hands, but Ben went straight for the other before his friend could let out a yell. The big guy was too busy to notice anything.

It would have been easy for Ben to kill him. Too easy. In the fraction of a second before he hit him, Ben's mind was racing through all the ways he knew of taking him down without inflicting fatal damage. Harder to do, but a lot less complicated after the fact.

So when the flying kick caught the attacker in the side of the neck, there was only enough force behind it to stun him and send him sprawling off the woman in a tangle of arms and legs.

The guy wouldn't be able to move his head for a month. But he'd live. He tumbled over, the big arms flailing, eyes and mouth wide with pain and surprise. The knife went clattering across the shingle. Ben doubled him up with a kick to the belly that was hard enough to wind him without rupturing stomach or spleen.

The other guy had already dropped the bag and was running away across the beach, heading for the steps that led back to the street. Ben thought about going after him, but a groan from the woman made him turn around. She tried to struggle up to her feet, but fell back, hair strewn over the ground. Her throat was mottled red, with angry fingermarks where the big guy had been strangling her.

Ben ran over to her and kneeled down beside her. 'Are you all right?' he asked urgently.

Five yards away, the big guy was staggering shakily to his feet, clutching his neck and stomach. He threw one look at Ben and made off, hobbling away after his friend.

Ben let them go. They weren't worth it. He turned back to the woman, gently took her hand and helped her sit up as she went into a fit of coughing. Her eyes were streaming, her breath coming in quick constricted gasps. She reached out with a trembling hand. 'My bag,' she wheezed in English.

Ben understood. The bag was lying three yards away, its contents spilled out over the pebbles. Makeup, purse, hairbrush, phone.

Asthma inhaler.

He snatched up the little blue spray. 'Is this what you need?'

She nodded urgently, grabbed it from him in a panicky movement. She jammed the spout into her mouth, pressed the plunger twice, shut her eyes for a second, then let out a long breath. Her shoulders drooped with relief. 'That's better.' She looked up. The look of alarm was draining quickly from her face, but her voice was shaking. 'You saved me.'

The accent was English. Home Counties, he guessed. He watched her for a moment. She was maybe in her early thirties. Her dark hair was loose about her face. She looked feminine, soft and vulnerable.

Ben glanced up the deserted beach. The two attackers had disappeared. 'You were lucky,' he said. 'Can you get up?'

'I think so,' she replied, sounding dazed.

He helped her to her feet. She was a little unsteady, her body leaning against his. The neck of her shirt was hanging open where the attacker had torn the buttons away. She noticed it, blushed and covered herself up. Ben glanced away and started gathering up her scattered possessions. He put them back in her shoulder bag and zipped it up. 'You should be able to find a cobbler in the town who can fix the strap for you.'

'Thanks,' she murmured.

'Are you with someone? Husband, friend?'

She shook her head. 'Travelling alone. Just passing through.'

'Do you have a place to stay?'

'I'm in a hotel across town.'

On the other side of the low harbour wall, the motor launch was pulling up at the westernmost jetty. It was exactly twelve noon. Ben didn't want to miss his ride, but he didn't feel right about leaving the woman on her own. For a second he regretted not having laid into the attackers harder. Should have damaged more than their pride. They might have wandered off in search of another victim. Or they might just as easily be watching from a hidden vantage point and waiting for another chance to get her. From the way she was glancing nervously up the beach, he knew she was thinking the same thing.

He didn't have time to deal with this. If he took her back into town and they reported the incident, there would be questions to answer to the local police, statements to take, hours of messing around – none of which would be any help to her.

There was only one thing he could do.

As he looked, a stocky guy in a baseball cap, white slacks and a polo shirt stepped from the motor launch. He tied it off and started walking down the jetty towards the dock, glancing up and down the quayside as if looking for someone.

Ben pointed at the launch. 'I have to get on that boat,' he said to the woman. 'I can take you somewhere safe, where you can get cleaned up and get some rest and a drink. Are you happy with that idea?'

She shot him a nervous glance. Doubt in her eyes.

'You can trust me.' He took out his passport and showed it to her. 'My name's Ben. Ben Hope. And I don't want to leave you here on your own. There's someone I have to meet. Come with me. It won't take long, and then we'll come back to San Remo together and I'll see you safely to your hotel. I promise.'

She hesitated, glanced again at Ben and across at the launch. She bit her lip in indecision. Then she looked back at the fallen knife, and shuddered visibly. That seemed to make up her mind. 'I'm Kerry,' she said. 'Kerry Wallace. And if you're sure it's all right, I'll come with you.'

'You're doing the right thing, Kerry,' Ben said. 'You'll be OK.'

The launch pilot was heading towards the walkway, glancing down in their direction. The guy returned Ben's wave.

Kerry was still a little unsteady on her feet. She brushed her hair back nervously, and Ben saw how pale her face was. Carrying her bag, he guided her gently across the beach and up the steps to the walkway. His jacket was lying crumpled on the hot concrete. He picked it up and handed it to her. 'You should cover up. You've had a shock.'

She accepted the jacket gratefully and pulled it around her shoulders. 'You're kind. Thank you so much.'

'It's nothing,' he replied. 'I'm sorry it had to happen to you.'

They met the launch pilot on the walkway. He smiled broadly. 'Mr Hope?'

Ben replied that he was.

'I am Thierry,' the man said breezily. His accent was unplaceable, somewhere between French and

Scandinavian. 'I am to pick you up and bring you to the *Scimitar*.' He glanced at Kerry. 'I was told you would be alone.'

Ben shook his head. 'This is Kerry Wallace. She's with me.'

Thierry shrugged. 'No problem. This way, please.'

They followed him up the jetty towards the bobbing launch. 'Are you sure this is all right?' Kerry whispered to Ben.

'As long as you're happy with it.'

'I don't have to be anywhere. I was just out walking, enjoying the sunshine.' She grimaced. 'I don't know what I'd have done without your help.'

'Don't think about it,' he told her. 'You'll feel shaky for a while, but it'll pass.'

Thierry fired up the boat engines as they climbed aboard. Kerry settled herself gingerly into a bench at the stern while Ben sat up front. The twin propellers churned up the water, and the launch powered away from the jetty and back out across the harbour.

After a couple of minutes Ben was watching the San Remo coastline shrink away and sink out of sight below the flat blue horizon. Thierry was taciturn, so he didn't bother trying to engage him in talk. Kerry sat quietly, still a little pale, holding his jacket tight around her shoulders as she gazed out to sea. Ben kept a watchful eye on her, looking out for signs of shock.

Twenty more minutes went by. The sea was flat and calm, a vast blue expanse stretching out as far as the eye could see all around them. The launch skipped gracefully over the water, sending up a light bow wave.

Ben was gazing back idly at the frothy wake, deep in thought, when Thierry's voice broke in on his reverie.

'There she is. The *Scimitar*.'

Ben turned to look. He'd been expecting an impressive yacht, but the sight of the enormous, sleek white vessel lying at anchor a few hundred yards across the water made him draw a sharp breath. The *Scimitar* was quite simply the biggest yacht he'd ever seen, her superstructure rising up as tall as a mansion on three stacked decks, the dappled reflection of the water shimmering along the huge length of her glittering white hull.

Thierry seemed pleased at his reaction. 'Beautiful, no? Fifty-four metres. What they call a superyacht.'

'And she belongs to Harry Paxton?'

Thierry's smile spread into a grin. 'You are kidding. He is not just the owner. He designed and built her. She is the flagship of the Paxton Enterprises fleet.'

Chapter Seven

The giant tri-deck yacht towered above them, dwarfing the motor launch as Thierry guided it around to the rear of the vessel and docked up. Ben gave Kerry an arm and helped her step up onto the boarding platform that jutted out a couple of feet above the whispering water. He followed her up a flight of steps to the lower aft deck. A couple of crewmen welcomed them aboard, shooting discreet but curious glances at Ben's companion.

Ben looked around him and tried not to be blown away by the opulence of his surroundings. He'd spent time in the homes of some extremely wealthy clients in the past, and stayed in some of the world's most overblown hotels. None of it meant much to him personally, but he had a pretty clear idea what luxury felt like. And the lower aft deck of the *Scimitar* had more luxury per square inch than anything he'd ever seen. The gleaming floor was some kind of exotic hard-wood. The long outdoor dining table was set for twelve. The Jacuzzi could accommodate twice that many. Ben could only guess at what the two decks above him looked like, let alone the interior.

A set of double doors swung open and a tall woman in a crisp white blouse and jeans walked up. 'Hi, Mr Hope. I'm Marla Austin.' She sounded Canadian. 'I'm Harry's assistant. Welcome aboard.'

'Good to meet you,' Ben said. 'Call me Ben.'

'Harry's just a little tied up on the phone right now,' Marla replied. 'He asked me to apologise. He shouldn't be more than twenty minutes.' She motioned towards a companionway that led upwards through a hatch. 'Would you like a drink? There's a fully stocked bar on the mid deck, right above us.'

'Can you take care of Kerry here?' Ben said. 'She's feeling a little unwell and could do with a lie down.'

'I got attacked,' Kerry said. It was the first time she'd spoken since leaving shore. 'Back on the beach in San Remo.' She blushed. 'Ben saved me. If he hadn't been there . . .'

Marla's eyes opened wide in shock. 'That's awful.' She glanced at Ben. 'I'll take care of her, Mr Hope.'

He thanked her, and watched as she led Kerry through the double doors inside the yacht. Left to wander around, he trotted up the steps to the next deck. It was even bigger and more opulent than the first. He spotted the bar in the corner, and went over to investigate.

Harry's PA hadn't been joking. The yacht had every thing, even his favourite single malt. What the hell was a former British army colonel doing living aboard this thing? He'd designed *this*? Ben was no expert, but it had to be worth at least fifteen million, maybe more. He was shaking his head in disbelief as he spooned ice into a Waterford cut-crystal tumbler and filled it with Laphroaig.

He looked at his watch. Harry wouldn't be around for another quarter of an hour or so. He explored the mid deck for a minute or two, marvelling at the wealth of it. Another companionway led upwards through a circular hole in the canopy above him and, fired by curiosity, he climbed up to see what was there.

He emerged onto the upper aft deck and took in the sweeping view of the sea. The breeze caressed his face and cooled him. He sipped the Scotch. 'Jesus, Harry,' he whispered to himself. 'What a life.'

Then a sound caught his ear. It was a strange sort of whistle, like something whizzing through the air. He turned to look.

By the time he spotted the solitary figure standing on the helipad at the far end of the upper deck thirty yards away, she'd already drawn another arrow from the quiver on her belt and fitted it to the bow she was shooting out to sea. It was a strange-looking weapon, almost futuristic, with large cam wheels on its limb-tips, telescopic sight, a complicated assortment of cables and a long stabiliser arm that jutted outwards from the handle like the barrel of a rifle.

The woman holding it was maybe twenty-eight, slim and lightly tanned, athletic-looking. Her long blonde hair was tied loosely back in a ponytail that blew gently in the breeze. She was wearing shorts and a sleeveless top that exposed the toned muscles of her shoulders and arms.

Ben couldn't take his eyes off her. She looked cool

and composed, completely zoned in and unaware of his presence as she focused on the floating island at least sixty yards away on the end of a long cable. In its centre was a round target face – a gold circle about the size of a dinner plate, tiny at that range, surrounded by red, blue and black concentric rings. The target was rising and falling gently on the swell. He guessed that made for a more interesting challenge.

He watched as she drew the string back, tension loading up in the bow's curved limbs, kinetic energy piling up behind the slim shaft of the arrow. All the best shooters he'd seen, the cream of the world's military marksmen, had that essential quality of stillness. That quiet assurance. It wasn't pride. It was the ability to lose themselves in the shot, to sublimate their ego completely so that, at the moment of release, they didn't even exist. Nothing existed except the target and the projectile. And he could see that same Zen-like, almost unattainable magic stillness in this woman as she stood there, oblivious of him watching her, poised like an Amazon against the sunlight, her body in perfect balance.

She released the shot. The bow tilted loosely in her hand as the tension left it. The arrow whipped through the air, covering the distance too quickly for the eye to follow. Ben shielded his eyes and saw it juddering in the centre of the yellow circle, right next to her previous shot. She certainly was good.

The woman nodded to herself, her face serene, just a hint of fierce satisfaction in her eyes. She reached for another arrow and brought it smoothly up to the bow.

Ben wondered who she was.

'That's Zara, my wife,' said a voice behind him, as if answering his thoughts. He turned and, for the first time in a decade, he found himself face to face with Colonel Harry Paxton.

The man hadn't changed physically, as far as Ben could see. He must have been fifty-four now, but he was still in great shape. He was casually dressed in jeans and a white cotton shirt. His greying hair was cropped short, just as it had been back in his army days. He had only a few lines to show for the intervening ten years. But somewhere behind the eyes, something had changed. There was pain there, some kind of emptiness. Ben had a feeling he was soon going to know more about it.

'She was the Australian Open champion when I met her,' Paxton said, nodding towards Zara. He smiled tenderly, a little sadly. 'We've been married eleven months now.'

Ben's eye lingered on her for just a moment. Then he turned and looked back at his old colonel.

'Hello, Benedict.' Paxton grasped Ben's hand and shook it with warmth and sincerity. 'It's so very good to see you again.'

'It's been a long time, Harry.'

'Too damn long.'

For a moment Ben thought about mentioning Helen. Saying how sorry he'd been to hear of her death. But it didn't seem right with Paxton's new wife standing just yards away.

'Thanks for coming at such short notice,' Paxton said warmly. 'You've no idea how grateful I am to you.'

50

'I knew you were a keen sailor,' Ben said. 'But this is something else. I'm extremely impressed.'

'My hobby became my business,' Paxton answered modestly, as though it was nothing. 'I'd always had an interest in designing and building yachts, but it wasn't until after I retired from the forces that I started getting into it more seriously.' He waved his arm across the sweeping decks. '*Scimitar* is the flagship of my little fleet. As well as manufacturing products to order for our clients, we run a charter business.'

Ben smiled at the idea of a yacht this size being so casually termed a 'product'. 'You've done pretty well for yourself.'

'As far as business is concerned,' Paxton replied, 'I can't complain. I've been lucky.' A dark look passed across his face, like a shadow. The sad look in his eyes suddenly intensified.

'But you didn't call me here to talk about business, did you?' Ben said.

Paxton sighed. 'No, I didn't. You've been very kind to come all this way. I owe you an explanation. Let's go somewhere private. Bring your drink.' He started down the companionway to the deck below.

As Ben went to follow him, he glanced back over his shoulder. Zara Paxton was laying down her bow, watching him from a distance. She waved tentatively, and Ben caught the flash of a smile before he looked away.

The interior of the yacht was even more spectacular than the exterior. Everything was burnished wood, and the carpets were thick and plush. Paxton led Ben through a series of corridors and opened a door. 'This is my private library. We can talk in here without being disturbed.'

Ben stepped inside the huge room and gazed around him at the floor-to-ceiling bookcases. He ran his eye along the spines of books. Shakespeare. Milton. Virgil. Row after row of military history and the age of sail. Where the walls weren't covered in books, gilt-framed oils of nineteenth-century warships glistened in the sunbeams that streamed through an overhead skylight.

Paxton motioned to a pair of burgundy Chesterfields. 'Please, have a seat.'

Ben sat down. The leather was cool against his back. He sipped his drink and watched Paxton for a moment. The colonel looked as if he was full of things to say, but didn't know where to start.

'What's this about, Harry?' Ben asked softly. 'You said you needed my help.'

'I'm sorry I was so mysterious on the phone,' Paxton said. 'It's something I can discuss only in person.' He walked over to a glossy antique sideboard that was covered with silver-framed photos. Some were of sleek white yachts in a variety of exotic locations, but most were family shots. Paxton picked one up, gazed at it for a moment, sighed and handed it to Ben.

Ben looked at it, wondering what this was about. The picture showed a man in his early thirties, rather bookish, serious-looking. Glasses, thin sandy hair, a slight belly, narrow shoulders.

'My son, Morgan,' Paxton murmured.

Ben glanced up in surprise. He'd known that Paxton

had a son, but the man in this photo wasn't what he'd have expected.

Paxton seemed to read Ben's thoughts. 'He took much more after his mother, physically. Our kind of life, the military life, wouldn't have agreed with him.'

'You talk about him in the past tense.'

Paxton nodded. 'I've made it quite obvious, haven't I? That's what this is about.' His throat sounded tight with emotion. 'The reason I asked you to come here is that my son is dead.'

'I'm so sorry,' Ben replied after a beat.

'He was murdered.'

Ben watched Paxton's eyes. It wasn't just pain in them now, but a depth of smouldering rage that was barely under control.

Paxton let out a long, trembling sigh, visibly struggling to stay calm. 'Let me get you another drink,' he whispered. 'Scotch, wasn't it?' He replaced the photo on the sideboard, reached for a decanter and topped up Ben's glass. He poured one for himself, drained it, refilled it.

Ben sipped the Scotch and waited for Paxton to go on.

Paxton slumped heavily in the matching Chesterfield opposite him. 'Morgan died in Egypt almost two months ago,' he said. 'He was found in his rented apartment. He'd been stabbed to death. There were thirty knife wounds in his body.' Paxton related the details matter-of-factly but his fingers were white against the crystal glass. He gulped back the last of the drink and set the glass down heavily on the table between them.

Ben watched every movement. He understood all too well what Paxton was going through. His heart went out to him.

But he still didn't understand why the colonel had called him here. 'What was Morgan doing in Egypt?' he asked. 'Did he live there?'

Paxton shook his head. 'Morgan is . . .' He paused, catching himself. Sighed and went on. 'Morgan *was* an academic at University of London. He taught history, specialising in Near Eastern Studies. That's what he was doing in Cairo. He was on a sabbatical, researching something to do with ancient Egypt.'

Ben listened intently.

'The police think it was an opportunistic robbery gone wrong,' Paxton continued. 'Whether he surprised the thieves, or they broke into the apartment while he was there, nobody knows. Or even cares. The Cairo police haven't caught whoever did it. They're not even close, and I don't think they're going to get results.'

'I'm so sorry,' Ben said again. 'I wish there was something I—'

'There is,' Paxton said, cutting him off. They locked eyes for a moment, and Ben tried to read the look. The sadness was still there, and the rage. But there was something else. The look of a planner at work, a tactician. The mind working hard through all that pain. Focusing, not folding.

Ben waited for the rest.

Paxton didn't keep him waiting long. 'You must be wondering why I called you here. The fact is, there's something I want you to do for me.'

Ben was silent. He could feel his neck and shoulders tensing up with anticipation.

'As you can tell, I'm not happy with the outcome of the police inquiry,' Paxton said. 'You wouldn't believe how sloppy and inept they've been.'

Ben had no trouble believing it – but he kept quiet.

Paxton went on. His voice was calm and controlled, his jaw set. 'As far as they're concerned, Morgan was just in the wrong place at the wrong time. These things happen every day, and they appear not to be pursuing it. Just one of those things.' Paxton paused and looked hard at Ben. 'And that's why I need your help. Justice hasn't been done.'

Ben waited. He was scared of what was coming.

Then Paxton came out with the thing he'd been dreading.

'I want you to go to Cairo,' he said. 'I want you to find whoever did this to my son. And I want you to kill them.'

Chapter Eight

'You were really unlucky,' Marla Austin was saying to Kerry. They were in the *Scimitar*'s VIP stateroom, far away from the library in which Ben and Paxton were talking. 'San Remo's normally a safe place. You don't hear of women getting attacked, as a rule.'

Kerry was reclining on a huge bed as Paxton's PA bustled around her. 'I still can't believe the way he handled those men,' she murmured, eyes half shut. 'He was so . . .' her voice trailed off.

Marla smiled at her from the foot of the bed. 'He certainly sounds like quite a guy,' she said. 'Now, you need to get some rest. You've had a nasty shock. I think your new friend and Mr Paxton will be talking for a while. I'll come back in an hour or so to check on you.'

'Thanks,' Kerry slurred in a sleepy voice.

'And I do think you should maybe see a doctor when you get back to port. Just to be sure. All right?'

'I will.'

'See you later, then. Rest yourself, OK?' Marla unfolded a blanket that was lying on an armchair. She laid it over Kerry. 'And if you get cold, there's a sweater there for you.'

'Thanks,' Kerry murmured again. 'See you.'

Marla tiptoed across the vast Oriental rug and slipped out of the stateroom. She shut the door quietly behind her and went about her business.

Inside the huge opulent room, Kerry lay on the bed with her eyes shut. She listened to the sound of Marla's footsteps disappearing up the passageway.

Once she knew she was alone, she opened her eyes and sat up straight, sweeping the blanket off her.

She scanned the room, alert and focused. The sleepy look was gone. She swung her legs off the bed and stood up. Strode across the room to where Marla had carefully laid her shoes and handbag. She picked up the bag, opened it and took out her asthma puffer.

She gazed at the little blue plastic pump for a second. Her eyes ran up its length to where the aluminium tube poked out of the top. Gripping the end of the tube between finger and thumb, she gave it a tug and it separated from the plastic body. She laid the plastic part on the chair next to her and turned the aluminium part over in her fingers.

It was the exact same size and weight as the medical product it was disguised to look like. The only difference was that, instead of containing a compressed solution of Salbutamol, the tube was hollow and housed a tiny electronic device. She shook it out. Coiled up with it was a miniature earpiece on the end of a thin wire. She fitted the mike into her ear and activated the device.

Somewhere miles above the earth, the GPS signal was instantly rerouted.

She knew her accomplices would already be listening on the other end, keenly waiting for her to report. It was all going smoothly so far.

'I'm on board,' she whispered.

'Copy,' said a man's voice.

'I'm going to take a look around.'

'Go easy,' said the voice. 'Don't get caught.'

'I won't,' she said softly. 'Out.'

She switched off the device, plucked the earpiece out of her ear and wound the wire around two fingers. She stuffed everything back inside the hollow Salbutamol bottle, and replaced it in the plastic body of the asthma pump. Slipping the pump in her pocket, she walked towards the door and opened it a crack. She peeked out into the corridor, glanced left and right. Nobody around. She slipped out into the passage. Her heart was thudding.

She knew she had to move fast. But she knew exactly where to go.

Chapter Nine

Ben and Paxton stared at each other in silence for a long moment.

Ben's glass was empty. He rotated it thoughtfully on his knee for a moment. Searched for the right words.

'I'm not a hitman, Harry,' was all he could answer.

Paxton reached for the decanter and refilled their drinks. 'It's a small community, our little world of ex-officers. Especially when it comes to men with your background. I've heard things on the grapevine. I know what you've been doing since you left the regiment. You didn't go into business, like me. Not conventional business, anyway. You tracked people down.'

Ben shook his head. 'You're making me sound like a bounty hunter. I found missing people. Kidnap victims, children mostly. That's what I did. And I certainly didn't do contracts.'

'But people died,' Paxton said, gazing at him steadily. 'At least, that's what I heard. Perhaps I was misinformed.'

Ben winced inwardly. 'No, you heard right. People died. But not like this.'

'Will you hear me out?'

Ben sighed. 'Of course. Go ahead.'

Paxton stood up and went over to one of the paintings on the wall. The gilt-framed oil depicted a naval battle, two sailing warships ripping into each other broadside on a stormy sea, jets of flame bursting through billows of white smoke, sails hanging in tatters. He gazed at it pensively as he went on.

'Let me tell you about my son. He was very unlike me. He was a man of intellect and philosophy, not a man of action. And I think he had problems coming to terms with that. He tried to follow in my footsteps, but it just wasn't him. He was a timid sort of man. That's not to say he didn't have talent. Somewhere inside him, I believe there was even the potential to be brilliant. But he wasn't ambitious. He had no drive, never really shone. Sometimes that frustrated me, and he knew it. Perhaps I was guilty of being too hard on him. I bitterly regret that now.'

Paxton turned away from the painting. 'Because the fact is,' he went on, 'that Morgan had one overriding passion in his life, which I never understood. It all started when he stumbled on something in the course of his research.'

'Stumbled on what?' Ben said, wondering where this was leading. He was still reeling from Paxton's request.

'You have to understand the academic mind,' Paxton replied. 'These aren't men who seek glory. It's hard for you and I to relate to that. They're men whose joy in life lies in things that we might consider trivial.' He paused. 'Morgan's great passion was a discovery he'd made to do with ancient Egypt. Some sort of papyrus relating to a minor political or religious upset that happened three thousand years ago. He told me a little about it, though to be honest I don't remember the details. It's not the kind of thing that would interest me, personally. But it meant a great deal to him.'

'And this was what he was researching in Cairo?'

Paxton nodded. 'He'd been working on it for a long time. When the opportunity arose to take a sabbatical year, his plan was to stay in Egypt for a few months. And so he'd taken all his research material with him. But when his body was found, all his belongings had been taken. They took his watch, his phone, his wallet and his camera. Even some of his clothes. And his briefcase, his laptop, everything. Which means that all his research is gone. It was all for nothing. All the effort he poured into it, the passion he had for it. All gone, because of some murdering little lowlife who thought he could make a bob or two passing on stolen goods.'

Ben didn't know what to say.

'I can't bear that my son is dead,' Paxton said stiffly. 'But what I can bear even less is that his legacy could be wiped out like that, like swatting a fly. I want him to have counted for something. Whatever it was that he was discovering, I want his academic peers to know about it and give him the due credit for it.' Paxton picked up the photo frame again and gazed at it, his face tight with emotion. 'If one of our soldiers died in action, we'd want him to be remembered. His name on the clock tower.'

Paxton was talking about the sacred SAS tradition

of inscribing the names of the regiment's fallen heroes on the clock tower at the headquarters in Hereford. 'A tribute,' Ben said.

'That's all I want for my son,' Paxton replied.

Ben thought for a long moment. 'I can understand that, Harry. I really can. And if all you wanted me to do was try to bring back his research material, that would be one thing. But you're asking for much more. You're asking me for a revenge killing.'

'Killing isn't anything new to you.'

Ben had to agree with that. 'But this is different, Harry. It's ugly.'

Paxton's eyes blazed for an instant. 'Who are they, Benedict? The worst kind of shit. You'd be doing the world a favour. And me.'

Favour. The word hit Ben hard. There was a lot of history behind it.

He looked down at his feet, his mind racing back in time. Half-repressed memories drifted in his imagination.

He looked up. 'May 14th, 1997. I haven't forgotten.'

'That isn't why I contacted you,' Paxton said. 'I don't want you to think I'm calling in old favours. I don't feel that you owe me anything, Benedict. Understood? I need you to believe that.'

Ben said nothing.

'I called you because I know you're the only person in the world I can trust,' Paxton said. 'And someone I know can see this through. I can't do it myself. I'm too close to it. It would kill me.'

Ben was silent.

'I would pay you, of course,' Paxton said. 'I'm a wealthy man. You can name your price.'

Ben hesitated a long moment before he replied. 'I need some time to think it over.'

'I can appreciate that, and I'm sorry for having sprung this on you.'

'One thing I can tell you right now. I don't want your money.'

'I appreciate that too,' Paxton said. 'But remember, the offer is there. You'd want expenses, at least.'

Ben looked at his watch. It was almost two in the afternoon. 'I know you want a quick answer. Give me until this evening. I'll call you and let you know my decision.'

Paxton smiled. 'Thank you. And whatever you decide, I'd like you to be my guest here on board tonight, for dinner. If your answer is no, then no hard feelings. If it's a yes, I'd like you to check out of your hotel and bring your luggage here. I already have a luxury cabin prepared for you. Stay here the night, and I'll brief you more fully before you leave for Cairo.'

Ben didn't reply. He was already working it over in his mind.

'Thank you again for coming all this way,' Paxton said. 'It was good to see you again, whatever happens.' He stood up.

At that moment, there was a knock at the door.

'Excuse me.' Paxton strode over and opened it. Marla was standing there. She was holding a phone in her hand. In the other was a neatly folded navy blue cotton jacket. Ben recognised it as his.

'I'm sorry to interrupt,' she said. 'It's Kazamoto,' she added quietly.

Paxton tutted under his breath. He took the phone from her. 'This might take a minute,' he said to Ben.

'I'll see you on deck,' Ben replied.

He left the study with Marla. 'How's Kerry?' he asked her out in the passage.

'Resting,' Marla replied. 'She had quite a shock, didn't she?' She handed him his jacket. 'She won't be needing this any more. I gave her something to wear.'

'That was kind of you.'

'Kind nothing. You're the one who saved her. A lot of people would have looked the other way.' She smiled. 'Anyway, I'll go and check on her again, now that your meeting's over.'

He thanked her, and headed towards the deck, jacket in hand. His legs felt heavy as he made his way back up the companionway. He stepped outside into the sunshine. The sea was shimmering blue, a gentle swell rocking the deck under his feet. He walked to the rail and looked out to the horizon. Reached into his jacket pocket for his Gauloises and Zippo. He slipped out one of the untipped cigarettes and lit up.

'Hello again,' a voice said.

He turned.

Zara Paxton was standing there. She'd let her hair down to her shoulders. It was waving in the breeze, catching the sunlight. She reached up with a slender hand to flick a curl of it away from her face and smiled, showing perfect white teeth. A twinkle of fun in her blue eyes.

He caught himself staring and glanced down at his feet, suddenly self-conscious.

'We weren't introduced,' she said with a soft laugh. He could just about detect the Australian accent in her warm voice.

'Mrs Paxton.' He held out his hand, and she shook it. Her hand was warm and tender, but strong.

'Please, call me Zara.'

'Ben Hope,' he said.

'Harry calls you Benedict.'

'Just Ben is fine.'

'Well, it's good to meet you, Just Ben.' Her gaze flicked down to the cigarette in his hand. 'Can I have a puff?'

Her familiarity took him aback. 'You can have a whole one, if you like.'

She grinned. 'No, just a quick puff. Harry can't stand me smoking on board. Or anyone.'

'I'll bear that in mind.' He offered her the cigarette, and their fingers brushed as she took it from his hand. She put it to her lips and took a drag on it, then passed it back to him. 'Thanks.'

For a few moments he couldn't think of anything more to say to her. There was a light in her eyes that he just wanted to stare at. Seconds went by, silence between them.

He finally broke it. 'I watched you shoot earlier. Hope you don't mind. You're very good.'

She smiled. 'I try.'

'Australian Open champion.'

'Missed out on the Olympics,' she said. 'Need to do better.'

Another awkward moment of silence passed. 'So you were in the SAS with Harry?' she asked. 'You're the first of his regimental comrades I've met.'

He shrugged. Didn't say anything.

'You don't like to talk about the army, do you?'

Her insight, her sudden serious look, took him aback. 'Not really.'

'You didn't like it?'

'I didn't like what it stood for,' he replied truthfully. 'That's why I left, in the end. But I didn't always feel that way. I loved it once. It meant everything.' Ben surprised himself with the way he was so open with her. He didn't generally discuss such things.

'Harry speaks very highly of you.' She paused. 'He told you about his son? So terrible.' She shook her head sadly.

'Did you know Morgan well?'

'Not that well,' she said. 'I only met him a few times. He and Harry didn't always see eye to eye. And I think Morgan had a problem with having a step-mother who was two years younger than him.' She paused. 'I know what it is Harry wants you to do.'

That surprised him. 'You do?'

'He told me. He just can't bring himself to go there and do it himself.'

Ben didn't reply.

'It must be so hard to visit the place where your son was murdered,' she went on. 'And to try to find his belongings.'

That was all Paxton had told her. Ben wondered how she'd react if she knew the rest of it.

66

'I was there with him in Cairo, when he had to iden-
tify the body. It was awful.' She shuddered. 'Poor Harry.
I really hope you can help, Ben.'

'I'm not sure yet whether I can or not.'

She nodded thoughtfully and glanced away from
him, looking out at the sea.

'So when did you two meet?' Ben asked.

'Eighteen months ago, in Sydney. I was organising
a charity event. He was offering the use of the *Scimitar*
for the occasion.'

'I thought you were a professional archer.'

She laughed. 'Have to be Korean for that. Anyway,
I don't work any more. Not since Harry and I got
married.'

'Harry's a lucky man,' he said, and immediately
wished he'd kept his mouth shut. Zara made no answer,
but he thought he saw her cheeks flush a little. She
turned her face from him.

Just then he heard voices coming from across the
deck, and looked around. Zara glanced over in the same
direction. Her husband was approaching, accompanied
by Kerry Wallace. As they came closer, Ben could see
that Kerry looked much more collected now. The pallor
in her cheeks had gone, and there was a lightness in
her step that hadn't been there before. He was glad she
was recovering from the ordeal on the beach.

Zara seemed to be studying her. 'Is that your wife,
Ben?'

'No, not my wife.'

'Your girlfriend, then?'

'Nothing like that. I don't know her.'

She frowned. 'But I thought – didn't she arrive with you?'

'It's a long story,' he said. In the background he could hear the burbling of the launch cutting around alongside the yacht's gleaming hull. He glanced over the side. Thierry was bringing it around to the boarding platform, ready to take them back to port.

Paxton walked up to Ben and shook his hand again. 'Remember, Benedict, whatever you decide, no hard feelings and I hope to see you this evening.' He turned to Kerry. 'It was a pleasure to meet you, Miss Wallace. Do take care. There are bad people out there.'

Kerry blushed. 'Thanks for looking after me. I'm very grateful to you, and to Marla. She was great. You're all very kind.'

'Please think nothing of it, my dear,' Paxton said with a smile.

'Shall we go?' Ben said. The launch had pulled up. He took Kerry's elbow to guide her over the side.

He looked back to say goodbye to Zara.

But she was gone.

Chapter Ten

Thierry dropped them off back at the jetty. Ben took out his phone to call for a taxi, but then saw one waiting on the quayside. 'I think that's for us,' he said to Kerry.

'They've thought of everything, haven't they?' she replied.

'They certainly have.'

The cab took them into the heart of San Remo, and dropped them outside Kerry's hotel. Ben walked her to the entrance of the lobby.

'I don't know what to say to you,' she said. 'I'm just so grateful you were there, and that you helped me the way you did.'

'Don't thank me,' Ben said. He took out his wallet and gave her one of the business cards he carried with him. 'My mobile number's on here. I don't think you'll need to call me, but don't hesitate if there's anything I can do. Promise?'

'Promise.' She flushed a little, then went up on tiptoe and pecked him on the cheek. With one last look, she turned and pushed through the lobby door into the hotel.

He started walking, and thinking back to what had happened on the beach. But, as he wandered back through the narrow, busy streets in the direction of his own hotel, he soon forgot about Kerry. There were more pressing things to think about. Of the two things that were weighing on his mind, he didn't know which worried him most.

The more he replayed Paxton's request in his thoughts, the more it made his head spin. He felt trapped by it. What was he going to do?

The other thing on his mind troubled him a great deal. It was something he'd never imagined could happen.

Every time he let his thoughts drift, he kept seeing Zara Paxton's face in his mind's eye. The sun on her hair and the sparkle of her eyes. He kept replaying their short conversation, the sound of her laugh. The warm softness of her hand on his. Kept thinking about the way he could have stood there on deck all day long with her, just talking, just being near her. And remembering the ugly little pang of annoyance he'd felt when Paxton had interrupted their brief conversation and he'd had to leave. Now all he could think about was that he was going to see her again that evening, in just a few hours.

He caught himself. *What the hell are these thoughts? What's wrong with you?*

Ben was furious with himself by the time he reached his hotel. He stormed straight up to his room, flopped on the bed and lay there for a while, his mind choked with conflicting emotions. They washed over him, pierced his skull, tormenting him. Feelings he'd thought he would never have again in his life. Not since losing Leigh.

He sat bolt upright on the bed.

You're lusting after the wife of the man who saved your life.

No, he thought, *it's more than that.*

Gritting his teeth with frustration he jumped up, strode over to the mini-bar and wrenched it open. There were some miniature bottles of whisky inside. He pulled them all out, gazed at them for a moment, then shoved them back inside. He didn't even feel like drinking. He didn't know what he felt like. It was all just confusion.

He slumped back on the bed. Fought to squeeze Zara from his thoughts – but all his mind did was race back to thinking about Harry. *What am I going to do?* he asked himself again.

Just when he'd thought he was out of it – out of that whole ugly world, done with field work and violence forever – fate was dragging him back in. This man wanted him to do murder on his behalf.

And yet Ben only had to cast his mind back to the events of May 14th, 1997, to remind himself just how much he owed Harry Paxton.

A day he'd never forget. There'd been a time, years ago, when the memory of it used to fill his dreams almost every night. Now the nightmare visited him only sporadically. But he'd never thought it was going to return to haunt him like this. He closed his eyes, and suddenly he was reliving the events as though it had happened yesterday.

* * *

71

For the entire decade of the nineties, the West African country of Sierra Leone, one of the most deprived and corrupt nations on the planet, had been consumed in violent civil war. Atrocities were committed wholesale – burnings, machete hackings and mass executions became commonplace. Towns and villages were razed to the ground as brutal gangs of self-styled rebels rampaged through the countryside, murdering and raping everyone in their path. Among the rebel fighters were child soldiers as young as eight, drugged and brainwashed into a state of zombie-like inhumanity, who had been handed automatic weapons and commanded to kill, kill, kill. Which they did, ruthlessly and without compunction.

Meanwhile, the rest of the world watched with little interest. Just another African tribal war. Just another Congo. Just another Rwanda. To the cold Western political mind, African lives were cheap, generally not worth intervening over. So the suffering and bloodshed went on unabated, and men like Ben could only watch and wait and hope that one day they'd be given the order that could help make a small difference to those innocent victims.

The worst of the rebel groups operating in Sierra Leone at that time had been a vicious militia force, several hundred strong, calling itself the Cross Bones Boys. Its thirty-year-old leader was a psychopathic despot known as The Baron, whose idea of amusement was to order the limb-hacking, followed not too quickly by the beheading, of entire village populations. Under his command, the militia was cutting a swathe of death through the country. Whatever political or idealistic motivation it might have started out with when war had first broken out had long since been perverted. For years, they'd been left pretty much to their own devices as civil war tore the country apart. There was so much blood soaked into the soil that it seemed nobody even cared any more.

But in May 1997, six years into the war, the Cross Bones Boys broke the unwritten rules by daring to kidnap, and then butcher, three Western aid workers. At that point, orders had come from on high that reprisals be carried out against The Baron and his militia. Ben's SAS squadron, headed up by Lt. Col. Harry Paxton, had been flown into the country aboard a UN aid aircraft and stationed clandestinely at the British Embassy in Freetown.

Officially, the SAS were never there. Unofficially, the mission objectives were simply to capture or kill as many of the Cross Bones Boys as possible, including The Baron himself, and chase off the rest. In theory, it was the kind of job the SAS were born for.

It hadn't been that easy in practice. With the whole country locked down in terror and suppression, MI6 intelligence agents struggled to gain any leads as to the whereabouts of the Cross Bones Boys and their leader. For two weeks the SAS squadron had waited on standby, ready to move at a moment's notice. It had been a frustrating, tense time.

Finally, agents had received a tip-off. The news was promising. In two days, The Baron and his second-in-command, Captain Kananga, would be passing through a Catholic mission on the banks of a river delta called Makapela Creek. The building complex had been deserted since back in 1992, early in the war, after the resident nuns and priest had been brutally slaughtered by another marauding rebel group. It was exactly the kind of place the Cross Bones leadership might hole up for a day or two and, according to the intelligence source, The Baron and Kananga would only have a light force of men with them.

An eight-man SAS team were quickly assembled and tooled up. A Chinook from RAF Special Forces 7 Squadron had flown them deep into the jungle. From the Landing Zone they'd trekked through the damp greenery and stifling heat. Reaching the Makapela Creek mission after dark, they'd got into position for the assault. It was meant to have been swift, surgical and decisive.

It hadn't quite turned out that way.

As the assault got underway, it quickly became clear that there was a much greater enemy force in the area than the intelligence reports had led anyone to believe. Militia soldiers suddenly burst out of hidden positions in the trees.

Hundreds of them. A rag-tag army swathed in cartridge belts, fired up with bloodlust and crack cocaine, heavily armed and running at them like demons.

Before anyone knew what was happening, a wild firefight had erupted across the whole mission complex. It had been mayhem, fast and furious and deadly. The jungle was lit up with the muzzle flashes of automatic weapons as the enemy started closing in. Gunfire exploded from everywhere. Within minutes the SAS team had found themselves encircled and cut off. They'd established positions in and around the buildings and fought back ferociously as bullets pinged and zipped all about them.

But they were massively outnumbered and, however many bodies piled up in the killing ground around the mission, more screaming Cross Bones Boys kept pouring out of the jungle. The SAS squad were in real trouble, and they knew it. Once they'd run out of ammunition, the militia rebels would close in to take them alive. The ensuing machete party would provide hours of macabre entertainment for The Baron.

One by one, Ben watched his teammates go down. Milne and Jarvis were blown to pieces by a rocket-propelled grenade round that ripped through the building they were firing from. Clark, the radio operator, had been crouched right next to Ben in the roofless wreck of the old chapel when he'd taken a .50-calibre machine gun bullet that left his head like a scooped-out walnut shell.

Ben had used his last grenade to destroy the concealed machine gun emplacement from where the shots had come. Moving low through the insane torrents of gunfire, he'd clambered over Clark's corpse and used the radio to call in air support. At that moment, he'd felt the hot punch of a bullet take him in the shoulder. He staggered, but stayed on his feet.

After that, Ben's memories were hazy. He remembered the searing heat of flames tearing through the mission buildings. The constant frenzied chaos of gunfire. The screams that pierced the night. The bodies of his comrades lying slumped where they'd fallen. The blur of shapes darting between buildings as the enemy kept on coming. His teammate, Smith, crouching a few yards away with his rifle tight against his shoulder, firing right, firing left.

Suddenly the sky had been filled with roaring thunder as the air support came storming in out of the night – two Lynx helicopters, spotlights sweeping the jungle, flame blazing from their miniguns. Trees snapped and fell, enemy soldiers were mowed down as others ran in a panic. The downdraught of the choppers blasted dust and vegetation into the air, tore the tin roofs from what was left of the mission buildings.

As Ben glanced up at the hovering aircraft, he was suddenly pitched forward on his face by a second bullet. His vision went dim. He fought to stay conscious, struggled to get to his knees. Tried to twist around to see who had shot him. He could feel hot blood spilling out of him.

He remembered rolling over onto his back. Through the haze of his fading senses, hearing another shot and seeing Smith crumple into the dirt nearby.

Out of the shadows stepped a man, silhouetted against the flames. He was holding a gun. Ben watched, dazed, as the man came closer and pointed the gun right at his head.

He remembered seeing the man come closer, step into the flickering firelight. The gun steady in his fist, ready for the killing shot. Behind the gun, the eyes in the black face wide and staring at him through the sights. Ben would never forget those eyes, bloodshot and wild, full of hate. They were burned into his brain forever.

After that, there had been a flurry of shots.

Then nothing. Just darkness and empty silence.

He was dead.

But suddenly, amazingly, he wasn't.

His next memory was of waking up in a soft bed in a military hospital. The first thing he'd seen when he opened his eyes was Harry Paxton sitting by his bedside, anxiously watching over him like a father with a sick child.

Eight men had gone in that day; only two had come out.

And if it hadn't been for Paxton, it would have been Ben inside one of the bodybags that had been choppered away from the smoking ruin in the aftermath of the firefight.

Harry Paxton, last man standing. It was one of those tales of heroism that was destined to become enshrined in regimental legend. For a long time afterwards, men had retold the tale – maybe they were still telling it now, years later. How Kananga, the Cross Bones militia captain, his forces scattering under air attack, had murdered Sergeant Smith and been just about to execute the injured Major Hope with a bullet to the head when Paxton had stepped in to save him. How the Lieutenant Colonel had selflessly got in the way of the bullet meant for the Major, before shooting Kananga with the last round from his pistol.

The rest of the story had come together gradually

as Ben recuperated in the hospital over the next couple of weeks.

By the time the reinforcement squad of paratroopers from 1 Para had arrived, it had all been over. Paxton's unit had accomplished its objective. The Cross Bones Boys were largely wiped out. Nobody ever knew what happened to The Baron. He'd either managed to escape, or never been there in the first place – but that didn't detract from the victory, and in any case he was never heard of again.

It had been one of the gravest losses of life in the regiment's history. Back in Hereford, the fallen had been laid to rest with full military honours. Amid the grief, Harry Paxton, arm in a sling from his bullet wound, was the hero of the hour. Plaudits and decorations had been heaped upon him, and soon afterwards he'd been given the promotion to full colonel.

As for Ben, nothing in his military experience had ever quite moved him the way Paxton's actions had done. He'd sworn he would do anything to return the favour to the man who'd saved him. Nothing – *nothing* – was ever going to stand in the way of that.

Chapter Eleven

Ben snapped back to the here and now, and glanced at his watch. Time was passing quickly, and Paxton was waiting for his decision.

But he already knew what he had to do.

There was no way he could refuse the colonel's request. He had too big a debt to repay the man. He couldn't just walk away.

One last time. Then the slate would be clean and it would be over. It was the least he could do for the hero who had saved his life.

And yet . . . the prospect of carrying out this task filled him with revulsion.

Unable to bear it any more, he jumped up and headed out of the hotel. The street outside was bustling with the first of the season's tourists. He filtered through the crowds and just followed his nose, trying to keep himself occupied with the ambience of the town, the architecture, the winding backstreets filled with interesting little shops, the colourful sprawl of spring flower displays that San Remo was famous for.

After a while he suddenly realised he'd wandered

near to the hotel where Kerry was staying. He checked his watch. A couple of hours had gone by since he'd left her there. He thought about going in to check on her, make sure she was OK. Maybe she'd have time for a coffee or something. The distraction would be good for him, to help get his head straight and calm his thoughts a little.

The hotel wasn't the finest establishment he'd ever seen, with a smell of damp in the air and a frayed path across the entrance to the reception desk. He guessed Kerry was a traveller on a budget, just passing through. It struck him how little he knew about her.

He walked up to the desk. Behind it was a bleary-eyed man reading a newspaper through a pair of dirty half-moon glasses. He peered over the top of them as Ben approached. 'Can I help you?' he asked in Italian.

'I'm a friend of one of your guests,' Ben replied. 'Her name's Kerry Wallace. I don't have a room number. Could you call her for me, please?'

The receptionist grunted, chucked down his paper and started leafing through the old-fashioned register on the desk in front of him. He flipped a few pages back and forth, peering through the dusty glasses at the columns of names.

He looked up. 'There is no Kerry Wallace here.'

'She's checked out?'

'No, *Signore*, there is no Kerry Wallace on the register. We have had no guest of that name.'

'She was here two hours ago. I saw her come in. Were you on duty then?'

The man's brow wrinkled with annoyance. He glared

heavily at Ben. 'I think perhaps you have the wrong hotel, *Signore*.'

Ben glared back at him. 'No, this is the right place. You're making a mistake.'

The receptionist let out an exasperated huff. He spun the register around on the counter. 'See for yourself.'

Ben ran his eye down the open pages. Frowned. Flipped a page. Scanned down the names. Flipped another page. Checked the dates going back a month. The guy was right. Nobody called Kerry Wallace, or Miss K. Wallace, or anything remotely resembling her name, had checked into the hotel.

'I'm sorry to have troubled you,' he said to the receptionist. 'My mistake.'

The man grunted again and flapped his newspaper back up in front of his face.

Ben left the hotel, puzzled. Had he got it wrong? He'd seen her walk in there. It was perplexing. He thought about it for a moment, and shrugged. A woman on her own, getting into trouble with men chasing her: maybe she'd wanted to be cautious and had given him a false name. But then again, she'd trusted him enough to go off to a strange yacht with him.

What the hell. It didn't matter that much. As long as she was safe. He had enough on his mind without worrying about Kerry Wallace.

He looked at his watch. He still had quite a while before he had to head back to the harbour for his dinner rendezvous on board the *Scimitar*. He walked on. It was warm and close, and dark clouds were beginning to gather overhead. The burning electric smell of a coming thunderstorm hung in the air.

He turned into the street where his hotel was, and the tall white building came into view a hundred yards further on. As he walked, he threw a casual glance to his right at a second-hand bookshop. It had a striped awning and stands of old hardbacks sitting out on the pavement. He'd always been drawn to those kinds of places, and sometimes when he was in Paris he'd spend a whole afternoon browsing around the bookshops by the Seine. It took him into a different world, helped him to forget the real one.

He glanced inside the shop. It was shady and inviting, and for a moment he was tempted to go inside, but decided against it. This wasn't the time.

Just as he was about to walk on, he noticed something inside the shop.

Some*one* inside the shop, browsing the shelves of dusty hardbacks.

She was wearing cream cotton trousers and a light blue silk blouse that accentuated the colour of her eyes and the gold of her hair. She turned to face him.

It was Zara Paxton.

Ben felt a surge of anger at the way his heart jumped when he saw her. He did his best to cover it up, and walked towards her with a smile. 'I didn't expect to see you here,' he said.

'Yes, what a surprise,' she laughed. 'I was shopping in the town, and I remembered this little bookshop. It's got a good poetry section.' She waved the book she was holding. 'I found this. Samuel Taylor Coleridge.'

'It's good to see you,' he replied uncertainly.

'Good to see you too.'

He stood there for a second, feeling awkward. 'I've decided what I'm going to do,' he said. 'I'm taking the job. Going to Cairo.'

'Harry will be so pleased. It's kind of you to help him.'

Another silence. 'Well, see you this evening, then,' he said. 'I'll be staying overnight on board, and I guess I'm leaving in the morning.'

'Ben, do you fancy going for a drive? I could show you the town,' Zara said suddenly as he was about to turn away. She looked down at her feet, tugged at a lock of her hair. 'If you feel like it, that is, and you've got some time. My car's just around the corner.'

He hesitated, nodded. 'Why not?'

She talked animatedly as they walked – a little too animatedly, he thought. Like she was nervous. So was he, and he didn't like the feeling. He worried that his answers to what she was saying were monosyllabic and trite. But the harder he tried to relax around her, the more he felt choked, and hated himself for it. *I shouldn't have agreed to this*, he thought desperately.

'This is it,' she said, pointing at a sleek black BMW Z4 Roadster convertible at the side of the street. She tossed her handbag in the back of the open-top car, bleeped the locks and they settled into the cream leather seats. She twisted the ignition and the engine rasped into life. As she put the lever in first gear, her hand brushed his. It was only the slightest contact, but she drew her hand away as though she'd touched a hotplate. She blushed. 'Sorry.'

'My fault,' he said, and cringed at his reply. *Jesus, Hope.*

They drove for a while, and she pointed out various architectural features of San Remo town. He listened, nodded, feigned interest. But he was more interested in her, and he felt bad about it. He shouldn't be here. This was all wrong.

But after a few miles around San Remo and its outskirts, something else was beginning to crowd his thoughts. Most normal civilians would have no way of telling when a professional surveillance team was following them. But Ben Hope was no normal civilian. He'd spent almost half his life watching his back, and a well-developed knowledge of surveillance techniques, coupled with a sixth sense for when he was being watched, was a combination he knew he could pretty much rely on.

Back in the streets after Kerry's hotel, he hadn't been so sure of it. Just a feeling. Then, when the big Suzuki Hayabusa motorcycle had passed three times as he walked, he'd started taking more notice. The rider was wearing a black leather jacket and full-face helmet with a tinted black visor, and he couldn't be sure – but it looked like a woman riding the bike.

When the dark blue Fiat slipped into the traffic behind Zara's Roadster and sat on their tail for three full kilometres, staying back in the traffic, trying too hard to make it look casual, he knew what was happening. The bright sunlight playing on the windscreen blotted out the faces inside. Two men, he thought. Who were they, and what did they want?

She noticed him looking in the driver's mirror. 'Something wrong?'

'Not exactly wrong,' he said. 'But not exactly right. Someone's following us.'

She looked at him in surprise, then peered in the mirror, frowning with concern. 'Are you sure?'

'Pretty sure.'

'Who?'

'I was wondering that myself.'

'What should we do?'

'We could stop the car, get out, walk back to that coffee bar we just passed, sit tight and see what happens. Or we could act stupid and try to lose them, in which case they'll know we know.'

'Who cares what they know?' she said. 'I'll lose them.'

'You think?'

'Hold tight.' She dropped down two gears and the engine note soared as she pressed hard on the gas. Ben felt himself pressed back into his seat. A gap opened up in the traffic ahead and Zara darted the sports car through just before it closed again. She laughed as she swerved across the road to avoid an oncoming van while a chorus of horns sounded angrily. She ignored them and stamped harder on the pedal. The BMW surged powerfully forward. Zara flashed through a red light, skilfully weaving in and out of more honking traffic.

Ben glanced back in the mirror. The dark blue Fiat was gone, left behind somewhere in the mayhem she'd created.

'How long did you say you've been living in Italy?' he asked over the noise of the engine.

'We're never in one spot for long. Harry takes the *Scimitar* all over the place. Why do you ask?'

'Just that you drive like an Italian.'

She smiled with pleasure. 'I'll take that as a compliment. Did I scare you?'

'Not yet.'

'I want to show you something,' she said. They were heading away from the town now, and out onto a winding coastal road with the sea on one side and sloping forests on the other. She took the bends fast and confidently, braked hard and took a turn to the left, accelerating smartly up a dusty single-track lane.

'Where are we going?'

'You'll see.'

The lane led steeply upwards, trees flashing by on each side. The air was heavy with the scent of flowers and vegetation. The storm was still gathering overhead.

Another couple of turns, and Ben was sure that whoever had been following them was truly left behind. But that didn't make him feel any happier about it.

Zara bumped the car down a rough track and pulled over onto a grassy verge. 'We're here?' he asked.

She smiled. 'This is it. We can walk the rest of the way.'

He followed her up the winding track through the trees. As they walked, her smile faded. 'Who would be following us, Ben?'

'I don't know.' Not *us*, he thought. Whoever it was, it was him they wanted. Which meant it was his concern, and he didn't want to burden her with it. He put his hand out to reassure her, touched her arm. 'It was probably nothing,' he said. 'I'm just paranoid. Wanted man in several countries. Too many unpaid parking fines.'

She laughed but didn't move away from the touch of his hand, and he dared let it linger there for a few seconds before snatching it away guiltily. She led him to a break in the trees up ahead. 'This is what I wanted to show you. Isn't it fantastic?'

Ben followed her gaze across the bay. From up here you could see the whole coastline, the sea stretching flat out to infinity. The sky was dull and leaden, but the view was spectacular.

'I come here sometimes just to look at it.' She paused. 'And to be alone.' She frowned up at the darkening clouds. 'Looks like we're in for some weather.'

As she said it, the first heavy raindrop spattered on Ben's shirt. Then another.

'Here it comes,' she said. 'We'd better take cover.' She pointed. A few hundred yards away, just visible through the greenery, a half-built house stood alone in a weed-strewn building site. 'Race you to that house,' she said. Her eyes were lit up with excitement, and her cheeks were flushed.

She took off, sprinting across the rough ground, and he followed her. The rain was coming faster and faster, soaking his shirt. As he ran he watched her, thinking how lithe and athletic she was. She jumped over a low fence and reached the half-finished house a second before him. They ran inside the shelter of the bare block walls, and listened to the rain hammering on the roof. She was giggling, only a little out of breath. Her silk blouse clung to her. She brushed her wet hair back from her face. 'That was fun. I win.'

He looked around him. 'Who owns this place?'

'Someone who ran out of money halfway through the build, I think. It's been like this for ages. Nobody ever comes here.' She wiped down her face and neck. 'God, I'm soaked through.'

The rain outside had become a storm. There was a flash of lightning, closely followed by a long, rumbling clap of thunder. 'This has been building all day,' she said.

Ben walked over to the glassless window and looked out. 'I love storms.'

'Really? Me too. I can never understand why people are afraid of them.'

Another lightning flash split the dark sky.

'You said you like to come up here to be alone.'

She nodded.

'Why do you want to be alone?'

She didn't reply for a moment. There was a silence, just the thunder crashing above them and the rain drumming on the tiles of the roof.

Then she said, softly, 'I need to get away from him, sometimes.'

'From Harry?'

She nodded again, biting her lip. 'Ben, I haven't been completely honest with you.'

He frowned, waited for more.

'You know earlier on, when we bumped into each

other in the bookshop and I told you I just happened to be in the area?'

'Yes?'

She paused. Flushed, turned away from him. 'I kind of lied. I wasn't interested in the bookshop. In fact, I've never been there before. I don't even like poetry.'

'I don't understand.'

'I was there because of you. I wanted to see you. But I got scared, so I hung around trying to pluck up the courage to go into the hotel and ask for you. I was about to walk away when you turned up.'

He sighed. Put a hand on hers. It was trembling. 'Zara, I—'

'I want to leave Harry,' she said, the words tumbling out. 'I'm not happy with him. Just when I was about to tell him it was over, we heard about Morgan's death. I couldn't do it to him then.'

He didn't reply. The rain was pounding even harder now, the storm right overhead. Lightning flickered in the sky, and another crash of thunder shook the house.

She ran her hands up his arms and pulled him towards her. 'I know what you think,' she breathed, her voice half drowned out by the roll of thunder. 'You think I'm just some frustrated wife looking for an adventure. But I'm not, Ben. It's not like that. When I saw you this morning, I . . . I've never felt . . .' she broke off.

He wanted to say he'd had the same feeling, but he couldn't find the words. It was all wrong, being here with her. She was Harry Paxton's wife.

She shivered again. Looked up at him with sadness

89

in her eyes. And at that moment, all logic deserted him. Their lips touched, just a little. Then the kiss became passionate.

He backed off, pushing her away. 'No. This isn't right. I can't do this. I owe everything to Harry Paxton. I mean everything.'

She looked up at him, blinking in confusion. 'What are you talking about? I thought you and he were just—'

'He saved my life, Zara. He took a bullet for me. Nobody's ever done that for me. I can't betray him.'

She stepped back, eyes widening. 'He never said anything about that.'

'He wouldn't. That's the kind of man he is.'

The storm was moving quickly on. The black clouds were dissipating, and rays of sun were filtering through. The rain stopped as suddenly as it had started.

Zara shivered. They stood for a moment in uneasy silence.

'We'd better get you out of those wet things,' he said, putting his arm around her shoulders. 'Let's go back to my hotel.'

Chapter Twelve

They didn't speak as Ben drove them back to his hotel. He pulled the car up and took Zara to his room. He didn't care about anyone following. That was something he could worry about another time.

As he sat on the bed and listened to the patter of the shower, he sank his head in his hands. He was wet through, but he didn't care. He felt terrible. 'Of all the women in the world,' he muttered to himself, 'I had to go and fall in love with this one.'

Love. He'd said it. The word hit him like a punch in the stomach.

Love wasn't an emotion that came too readily to Ben, and normally he would have laughed at the idea of love at first sight. But, no matter how crazy it seemed to him, he knew that was what had happened. There was no other way to say it. No point in denying it. No point in trying to understand it. There was just something about her, and the thought of her so close was driving him wild.

He heard the shower stop running, and a moment later the hum of the hairdryer. He closed his eyes and lay back on the bed. After a couple of minutes the bathroom door opened and Zara came out, wrapped up in a white bathrobe. She walked to the window, her eyes averted from him, and stood with her back to him. He stood up, wanting so badly to go over to her and hold her, kiss her. But he fought it, and turned away to get himself a drink at the mini-bar. It would have been so easy to let too much happen. Nothing could – that was a forbidden zone. They had to go back to the yacht together and face Paxton at dinner – there was no way Ben could go through that, knowing he'd given in to what he was feeling.

After a while, Zara's clothes had more or less dried out on the heated rail in the bathroom. She changed and brushed her hair while he quickly towelled his own and put on a dry shirt. They walked downstairs in silence. Ben checked out, paid his bill and they went out to the car.

Thierry was waiting for them at the jetty with the motor launch. Dusk was beginning to fall by the time they boarded the *Scimitar*.

As they came on deck, Harry Paxton was standing at the rail watching them. When he saw the bag in Ben's hand, his face broke into a smile.

'Look who I happened to run into in town,' Zara said to her husband. 'Just think, we bumped into each other in this little bookshop. Don't you think that was an amazing coincidence, Harry?'

Ben winced inwardly at the way she said it. Explaining too much. She wasn't a great liar.

But Paxton didn't seem to pick up on it. He was all smiles and charm as he got a crewman to take Ben's bag and show him to his cabin below.

The cabin was more like a luxury hotel suite, a three-room apartment with glistening walnut panelling, Persian rugs and antique furnishings. But to Ben it felt like a gilded cage, and he wasn't looking forward to the prospect of dinner with Paxton and Zara. He killed time in the vast cabin, leafing desultorily through some yachting magazines he found on a coffee table. The drinks cabinet in the living room was richly stocked with vintage wines, cognac and single malt Scotches. He filled a crystal tumbler with Glenmorangie and sat drinking it, staring into space, struggling to keep Zara out of his thoughts. Then he showered and shaved quickly, rummaged through his bag and changed into the only spare clothes he had left, a pair of black jeans and a black roll-neck sweater.

After half an hour there was a knock on his door, and the same crewman informed him that dinner was served.

The huge dining room was as opulent as anything on board a luxury cruise ship. Paxton greeted him, wearing an open-necked shirt and grey flannels. 'It's a bit showy, I know,' he said, gesturing at the room. 'But when your business is persuading oil billionaires and Japanese business tycoons to part with their money, you need to make a big impression. My clients expect the ultimate.'

There were three places set at the long, burnished dining table. Paxton showed Ben to the top of the table – 'As you're the guest of honour.'

Ben sat, glancing down at the array of silver cutlery and the sparkling glassware in front of him. A door opened and Zara walked in. She looked stunning in a grey cashmere dress that was cut diagonally across the shoulder. Her hair was piled up in loose curls, and she was wearing a simple but elegant gold necklace. Ben struggled not to stare as she walked the length of the table and sat down facing her husband.

Staff brought in the first course, a dish of seafood pasta. Paxton reached for a bottle of Pouilly-Fumé that was sitting in an ice bucket, and poured out three glasses. 'I want to thank you once again for deciding to help me,' he said to Ben. 'You don't know what it means to me.'

Ben sipped the chilled wine.

Zara was avoiding his eye. She raised her glass, and spilled some wine on the tablecloth.

'Are you all right, darling?' Paxton asked with concern. 'You seem a bit preoccupied.'

'It's nothing,' she said. 'I always get a headache after a thunderstorm.'

Paxton seemed surprised. 'You love storms.'

She flushed a little. 'It's OK. It'll pass.'

They ate. Conversation was sporadic, Paxton avoiding any mention of Morgan. Ben quickly ran out of small talk. Zara was quiet, toying with her food. The first course dishes were taken away, and the Steak Wellington main course arrived on a silver platter.

At a certain point Zara put down her knife and fork. She dabbed her lips with her napkin and pushed her chair away from the table. 'I'm really sorry about this.

But you'll have to excuse me. My headache's getting worse, and I have to go and lie down.'

Paxton was straight up on his feet, fussing over her. 'You should have said, darling. You go and rest, and I'll get you a painkiller.'

Ben was left alone for a few minutes as Paxton escorted Zara from the room. He knew she was lying – he'd have made some excuse to escape the atmosphere, too, if he could. The way Paxton so obviously cared for her made him feel even worse than before.

He was almost thankful that tomorrow he'd be leaving for Cairo, on a mission to avenge a man he'd never met.

Paxton returned a few minutes later, full of apologies for leaving his guest unattended. They finished eating, and Paxton invited Ben into an adjoining lounge that looked like a salon from the Palace of Versailles. He offered Ben brandy, and they sat and talked about the yacht business.

Finally, Ben had had enough of skirting around the main issue. 'We need to talk about Cairo.'

Paxton glanced at his watch. 'It'll have to wait until tomorrow. I'm afraid I have an engagement this evening. There's a chopper coming to pick me up for a business meeting in Monaco. One of my more eccentric clients, a Hollywood star who thinks everyone has to come to him. And of course they do.' Paxton smiled grimly. 'Make yourself at home. We can talk in the morning, and I'll tell you everything you need to know.'

Paxton left a few minutes later, and Ben heard the

helicopter come and go. He was glad to be alone again, even though his thoughts were in turmoil. He lounged back in his armchair and drank another large glass of brandy, trying to relax. But it wasn't working.

He wandered back through the maze of corridors and passages, glancing at the rows of gleaming wood doors. Caught himself wondering where Zara was.

Back in his cabin, he grabbed the bottle of Glenmorangie and a glass, slouched on a sofa, aimed the TV remote at the big screen on the wall and flicked through dozens of satellite channels before settling on some mindless zombie movie that he watched idly for a while. Eventually he switched it off and sat in darkness. His thoughts passed back and forth like conflicting voices in his head.

It's not right for Paxton to be asking me to do this for him. I don't know these men I'm supposed to kill. They're nothing to me. I have no personal reason to harm them.

But it's only a job. You've done it before.

Not like this. Not since the army. You swore you were never going to do that again. You gave up fighting other men's wars and killing other men's enemies.

Are you just trying to justify your feelings for this man's wife? You want to be with her, take her away from here. So you're looking for excuses.

He kept on like that, argument after counter-argument, until he felt exhausted. The fact was, he was here; and just being here, on board for the night, was as good as giving his word to Harry Paxton. Like it or not, he was committed now.

A sound made him sit up, suddenly alert. He

listened. Nothing. Just the whisper of the waves against the sides of the vessel.

But then he heard it again. A gentle tapping on his door.

'Who's there?' he called softly.

A crack of light appeared in the doorway, widening until he could see the figure there. It was Zara.

She slipped into the room and snicked the door shut behind her, closing out the light and merging with the shadows. He saw her dark shape move silently towards him, and step into the patch of moonlight that was shining in through the porthole.

'Zara, you can't be here,' he whispered.

'I had to come,' she said, sitting beside him on the sofa. She moved close, and he could smell her perfume. 'I need to be near you.'

'Why?' he said falteringly.

'I think I'm falling in love with you.'

'Don't say that.'

'It's the truth. I can't help it.'

'Harry loves you,' he said. 'I can see it.'

'It's over between me and Harry. It has been for months.' She let out a sigh. 'Sometimes things just don't work out. It's nobody's fault.'

'If he knew . . .'

'I know. It would destroy him. But you feel the same way, don't you?'

He couldn't answer.

'Don't you?' she repeated, a little more urgently. Her hand slipped into his, and she moved closer. The warmth of her body made his heart beat fast.

He didn't speak.

'You do, don't you? I know you do.'

Then she kissed him, and he could feel the quickening of her breathing.

'Harry's gone for a few hours,' she whispered, breaking the embrace. Her arms encircled his neck and she moved forwards to kiss him again.

He gently took her wrist and pushed her back. She sat there gazing at him in hurt bewilderment.

'I already told you this can't happen,' he said softly.

'I'm going to leave him. When this is over, when you do this job for him and he's not suffering so much. I'll wait a while, a month or two. Then I'm out of here. So it makes no difference what happens here between us tonight.'

'I can't do this to the man who saved my life.'

'I want you,' she said. 'I want to be with you.'

'I want you too,' he replied. 'But you have to understand. I'm not free to make that decision.'

'But you love me.' Tears glistened on her face. He wanted to kiss them away.

He hesitated. 'Yes,' he whispered.

'Is it so wrong, if it's love? If we didn't plan it this way, if it just happened to us? Why is that wrong? People do fall in love.'

'I'm sorry,' he said. 'It's just the way it is. Can't we be friends?' But it sounded empty and hollow to him even as he said it. He knew it could never be.

She pulled away, standing up and moving back into the shadows. 'I won't be here when you leave tomorrow.'

'Zara—'

'Goodbye, Ben.'

He watched her slip back to the door. The chink of light appeared and disappeared as she left the room.

He leaned back and closed his eyes. His thoughts swirled. He lost all track of time.

It had been a long time since he'd felt this lonely.

Chapter Thirteen

The feeling of loneliness was still with him when he woke up early the next morning. He sat up in bed and watched the sun break away from the flat blue horizon and begin its climb up across the lightening sky. The sea was a little choppier today, and there was just the slightest perceptible sense of motion as the superyacht rode up and down on the swell.

After a few minutes he rolled out of bed and forced three fast sets of twenty press-ups out of himself on the soft carpet. It helped to shift his focus and settle his restless mind, but not enough. He paced up and down for a while in the luxurious stateroom, finding the opulence of it almost oppressive. Then he went for a shower in the massive ensuite bathroom. Afterwards, he found a dark blue bathrobe on a rail and put it on, noticing in the mirror that it had the yacht's name embroidered in gold across the right breast. He wandered back out of the bathroom and flopped on the bed.

What a situation. He closed his eyes and tried to empty his mind, but it wasn't working. He grabbed his

Omega from the bedside table and looped it over his wrist, noting that it was after eight. He reached for the phone and punched in the number of the office in Normandy. He was expecting Jeff to answer, but the voice that greeted him on the other end was Brooke's.

'You're still there,' he said.

'You're losing it, Hope. I'm here for a few days. We talked about it, remember?'

He did. 'Sorry,' he muttered.

'I was kind of hoping you'd be back today.'

'No chance of that.'

'Where are you?'

'I'm still in Italy. But I won't be here much longer.'

'You'll be back tomorrow?'

'No. That's what I was phoning about. I'm going somewhere else.'

'So mysterious. Am I allowed to know where?'

'Cairo.'

She paused. 'Why?'

'Don't ask.'

'How long for?'

'I don't know,' he answered truthfully.

'You're being a bit weird, Hope.'

'I know. I'm sorry. There's nothing I can do about it.'

'What's wrong?' she asked, sounding anxious.

'Nothing's wrong. Tell Jeff I'll be back there as soon as I can.'

'I'm worried about you,' she said. 'Talk to me, Ben.'

'Nothing to be worried about. I'll see you again soon.'

After the call was over, he dressed and wandered up

on deck. Part of him was hoping Zara would be around, but another part dreaded it.

Out on the lower aft deck, the long table was set for breakfast. The scent of freshly percolated coffee drifted on the sea breeze. A basket was filled with warm croissants and pain au chocolat, and a jug of orange pressé sparkled in the sun. Zara was nowhere to be seen.

'My wife sends her apologies,' said Paxton's voice behind Ben. 'She had an early dental appointment and won't be joining us. Said to say goodbye to you.'

Ben turned. 'Morning, Harry.'

Paxton was smiling. 'Did you sleep well? I hope the noise of the helicopter didn't wake you.'

'I slept fine, thanks,' Ben said. 'How was your business meeting?'

'It went very well.' Paxton motioned at the table. 'Please, take a seat. Have some breakfast. I can have the chef prepare you bacon, eggs, anything you want.'

'This is fine, thanks, Harry.' Ben reached for a croissant, poured coffee into his cup.

They chatted over breakfast for a few minutes. 'I still don't know how to thank you for what you're doing for me,' Paxton smiled, the sadness in his voice tinged with warmth. 'You're booked on a Swiss International Airlines flight from Nice at eleven. There are a few particulars I wanted to run through with you. When you're finished, perhaps we could go down to the library?'

Ben put down his empty cup. 'I'm finished. Let's go.'

The first thing he noticed when he walked into the library was the attaché case on the table. Paxton went over to it, took out a slim card folder and handed it to Ben. 'These are all the details,' he said as Ben leafed through the contents. 'The address of Morgan's rented flat in Cairo. A copy of the coroner's report, and of my correspondence with the homicide department, for what it's worth. Your tickets will be waiting for you at the airport.' Paxton reached back inside the case and took out a thick envelope. He handed it to Ben.

'What's this?'

'Your expenses,' Paxton said.

Ben looked inside at the fat wad of banknotes.

'Egyptian currency,' Paxton said. 'Three hundred thousand Egyptian pounds. That's about forty thousand Euros, give or take.'

'That's too much, Harry. Take some back.'

Paxton shook his head vehemently. 'Keep it, please. Spend as much as you want and, whatever's left over, change it back to whatever currency you need for yourself.'

Ben shrugged. 'If you insist.'

'I absolutely do.'

Ben ran his eye along the row of pictures on the sideboard. He skipped over a photo of Zara in a swimsuit sitting by a pool in some exotic place. Next to it was a picture of Morgan. 'It might be useful for me to have a picture of him,' he said. 'Something recent, so I can ask around. It might jog a memory.'

Paxton picked one up and handed it to him. 'This

was taken the last time I saw him, just before he left for Cairo. One of the rare times he ever came to stay with us on board.'

Ben looked at the photo. It showed Morgan sitting in the *Scimitar*'s dining room, looking a little flushed and uncomfortable, holding a champagne glass. He was wearing a lightweight blazer, white with thin blue pinstripes. Ben could see the edge of a chunky gold watch protruding extravagantly from his cuff. It seemed somehow incongruous on him.

'Expensive-looking item,' he said. 'Was that the one he was wearing on his trip? You mentioned it was stolen.'

Paxton nodded sadly. 'A Rolex Oyster. He always wore it. It was a present from his mother. She had it engraved. He treasured it.'

'Tempting chunk of gold for a thief.'

'I know. Morgan wasn't especially streetwise. Academics live in their own little cocoon. I warned him about the watch, advised him to leave it here so that I could put it in the safe. But he didn't want to know.' Paxton let out a long, trembling breath. 'I should have been more insistent. I let him go out there and make himself a target. It was my fault.'

Ben was wishing he hadn't mentioned the watch. 'Don't beat yourself up, Harry. They might just have been going after his wallet, his computer, his phone, even his shoes. He was a wealthy Western tourist. It happens. People get murdered for a lot less.' He waved the photo. 'Can I take this with me?'

'Take it,' Paxton said. 'I have a copy.'

Ben removed the picture from the frame and slipped it into the folder with the other papers. There wasn't much, but he was already forming his plans. He put the folder in his bag and buckled the straps. 'I'm ready.'

Paxton looked pleased. 'Good. There'll be a taxi waiting for you at Porto Vecchio to take you to the airport.'

As Ben was about to leave, Paxton suddenly and unexpectedly embraced him. Ben could feel the tension in the man's body.

'I love my wife, Ben,' Paxton said in a low voice.

Ben recoiled at the words but tried to hide it. 'I know that, Harry.'

'I'm too old for her. I don't even know what she sees in me. But I love her more than anything. She's all I have left in the world.'

Ben just nodded.

Paxton patted him on the back, drew away and wiped away a tear. He collected himself quickly. 'I'll wait for your call, then.'

'I'll be in touch, Harry.'

Ben stepped off the launch at Porto Vecchio and got into the waiting taxi. Forty-five minutes later he was back at the Côte d'Azur International Airport across the border in Nice, grabbing his bag out of the boot and heading across the car park towards the airport terminals.

He wished he were getting on a plane back to Normandy, not boarding a flight bound for Amsterdam and then on to Cairo. He felt trapped. He thought of Brooke and Jeff, wondered what they were doing at that moment. They felt a long way away. He suddenly realised how much he missed having them around.

He was halfway across the tarmac when the sound of a car approaching fast made him turn. Zara's BMW Roadster had pulled in off the street and was speeding towards him. The car screeched to a halt five yards away from where he was standing and the door flew open. Zara jumped out and came running up to him. Her face was tense.

'What are you doing here?' he asked, bewildered.

'I couldn't let you go without seeing you again.'

'You followed me all the way from San Remo?'

'I had to say goodbye. I'm sorry I walked out on you last night. It was stupid of me to run away like that.'

'It was better that you didn't stay.'

'I meant what I said. That I love you. I do. I want us to be together. I'll find a way, some way that won't hurt Harry.'

'Don't talk like that. I can't listen to this. It's not right.'

'You know it's right,' she said. 'We both do.' She held him tight. He stroked her hair as she moved her face up to his. The struggle was killing him. He gave in to the kiss. They embraced for a few seconds, and then he pushed her away reluctantly, his throat tight. 'I've got to go. I'm going to miss this flight. I've got business to take care of.'

'Stay with me. Take the next flight.'

'You know I can't do that.'

She reached up and gently caressed his cheek. 'Take care.'

'You too,' he said.

'When will I see you again?'

'I don't know.' He turned to go, tearing himself away.

'Call me,' she said as he walked off. 'Promise you'll call me.'

He wanted to turn back and hold her again, be with her, take her somewhere where they could be alone. But he kept walking. Just before he pushed through the doors into the terminal building, he glanced back. She was standing there by her car, a small, forlorn figure in the distance. She waved. He sighed and entered the building.

Across the car park, two men had been sitting in a car watching the whole thing. The driver had been about to get out to follow their target inside the airport to find out what flight he was getting on.

Then the BMW had screeched up and the Paxton woman had jumped out. The man had ducked back inside the car, not wanting to be spotted.

He turned to his companion in the passenger seat, who was wearing a white foam neck brace. 'What's going on here? What the hell is she doing?'

The passenger looked grim as he watched Zara Paxton with her arms around the target. 'Christ,' he groaned. 'She wasn't supposed to get emotionally involved with him.' He glanced at his colleague, wincing at the pain that the movement cost him. 'You think she's told him anything?'

The other one sighed. 'I don't know. We'd just better pray she isn't going to fuck this whole thing up for us.'

Chapter Fourteen

Pierre Claudel was a master at what he did. In the shadowy circles in which he moved, his name was a whispered legend. The truth about his life was a closed book, and he preferred to keep it that way.

At the age of forty-two, he was a confirmed member of the Cairo rich list. He was tall and suave, always well-dressed, impeccably mannered and extremely eligible. He played tennis and polo, enjoyed fine art and fine wine, had a private box at the opera, could recommend the best restaurants and hotels in any city in the world, and was seldom seen in public without the latest addition to the procession of expensive, but always eminently replaceable, women who passed through his life and bed. He drove a bright red Ferrari and lived in a mock Tuscan villa set in 1.6 acres of clipped and manicured country parkland in Hyde Park, one of Cairo's most exclusive gated communities.

As to where all this had come from, Claudel was highly secretive about the nature of his business. When asked what he did, he would just smile his charming smile, give a modest little wave of his hand and reply that he specialised in cultural exports. That answer was good enough for the small-talking country-club elite and the women he seduced at the city's fashionable high-society parties. They didn't need to know the truth. Nobody did.

A long time ago, back in his native France, Pierre Claudel had been a passionate archaeology scholar. As a young student he'd worked himself mercilessly, graduated top of all the classes he'd ever taken and formed the makings of a glittering career in academia. He'd taken a lecturer's post at the Sorbonne, where some of the students were older than he was. He'd done well, settled into a comfortable if not terribly luxurious lifestyle. Found himself a nice girlfriend, Nadine, and moved into a flat together. A little car, a little dog, a cosy little Parisian routine. Talk of marriage, starting a family one day.

It would have satisfied a lot of men, but that wasn't the way Pierre Claudel's mind worked. He wanted more. And within a year or two, he was becoming restless.

Then, at the age of twenty-seven, his passion for Egyptology had brought him to his first excavation in the Western Desert and he'd felt the first kiss of adventure. He'd been hooked. It suddenly hit him what he should be doing with his life. Fortune and glory were the promises that lurked under the sands, and he was going to find them.

On his return to France he instantly started winding up his old life there. He quit his job, left Nadine weeping over a brief note on the kitchen table. With his whole world in a suitcase he boarded a flight, stepped down on the hot Egyptian soil and never looked back.

The new, reinvented Claudel installed himself in the cheapest rented rooms he could find in Cairo, and immediately got down with fierce enthusiasm to setting up his new business. He became, in effect, a professional tomb robber. And within a year of starting up his operation, he was already on the fast track to becoming a very wealthy man. He could still remember the day he'd made his first million. *This is fucking easy,* he'd thought.

And years later, that was still exactly how he felt about it. It was easy. Ridiculously easy. He was damn good at it, and it had been very, very kind to him.

He liked to think that his profession was older than prostitution. Ever since the earliest civilisations had started honouring their dead by burying them with precious objects, there had been opportunities for men like him. He wasn't the kind of idiot that the Egyptian Antiquities Police would catch, shovel in hand, digging at the foot of the Step Pyramid at Saqqara. Claudel's operation was slick and sophisticated. And safe. He made sure that the guys doing the actual thieving never knew who they were working for, while he himself never even went near the desert. The wine bars and top class restaurants and golf courses were the places he carried out his business, and that suited him fine. Hot sand was bad for his handmade Italian shoes.

Claudel had travelled everywhere in the course of his trade – Rome, Athens, Ankara, Beirut, Damascus, Delhi were all potential sources of prime merchandise for him. But Egypt was the real deal. Egypt was where it was truly at, and he wasn't the only greedy piglet suckling on her fat teat. Everyone with half a connection was muscling in for a piece of the action. Even government officials trusted with the job of protecting Egypt's heritage had been caught amassing huge fortunes by squirrelling artefacts to private buyers in Europe and the USA. Pharaonic slate palettes, pottery, glazed figurines, bronze statuettes, amulets, gold trinkets, carved stone heads, tapestries, even furniture – not to mention the wealth of items left over from the Graeco-Roman period. There was a veritable avalanche of stuff pouring out of the country.

Claudel was careful never to let the artefacts too close to him. There was no Egyptian art in his home, not a scrap of anything that the Ministry of Culture or the Antiquities Police could ever catch him with. They'd never come close to suspecting him, but if they ever did come knocking on his door he'd be only too happy to show them around the place. Everything he personally owned was legit. Nobody could ever know that he'd paid for his collection of Ming vases by tunnelling through the wall into a storeroom used to house artefacts at a temple in Karnak and making off with a truckload of statues. He'd never even seen them. Even before they were his, they were sold.

It had been the same with the priceless Louis XIV desk in his study, a trade for a Ptolemaic-era gold mask lifted from a mummy at the necropolis of Deir-el-Banat. One of his first really big sales. He could still remember it well. The tombs had been nice and shallow, sometimes just a metre under the surface. Grab and go. By the time the authorities had rolled up, all the good stuff was gone. They could keep the bones and bandages. Claudel had little use for dusty old corpses.

And that was the way it had continued. Fifteen years on, business had never been more brisk. The appetite for Egyptian antiquities was as hot now as it had been in ancient times. Occasionally, an eagle-eyed Egyptologist would spot the stolen goods that cropped up in the auction rooms of Christie's and Sotheby's and the alert was sounded. The trail would sometimes lead back to the source and heads rolled, especially when the Ministry of Culture boys got together with Interpol to hunt down the crooked dealers. But Claudel was far too clever to let that happen. He'd made a fine art of creating buffers and paper trails to protect himself, and in any case most of his trade was with private owners. Unscrupulous connoisseurs were always keen to expand their collections, and blush-making sums of money would change hands – even if the artefacts could never be openly displayed.

So, Pierre Claudel was a man with just about everything in life. But it was in his nature to want more, as it had always been. He would stand at his balcony in the mornings, sipping espresso, and gaze out towards the desert far away. The sands still held many secrets. There were still undreamed-of fortunes to be made out there. He yearned for one really big find, something he could retire on. Some of the legendary treasures of ancient Egypt were still undiscovered – like the fabled tomb of Imhotep, one of the nation's earliest and most influential rulers, a man long thought not even to have existed. Armies of archaeologists and historians were out there and had been for years, scouring the sands for that elusive prize. If only he could snatch something of that magnitude out from under their noses – what a coup *that* would be. Something like that would set him up for life and for twenty lives afterwards.

He would lie awake at night, just imagining it.

Then, one day in late September, seven months ago now, Claudel had had a call that changed his life.

The minute he'd heard the man's voice on the other end, he'd known this was serious, heavy shit. Normally he'd have slammed the phone down or demanded to know where they'd got his private number. But instinct had told him otherwise, and he'd listened to what the man had to say.

As a result of the call, a meeting had been set up. Not in the city, but in the desert. The man had been insistent on that point. Claudel had been uncomfortable with the idea, but his gut feeling again directed him to go with it. So he'd driven out there, alone as instructed. It had been a long, hot, dusty drive. The meeting place was a spot he knew from years ago, one that had never been worth visiting again. Whatever scraps the lonely ruined temple had to offer had been pilfered centuries ago. Now it just stood there, neglected and half buried in the sand, in the shade of a towering escarpment miles from anywhere.

As he'd pulled up and stepped out into the searing sun, Claudel had sensed he was being watched from the escarpment high above. Time had passed. He'd paced up and down, checked his watch impatiently. The heat of the sun was giving him a headache. He wasn't used to roughing it any more. He'd been just on the point of leaving when four off-road vehicles had appeared out of the shimmering heat haze and bounced across the dunes towards him.

He'd shielded his eyes from the sun and watched them approach. The ten men who climbed out of the dusty vehicles weren't the kind he normally did business with. Most of them looked like ex-soldiers, or mercenaries. Nobody was smiling. Several of them were carrying stubby automatic weapons on slings over their shoulders. Claudel didn't generally come into contact with guns in the course of his work, and he didn't much like them. These had evil-looking, curved magazines, folding stocks, a brutal military appearance to them. They looked scuffed and worn with use, and he could only wonder how many people had been shot with them.

But it was too late to run now. He was committed – to what, he didn't yet know.

Claudel had been shoved against his car and frisked for weapons and wires. 'Watch the suit,' he protested.

'He's clean,' the tall bearded one had muttered. They released him and he dusted his clothes off indignantly. The men signalled across to one of the jeeps, and only then had Claudel noticed the eleventh man, the one who'd hung back, sitting smoking in the rear seat, quietly watching from a distance.

The man had stepped down from the vehicle and

walked across the sand. His face was long and lean, the dark curls receding across his high forehead. He was wearing khaki trousers and a loose-fitting shirt that billowed in the warm breeze, the black rubber butt of a pistol protruding from a Cordura holster on his hip. He carried a slim briefcase in his left hand. He was slightly built, not tall, not physically striking or intimidating in any way. But he exuded an air of menace that seemed to come from somewhere behind those deep, dark eyes.

Claudel had looked into them and he couldn't tell what the man was thinking. That scared him most of all. Something told him those eyes had seen things he couldn't imagine. This was a man without any trace of kindness or humour or compassion. Even the rest of the group had almost visibly shrunk away from him as he moved past them.

The man had strode up to Claudel. Stood with his boots planted apart in the sand and gazed at him impassively. 'My name is Kamal,' he said. His voice was soft, almost gentle.

Claudel could sense the rest of the men watching him. The burly one with the baseball cap, the least mean-looking of the bunch, glanced nervously at Kamal. Another one, a ferret-like little guy with a shaven head and an ammunition belt wrapped around his torso, was fingering his gun.

Then Kamal had beckoned to Claudel and walked towards the shade of the rocks. The Frenchman had followed, feeling the sweat run down his temples, not just from the heat. His neck and shoulders ached with tension, expecting a bullet. He racked his brain as he walked. What had he done? Had he offended someone? Stepped on the wrong toes?

But then Kamal had done something unexpected. He sat down in a shady hollow in the rocks and motioned to Claudel to join him. 'I know who you are, and what you do. You can help me.'

Claudel eased himself down on a rock. 'I don't know what you want,' he replied hesitantly.

'I want to show you something.'

Then Kamal had opened the case. Inside it was a large manila envelope. He handed it over. Claudel frowned at it, looked inside and saw that it contained a series of glossy colour prints.

Kamal was watching him expectantly. Claudel shot him a baffled look, then started leafing through the photos. They showed a stone slab, ancient and pitted, covered in sand-dusted hieroglyphs.

'You can read them?' Kamal asked quietly.

Claudel nodded distractedly. He was already deep into them. He could feel an icy tingle running down his neck, down his spine as his eye traced the lines of symbols, converting them into words. He suddenly broke away from them and looked up. 'Where did you—'

'Read,' Kamal said, interrupting.

Claudel's fear was gone now. He read on.

'What does it say?' Kamal asked.

Claudel studied the glyphs again for a moment, struggling to condense their meaning. 'Amun is content,' he read slowly out loud. 'The Heretic of Amarna shall be denied, the treasures restored to their rightful place.'

Kamal smiled. 'An educated man. I had to have it translated.'

But Claudel wasn't listening. The icy tingle was intensifying into a mounting excitement that made him breathless.

The Heretic of Amarna shall be denied.

The Frenchman couldn't hide the tremble that made the glossy photo in his hands flutter.

It couldn't be. Amarna, the city in the sands. The heretic pharaoh. The ancient story of the three High Priests who'd defied him. Claudel knew what this was about. Treasure. Big time.

But it was just a legend. A myth. Dismissed by every Egyptology scholar in the world as fantasy and nonsense.

Could it be true after all? Surely not.

But what if it was?

He suddenly felt as giddy as a schoolboy. This could be it. This could be the big one. The thing he'd been waiting for. The biggest discovery of his career. Maybe the biggest haul in history. If even half the discredited legends were true, it would be like finding Tutankhamun's tomb all over again. And then some.

He looked up, meeting Kamal's eye. 'It's incredible.'

Kamal smiled in satisfaction. 'That's what the other guy said, too.'

Claudel frowned. 'The other guy?'

'You're my second opinion. Don't take it personally.'

Claudel was suddenly tense with fear. 'Who else have you told about this?'

'A curator at the Egyptian Museum,' Kamal said. 'We paid him a visit at his home last night.'

118

'What?' Claudel gaped in horror. 'Who?'

'Beng.'

'You told Beng about this?'

'Don't worry. He won't be telling anybody.'

'Why not?' Even as he said it, Claudel knew it was a stupid question.

'Because I decided I didn't like him,' Kamal replied. His voice was casual, his posture was relaxed as he lounged easily on the rocks. But Claudel caught the look in his eye.

It unsettled him for only a moment. Nothing could tear his thoughts away from this.

Claudel read on, and his jaw dropped open.

'What does it say?' Kamal said.

'Beng didn't tell you?'

'He did. But I like hearing it. And I need to know that you're capable of helping me, before I decide to make you my offer.'

'What offer?'

'Just read it to me,' Kamal said testily.

Claudel ran his shaking finger along the lines of symbols. This was a test, and he knew it. These guys were more than capable of leaving him out here if he didn't satisfy. But at the same time that hardly seemed to matter to him. All that mattered was the image he was holding of the ancient hieroglyphs.

'It talks of . . . untold riches,' he had said falteringly. 'Gold and other treasures, more than men can imagine. And a cache a hundred times greater. No, wait. I'm getting it wrong.' He bit his lip, staring hard at the photo in his hand. 'A *thousand* times greater.' He looked

119

up, baffled, his excitement growing even more. 'A thousand times greater than what?'

'Than the one we already found,' Kamal said simply. He gestured to the others. 'Fekri, Naguib. Bring it here.'

Two of the men had trotted over to Kamal's jeep and lifted something from the passenger seat. The object was three-foot long, wrapped in sacking cloth. The men didn't look weak, but the strain was showing on their faces by the time they'd heaved it across the sand to the rocks. Their rifles clattered against their backs as they struggled with the heavy weight. Kamal motioned again and they laid the object end-up on the ground. Stood back, breathing hard, wiping their sweaty hands on their trousers.

Claudel had stared at the thing. *What the hell . . .*

'Uncover it,' Kamal had commanded.

The Frenchman had reached out tentatively, grasped the edge of the sackcloth and tugged. It fell away.

The sun glinted on the object. Claudel almost felt bathed in golden light. He gasped, blinked, rubbed his eyes, gasped again. It wasn't true.

But it was. He was looking at a glittering statue of the cat goddess, Bastet. A surreal sight out here in this wilderness of sand and rock. He reached out a trembling hand. It wasn't gilt. It was solid gold. Maybe a thousand pounds in weight. He caressed it in awe. The single biggest piece of gold he'd ever been this close to. And if he was right about what it was, nobody had laid eyes on it for more than three thousand years.

Claudel's famous composure had slipped completely at that moment. He'd crawled around the statue on his hands and knees. He didn't care any more that he was ruining his suit. As he moved around the incredible object, running his fingers feverishly over the cool, smooth, bright gold, Kamal had told him where he'd found it. He told him about the old Bedouin fort far away, lost in the oceans of sand. About the dry well. The buried stone chamber that the well diggers had narrowly missed. The way he'd exposed part of it when he'd shot the man trapped at the bottom of the shaft. He related it calmly, matter-of-factly, as though it was nothing. As though it had been his destiny to find it.

Kamal motioned at the shining statue. 'And this is just a token I brought to show you. There was enough to fill a small truck. We're rich.'

Claudel wiped sweat out of his eyes. *And the hieroglyphs spoke of a cache a thousand times bigger?*

Kamal pointed at the Frenchman. 'Now *you're* going to help me become much richer.'

Claudel gave a bitter laugh. 'And then what? I end up like Beng?'

'Only if you disappoint me,' Kamal said. 'Or if you try to cross me or deceive me in any way whatsoever. I'm not unreasonable.'

Claudel had glanced over his shoulder at the men standing nearby. His eye lingered on the guns. 'I'm sure,' he had muttered.

'And I'm not interested in cultural treasures,' Kamal went on. 'I just want the money. I have my own plans.' He leaned forward on his rock, fixing Claudel's eyes with his. There was something mesmerising about his gaze. 'So here's my offer,' he continued. 'From now on, you work for me. I need a fence. You'll use your contacts to dispose of the items we found, and you'll arrange for the funds to be placed in a Swiss bank account. You'll have all the details.' He had paused, watching Claudel with a fierce intensity. 'And then we're going to find the rest of this treasure. You and I, partners.'

Claudel had just gawked back at him.

'It's your decision,' Kamal had said. 'Either we have a deal, or you die here today. Nothing personal. It's just business, you understand.'

In the background, one of the men had racked the cocking bolt on his weapon. The zinging metallic sound had sliced through the stillness and made Claudel shudder.

'Oh, I think we have a deal,' he'd said.

Now, seven months later, Pierre Claudel still couldn't forget that day in the desert. And he never would.

Chapter Fifteen

Cairo

Al Qâhirah. The name meant 'The Conqueror' in Arabic. Fourteen hours after takeoff from the south of France, the 747 made its descent out of the blazing, red-gold sunset.

Peering out of the windows across the aisle, all Ben could see on one side was the endless expanse of desert. On the other, the city looked like a gigantic oasis in the sands. A seething megapolis of eighteen million people, the largest city in Africa and the Middle East. The Nile wound through its heart, sparkling under the setting sun, its waters flanked by the vast urban sprawl that had grown up on its banks for thousands of years. High-rise blocks, domes and minarets stood silhouetted against the dramatic reds and golds of the sky. More than any other North African capital, it was a city of contrasts. The ancient and the modern. Extremes of wealth and poverty. A melting-pot of beauty and culture, filth and pollution.

It had been a few years since Ben's last visit here,

when he'd been searching for a missing girl. That had been a tough assignment, but he'd made a few contacts. One in particular might be useful to him this time around. That could wait, though. He knew where he had to go first. He reached into his pocket for the address Harry Paxton had given him.

Dusk had fallen by the time he cleared the airport. The city was coming to life as the temperature cooled and night fell over the skyline. Ben's taxi sped down a multi-lane highway that snaked through the urban sprawl, past giant billboards in Arabic and English and the lights that shimmered on the dark waters of the Nile. The taxi cut across town, skirted the fashionable and wealthy areas and then headed into districts that were rundown and neglected. The driver pulled up in a narrow street. Ben paid him, thanked him in Arabic and got out.

A wind was gusting in from the Sahara, bringing squalls of sandy dust that drifted across the pavements. Ben walked to the apartment building that had been Morgan's last place of residence and gazed up at the plain concrete façade. It was about as remote from the luxury of the *Scimitar* as you could get. The thump of hard rock and a blaring TV drifted down from open windows, blending together into a discordant mess of sound.

He tried to imagine Paxton's son in this place. It was going as native as a man like him would dare. Slumming it, as far as a sheltered middle-class guy on a cushy university salary could slum it. Checking into a hotel would have been too much of a tourist thing to do. This must have been Morgan's idea of being adventurous. Maybe he'd entertained some schoolboy explorer fantasy, some romantic notion of what it meant to be coming to Africa in search of ... what, exactly? Ancient secrets? Academic fame and glory?

And out in these streets, with his gold Rolex and dapper little blazer, the hapless Morgan Paxton would have stood out like a beacon for every opportunist crook for miles around. The complete opposite of his father, a man who could speak a dozen languages and blend in just about anywhere in the world.

Ben stepped inside and walked to the foot of a curving staircase. Graffiti on the wall had been thinly painted over, as though someone was making a half-hearted effort to maintain the place. He climbed the staircase to a landing. There were four doors off it, scratched and worn. One of them opened. An angry-looking young guy came out and walked past him and headed down the stairs, followed by a teenage girl who looked like she'd been crying.

Happy place, Ben thought. He checked the numbers on the doors and walked up another floor. The heavy bass of music throbbed through the walls. A baby was howling somewhere, mixed with the sound of a woman screaming, a door slamming, something breaking. He paused, listening. It sounded like a couple having a violent row. The music thumped on. It was a noisy place. The kind of place you could get stabbed to death in your own room and nobody would hear. Or care.

He climbed another flight. Checked the numbers on the doors again. This was it.

The door to what had been Morgan's apartment was ajar. He pushed it open quietly and walked in. Whatever police investigation there had been, it was done with now. Although shabby, the room was clean and tidy and looked all ready to move into.

'Can I help you?' asked a voice in English.

Ben turned. A burly guy was coming out of the kitchenette. He was heavily bearded, and the dark eyes were locked aggressively on Ben. He wore a vest with a suit jacket over the top of it. In one chubby hand was a metal toolbox with a hammer and a wrench sticking out of it. He might have been a caretaker, but a small-time landlord spotting a Westerner in his place would be more likely to start talking English in the hope of making a quick sale.

'Flat looks empty,' Ben said. 'Anyone staying here?'

'It's available.'

Ben pointed at the toolbox. 'Problem with the plumbing?'

'No problem. You need a place?'

'Maybe.' Ben walked around the room, glancing around him here and there. Through a doorway he could see the small, simple bedroom. The single bed was stripped to the mattress. A neat pile of white cotton sheets lay folded on a chair. A plain chest of drawers with a cheap lamp. Above the bed was a framed print of the Sphinx, to satisfy any tourists who might want to slum it the way Morgan did. The bedroom looked exactly like the photo in the police report – except for the sprawled corpse on the bed, the blood spattered up the wall and the slick of it across the floor.

Now, two months later, nobody would ever have guessed the place was fresh from being the scene of a brutal murder.

'You got satellite TV and Internet,' the landlord said. 'It's a good deal.'

Ben nodded. 'Friend of mine stayed here. Know who I'm talking about?'

The big guy made a dismissive gesture. 'Am I supposed to remember all the people that live here?'

'What about the ones that die here? You remember them?'

The guy's face crunched into a scowl. 'Who *are* you?'

'Nobody,' Ben said. 'Just someone who doesn't like the idea that an innocent man got knifed right here in this building. Your building. I wouldn't like to think that someone talked to someone about the soft Westerner with the gold Rolex. Easy money, if you know where to find it.'

The man's face was reddening under the thick beard. 'I don't like these questions. You want the place or not?'

'Just thoughts, that's all.' Ben reached for his wallet. Shelled out some of the banknotes Paxton had given him. He didn't bother counting. 'Is that enough for a week's rent?' he asked. He could see from the landlord's eyes that it was more than enough.

The landlord reached out for the money. Ben pulled it back out of reach. 'You live on the premises?' he asked.

The man smiled, less guarded now. The cash had

broken the ice. It had that effect on people. He jerked his head upwards. 'Top floor.'

'You found the body?'

The man nodded again. 'The door was open. I could see the blood on the wall.'

'Did you ever see my friend with anyone? Did he have visitors?'

'Not that I know of. I never saw anything. But I mind my own business.'

It might be true, or it might not. Time would tell. 'I'll take the place,' Ben said. He handed the guy the money.

When he was alone, he opened all the windows to let some air in. Traffic rumbled past in the street below. He took the slim folder out of his bag. He'd studied the coroner's and police reports on the plane, and he pored over them again for a few minutes now. The police reports were signed by the officer in charge, whose name was Ramoud. It was just as Paxton had said. The investigation had been pretty cursory.

Ben put the reports aside and looked at the photos again. They weren't pleasant viewing. It must have been terribly hard for Paxton to see the mutilation done to his son's body. The pathologist's assessment was that the murder weapon had been some kind of heavy blade, a machete or similar.

Ben chucked the photos down and looked at his watch. Time was passing and he didn't want to hang around in Cairo any longer than he had to. He replaced the papers in the folder and slipped it into his bag. Slung the bag over his shoulder. Locked the door behind him and headed back down the stairs into the night air.

He knew exactly where he was going from here.

He hailed a battered Mercedes cab and the driver took him east of the river, to where the streets became narrow lanes and crowded tenements jostled for space among the hundreds of ancient mosques. Ben had the taxi driver pull up and wait for him near the slum settlement of Manshiyat Naser, the place known as Garbage City. He got out and walked through the long shadows of the cramped alleys.

He heard the plod of hooves on tarmac as a donkey cart passed under a faint streetlight. The cart was being driven by a young boy. It was stacked ten feet high with the stinking rubbish that was brought into this part of the city for the locals to sift through for anything they could recycle or sell. A whole industry built on the things people threw away. That was this boy's future, Ben thought.

The boy's eyes met his for a fleeting moment, and the cart passed on into the darkness.

Three minutes later Ben was walking in a familiar doorway. The place was worse than Morgan's apartment building, a lot worse. It hadn't changed much since he was last here. And he was pretty sure his contact wouldn't have changed much, either.

Abdou was a guy you went to if you needed something. All kinds of things – as long as they were shady enough. Ben knew a little about his business. He was an entrepreneur with all nine fingers stuck in a lot of dirty little pies across the Cairo underworld. The tenth finger had been the one he'd stuck into the wrong person's affairs. That someone had snipped it off a long time ago with a pair of bolt croppers – a gentle reminder of his station. Ever since then, Abdou had shied away from dealing in the hotter stuff – the dope, girls and guns – but he still knew all the angles and a lot of people who didn't always want to be known.

The crumbling apartment building stank worse than the garbage-laden air outside. A yellow light bulb flickered on and off, and the walls dripped with condensation. Ben took the stairs two at a time and didn't slow down for the door. It burst in and smashed off the wall as he strode into the dark hallway.

Abdou came darting out of his office, a pistol cocked and ready in one wizened hand, his finger-stump clawed around the grip. The bald, gaunt old man might have looked wasted and harmless, but Ben knew appearances were deceptive. Hidden in the shadows, he ducked into a doorway as the Egyptian came running down the hall. He stepped out suddenly. Knocked the gun flying from the old man's hand.

Abdou swore as he recognised him. Quick as a cobra, his other hand darted inside his jacket and Ben had to twist out of the way as the knife flashed across his ribs. He caught the wrist and spun the old man around into an armlock. The knife dropped to the floorboards.

'You're slowing down, Abdou,' Ben said in Arabic.

Sweat trickled down the old man's bald skull as Ben held him powerless. 'Bastard,' he spat. 'You promised me you'd never show your face here again.'

Ben shoved his wiry frame back towards the office and sat him down hard in a chair. The walls were peeling. Fat black flies buzzed around the single naked bulb that hung in the middle of the ceiling. Abdou's desk was littered with the stuff of his trade – curled-up sheaves of money, photos, blank passports. Behind the desk, a safe was bolted to the wall. Ben didn't even want to know what was in it.

Keeping an eye on the angry old man, he scooped the fallen pistol off the floor. The Czech CZ75 9mm semi-auto fitted snugly into his hand. It was an old school kind of weapon, the kind Ben liked. All steel, rugged and solid, high-capacity magazine, clean and oiled, silencer fitted. Useful. He checked the chamber and magazine. It was fully loaded.

'Looks like I lied,' he said. 'Nice to see you again, Abdou.'

'I had a hell of a lot of heat on me after the last time,' the old man grated. 'And you knew there would be. English bastard.'

'Half Irish,' Ben said. 'That's a hazard of your chosen profession, my friend. If you're going to inform on kidnappers, you have to expect they might get upset.'

Abdou was rubbing his wrist. 'What do you want?'

'This is my last ever job. I want to get it done and go home. So let's make this easy on both of us. All I want from you is a name or two. Maybe three. Then I'm gone. I was never here. And you'll be a little richer. Easy money.'

The gaunt face wrinkled in disgust. 'That's all you wanted last time, too. Almost got me killed over it.'

'You still have nine fingers left,' Ben said. 'It can't have been that bad.'

'And I plan on keeping it that way.'

Ben smiled. 'Nothing so hot this time, Abdou. I promise. I just want to know where I can buy a watch.'

'That's it? A watch?'

'That's it.'

'Looks to me like you already have a watch,' said the old man pointedly, looking at Ben's Omega.

'But say I wanted something a little more special and I wasn't inclined to pay the full price. Where could I go?'

Abdou shrugged. 'Anywhere in Cairo. Any one of a thousand guys. Take your pick. How should I know?'

'Come on, Abdou. You can do better than that.' Ben took out a wad of money and held it there under the old man's hungry gaze. 'The watch I'm looking for would have hit the market in the last couple of months. A gold Rolex Oyster. Very distinctive. I'm prepared to offer top dollar for it. No messing around.'

Abdou's eyes narrowed suspiciously. 'Why?'

'Let's just say it's of personal interest to me. I'd like it back.'

'Nobody gets hurt?'

'Nobody who didn't bring it on themselves,' Ben said.

The old guy thought about it for a moment. Then his old face crinkled. Ben knew what he was thinking. *What the hell. I still have nine fingers left.*

'I can give you a list of names,' Abdou said. 'If your watch is still in Cairo, someone will know.'

Ten minutes later Ben was back out in the street with the CZ75 pistol in his waistband. In his pocket was a notepad page with five names, five addresses. He walked to the waiting taxi.

It was going to be a long night.

Chapter Sixteen

Within an hour, five names had dropped to three. Abdou's list wasn't turning out as productive as Ben had hoped. The first address he went to, west of the river, was just a sea of rubble with Portacabins and cranes throwing long shadows in the moonlight. A billboard told him the area had been demolished to make way for some new retail development.

When the second place turned out to be deserted, derelict, Ben was beginning to suspect the old man had tricked him, and began to think about paying him a return visit.

But then the third address raised his hopes again. Ben got the taxi to drop him off a few hundred yards away and walked the rest. The pawnshop was just as Abdou had described it, tucked away from the street. There were enough furtive-looking guys hanging around in the neighbourhood to make Ben think it was exactly the kind of place a certain type of opportunist thief would go to dispose of an especially hot item. Abdou had said the proprietor, Moussa, was one of the best fences in Cairo. The hanging Fender guitars and digital camcorders in the barred window were just a front. The choice stuff was locked away upstairs in Moussa's private quarters.

The place was easy to break into through a side entrance. Ben entered silently, followed the sound of the beeping alarm keypad to the control box and ripped it off the wall. He took a mini Maglite from his bag and flashed it discreetly around him. The shop was an Aladdin's cave of bric-a-brac, most of it useless junk. Raking through the place, Ben found a glass cabinet stuffed with watches: Sekonda, Timex, Casio, Citizen. Nothing too prestigious on open display – but he hadn't expected there to be.

Through a bead curtain, up a flight of steps, moving silently in the darkness. He drew Abdou's pistol from his belt. A yellow streak of light under a door, the sound of a TV – canned laughter, some imported comedy show. The volume was turned up high enough to have drowned the beeps of the alarm. Ben smiled in the darkness. *Careless.*

The door was flimsy and gave way on the first kick.

Moussa was alone. The room around him was strewn with fast-food packaging and bachelor debris. He was sitting on a sofa in his underwear facing the TV, a big spoon in one hand and a tub of ice cream in the other. He spun around in panic as the door crashed in, long black hair whipping around and his thick beard parting in a gape of horror. The spoon and the ice cream dropped out of his hands as Ben strode up to him, grabbed his beard and dragged him down off the sofa onto the floor. The pawnbroker sprawled on his back, blinking, too shocked to make a sound.

Ben was a big believer in simplicity, and the approach he used to get the truth out of people was as simple as he could make it. It was a system that had worked for him many times, in a lot of situations, and when it was the appropriate course of action it never failed. It was the ultimate test of sincerity.

He planted a foot on Moussa's chest, pointed the CZ75 in his face and watched his eyes. 'I have a couple of questions,' he said softly.

Five minutes later, Ben's heart was sinking again. The man knew nothing. He was slumped against the wall, his hair slicked with sweat and tears, mouth hanging open in shock. He'd passed the test. All Ben could do was move on to the next name on the list.

He laid a couple of banknotes on a table as he walked back to the shattered door. 'Thanks for your time,' he said, and left.

It was after midnight by the time he made it to the fourth place on his list. As the taxi rolled up, Ben did a double-check that the address was right. It was.

He opened the car door and stepped out into the sultry night air. Not the kind of environment he would have expected to find one of Abdou's contacts. It was a nice, respectable, middle-class street of neat white houses and trim little gardens. The pavement was lined with trees, and the cars parked along the kerb were relatively new, clean and well cared for. The kind of place a schoolteacher would live. Not rich, not poor, not particularly exciting and completely safe. It might have been the perfect cover for someone in Abdou's line of work. Or then, Ben thought, it might be a complete wild card.

He looked up at the house. There was a light on upstairs, shining through a gap in closed drapes. A movement from inside. Someone getting ready for bed, maybe. He hesitated for a moment, creaked open the small wrought-iron gate and walked up a path to the front door. He rang the bell. A minute went by, and then he heard sounds from inside. A woman's voice speaking Arabic. Footsteps coming down the stairs. A little scrape of metal from the other side of the door told him that someone was sliding aside the cover of the peephole to see who was there. The door opened a crack, pulling the security chain taut.

A woman's face appeared in the gap. She was perhaps in her late thirties, but she looked tired and careworn. There were lines on her brow and flecks of grey in her black hair and her eyes narrowed with suspicion as she peered out at him.

Through the three-inch aperture Ben could see a pair of teenage boys behind their mother in the hallway. Both were dressed in T-shirts and shorts, hair tousled as if they'd climbed out of bed in a hurry to see who the mystery visitor was. One was about thirteen, the other maybe a couple of years older. The elder one was trying hard to look strong and protective. Ben guessed that meant there was no father in the household. Behind the two kids, the hallway was littered with crates and cardboard boxes. It looked as though the family were either in the middle of moving out, or moving in. This wasn't looking promising. He glanced again at the name on his list.

'Mrs Hassan?' he said to the woman in Arabic.

'Who are you?' she asked. 'It's late. What do you want?'

'I need to talk to your husband, Mrs Hassan. Can I come inside?'

She hesitated, shook her head. 'My husband's not here any more.'

'Where can I find him? It's important.'

'Whatever business you had with him, you're too late.'

'Where did he go?' Ben asked. But the look of intense sadness on the woman's face was already telling him the answer.

She didn't reply. Hung her head and wiped an eye. The elder of the two boys stepped up to the door, reached for the security chain and unhooked it from its fastening. He opened the door and stood in the doorway, defiance in his eyes, doing his best to bristle and puff out his narrow chest and shoulders. It was a brave thing to do, Ben thought. A boy standing up and being a man. A turning point in his young life. That took a lot of guts.

He smiled at the kid. 'I didn't mean to upset anyone.'

'My father is dead,' the boy said. 'Go away. Leave my mother alone.'

Ben cast his eye around the hallway. There was a desolate air about the place. What had once been a family home was now just an empty shell full of memories these people wanted to get away from.

'Who are you?' the woman said again, laying a hand on her son's shoulder. 'You are not from the police.'

'No,' Ben said. 'I'm looking for something and I thought your husband might be able to help me.'

'He was ill for a very long time,' she said, beginning to cry. 'He had diabetes. First they cut off one leg, then the other. Now he's dead. I don't care what you were looking for. I want you to go.'

He watched the tears streaming down her face, and his heart went out to her. There was little point in apologising for disturbing what was left of her family in the middle of the night.

He turned and left. Heard the door shut behind him as he made his way back down the path to the little gate. The taxi driver was slouching behind the wheel, one arm hanging loosely out of the window. Ben opened the door and climbed in the back seat with a sigh.

'Where now?' the driver said lazily.

Ben dug the crumpled list back out of his pocket and unfolded it. Now there was just one name left at the bottom.

Mahmoud Barada. Nightclub owner and entrepreneur on the side. Buyer and seller of pretty much anything he could turn a dollar with.

Ben read out the address to the driver and felt the acceleration press him back in his seat as the taxi lurched away.

He closed his eyes and leaned his head back against the warm leather as the car sped into the heart of downtown Cairo. This was the last chance. If it led nowhere, he was going to have to rethink his options.

His mind drifted until the taxi driver's voice broke in on his thoughts. 'We're there. You want me to hang around?'

'I won't be long.' Ben stepped out of the car.

They were at the end of an unmarked alleyway. Coloured neons flashed on crumbling brickwork and the huddled shapes of people in the shadows. Buying and selling. There was a lot of it going on. As Ben walked up to the nightclub entrance a girl came up to him and offered him a good time. She might have been Somali, and wasn't more than seventeen. He walked past her and paid some money to the beefy guys at the door. The music was pumping out into the street, a blend of hip-hop and Eastern.

Ben walked inside. As one o'clock drew closer, it seemed that the party was just beginning to groove. The place must have been a warehouse or storage depot at one time. The air was thick with the heat and smell of a thousand tightly packed bodies, black, white and everything in-between. Through the heavy bass throb of the music he could hear half a dozen different languages as people yelled at each other to be heard.

There was a long bar at the far end, where at least a hundred people were jostling and shoving to get served. Above it was a scaffold construction with scantily clad dancers, their bodies shining and writhing in the strobing lights. Around the edges of the room were nooks and tables screened by palm leaves. Couples sat close, heads almost touching so that they could talk in the din.

Ben pushed through the throng that swarmed at the bar.

'You can't miss him,' Abdou had said. And Ben didn't. Barada fitted the old man's description of him exactly. He was the only person at the bar who wasn't trying to get a drink. He leaned on his elbows with his back against the shiny counter, surveying his enterprise with a look somewhere between smug satisfaction and cold contempt. His flowery shirt was open halfway to the waist, buttons straining across his belly. He was about forty, greasy thinning hair tied back in a ponytail, his face pitted with old acne scars.

Ben walked up to him and saw the cold gaze swivel to meet his. Barada gave a curt nod as if to say, *What the fuck do you want from me?*

Ben's eye ran across Barada's broad chest and down his arm. The left forearm sticking out of the rolled-up shirt sleeve was thick and hairy. Around the wrist, flashing in the swirling lights, was clasped a chunky gold Rolex.

Ben moved closer, close enough to smell the booze and garlic on the man's breath and shout in his ear. Barada looked like he was ready to listen.

'I have a business proposal for you,' Ben said.

The man's face was deadpan. He stared for a beat, peeled his heavy frame off the bar and gestured to follow him. Ben watched the wide back muscle its way through the crowd. Barada spilled a girl's drink out of her hand and didn't look back. The hand with the Rolex swatted open a door marked 'PRIVATE' and Ben followed him through. The door swung shut, damping the thud of the music. On the other side of it was a dark, winding corridor. Barada kept walking, and Ben walked behind a few paces. A few yards along the corridor, light was shining out of a half-open doorway. Barada thumped on the door, shoved it open, kept walking past.

Two large men appeared in the doorway. Behind them in the room was a low table scattered with beer bottles and a big screen was showing an action movie, cars exploding and machine guns rattling.

The two guys stepped out into the corridor, staring hard at Ben, then followed as Barada led the way up a flight of steps. He shoved open another door and they were inside an office. The décor was seventies porn king. Barada walked around behind a desk, settled heavily into a chair. He motioned to the heavies, who stood either side of the door, hands crossed over their stomachs, gazing at Ben as if just waiting for the command to take him apart.

Ben walked up to the desk and dumped his bag on it.

Barada gazed impassively up at him. 'So what do you want? You speak English, right?' He spoke it with the phoney transatlantic twang of someone trying too hard to sound cool.

'I want to see your watch,' Ben said.

Barada grimaced, confusion quickly slipping into impatience. 'You said you had a business proposal.'

'I do. You let me see your watch, and I don't kill you. That's the deal.' Ben slipped out the CZ pistol and pointed it in Barada's face. He didn't take his eyes off the fat man but sensed the sudden shift behind him as the two heavies moved his way.

'Stay,' he said.

Behind him, the two guys stopped dead.

'Back against the wall,' Ben said.

The heavies backed up. There was silence in the room, just the muffled thump of the beat shaking up through the floor.

Barada chuckled as he peered down the barrel of the 9mm. 'You've got some incredible fucking nerve. These two guys can break you into small pieces.'

'Take it off,' Ben said, pointing at the watch. 'I want to see it.'

Barada hesitated. 'You some kind of weirdo?' he demanded. 'Got a watch fetish or something?' But he did what he was told. He undid the clasp. The bracelet opened up and he shook it down his wrist and slipped it over his big hand. He passed it to Ben.

Ben flipped it over and ran his eyes over the back. Neatly engraved in fine italic script on the gold backplate were the words 'To Morgan, with love from Mummy'.

Ben looked down at Barada. There were some beads of sweat breaking out on the man's brow but he was doing his best to look collected. Ben lowered the gun a few inches, still aware of the glowering heavies behind and on either side of him. 'OK, I'll take it.'

'What do you mean, you'll take it?'

'I want it.'

'It's mine. You can't have it.'

'I'm buying it,' Ben said. 'Double whatever you paid for it.'

'Or?'

Ben clicked off the safety.

Barada snorted. 'What, you stick a gun in my face, you tell me you want my Rolex but you want to pay for it?'

Ben smiled. 'Do I look like a criminal to you?'

'So what the fuck are you, some kind of mummy's boy who wants his watch back? You're Morgan, right?'

'Morgan's dead,' Ben said. 'And I think whoever sold you this watch killed him.'

Barada shrugged. 'Not my concern. I buy and sell stuff. I'm just a businessman. I don't ask questions.'

'That's fine,' Ben said. 'But you can answer one for me. I want to know who sold you this.'

'I forgot.'

Ben laid the Rolex on the desk. Still pointing the gun at Barada, he reached into his bag and took out a thick wad of notes. He slapped them down on the desk beside the watch. 'That's forty thousand Egyptian pounds,' he said. 'For the watch and the information. I'm guessing that's a lot more than you paid for it. Give me what I want, then I'll go away. Nobody has to get hurt. You can buy another watch just like it in the morning. Deal?'

Barada gazed wistfully at the Rolex. 'It's a limited edition. No longer produced.'

'You're breaking my heart.'

Then Barada's eyes moved from the watch to the pile of money. 'Seems like you want this pretty badly. What's your intention, if I give you this information?'

'Not your concern,' Ben said. 'You're just a businessman, remember?'

Barada smiled, relaxing a little. 'I like your style. You've got balls, coming in here like this. You want a girl or something? Stick around a while, have a drink.'

'I want what I asked for. Nothing more, nothing less. Just a name and an address.'

'Maybe we can do business,' Barada said. 'What the fuck. They're shits anyway.' He grabbed a pad from his desk, reached for a pen and scribbled two names and an address. 'Couple of dealers. Lowlife druggy bastards. They live in a stinking rat-hole apartment across the river. Mostly stoned out of their heads. They owed me money, said they didn't have it. I could have had their legs busted, but I liked the watch.' He shrugged again and tore the page off the pad. 'But I guess it's only a watch.' He reached for the money and slipped the note across the desk.

Ben picked it up and read it. 'This information had better be good.'

'It's good,' Barada said, stuffing the money away in a drawer. 'And if you put a couple of bullets in their heads, nobody's going to cry over it.'

Ben slipped the note inside his pocket. He lowered the gun. 'How long since you got the watch from them?'

'Couple of weeks, give or take.' Barada paused, looking expectantly at Ben. 'So we're cool?'

145

'Maybe,' Ben said.

'You sure you don't want that drink? What's your name, anyway?'

'Another time.'

Chapter Seventeen

It was after one when Ben found the place, a sad-looking tenement building right next to a breaker's yard. Everything was marked with neglect. A cat darted out of the doorway as he approached, carrying a struggling rat in its teeth. He walked through an entrance hall that smelled of stale urine and was dimly lit by a flickering bulb. Climbed the stairs to the fourth floor and came to the door he was looking for.

It wasn't even locked. He walked right in and the stink of the place hit him. He paused, letting his eyes adjust to the blackness. Ahead of him was a short passage, littered with junk. He made his way along it and opened the inner door.

The room he walked into was bathed in the dull glow of a sideboard covered in flickering candles. Wax dripped down the wood, hardening on the floor. Somewhere in the shadows, aggressive rap music blared from a tinny stereo. The air was oppressive, thick with the mixed odours of stale booze and smoke and sweat – the smell of a space whose inhabitants didn't care about their own lives.

A bare mattress lay on one side of the room and Ben could make out the shapes of two sleeping bodies in the candlelight. A man and a woman, both naked, arms and legs entangled, half covered by a rumpled sheet.

Across on the other side, nearer to the candle-glow, was a table. Ben took in the razor blade, the rolled-up banknotes, the little mound of white powder and the half-snorted line of it that the table's single occupant hadn't managed to finish before he passed out. He was slumped on a low stool with his arms spread across the table, his forehead resting on the glass. Ben watched him for a moment. He was breathing slowly, deeply. He looked young, early twenties, scrawny with a patchy beard.

A yard from the table, a second woman was lying sprawled, her bare legs kicked out on the rug. Ben stepped over to her and crouched down to take a look at her. She was maybe twenty and looked European, with dirty blonde hair and what could have been a pretty face if it hadn't been pressed down against the floor of a dingy drug den. She was just as out of it as her friends. She was wearing some kind of lightweight blazer, striped cotton that had ridden up to reveal her skimpy knickers and an angel tattoo across her coccyx.

Something about the striped garment looked very familiar. Ben reached for a candle and brought it closer to inspect. He was pretty sure it was the same one Morgan Paxton had been wearing in the photo.

He flipped on a light switch. The room was suddenly bright, but that didn't do much to stir its occupants.

The girl on the rug seemed to sense something, and lifted her head a couple of inches. The naked couple on the mattress didn't move, and neither did the young guy at the table.

Ben turned off the shrill music and walked back over to the table. He leaned down so that his face was just a few inches from the glass. He took a deep breath and blew hard, scattering the white powder into clouds of dust.

That got the attention of the young guy. He suddenly woke up, eyes snapping wide open. He lurched unsteadily to his feet and made to grab Ben by the shirt, shrieking in Arabic, 'You fuck! You *fuck!*'

Ben twisted his wrist into a lock and threw him back down. There was no strength in the guy's wasted arms. He slumped sideways and rolled off the stool, gasping.

The girl on the floor slowly dragged herself across the rug and started burying her face in it, snorting up the fallen coke. Ben hauled her to her feet, moved her to an armchair and lowered her into it. He stripped the blazer off her. 'Don't hurt me,' she pleaded in English.

'I'm not here for that,' Ben said. He stuffed the blazer into his bag and took out the pistol. The girl started screaming, and it woke the two on the mattress. The naked woman was suddenly alert, staring at Ben in horror and pulling a sheet around her.

'Get some clothes on,' Ben said to her. She nodded. Stood up, legs trembling, and started pulling on jeans and a loose top.

'Now get out of here,' he said. 'Don't come back.'

The women left, staggering out of the door.

Now it was just Ben and the two guys. He stepped over to the one who was still lying slumped on the floor, muttering to himself. Grabbed a fistful of the guy's hair and dragged him kicking and hollering over to the mattress. He dumped him down next to his friend, who was coming around, struggling into his trousers and groping for his shirt.

Ben stood over them. Pulled back his left sleeve and saw their half-open eyes flicker to the gold Rolex that he was wearing alongside his own Omega.

'Recognise this?' he said.

No response, but there was a glimmer of understanding in their faces. Now they knew what this was about. The younger one glanced away nervously. His hands were shaking.

Ben walked to the door and peered out into the corridor. The women were long gone. He shut the door, locked it and put the key in his pocket. He checked the window. It was barred, and there was no balcony or fire escape. He glanced back down at his two groggy, blinking, mumbling prisoners. Satisfied that they weren't going anywhere, he did a quick search of the flat.

Apart from the main room, there was just a kitchenette with a greasy stove and a cockroach on the wall. Off that was a door to a tiny cubicle with a stinking toilet. On a chipped sideboard in the kitchen he found a knife. A very big knife. It had a tarnished brass hand-guard, like a sabre, and the broad blade in the leather

150

sheath was twelve or thirteen inches long. It made him think about the brutal wounds on Morgan Paxton's body. The kind of wounds that a heavy hacking blade like this would inflict.

He left it lying there. Stepping away, he felt a loose floorboard under his foot. It lifted up at one end when he stamped on it. He kicked it away, revealing a hollow space under the floor about eight inches high. There was a crumpled plastic bag stuffed inside.

He kneeled down next to the hole and used the gun to fish the bag out by its handle, then scattered the contents out on the floor and sifted them about with the pistol muzzle. There was a bundle of banknotes held together with an elastic band and a few other papers. Those didn't interest him. What did interest him were the debit and credit cards in Morgan Paxton's name, and his British Library membership card. Then among the papers he found a UK passport. He flipped it open with the gun and Morgan's face stared up at him from inside.

He left the evidence where it lay. If there'd been a doubt in his mind, it was gone now.

As an afterthought he crouched down lower to the floor and stuck his whole arm inside the hollow space. It was a long shot, but these guys were such amateurs that anything was possible.

His fingers made contact with something that wasn't wood or masonry. It felt rounded and smooth and plasticky. He grasped it and felt it move. A few inches, and he could see it. The manufacturer's logo in silver letters on black plastic. It was a small laptop computer.

He pulled the machine up out of the hole and set it down on the floor in front of him, resisting the temptation to flip open the lid and turn it on. No time for that now. He just stared at it instead. Was this Morgan Paxton's laptop? The chances were that it was. Either the thieves hadn't got around to selling it yet, or they'd fancied keeping it for themselves.

Ben grabbed the machine and carried it back into the main room. The two guys were still lying there, slumped against the wall. One of them was trying to say something. Ben laid the laptop carefully down on the glass-topped table. He stepped towards his prisoners, took the gun from his belt and pointed it at them.

'Why did you have to kill him?' he asked in Arabic. 'Don't you know what you've brought on yourselves, doing that? All for a line of coke. Is it worth it?'

'I didn't do it,' the younger one blurted out, suddenly finding his voice. His face was twitching as he watched the gun. He pointed a finger at his friend. '*He* stabbed the guy. I told him not to. But he just kept sticking the knife in.'

'You think I care which one of you put the knife in?' Ben said.

The younger one was crying now. The other just stared in dumb terror.

'What happened to the case and the papers?' Ben asked. 'I know they were there. You took them. Don't lie to me.'

No reply. Just the quiet sobbing from the younger one. Then the older of the two guys spoke for the first time. 'We burned the papers. Sold the case.'

Ben nodded. *So be it.* Now it was time to finish his job.

He stepped back from them. Two steps. Three. He raised the pistol and let the sights hover on their bodies. He moved his thumb up to the safety lever and nudged it until he felt it click to the fire position.

The two were squirming. The younger one put his hands out, as though he thought he could shield himself from the strike of a 9mm jacketed bullet moving at close to the speed of sound. A dark stain was spreading over the crotch of his jeans.

Ben felt the cool, smooth face of the trigger against his finger. All he had to do was shoot these two scum-bags, pick up what was left of Morgan's things and get out of here. Nobody would even know they were dead, until the rotting-corpse stink found its way under the door and out into the hallway. In the Cairo heat, maybe less than two days. But that was plenty of time. There was no way the two women were going to run to the police, either. He was home free. All he had to do was pull the trigger.

You owe this to Harry Paxton, he thought.

He let the sights settle on the older of the two. His friend was probably telling the truth – this one was the killer. He had a harder look about him, even facing death.

Shoot him first, then the other. The debt to Paxton would be paid. Ben could go home and forget the whole thing.

But staring down at the two pathetic forms through the sights of the Browning, Ben knew he'd never forget.

He'd sworn that he was never going to do this again, and it would be a broken promise to himself that he'd never be able to forgive.

The gun wavered in his hands. He let out a long breath. Voices argued in his head.

They're shits. They deserve it. Look what they did. You saw the photos.

But your days of killing to order are behind you. You're not SAS any more.

Two bullets. Then it's done. It's not like it would be the first time for you.

No. You can't.

I'm sorry, Harry.

He lowered the gun. The two men were staring at him, wide-eyed, following his every move.

He clicked the safety back on, let the pistol dangle at his side.

'OK,' he said to them. 'Here's what we're going to do.'

Chapter Eighteen

Three minutes later, the two junkies were lying bound and gagged on the rug. Just two parcels waiting to be delivered, as Ben made his preparations. He carefully wrapped Morgan Paxton's striped cotton blazer around the laptop for protection, and slipped it into his bag. Then he fetched a rag from the kitchen, sat on the stool at the glass-topped table and stripped down Abdou's CZ75 into its component parts. He used the rag to wipe everything down and reassembled the pistol, careful not to leave any prints.

The two prisoners craned their necks to eye him nervously as he worked. He ignored them. When the gun was back together he stood up and walked over to the older one. Holding the weapon butt-first with the rag, he grabbed the junkie's right hand and smeared his prints all over the frame, slide and trigger guard. He walked back into the kitchen and stuffed the gun into the hole under the floor along with the rest of the evidence.

Locking the door behind him, he left the flat and made his way silently down the stairs to ground level.

The taxi was still there, dusty under the faint street-lights. The driver was lounging smoking in his seat, clearly enjoying what was turning out to be a lucrative and easy job for him. Ben smiled. The guy was about to get a shock.

He climbed the stairs back to the junkies' flat, unlocked the door and went inside. Nothing had changed. The two strained to peer up at him as he walked up to them. Their eyes were bulging, faces red, veins standing out on their foreheads. He grabbed the older one by the shirt collar and hauled him across the floor. The guy struggled and mumbled behind the gag. Ben dragged him along the passageway to the door, out into the hallway. He let the guy's head crack down on the floor as he let him go to lock the door, then grabbed him again. 'If you think I'm carrying you down,' he said, 'you're much mistaken.'

The descent was fairly brutal, and after bumping down three flights of urine-smelling concrete stairs the guy's protests had dwindled to a sobbing whimper. Ben heaved him up over his shoulder, glanced up and down the dark street to check nobody was around, and carried him across to the car.

The taxi driver was already out of his seat. His laid-back composure slipped a little when he saw the bound, gagged prisoner. 'What are you doing?' he gasped.

'I'm making a citizen's arrest.' Ben opened the boot of the car and dumped the writhing body inside. 'Leave it open. There's another one to come.'

A couple of minutes later, both prisoners were stuffed in the boot. Ben slammed the lid. There was a muted squawk of pain and fear from inside. He checked his watch. It was after three in the morning. He turned to the taxi driver. 'Last call,' he said. 'These guys are going to jail.'

The taxi driver grinned and shook his head. 'You are one crazy motherfucker,' he said as he slipped back in behind the wheel.

'Tell me about it,' Ben answered. He climbed in the back, slammed the door and the car took off again, riding a little low at the back.

Down at the police headquarters, Ben went up to the main desk and asked for Ramoud, the officer in charge of Morgan's case. He refused to talk to anyone else. After some consternation and a lot of whispering, someone went to fetch him. When he finally came breezing out of a doorway, Ramoud looked cartoon-like, small, fat and bald in a double-breasted grey suit.

Ben didn't say much. He led the policeman out to the car, opened the boot and let him see what was inside. Then he told him what it was all about, what these people had done and where the evidence was that could prove it hands down. A cast-iron, slam-dunk guaranteed conviction.

The prisoners were bundled out of the car and dragged inside the station to be processed and thrown in the cells. Ben watched them being marched away. Stepped back outside, handed his driver a clutch of notes, thanked him and let him go.

Ramoud reappeared, eyeing Ben curiously. He gestured to follow him, and they made their way through labyrinthine neon-lit corridors until they came to a small office. Ramoud showed Ben to a chair and offered him coffee in a foam cup. It was tepid and tasteless but he welcomed it. Fatigue was wearing him down. It was four in the morning and he'd been on the move for a long time.

He had no objection to giving his name and letting Ramoud see his passport. As far as anyone was concerned, he'd done nothing wrong, broken no laws. He filled in a couple of forms, signed and dated them and slid them back across the desk.

'I have a few more questions,' Ramoud said with a smile.

'Fire away,' Ben replied. He knew they wouldn't be too tough. The arrest wasn't exactly standard procedure, but he got the feeling that the police chief had no problem with someone else doing his work for him. Ben guessed he wasn't in for much of a grilling – and he was right. Ramoud skirted none too subtly around the whole issue of exactly how Ben had come across his information. He didn't even ask what was in the bag, and Ben didn't volunteer any information about it. The laptop and the blazer were strictly for Harry and, besides, he didn't want to bring heat down on his informants. Barada was what he was, but Ben didn't have any personal issue with the man. Plus, the night-club owner might be inclined to go after Abdou, and the old crook didn't deserve to lose any more fingers. At least, not over this.

Ramoud scrawled careless notes as Ben gave his statement. Now and then he would stop, chew the end of his pen and look up to ask another question. The answers Ben gave were ludicrously vague and would have attracted the deepest suspicion in any European police procedure, but Ramoud seemed perfectly satisfied and kept scribbling.

Ben smiled to himself. Corruption had its place, sometimes.

By 4.30 a.m., the detective had the paperwork wrapped up and seemed happy. He gave Ben his solemn assurance that he had men already dealing with the evidence and that, if it were half as incriminating as it sounded, the two guys were in the deepest shit imaginable.

Ben didn't reply. From what he'd heard about the brutality and torture record of the Egyptian police, he had the impression that Morgan's killers weren't in for a pleasant time. That was fine by him, and it was the best payback he could offer on behalf of Harry Paxton.

'Then we're done?' he said.

'You are free to go. You have done the city a service. I thank you once again.'

'I need to call a cab.'

'No need. I will have one of my men drive you home.'

'Thanks.' Ben checked his watch. It was 4.35 a.m. and he was looking forward to getting some sleep.

'You wear two watches,' Ramoud observed.

'I travel a lot. Different time zones.'

'You can get one watch that will do all that.'

Ben smiled. 'I'm old-fashioned.'

Chapter Nineteen

The Claudel Residence,
Hyde Park, Cairo
4.45 a.m.

Pierre Claudel couldn't sleep. He climbed out of bed, wandered out onto his balcony and watched the night creep towards dawn.

He was so weary. His senses felt bombed to numbness with stress. Ever since that day in the desert when Kamal had told him about his discovery, Claudel's mind had been in turmoil. Two things had been constantly in the foreground of his thoughts, and he was thinking about them now as he reflected back over the events of the last few months. The worst time of his life.

The first preoccupation burning a hole in his brain was the frustration of knowing that the treasure was out there somewhere, but having no idea where to find it. Kamal had offered him ten per cent. Maybe not overly generous, but ten per cent of a gigantic fortune could still set him up for life. His hustling days would be over.

He couldn't wait for it to happen. Up until that

day in the desert, he'd felt pretty rich and successful. Now, in comparison to what he could get, *might* get, desperately *longed* to get out of this, he felt poor and miserable and shabby. The feeling was as though something had crawled under his skin, making his flesh creep.

The second major preoccupation was Kamal himself. Kamal terrified him. While Claudel couldn't stop thinking about the treasure, another part of him bitterly regretted that he'd ever joined forces with this man.

What scared him even more, and kept him awake at night staring up at the dark canopy of his four-poster bed, was the knowledge that Kamal was fast running out of patience. Not even the million dollars that the first haul of treasure had generated, now sitting pretty in a numbered Swiss bank account minus Claudel's ten per cent fence fee, could placate the Egyptian. He was getting jumpier by the day. Weeks were ticking by like seconds, merging into months, and still Claudel wasn't coming up with anything.

It wasn't for lack of trying. He'd driven out across the Western Desert with Kamal and his men. A long, hot, dusty and exhausting trek that almost killed him. They'd found the Bedouin fort, and Kamal had shown him the well. Claudel had nervously clambered down there on a rope, examined the shattered empty chamber where the cache of gold had been. He'd frantically pored over every inch of the stone carvings, searching for more hieroglyphs that hadn't been in the photos and might yield a clue. But there was nothing. The trip to the fort turned out to be a complete waste of time.

Back in Cairo, Claudel had considered his options. They were disturbingly limited. There were few people in the world whom he trusted, and he was especially cagey about letting anyone else in on the treasure hunt. But in his desperation he'd been forced to put out feelers in the shadowy world of illicit antiquities dealing. He'd sat back, chewed his manicured nails down to the quick and hoped his enquiries would offer up some kind of lead.

The silence of the phone seemed to taunt him.

Meanwhile, Kamal had invaded his life like a disease. He'd taken a liking to the luxury Hyde Park villa, started spending more and more time there and generally treated it as his home. He'd sprawl in the armchair that had once belonged to the inventory at Fontainebleau Palace, a glass of red wine precariously perched on Claudel's irreplaceable period satin upholstery, stretch his boots out on the white cashmere silk carpet and flick ash from his Davidoff cigar all over the place. It made Claudel cringe, but he knew better than to complain.

If he hadn't been so damn scared all the time, he might have chuckled at the irony that one of the city's most exclusive gated communities, designed to keep undesirable elements away from the homes of the rich, had become Kamal's luxury refuge. It was a perfect hideout for him – the guards at the gate were used to seeing Claudel's van come and go. As long as the drivers showed their private pass, vehicles were just waved through without a second glance, without any clue that heavily armed men were riding in the back.

It had quickly descended into a nightmare. Claudel

couldn't go anywhere in his own home without some hostile-looking hard guy eyeballing him. Couldn't bring anyone back to the house. No women. He was like a prisoner. He stopped going to parties. Friends were calling him to ask if he was ill, and he'd been fobbing them off with all kinds of lame excuses. He'd started drinking more, too, to calm the palpitations he'd started getting. One day he'd gone down to his wine cellar to fetch a bottle for himself, and he'd found a stack of weapons and ammunition down there. He'd nearly had a heart attack. But he could say nothing.

Then suddenly, eight weeks ago, after five months of anxious torment, the phone had rung. Claudel picked up. It was Aziz, one of the contacts he'd called in months before. They'd worked together on a few jobs in the past. When he wasn't stealing antiquities, Aziz freelanced as a tourist guide. As far as anyone in the business could be trusted, Claudel was reasonably sure of him.

'That thing you told me about. You still interested? I might have information.'

Claudel gripped the phone tightly. 'I'm definitely still interested.'

At that moment, Kamal appeared in the doorway. He watched and listened, head cocked curiously to one side. His eyes narrowed.

Aziz chuckled on the line. 'Let's talk about my cut first. Pierre Claudel doesn't get this jumpy if there isn't a pile of money involved.'

Claudel darted an impatient glance at Kamal. 'Five per cent of whatever I get. The usual.'

'Fuck you. Make it ten per cent and I'll tell you what I just heard.'

Claudel gritted his teeth. 'Six.'

'Eight.'

Claudel sighed. 'OK. Eight.'

Aziz sounded satisfied. 'I imagine you don't want to discuss this on the phone. Meet me at Café Riche. I think you'll find it worthwhile.'

'Café Riche,' Claudel repeated. 'Give me half an hour or so.'

Kamal wagged his finger. 'Tell him to come here.'

Claudel covered the receiver with his hand. 'I don't bring business associates up to the house. That's a rule.'

'I just broke it,' Kamal said, raising a warning eyebrow.

Claudel paused, sighed, spoke back into the phone. 'I can't make that appointment, Aziz. Come up to the house. You know where it is. Yes, as soon as you can.'

Once the call was over, Claudel and Kamal waited. Paced, checked their watches, paced some more. Nothing was said, tension building like static between them. After an anxious half-hour, Claudel heard the crunch of tyres on gravel and saw Aziz's car pulling up outside.

Aziz walked into the villa and glanced around him. 'Nice place,' he started saying.

But he hadn't gone three steps inside the marble-floored hallway before Kamal's men hauled him through to the living room, dumped the panicking man in a chair and surrounded him.

'You had something to say,' Kamal told him.

Claudel pushed past, trying hard to hide his fury.

'Let me talk to him.' He leaned down and looked earnestly at Aziz. 'I can't explain, my friend. But it's very important that you tell me what you know.'

Aziz glanced up at the circle of hostile faces and started babbling nervously, spilling out his story. Four days ago, he'd been hired as a guide by an Englishman who'd introduced himself as Dr Morgan Paxton. The guy had wanted Aziz to drive him out to the pyramid cluster at Abusir, seventeen kilometres south of Cairo.

The tomb complex of Sahure, Claudel thought. The second ruler of Egypt's Fifth Dynasty of kings, buried a thousand years before Akhenaten's reign. 'What for?' he asked. 'What did this Paxton want there?'

'I don't know,' Aziz replied 'He didn't say.'

'Tell me about this Englishman,' Kamal cut in.

Aziz glanced from one man to the other and babbled on, talking so fast he kept tripping over himself. 'An academic. Nerdy. Sandals and socks and a little blazer. Not the most streetwise kind of guy – didn't have the sense to cover up his Rolex. When we got there, he wanted to go off on his own. I told him there were snakes. He said he didn't care about the snakes, and that I was to wait for him in the car. He seemed really cagey about letting me go with him, like he wanted to keep it to himself. But there was no way I was going to sit cooking in the car. So I got out and sat in the shade and waited for him. If the crazy foreign bastard wanted to get himself lost or bitten, that was his problem.'

Claudel was painfully aware of the mounting impatience on Kamal's face. 'Just tell us what happened, Aziz.'

'I waited about an hour. Then I saw him walking back. No, not walking, running. He was covered in dust and cobwebs, all out of breath, red in the face, excited as hell. Like a kid. He was punching the air with his fist. I thought he'd gone crazy. He kept muttering to himself.'

'Muttering what?'

'I don't remember the exact words. But as soon as he said it, I remembered your call that time. That's why I phoned you.'

'What did he say?' Claudel asked feverishly.

'It was something about Amun being happy. And something about the heretic.'

Claudel felt the blood rush to his face. 'Amun is content; the Heretic of Amarna shall be denied?'

'That's it. That's what he said.'

Claudel tried to think. What was the connection? 'Did he say anything more?'

'No.'

'You're absolutely sure about that? It's important.'

'I told you, he didn't say anything. He was just cackling and laughing to himself, like a nut. Then he had me drive him back into Cairo, as fast as I could. He started getting nervous, looking at his watch. Told me to head for the Egyptian Museum, but we missed it by five minutes. He looked pretty pissed off, but he didn't say why or what he was looking for there.'

'And then?'

'And then he had me drop him off at his apartment building. Said he'd call me if he needed me again. That's it.'

'But he hasn't called?'

'No.'

'But you know where he's staying?'

Aziz blurted out the address.

Kamal stood over the frightened guide with his arms folded and a cold look in his eye. There was silence in the room.

Claudel's mind was racing. It was either a disaster, or it was a break. It was clear that this Paxton person knew something. He was an academic. Maybe a history or archaeology scholar of some kind. What had he stumbled on? How much did he know? Who else had he told? The thought made Claudel break out in a cold sweat.

'I want to talk to this Paxton,' Kamal said, breaking the silence. He motioned to his men. 'Emad, Farid, Mostafa, go and fetch him. Bring him here.'

This isn't your fucking house, Claudel wanted to scream as the three men obeyed instantly and left the room. But he was too afraid to say a word.

Kamal turned back to Aziz. 'Would you like a drink?'

Aziz glanced nervously at Claudel.

Kamal smiled. 'Come on. A little glass of something.' He moved to the drinks cabinet, opened the doors and scooped up one of Claudel's fine cut-crystal wine glasses.

It had all happened before Claudel could react.

Kamal's eyes flashed at Tarek, the leathery one, and the burly Youssef, who were standing behind Aziz's chair. They gripped the man's shoulders, pinning him down in it. Aziz opened his mouth wide in protest, and Kamal stepped quickly up to him and rammed the glass into it.

Aziz tried to scream. Kamal slowly pushed with his palm against the base of the glass until the guide's cheeks were bulging and his eyes were darting crazily from side to side in his panic. He struggled and flailed against the hands holding him down.

Kamal let go of the glass, leaving the stem and base sticking out of Aziz's gaping mouth. He moved his hands either side of the man's face. Balled them into fists. Then crunched them against Aziz's cheeks.

Claudel heard the sickening crack of the glass breaking inside Aziz's mouth. Kamal's eyes were wide and bright. He pinched Aziz's nose with the thumb and forefinger of his left hand. Used the heel of his right hand against his chin. Aziz was trying to spit, but all he could do was swallow. His screams were stifled against Kamal's hand. Blood welled out of his mouth, gushing down his throat and chest.

Then Kamal let him go. Aziz writhed screaming out of the chair and collapsed to the floor. A blood-choked gurgle came from his lacerated lips.

Kamal hadn't stopped smiling the whole time. He watched for a few more seconds, then took the pistol from behind the hip of his jeans. Worked the slide, pointed it down at Aziz's head.

Aziz stared up. The bottom half of his face was slick with blood. His mouth was contorted. His eyes were pleading, full of terror. Then a hole appeared between them and he slumped to the floor with the back of his skull punched out.

Claudel stood numb with horror, deafened by the gunshot. He gaped down at the bloody corpse, and the stain that was seeping through the cashmere carpet. 'What did you just do?'

'He knew too much,' Kamal said. 'Get rid of him. Now we'll soon see what this Paxton knows.'

But an hour later, there had been more bad news. By the time Kamal's three men had got to the apartment building, police were all over it and there was a bloody corpse on a stretcher being loaded into the back of an ambulance. Dr Morgan Paxton's corpse.

Someone had got to him first. But who?

The news had said it was a robbery gone off the rails, but Claudel didn't trust it. He spent six straight hours on the phone, trying to find out more about the Paxton murder. Nobody seemed to know anything, not even his cop contact. Sergeant Hussein of the Cairo Municipal Police had proved a useful, if expensive, ally in the past when Claudel needed information, or for the cops to look the other way. But Hussein had nothing for him this time.

The Frenchman sank deeper into despair. What if the killer had taken information from Paxton? What if someone else beat them to the treasure?

His life would be over. Ended. The way Kamal kept glaring at him, he was scared that that time would come even sooner.

All that had been two months ago. Since then, Claudel had been like a zombie. Time seemed to have stopped. He couldn't drag himself away from the news, convinced every time he turned on the TV that he'd be greeted with an announcement of a major archaeological discovery out in the desert. He'd driven out to the Abusir pyramids, south of Cairo on the edge of the great sands, desperately searching for whatever it was that this Paxton might have found there. The place was a broken-down wasteland of scattered rocks and dust. He'd spent hours there, wandering among the ruins, digging aimlessly in the sand. To no avail. He just didn't know what he was looking for.

Back at the villa, Kamal came and went, sometimes staying a couple of days at a time, sometimes disappearing for a week. Claudel did his best to avoid him, and didn't even want to think about what he might be up to during his absences. Each time he saw the van pull in through the gates he had the same chilling fear that today was the day Kamal would finally give up on him and put a bullet in his head. Claudel felt more and more as if he was living on borrowed time. It was like waiting for death.

He stood there on the balcony, his mind returning to the present as he watched the lazy red disc of the sun slowly begin its climb in the eastern sky. He sighed.

His phone rang on his bedside table. He wandered over to it, picked it up wearily and stabbed the reply button. Who could be calling him at this time of the morning?

It was the cop, Hussein.

'You know what time it is?' Claudel said irritably.

'This can't wait. I thought you'd want to know.'

Claudel tutted. 'What?'

'You know you asked me about the Paxton business?'

A faint glow of hope crept into Claudel's burnt-out brain. 'Yes?' he replied cautiously. He listened as Hussein talked, and his eyes began to widen.

'A citizen's arrest, you say?'

'Brought in trussed up like a couple of chickens,' Hussein said. 'And the way things are looking, they're dead certs for the Paxton killing. They confessed inside of ten minutes. Probably swing for it. But here's the strange bit. While we were locking them up, one of them was raving about the guy who brought them in. This crazy foreigner who'd stormed into their place, interrogated them about Paxton, beaten the crap out of them and stolen all their stuff.'

'Who the hell is he?'

'Somebody professional,' Hussein said. 'By all accounts, he mowed them down like grass.'

Suddenly there was blood flowing in Claudel's veins again. 'You have a name for this guy?'

'I can do better than that,' Hussein said. 'A police car just took him back to his apartment. Not five minutes ago. He's staying at the same place Paxton did.'

Chapter Twenty

Ben was drifting in and out of a doze as the unmarked car drove him back. It pulled up outside the grim apartment building. He thanked the driver for the lift, got out and watched the police car's taillights disappear down the street. It would soon be dawn. He wearily climbed the stairs, let himself into the rented flat, switched on the lights and flopped in an armchair.

He felt suddenly deflated, melancholy. Morgan's killers had been taken care of, but what good was it going to do anyone? The whole thing had been depressing and ugly, and now he was glad it was over. All he wanted to do was go home.

His eyes were heavy. Sleep beckoned, but he didn't want to use the bed. Kept imagining Morgan's body sprawled over it. But there was a sofa in the living room that seemed comfortable enough. He'd slept in a lot of worse places in his time.

He turned off the main lights and put on a small corner lamp that flooded the room with a soft glow and almost made it seem cosy. He settled down on the sofa, letting his muscles relax and exhaustion take over.

But it was no use. He knew he couldn't sleep until he'd taken a look at the computer. Jumping up, he grabbed his bag and carried it back to the sofa. Sitting on the edge, he pulled out the laptop. It was still rolled up inside the striped blazer.

As he unwrapped it, a small scrap of paper fell out of the blazer's breast pocket and spiralled down onto the carpet. He laid the computer down next to him on the sofa and bent to pick up the paper. Unfolding it, he saw it was a receipt stub from a Cairo grocery store, showing the purchase of some tinned food and a bottle of beer. Across the pale columns of figures, someone had scribbled a phone number in biro.

Ben read the number three times before his tired eyes registered that it was a UK landline number. The area code was 01334. It wasn't one he knew. Then there was the main number, and below that was what looked like a three-digit extension number, maybe for an office – 345.

It might be important, or it might not. Ben folded the receipt and replaced it in the blazer pocket, making a mental note to tell Harry about it when he saw him. He bundled the blazer back in his bag, slipped the gold Rolex off his wrist and dropped it inside as well. He laid the bag on the floor, settled back on the sofa with cushions propped behind his head and the slim computer resting on his stomach. He flipped open the lid and pressed the power button. Waited as it loaded itself up.

Morgan's screensaver was a shot of some archaeological dig in the sands. Ben clicked on the 'My

Documents' icon and a list flashed up. It was a short one. He scrolled down, looking for anything promising. Then he came to it.

THE AKHENATEN PROJECT

Akhenaten. Ben dimly recalled the name from his theology studies. The so-called heretic pharaoh whose turbulent reign, more than a thousand years before Christ, had wrought havoc on Egypt's economy and morale. Was this the subject of Morgan's research? So this was what it was all about – some obscure pharaoh? Hardly a big deal. Ben clicked on the document, wondering what he was about to find.

The screen suddenly went blank. A box flashed up, asking him to enter a user name and password. Above it, a curt line of text informed him: 'Automatic access disabled. This file is stored in a password-protected vault.'

Access denied. He tried again.

Same response. The way was barred.

He gazed at the screen for a second. Shrugged. It wasn't his problem. Harry might be able to access the document – if Morgan had talked about it, he might know the password or be able to guess it. But there was no way Ben was going to get in, and he didn't care that much. He yawned.

But then he thought about Harry, far away, sitting surrounded by all that luxury and probably unable to relax for a single moment as he waited for Ben to report back to him. The man's whole life was on hold.

Then Ben remembered that the apartment had Internet access. *What the hell.* Now was as good a time as any. He kicked his legs off the sofa, stood up and carried the whirring laptop over to the desk. He found a curled-up wire hanging out of a phone socket, and on the end of it a plastic mini-connector that matched up to a port on the side of the computer. He clicked it into place, and in a few moments he was online. He logged on to his webmail account and typed up a quick message:

Harry – Job completed. Coming back tomorrow, will talk soon. In the meantime, attached is Morgan's research file. Encrypted document, hope you can access. B

He attached the Akhenaten Project file to the message, hoping it would work. It did, and when he hit 'send' the message disappeared into the ether with no problems.

That was it, then. He'd done his best.

He yawned again, more deeply this time, walked back over to the sofa, turned out the side-light and stretched out. A couple of hours' sleep was all he could expect before heading to the airport. Then back to San Remo to deliver Morgan's belongings to Harry, and then on to Normandy and Le Val. He relished the idea.

What he didn't relish so much was seeing Zara again. He didn't know if he could bear it. Maybe he should arrange for Harry to meet him at a bar in town and hand the things over there. He nodded to himself sleepily. That's what he'd do.

That was his last thought before he drifted off.

Outside his window, dawn was breaking over Cairo. The city was beginning to grind back into life, the traffic rumble slowly building and the heat returning as the sun began its climb over the desert.

Ben slept. In his dreams he heard the gunfire and the screaming again. Saw the faceless man, the eyes full of hate behind the gun. He saw Zara, smiling at him through a haze.

Then he was waking in a panic and springing to his feet as the door of the apartment burst open and four heavily armed men crashed into the room.

Chapter Twenty-One

Ben stood, frozen, disorientated. There was nowhere to run, nothing to hand that he could use to defend himself and he could only watch as the men swarmed into the room and positioned themselves around him.

Four gun muzzles pointed right at his head. AKS-74U assault weapons, the radically cut-down version of the Kalashnikov rifle. The Russian military had nick-named the gun the 'okurok' – the 'cigarette stub'. Uselessly random and inaccurate at long range, but devastating at close quarters as a high-capacity, high-powered submachine gun, it was a favourite tool of terrorists. Whoever these guys were, their armament alone told him they were serious. And he could see from the way they moved, slick and professional like trained soldiers, that they'd done this kind of work before.

'Search the place,' said the one in the long black coat.

Ben knew instantly that he was the leader. The other three were the brawn, but he was the brains. He wasn't the kind who felt he had to pump iron or shave his head to look scary. It was all in the eyes. There was a wild ferocity in them, an imperious air of complete self-belief. Ben had no trouble believing that this guy would be the first to hose a full magazine of 5.45mm high-velocity rounds into him if he so much as twitched a finger. There was no doubt he was the most dangerous man in the room.

Except for one. They didn't know who they were dealing with.

Not yet.

They frisked him, rifled through his wallet, took a look at his passport, and dumped them on the floor. The leader and the big bearded one kept their weapons glued to him as the shaven-headed one and the older, leathery one swept through the apartment. It was a quick search. There was little to find except Ben's well-worn army bag and Morgan's laptop. The leathery guy laid them both on the desk.

'Down on your knees,' the leader commanded.

'I don't think so,' Ben said.

The leader gestured. 'Mostafa.'

The big guy with the beard stepped towards Ben. He was about three inches taller and at least sixty pounds heavier. There was a lot of muscle behind the blow that sent Ben sprawling to the floor. He was ready for it, but it still drove the wind out of him. He struggled to his knees, gasping.

'Better,' the leader said. 'Now where are Paxton's things?'

'I don't know what you're talking about,' Ben said.

The leader snorted. His gaze flicked away and landed

on the bag. He slung his AKS over his shoulder and strode across the room. Grabbing the bag, he upended it and spilled its contents across the desk. The wads of banknotes landed in a small pile. The man raised an eyebrow as he sifted through the stacks of money. He snatched up Morgan's crumpled blazer, gazed at it coldly, and flung it aside.

Then he picked up the Rolex and examined it, flipped it over and studied the inscription on the back. 'You don't know what I'm talking about. Yet you have Paxton's watch. It makes me wonder what else you have of his.'

He laid the watch down on the desk and picked up the slim card folder that Paxton had given Ben. Opening it out on the desk, he rifled through the documents inside. His eyes skimmed quickly over the police and coroner's reports, the photographs. His hand moved across to the laptop and flipped open the lid. The machine lit up, showing Morgan's archaeological dig screensaver.

The leader peered at it and a small smile curled on his lips. He reached down, twirled a finger on the mouse pad and clicked. His smile widened. '"The Akhenaten Project"', he read aloud. 'Very interesting. Now let's see what we have here.'

He double-clicked and waited. Then he did it again. The smile melted away. He turned and glared at Ben. 'The file is encrypted.'

'I could have told you that,' Ben replied. 'Saved you the trouble.'

Cold fury filled the man's face. 'Tell me the password.'

'I've no idea what the password is,' Ben said. 'It's not my computer.'

The leader motioned to the big guy again. The powerful kick caught Ben in the ribs and sent him sprawling back down on the floor. White pain flashed through him. He saw stars. But he wasn't about to let them see him beaten down. He struggled back up again, blanking out the agony.

The leader walked up to him, stood over him. Unslung his AKS and shoved the muzzle hard against Ben's temple. 'The password,' he repeated.

Ben coughed, waiting for the pain in his ribs to subside. He didn't think anything was broken in there. 'I told you. I don't know the password. I've no idea what's on the file.'

'Your friend didn't tell you?'

'Morgan Paxton wasn't my friend.'

'No? You have his things. You're living in the same apartment. You were hunting the men who killed him.'

Ben's mind was working hard as the pulse in his temple throbbed against the cold steel. Who the hell were these people? 'I was sent here,' he said. 'I'm a private detective.'

'Who sent you?'

'Jennifer Paxton,' Ben lied. 'Morgan's mother in England.' He knew that giving Helen Paxton's real name could easily lead them back to Harry, if they checked. Which Ben couldn't afford to assume they wouldn't. The leader looked like the kind of guy who would check everything.

'She paid you all that money?'

'She wanted me to find her son's killers and bring back his belongings. She doesn't know what he was doing here, or what's on the computer. She doesn't care, and neither do I. She just wanted his things. Sentimental value.'

The leader drew away the weapon. 'Sentimental value,' he echoed thoughtfully. He crouched down and his cold eyes bored into Ben's. 'My name is Kamal. And I'm not that sentimental.'

Ben met his gaze and said nothing.

Kamal stood up and walked back over to the desk. He laid down his gun, grabbed the laptop and shoved it back in the bag together with the documents, the wads of banknotes and the blazer, and slung the bag over his shoulder. Then he paused, looked thoughtfully at the Rolex for a second, slipped it on and did up the clasp. 'Nice watch,' he muttered, admiring it on his wrist. He grabbed up his AKS and slipped it under his raincoat.

'Kill this piece of shit. I'll be waiting in the van.'

Chapter Twenty-Two

As Kamal left the apartment he caught a last glimpse of the foreigner. Down on his knees, face white, eyes pleading as the men closed in around him for the kill. He'd seen a hundred pathetic lives ended that way. At that moment, facing a humiliating death, knowing that the sum total of their worthless existence was about to be snuffed out like a cockroach under the sole of a shoe – that was when Kamal felt most repulsed by his victims. That last undignified reaction in itself justi-fied stamping them out. He couldn't bear to be in the room with them any longer than he had to. Human detritus. Food for worms.

The foreigner was begging now. 'Please! Don't kill me! I've got a wife and child!'

Kamal smiled as he shut the door. He glanced left and right. There was nobody around. He made his way down the spiralling stairs, past the empty landings, and out into the street where the plain white van was parked across from the building. The early morning sun was already getting hot. He crossed the road and climbed up into the cab, slipped the stubby assault weapon out from under his coat and laid it down in the footwell. Kamal leaned back in his seat and watched through the dusty windscreen as the scattering of passers-by went about their business.

He looked at his shiny new watch. The men wouldn't be long doing what they had to do. He was impatient to get back to Claudel's house and try again to get into the laptop file. He was sure he could crack the password. How hard could it be? That French prick would have ideas, anyway. They'd spent a lot of time talking about all this history stuff. Stuff that would have been incredibly boring to Kamal, if it hadn't represented unimaginable wealth. That kind of brought it to life for him.

Then again, why wait? He had a minute or two. The men would probably be finishing off the foreigner about now. Once they'd got bored of watching Mostafa smack him around, Tarek would hold him while Farid slit his throat. Then they'd close up the apartment and make their way downstairs. Maybe stop for a cigarette in the hallway. There was time enough to have another quick look at the file.

He reached for the bag. It was battered and worn, but he liked it. Deciding to keep it, he undid the fastenings, slipped out the laptop and powered it back up. First, he clicked into 'My Documents' and tried again with the little icon labelled 'The Akhenaten Project'. He got the same response as before. 'Access denied'.

No problem, he thought. He cast his mind back to his talks with Claudel, pondered for a moment, then clicked on the box that said 'Enter password', and typed the word 'amun'.

Kamal didn't remember exactly who Amun was. Some god who'd meant something in ancient times. It only meant anything now if it could unlock the file, lead him to his money.

It didn't. Access denied.

But it was no big deal. Plenty more options.

He typed 'amuniscontent'. No joy.

He typed 'heretic'. That was denied as well.

He swore violently, slammed the computer shut and shoved it back in the bag. Looked at his watch again, glanced, seething, at the window of the building. What the fuck was keeping them up there?

His patience snapped. He reached down into the footwell and snatched up the gun. Slipping it under his coat he went storming back across the street. The precious laptop in the bag slapped against his hip as he walked.

As Kamal strode up to the entrance, an old man was coming out of the building holding a small child by the hand. The child looked up at Kamal with inquisitive eyes, and the old man shot him a fearful glance.

Kamal didn't slow down. He marched straight ahead through the entrance, shoving the old guy roughly out of the way. He didn't even look back, but the sound of the old man's pain and confusion as he stumbled and fell against the wall, and the cry of the distressed child, pleased him.

Kamal took the stairs three at a time. He reached the landing where the apartment was and strode fast up to the door. It was open a few inches. He could hear no sound, no voices, coming from inside. He frowned. His instincts dictated caution, and he always trusted his instincts. He brought the AKS out from under his coat and held it at hip level, flipping off the safety. Then he jutted out his chin and marched in through the open door.

He stopped. Blinked and stared.

Two of his men were lying on the floor. Mostafa's bulk was spreadeagled on his back with his arms flung outwards at his sides. He had a squashed red mess in the middle of his face where his nose had been rammed backwards into his skull.

Tarek was sprawled in a heap at an angle to him. He had a crushed trachea. It had been stamped on. There were bubbles of blood around the corners of his mouth, trickles of it down to his ears. His eyes were staring up at the slowly rotating ceiling fan.

Farid was sitting in a chair by the desk. One leg was bent under him, the other stretched out in front. His hands lay limply in his lap. His shaved head was on backwards.

The room was eerily undisturbed. Barely a sign of a struggle. The foreigner's wallet and passport had disappeared.

And so had the foreigner himself.

Kamal's mouth hung open. He suddenly felt cold, unnerved. Who the hell was this man, to have done this?

He was still standing there agape, his gun dangling loose at his side, when the door swung quietly shut behind him.

Chapter Twenty-Three

Ben clicked the door shut and walked into the room. In his hands was the stubby AKS he'd taken from one of the men. He had it trained precisely on Kamal's head. At this range, he didn't need to use the sights. A three-shot burst at three yards, and the walls would need yet another fresh coat of paint.

'Lose the gun,' Ben said.

Kamal was pale. 'Who are you?'

'Lose the gun,' Ben repeated. 'Or I'll kill you. I won't ask you again.' As he said it, he could see how fast Kamal was recovering from the surprise. He wasn't their leader for nothing. He was a far more redoubtable adversary than any of them. Quick, smart and very mean. Ben's senses were on full alert and his finger was on the trigger. The AKS probably had a pull of about six pounds, maybe seven. He had about five pounds on it already.

Kamal frowned. Glanced down at the gun that was still hanging at his side. He relaxed his fingers, and the weapon dropped straight down to the floor, an inch from his feet.

'Kick it away,' Ben said. 'And let's have that Glock, too.'

Kamal paused a beat. *I'm impressed*, his eyes said. He nudged the AKS with his shoe. It slid across the floor. Then, very slowly, he drew back his long coat until it cleared the Cordura holster on his belt. He unsnapped the retaining strap and eased the pistol out between forefinger and thumb. Held it out at arm's length and flicked his wrist. The gun clattered to the floor a couple of feet away.

He kept his eyes on Ben the whole time. There was a glitter of something in them. As though he found the whole thing *amusing*.

'Now it's going to be your turn to talk,' Ben said. 'I want to know a few things. Like what you want with Morgan Paxton's research.'

Kamal gazed down the muzzle of Ben's AKS, then looked up, fixing him with a cocky glare. The faintest hint of a smile appeared on his lips. 'You would just love to know, wouldn't you?'

'Then make me happy.'

'You'll find out soon enough,' Kamal said. 'You all will. The day is coming.'

Ben frowned. 'What does that mean?'

But Kamal just smiled more widely. He took a step backwards, over one of the bodies, away from Ben, towards the window.

Ben took a step forwards, keeping a steady distance between them. 'Don't move any further,' he warned.

A sudden sound behind him made him whirl around, ready to fire. For an instant he thought there were more of them.

It was the landlord. He was bleary-eyed and unshaven, wearing a vest and shorts. 'I thought I heard someth—'

His voice trailed off mid-word. He took in the guns. The corpses. His face froze into an expression of horror.

Ben turned back to Kamal, but it was already too late. Two seconds was too long to leave a guy like him unguarded. Kamal plucked his hand from his coat pocket and lobbed something across the room, then turned and crashed through the window and out onto the fire escape.

The object rolled across the floor.

Fragmentation grenade.

Ben dived back through the open door, hauling the landlord with him out into the hallway. The guy was heavy and clumsy. As Ben yanked him out of the way of the impending blast, he crashed down on him with all his weight.

About half a second after that, the grenade detonated in the confined space. The explosion ripped through the apartment. Shrapnel tore into everything and a fireball rolled out of the doorway as the frame and door shattered into a million tumbling splinters. The wall burst outwards into the hallway, pieces of masonry spinning through the air.

In the aftermath of the blast was the stunned, deafened, disorientated silence that follows every explosion. Through the smoke and dust Ben could see his hand lying in front of his face. It was white with powdered masonry, spattered with blood. He struggled to focus. Saw his fingers twitch and contract into a fist, and realised the hand was still connected to his body.

Something was pressing down on him, making it hard to breathe. He tried to get up, heave the weight off him. It was the body of the landlord, crushing him. A big arm fell limp at the man's side.

Ben rolled out from under him. Through the terrible ringing in his ears he could hear the high-pitched whine of smoke alarms and, somewhere beyond that, the screams of a woman. He staggered to his feet. Looked down at the landlord. The man was dead. His chest and face were a bloody mess from where he'd absorbed the blast of lethal shrapnel.

Ben checked himself all over with trembling hands. He knew he could be badly injured, even if he didn't feel it yet. Smashed nerve endings and pumping adrenaline could mask just about anything in the first moments before you even knew you were hit. But all the blood on him belonged to the landlord. He didn't have a scratch on him.

Then he remembered. *Kamal.*

With his ears still whining from the blast, Ben leaped over the dead man, sprinted down the burning hallway and bounded down the stairs four, five, six at a time. Burst out into the street. A crowd of people had gathered, pointing up at the smoke that poured from the apartment window. Three or four of them were already on their phones, calling for emergency services.

People stared as Ben streaked past, broken glass crunching under his feet. He couldn't see Kamal anywhere.

An engine revved. The grating roar of a diesel being pushed way too hard. Someone in a desperate hurry.

He whipped around just in time to see Kamal peering wild-eyed out of the van window before it lurched away from the kerb across the street and took off, smoke belching from its exhaust.

Ben sprinted after it. Running for all he was worth, he caught up with the van. His straining fingers closed around the black metal handle of the back door, and he felt the joints of his wrist and elbow and shoulder being stretched as the vehicle accelerated manically down the street. He held on. The van picked up more speed and now he was running in giant strides, the road flashing by under his feet. He tried to wrench the door open, so that he could clamber inside and get at the driver.

But the doors were locked. The van kept accelerating, engine screaming up through the gears. Ben lost his footing, stumbled and felt his knee grate on the road as he went down. For a short distance he was dragged along. Somehow he regained his footing and he was running again. His fingers were screaming to let go of the handle.

A blare of horns. The van swerved to avoid an oncoming vehicle. Ben was thrown sideways and the handle was torn from his grip. He tumbled and rolled on the tarmac and came to a stunned halt at the kerbside.

As he looked up, all he could see was the back of the white van rapidly disappearing into the distance. At the top of the street it skidded left, and then it was lost in the traffic and out of sight.

Ben thumped the road with a bleeding fist. He was

aware of the people staring at him from the pavement. Someone was yelling in Arabic, words he didn't register.

He clambered painfully to his feet, and started walking in the same direction as the van. He didn't look back.

He was half a block away by the time he heard the howl of approaching sirens.

Chapter Twenty-Four

Ben walked for twenty minutes under the hot sun, ignoring the pain from the kick to the ribs, his grazed knee and scuffed hands. The worst of the blood was on his shirt, from where the dead landlord had bled all over him. He covered it with his jacket, and from more than a few yards away he didn't look too alarming.

He bought a fresh T-shirt, a pair of imitation Levis and a litre of bottled water from a street market. He was thankful he still had his wallet, and just about enough cash to get him out of Egypt. If that was what he needed to do: he wasn't sure yet what his next move should be.

In a secluded alleyway nearby he stripped off his old clothes, washed himself down as best he could and put on the T-shirt and jeans. He bundled up his old things and stuffed them into a skip, drank what was left of the bottled water and wandered back out into the street feeling a little refreshed.

After a few more minutes of walking, he came to a café-bar with tables and chairs outside. He took a seat in the shade of a parasol and ordered strong black coffee. He drank a pot of it, ordered another, and sat there quietly until the caffeine rush began to focus his thoughts.

He thought about what he'd just done. *Had to do.* There'd been no choice – but that didn't make him feel any better about it. He'd sworn he was never going to kill again, but just when he'd thought he'd done the right thing by handing Morgan's assassins over to the police, here he was again being dragged back into the familiar old world that he'd worked so hard to escape from. Could he never get away from it? Was that really his destiny in life?

He sighed. Then his thoughts turned to Morgan Paxton. One thing was clear now. Whatever this apparently unassuming, naïve academic was into, it was obviously much bigger than just scholarly research. A man like Kamal could have been attracted to this Akhenaten Project for only one reason. Money, or the promise of it. And when the prospect of wealth and ancient history were brought together in the mix, that amounted to a formula that could produce only one simple answer.

A treasure hunt.

The question was, had Morgan known just how big this was? Ben thought about it for a while. He retraced Morgan's steps in his mind. The guy had come to Egypt on his own. Not as part of some research team, but independently – and he'd encrypted the file on his computer. That didn't look like the behaviour of an ordinary academic researcher. In all kinds of other ways, Morgan might have been the typical egghead scholar, but this looked like deliberate, calculated secretiveness. People didn't actively protect information unless they thought it had special value. He'd known what he was into, for sure.

But then there must have been leaks in Morgan's security. He might have been acting cautious, but he was still an amateur at this game. And he was a stranger in a strange land. The kind of guy who could draw – and had drawn, fatally – all kinds of the wrong attention. Maybe he'd needed help for his project. Maybe he'd been foolish, talked to the wrong people to get that help. People who knew people, one thing leading to another until, next thing he knew, he had someone like Kamal on his trail.

Kamal. Ben visualised the man's face. Who was he? Someone committed, dedicated – but to what? *The day is coming*, he'd said. Ben didn't know what he'd meant by that – but it didn't sound good.

And now he had to figure out his next step. One thing he couldn't avoid was the call to Harry. A call he wasn't looking forward to making.

He took out his phone and dialled Harry Paxton's personal number. Paxton picked up after three rings.

'Harry. It's Ben.'

'I got your email,' Paxton said.

'Were you able to open the attachment?'

'I haven't tried. I was more interested in hearing what you had to report. So tell me, Benedict. It's over? You've done it?'

Ben paused and bit his lip. There was no easy way to tell Paxton this. Start at the start. 'I found the men who killed Morgan,' he said. 'They were just petty thieves who got in too deep. They still had some of his things.'

'And you dealt with it? The way we talked about?'

'Yes, I did deal with it, Harry. But not quite the way you intended.'

There was a silence. Then, 'What do you mean?'

Ben let out a long breath. 'I couldn't go through with it, Harry. I told you at the time, it's not what I do. They're in police custody now. They'll be on murder, firearms and drugs charges that'll see them locked away for a long, long time. Drugs alone carry a twenty-five-year hard labour sentence in Egypt. They might well even get the rope for it. But it's out of our hands now.' He paused. 'I'm sorry. I know it's not what you wanted. But it's the best I could do.'

Paxton was quiet for a few moments, and Ben could feel him thinking. Adjusting to the idea.

'I suppose you had to do what you felt was right,' Paxton said eventually. 'I appreciate that. I admire your integrity. I really do. You're a good man, Benedict.'

'I have to warn you,' Ben said. 'There's more to it. Complications. There are other people interested in Morgan's research. Very dangerous people. They weren't the ones who killed him, but I think they would have if there hadn't been the robbery. It was just a question of who would get to him first. I'm sorry. I know this is painful to hear.'

'I'm stunned,' Paxton said after a moment's silence. 'Are you sure about this?'

'Pretty sure,' Ben said, feeling his bruised ribs. It hurt to breathe, and it hurt even more to move. He ran through what had happened. 'And so I've lost most of what I retrieved,' he finished. 'I'm really sorry.'

'Never mind the computer and the watch,' Paxton said. 'The important thing is that you're all right. But who are these people?'

'I don't know. I just know that Morgan's research went a little beyond pure academic interest. And I think he knew it, too.'

'It must all be in the file you sent me,' Paxton said.

'I'm sure it is. Did he ever mention something called The Akhenaten Project to you?'

'I don't recall. I don't think so, but then again he was always talking about names and dates from history. This god, that pharaoh. I never really paid it much heed.'

'That's fine,' Ben said. 'But now we have a problem. I need to know what to do next. Whatever Morgan was into, I'm very concerned that these people might come after you. You're the next of kin. They might think you know something. I fobbed them off with a lie, but it might not deter them for long.'

'So what are you saying?'

'I'm saying that perhaps I need to stay here in Egypt a while longer. Find out who these people are and stop them before they do any more harm.'

Paxton was quiet for a moment. 'I don't want that, Benedict. I asked you to do something for me, and you did it. You've done enough for me. I'll be eternally grateful. As for these people, whoever they are, I think I can look after myself. I haven't quite forgotten everything I learned in the army. Let them come. They'll be surprised at the reception they'll get.'

'You don't want this kind of trouble, Harry,' Ben replied. 'Believe me. It's not worth it. Your fighting days are over. You've started a new life. Get on with it. Think of Zara, if nothing else. Remember, she's vulnerable, if they link this to you.'

Paxton didn't reply.

'You're on a yacht,' Ben continued. 'You can move from place to place untracked, and you can run your business from anywhere. So stick a pin in the atlas, find yourself a nice warm paradise somewhere and set sail. That's my advice. I don't think these guys have got a long reach, but play it safe.'

There was another long silence on the phone. Then Paxton said, 'Perhaps you're right. Maybe there's some other way to honour Morgan's memory. I could donate some money to a museum in his name. Set up a trust fund for young researchers.'

'That sounds like a good idea, Harry. And there's one more thing. If I'd known what I know now, I'd never have sent that file to you. I'd have wiped it. And I think that's what you should do. Delete it from your computer, right now.'

'I'll do that,' Paxton said.

'And will you promise me you'll relocate?'

'As soon as it's feasible. I promise. You're right. I need to think of Zara.' Paxton paused. 'Will you be coming back to San Remo, to see us while we're still here?'

Ben didn't reply.

'After what you've been through, I'd like you to be my guest here for a few days,' Paxton said. 'So would Zara. She seemed very much to enjoy your company.

I sometimes think she's a bit lonely,' he added wistfully. 'I'm always up to my eyes in business. She'd love to see you again.'

Ben squirmed. *Jesus.*

'Maybe some other time, Harry. If I'm not staying here, I've really got to be heading back home.'

'I'm disappointed,' Paxton said. 'I would have liked to be able to thank you in person, show you how truly grateful I am. But I understand you have affairs of your own to attend to. I hope you'll at least let me wire you the money you lost.'

'Forget it, Harry. I don't want it.'

'You earned it.'

'I didn't do much,' Ben said.

Paxton paused. 'Keep in touch, won't you?'

'See you around, Harry. I'm sorry I couldn't do more for you.'

Ben ended the call. He sat still for a moment, deep in thought.

'Right,' he muttered to himself. 'Time to go home.'

Chapter Twenty-Five

Claudel was flicking through a book in his study when he heard the van skid up on the gravel outside. A few seconds later, Kamal came bursting into the villa. Rapid footsteps across the marble floor of the hall. The study door flew open. Kamal stormed into the room, clutching a laptop to his chest. He strode over to the desk and thumped it down, sending papers fluttering.

'What's that?' Claudel asked nervously. He could almost feel the heat of the aggression that was pouring off the man.

Kamal's eyes flashed with fury. '*That* is your whole life, until you can figure out what's inside.'

Claudel flipped the lid open and switched on the machine. As he sat poring over the screen, Kamal was pacing up and down, almost manic with rage. He tore a valuable second edition of Gibbons' *Decline and Fall of the Roman Empire* from a bookshelf and hurled it across the room. It smacked against the wall. The binding burst apart and it fluttered to the floor like a dead bird. 'I'll have that bastard's head on a *plate*!' he screamed.

'What happened?'

'Three of my men are dead, is what *happened*.' Kamal roared the last word. He grabbed a delicate eighteenth-century upholstered chair, threw it down and stamped it into pieces. 'Fuck! Fuck! Fuck!' Pieces of wood spun across the study floor.

Claudel looked away. He knew better than to ask too many questions of Kamal when he was in this mood. He returned to the computer, and quickly found the Akhenaten file. His eyes brightened. Then he tried clicking into it.

'This file is encrypted,' he said, looking up.

'I know that,' Kamal raged. 'You take me for a fucking idiot?'

Claudel looked back down at the screen and felt a trickle of sweat run down his neck. 'I'm not a computer person,' he protested weakly. 'How am I supposed to crack an encrypted file?'

Kamal stormed over to him with his teeth bared in anger. 'I don't care how you do it. You figure this out. Understood?'

Claudel was already running through his options, thinking of all the people he knew who could help. *Hisham*, he thought. Hisham was good with computers.

But no sooner had the thought occurred to him, than his heart sank again. He couldn't call Hisham. If he failed, Kamal would just shoot the guy, or worse. Anyone Claudel brought in on this situation was condemned to death. He thought of what had happened to Aziz. He thought about him all the time, couldn't get the image out of his mind. He'd been having nightmares about it.

No. He was on his own.

He looked desperately up at Kamal. 'The password could be anything.'

'Then try everything,' Kamal said. 'Starting now.'

Chapter Twenty-Six

Normandy

It was a long journey home, and it was late when Ben finally arrived back at Le Val by taxi. The moon was full, bathing the cobbled yard in milky light. He paid the driver and stepped out, stretching his legs. Watched the car drive off into the darkness up the long, winding drive.

He looked around him. The homely smell of the wood-burning stove was drifting across from the farmhouse, and there was a light on behind the curtained kitchen window. Across the yard, the trainees' accommodation block was dimly lit and he heard someone laugh in the distance.

He heard the sound of running paws, and a shaggy shape hurled itself out of the shadows to greet him.

Ben patted the dog affectionately as it jumped up to lick his face. 'Hey, Storm. Good to see you too, boy.' And he meant it. It was good to be home. He wearily climbed the three steps to the farmhouse door, turned the big brass handle and stepped into the hallway.

The place was warm and welcoming. Someone had a CD playing in the kitchen. Ben recognised the music. It was one of his own collection: Art Blakey and the Jazz Messengers. He walked down the flagstone passage and pushed open the oak door. All he could think about was a large glass of red wine, a chunk of local cheese and a hunk of bread.

Brooke was sitting alone at the kitchen table, reading a novel. In front of her was a steaming mug that smelled like cocoa. She looked up as Ben came in. Her hair was damp, as though she'd just got out of the shower, and she was wearing an emerald green bathrobe. It brought out the green of her eyes, something Ben had never noticed about her before.

She put down her novel, and smiled warmly. 'You're back.'

'You're still here,' he said.

'I told you I was going to hang around for a few days, remember?' She peered at him and her smile faded. 'Christ, Hope. You look like shit.'

'Thanks.'

'Honestly. Your eyes are like two burnt holes in a blanket.'

'That makes me feel even better,' he said, making a beeline for the wine rack.

'What happened?'

'Nothing I really feel like talking about.' He grabbed a bottle and the opener, and set about tearing away the foil to get at the cork.

Brooke stood up. She came over to him and laid a hand on his arm. 'Go and sit down. I'll do that.'

She pointed at the huge cast-iron pot that was sitting on the range. 'There's still some of Marie-Claire's cassoulet. To die for, I'm telling you. Blew my diet completely. You hungry?'

He slumped in a wooden chair. 'Like I've never eaten in my life.'

Brooke pulled the cork out of the bottle, glugged wine into a large glass and set it down in front of him. He knocked it back, reached for the bottle and refilled it.

'Bad day at the office, then,' she said over her shoulder as she ladled a pile of the stew into a saucepan and started warming it over the gas flame.

He didn't reply. Sat and drank as she served the food onto a plate and brought it over to him. There was concern showing in her eyes.

'Thanks for this, Brooke,' he said through a mouthful of the stew. 'You don't know how glad I am to be back.'

She sat down beside him at the table and rested her chin on her palm, watching him eat. 'How come you don't want to tell me what happened? What took you to Cairo?'

'I was just helping a friend.'

'This Paxton guy?'

He nodded.

'But it's over now?'

He nodded again.

Brooke snorted. 'Well, whatever you were doing out there for him, I hope he appreciates it. You should see yourself.'

'I just need a rest. I'll be fine in the morning.' His plate was empty and he drained the last of his glass of wine. 'So what have you been up to?' he asked her, abruptly changing the subject.

'Relaxing, mostly. Waiting for you.'

'I told you not to wait for me,' he said.

She shrugged. 'Jeff's been teaching me to shoot. Says I'm good at it.'

'Uh-huh,' he grunted, reaching for the bottle again.

'You going to drink the whole thing?'

'Maybe.'

'Someone's been calling for you,' she said. 'Phoned three times this evening. A woman.' She paused, watching his reaction. 'Someone called Zara. Sounded Australian.'

Ben's glass stopped halfway to his lips. He set it down heavily on the table. 'Shit,' he muttered.

Brooke smiled, raising an eyebrow. 'Someone you ran into on your travels?'

'You might say that,' he replied sullenly.

'Seemed very anxious to talk to you,' Brooke said. 'I'm sure she'll call again.' She leaned forward on her elbows. 'So what's she like, Ben?'

'Who?'

'Don't play games. You know who I mean. Zara.'

He stared at her. 'What's it to you?'

'Whoo. Testy. Must have hit a nerve there.'

'Leave it alone, Brooke. I'm tired, OK?'

'Is she pretty? Sounded pretty.'

He stood up, grabbed his glass and what was left of the bottle. 'I'm going to bed.' As an afterthought he grabbed another bottle from the rack and tucked it under his arm as he headed for the door. 'See you in the morning,' he muttered. 'I'll be up late.'

'What if she calls again?'

'Tell her I've died or something,' he said. Then he banged through the door and climbed the stairs.

He'd been right about the late morning. It was well after ten o'clock when he came plodding down the stairs holding three empties. The two wine bottles, and the whisky he'd washed them down with. His mouth felt thick with the aftertaste of stale booze, and his head was heavy.

It hadn't been a good night. He'd thrashed about restlessly for a long time, trying to sleep. But it had been no use. He couldn't stop his mind from whirring around and around in circles, working over all the things that had been happening. Eventually, he'd given up. Sat up on the rumpled sheets and put the light on and just sat drinking until well after five in the morning.

The faces of the three men he'd killed had haunted him long into the night. Even when he'd polished off the second bottle of wine and moved on to the whisky he kept in the wardrobe, he hadn't been able to still his mind.

When he wasn't thinking about the things he'd had to do in Cairo, he was thinking about Zara. He thought of the brief time they'd spent together. Seeing her in the little bookshop in San Remo. Running through the rain to shelter from the thunderstorm. The touch of her hand on his arm. Her firm body close to his. Her smile, her laugh, her tears.

Why was she calling him? He dreaded having to talk to her, if she called again. And he knew she was sure to.

What if she wanted to meet him? He knew that just the sound of her voice might destroy his resolve – that he'd give in and agree to meet up with her somewhere. That just couldn't happen.

Part of him was thankful that Harry had agreed to haul anchor and relocate the *Scimitar*. Zara would be far away, and in time his feelings would diminish. But it also meant he probably would never see her again, and right now he wasn't sure he could handle that.

He was still feeling racked with the same uncertainty, and hating himself bitterly for his weakness, as he stepped out into the morning drizzle. He was heading across the yard to dump his empty bottles into the recycling bin when he heard Jeff Dekker's voice call his name.

He turned. 'Hi, Jeff.' His voice came out as a croak.

Jeff trotted up to him. The trousers of his fatigues were spattered in mud up to the knee. 'Glad to see you back. Are you taking the eleven o'clock pistol shooting group?' He glanced at the empty bottles and looked more closely at Ben's face. 'Jesus, mate. You look like—'

'Like shit. So everyone keeps telling me.'

'Are you OK?'

'I just need to get my head together. I was thinking of going for a good long run.'

'You look more like you need to rest.'

'I'm sick of resting. Running will relax me. Listen, if anyone calls for me—'

'Like Zara, for example?' Jeff grinned.

'Give me a break. Not you as well.'

'She sounded hot. Anything you'd like to tell me, Ben?'

Ben sighed. 'Yeah. Mind your own fucking business.'

'She's bound to call again,' Jeff said. 'You can't put her off forever.'

'I don't want to talk to her. Tell her anything you like. I've gone off and joined the Trappist monks, OK?'

'If she wants to come here, I'm not going to put her off,' Jeff said. 'I'm no Trappist monk.'

'Do me a favour, Jeff.' Ben walked over to the recycling bin and tossed the bottles in one at a time. He whistled for Storm. The German Shepherd burst out of one of the barns, halted suddenly, stiff and alert, then came running over.

Ben ran his fingers through the dog's thick coat. 'Come on, boy. Let's go and run some of the crap out of our system.'

Two hours of punishment later, as the drizzle turned into sheeting rain over Le Val, Ben and the dog returned to the house bedraggled and soaking. Storm shook himself in the yard and trotted over to his kennel. Ben walked up to the house and went into the kitchen.

Jeff Dekker and the six-strong group for the new Counter Attack Team training course were all sitting around the long table eating lunch. Jeff was in the middle of entertaining them with a funny anecdote when Ben walked in. Faces turned to look. 'Everyone, this is Ben Hope,' Jeff said, breaking off his story. 'Come and join us, Ben. I was just telling them about that time when—'

'Great to meet you all,' Ben interrupted him shortly. 'Have a good lunch. Maybe see you later.' He strode up to the wine rack, dripping rainwater across the flagstones, and grabbed a bottle. Snatched a cold chicken leg from the platter in the middle of the table and headed for the door. The room had gone quiet and he could feel all eyes upon him, but he didn't care. He shoved through the door and headed for his quarters.

Upstairs, he dumped the bottle and the chicken leg on his desk, stripped off his wet clothes and left them in a heap on the floor as he went for a shower. He spent a long time under the water, turning it up as hot as he could bear it. Afterwards he towelled himself dry and changed into a pair of jeans and an old sweatshirt. Flopping on the couch, he munched desultorily on the cold chicken and gulped wine from the bottle. It didn't do much to take the edge off his mood.

He was just thinking of going downstairs to fetch more Laphroaig from the cellar when his phone rang in his pocket. He dug it out, and his thumb hovered over the reply button for a moment before he decided against answering it. It rang insistently until his answering service kicked in, then went quiet.

You fucking coward, he seethed at himself. *It might not even have been her. You never going to answer your phone again?*

A few moments later, it rang again. He took a deep breath and answered on the second ring.

He had a message. It was Zara.

Her voice sounded small and timid. 'Ben, it's me. Where are you? I've called and called.' A pause. 'There

209

are things I have to talk to you about. Important things. Call me back soon, all right?' Another pause. 'Love you. Miss you.'

Then the robotic voice of the answering service was again in his ear. 'To listen to the message again, press 1 . . .'

He couldn't bring himself to delete it. He listened to it again. Decided to call her back. *Fuck it.*

He was just about to phone her when there was a thumping on his door and Jeff walked in and stood over him with his arms folded.

'What was that all about?' he demanded.

Ben looked at him blankly.

'Jesus, Ben. What's got into you? The way you behaved in front of those guys.'

'They're ex-soldiers, Jeff. They're not a bunch of social workers.'

'They're our *clients*, Ben. That's what they are. Remember that business you used to run?'

Ben didn't reply.

'I've never seen you like this before, mate,' Jeff said. 'I don't know what the fuck's going on inside your head, but you need to snap out of it sooner rather than later.'

Ben just sighed and looked down at his feet.

Jeff glared at him a second longer and then left the room, slamming the door behind him.

Chapter Twenty-Seven

The following morning

The acres of woodland around Le Val were deep enough to lose yourself in, and Ben meant to do just that. He knew all the little tracks and paths through the forest. Some of them had been there forever, probably created by deer and wild boar, and some of them he'd made himself. Over fallen trees and up earth banks, across the stream and through dense ferns, he ran until his body was screaming for rest.

In a tiny clearing in the forest was one of the features of Le Val that he loved most – the ruin of an old church dating back to the thirteenth century. There was nothing left but a few crumbled stone walls and the remnants of a tower where generations of doves had made a home for themselves. At its foot was a slab of stone nestling among the wildflowers, where he liked to sit and think, listening to the doves burbling and cooing in their nests. That was where he headed now, with the dog trotting along behind him.

He sat and listened to the sounds of the forest.

Everything was so tranquil. It was a beautiful spring morning. The sky was blue above the trees, and the birds were singing. He should have been happy. This place was his home now.

He knew he had to get a grip on himself. Jeff had been right. If he wasn't careful, he was going to start neglecting his business and everything he'd worked so hard to build was going to slip through his fingers.

But the way Ben was feeling right now, he wanted to shy away from everything. He felt empty inside. He didn't want to have to deal with people, or have to take care of all those thousands of little tasks that just last week he'd have attended to with enthusiasm.

There was only one person in the world whose company he longed for. The one person he wasn't free to be with. He'd left his phone back in the office, avoiding the inevitable call from her.

He sighed and took out his cigarettes. Jogging and smoking, he thought. First the detox, and then the retox. *Great going, Hope.* But he didn't care. Storm watched curiously as he sat there blowing smoke rings that drifted over the ruined walls.

The dog snapped to attention, suddenly alert, ears pricked up. A second later Ben heard the snap of a twig. He turned.

Stepping out of the trees, Brooke peered through the ivy-tangled Gothic archway and spotted him sitting there inside the ruined church. 'Found you,' she smiled, approaching. The way he was looking at her, she didn't think he was too happy to have been found. Then he smiled back – but she could see the sadness in his face.

She walked under the arch towards him. 'Mind if I join you?'

He didn't reply, but shifted along the stone seat to make room for her. Brooke sat down beside him, her knee touching his.

'I didn't know anyone else knew about this place,' he said.

'I've been exploring. I love it here. And I had a feeling it was the kind of spot Ben Hope would disappear off to when he needed to be alone.'

'You know me pretty well, don't you, Brooke?'

'Pretty well,' she said. 'Well enough to know that something's eating you.'

'I'm sorry. I know I've been shit company.'

'I've had better, that's for sure.' She put her hand on his arm. 'Tell me what's bugging you. You've been like a hen on a hot griddle since you got back. It's something to do with this Zara who keeps calling. Right?'

He tossed his cigarette stub away and watched it smoulder in the leaves for a moment, then crushed it with his boot. 'I told you, I don't want to talk about it.'

'I think you need to talk about it.'

'There you are, sounding like a psychologist again.'

'I want to help you,' she said. 'Won't you let me? I don't like to see you suffering like this.'

'It's my problem,' he said. 'I'll deal with it.'

'But it matters to me. A lot.' Brooke wondered if she was saying too much.

He reached out and touched her nose with brotherly affection. 'You're a good friend to me, Brooke.'

I don't want to be your friend, she thought. 'So am I right?' she asked.

'Right about what?'

'Right about this Zara.'

'You're right. It's to do with Zara. Zara Paxton.'

'Paxton. As in Harry Paxton?'

He nodded glumly.

'Daughter? Sister?'

'Wife.' Ben turned to look at her. 'I'm in love with her.'

Brooke frowned. 'In love,' she repeated. 'Since when?'

He sighed. 'Since the first time I saw her. In Italy.'

'But that was just a couple of days ago,' she said.

'That's right.'

'Love at first sight? Come on.'

'It's corny, isn't it?' he replied with a chuckle. It sounded mirthless and hollow. 'Stupid. But that's how it is and I can't seem to shake it out of my head.'

Brooke stiffened a little. 'This is something of a surprise, Ben.'

He snorted. 'And for me. You think I'm happy about it?'

She bit her lip thoughtfully. 'Does Zara feel the same about you?'

'Now you really do sound like a psychologist.'

'Does she?'

Ben sighed. 'She says she does.'

'I guess that would explain all the phone calls. And does the colonel know about this affair?'

'It's not an affair,' Ben said defensively. 'Nothing's happened between us.'

'But does he know?'

'Of course he doesn't. And he's never going to, because nothing's ever going to happen.'

'What do you mean?'

'Why do you think I'm not answering her calls?'

Brooke glanced knowingly at him. 'Because you're scared of what you're feeling.'

Ben said nothing to that.

'Can I level with you?' she said.

He lit another cigarette. 'You're going to anyway. Why ask?'

She measured her words, not wanting to say what she was about to say. 'Here's what I think. If you love this woman and she loves you, why don't you just go for it? You've been through a terrible time the last year or so. You've been as down as anyone can be. Who wouldn't, after what happened to Leigh?'

She paused thoughtfully, then went on. 'What I'm trying to say is, if now all of a sudden you've found someone new that you can love, that makes you one of the luckiest guys in the world. Don't fight it. We only go around once, Ben.'

'You don't understand. Harry Paxton saved my life.'

'I know that. So you feel you have a debt of honour to him. That's admirable. But are you prepared to throw away a chance of real happiness over it? If anyone deserves a break, it's you.'

He didn't reply.

'In addition to which, I'm guessing that this Cairo

trip was all about paying the debt back. So how much more do you think you owe this Paxton guy?'

Ben smiled faintly. 'I didn't exactly pay it back. Not quite.'

'Get back to the house, Ben. Pick up the damn phone and talk to her. You need to go with your heart.'

There, she thought. She'd said it. Just about the hardest thing she'd ever had to say to anyone. She wanted to reach out and hold him, tell him how she really felt about him.

'What's wrong with your eye?' he said suddenly.

She reached up quickly and wiped away the tear that was clinging to her lashes. 'Nothing. Just a speck of dust.'

'Let me have a look,' he said, bending towards her.

She turned away. 'No, it's all right.' She took a tissue from her pocket and dabbed her eyes.

'Come back with me to the house,' he said. 'I need to talk to Jeff. Apologise to him for the way I've been acting up. And you can rinse out that eye.'

'Think I'll stay a while. I like being alone here.'

'You're sure? Know your way back?'

'Found you here, didn't I?'

As he was leaving, he reached down and touched her shoulder gently. 'I'm glad you're my friend.'

He walked away, the dog trotting along at his heel.

Brooke watched him slip away into the trees. Once she was alone, she buried her face in her hands and cried.

Ben walked into the office to find Jeff sitting at the desk filling out some paperwork.

He came right out with it. 'Jeff, I'm sorry I've been acting like a prick the last couple of days.'

Jeff grinned. 'Yeah, you have. But I forgive you, mate.'

'I need something to do.'

'You can finish this paperwork. I've been breaking my balls over it all morning. How's that for a punishment?'

'That'll do to begin with,' Ben said. As he was about to start leafing through the paperwork, his mobile started ringing from the corner of the desk where he'd abandoned it earlier.

'Aren't you going to answer that?' Jeff asked.

'It's her.'

'Better get yourself a new SIM card. Because otherwise you might as well toss that phone in the river, if you're never going to answer it again.'

'I don't know what to say to her.'

'For Christ's sake.' Jeff snatched the phone up. 'Le Val.' He listened for a moment, glanced at Ben. 'Sorry, he's not available right now.'

There was a pause as Jeff listened to the caller talking. Ben could just about make out the sound of their voice. It was a woman. *Zara*. He knew it.

'OK, hold on.' Jeff pulled the phone away from his ear and covered it with his palm. 'She says it's extremely important.'

'Jeff . . . don't do this to me.'

Jeff shook his head. 'You don't get it. It's not Zara. It's someone called Kim Valentine.'

'Who?'

'Says you know her.'

'I don't know any Kim Valentine.'

Jeff thrust the phone at him. 'You'd better talk to her.'

Ben reluctantly clapped it to his ear. 'Ben Hope.'

'We need to talk,' said the woman's voice on the other end.

'I don't know you.' But, even as he said it, he was thinking he'd heard that voice before.

'Yes, you do,' she said. 'You just don't know it yet.'

Then Ben was holding a dead phone. 'She hung up,' he said to Jeff.

Suddenly it rang again in his hand. He answered it. This time it was a video call, and Ben stared at the woman's face on the tiny screen.

The image was clear. There was no mistaking it. She looked a little different – now the dark hair was scraped back tight in a ponytail, and she wasn't wearing makeup. But she was definitely the same woman.

'Now you know,' said Kim Valentine.

It was Kerry Wallace. The woman he'd rescued on the beach in San Remo.

Chapter Twenty-Eight

Ben couldn't believe what he was seeing. He shook his head in bafflement.

'We need to talk,' Kim Valentine said again. 'There are things you need to know.'

He just stared, said nothing.

'I know this comes as a surprise for you,' she said. 'But it's vitally important that you hear what I have to tell you.'

'What's this about, Kerry? Or Kim, or whatever your name is today.'

'Forget Kerry. Kerry never existed.'

'Which means you set me up,' he said. 'The whole thing on the beach was a fake.' Now he understood the reason he hadn't been able to find her at the hotel. 'Why did you do that?'

'That's what I need to talk to you about.'

'Then I think you'd better start talking right now.'

She shook her head. 'It's complicated. Better that we meet in person. Face to face.'

'You want to talk to me face to face, you come here

and explain yourself. I'm not going all the way back to San Remo.'

She shook her head. 'We're not in Italy any more. We're in Paris.'

'Why Paris?'

'There are reasons.'

'Who's *we*?'

'My associates. You've already met them. One of them is still wearing the neck brace you put him into.'

'I should have broken his spine,' Ben said. 'Maybe I will.'

'You'll feel differently when you hear what I have to say,' she replied. 'So, will you meet us? I guarantee you won't regret it.'

Ben hesitated. 'You've already tricked me once. What makes this any different?'

'I'm sorry it had to be that way, but I had no choice.'

'I have one,' he said. 'I can just end this conversation right now.' He switched off the phone, and the screen went dark.

'What was *that* all about?' Jeff asked as Ben started pacing up and down the office. Ben didn't reply. He stopped pacing and gazed at the phone in his hand. He had to know more.

He called back.

She answered on the first ring. 'Knew you'd call back.' There was a note of relief in her voice as well as triumph.

'All right. I'm listening.'

'How fast can you get to Paris?'

He looked at his watch. It was approaching midday.

'I can be there this afternoon. Three hours, give or take.'

'Call me when you get there. I'll give you the address to come to.'

'Then I'll see you later, Valentine.' Ben ended the call and shook his head, as if to clear it. He let out a long breath.

'Off again?' Jeff said. 'More travels?'

'You won't know I'm gone.'

Jeff smiled a long-suffering smile. 'Don't worry. I can take care of things.'

They both turned as the door swung open and Brooke walked in. She was wearing a serious expression, and the same black jeans and green combat jacket she'd had on when Ben had picked her up at the airport. The holdall in her hand looked packed. She dumped it on the floor at her feet. 'I'm leaving now,' she announced.

Ben thought he could hear a certain coldness in her voice. 'I thought you were sticking around for a few more days,' he said.

'There are things I have to do in London. Better I get back.'

He shrugged. There didn't seem any point in arguing with her. 'I'm leaving for Paris in a few minutes. I can drop you off at the airport on my way.'

She arched an eyebrow. 'Paris?' she echoed pointedly. 'Meeting someone?'

'Yes, I am. But not who you think.'

'I don't need a lift, anyway. I already called a cab. They'll be here any minute.'

'Thanks for talking to me earlier, Brooke.' Ben patted her shoulder. But something was wrong. He felt the muscles tighten and she flinched away.

'Have a wonderful time in Paris,' she said stiffly.

'It's not exactly a pleasure trip.'

'Whatever.' She glanced at her watch. 'I think I'll walk up to the gate and meet the cab there. See you next week, Jeff.' She snatched up her bag.

'Look forward to it,' Jeff replied. 'Safe journey home.'

Then Brooke was gone. Ben watched through the window as she marched across the yard with her holdall on her shoulder. 'Something's up with her,' he murmured. 'I don't know what.'

'Don't you?' Jeff said with a chuckle.

Ben turned to him. 'What?'

'Come on, mate. Are you blind or just thick?'

'What do you mean?'

'You really can't see it, can you? She has a serious thing for you.'

'Don't be daft. You know Brooke. She likes to flirt and joke around. She doesn't really mean anything by it.'

'Doesn't flirt with me,' Jeff said. 'Wish she would.'

'You're talking crap. She and I are just friends.'

Jeff lounged back in his chair and cupped his hands behind his head. 'Whatever you say, Ben. Whatever you say.'

Chapter Twenty-Nine

But Ben had more to think about than Brooke. He dashed up to his quarters, packed a few things in a leather overnight bag, and headed back across the yard to a squat brick building between the gym and the trainee block.

It was no more than a hut. The door was riveted steel, a foot thick, and beside it was a wall-mounted keypad console shielded from the elements under thick plastic. He punched in a number. It was changed every week, and only he and Jeff knew it.

There was nothing inside the building, just a square hole in the concrete floor and a flight of steps leading downwards. At the bottom of the steps was another heavy door and another keypad. He dialled in the twelve-digit passcode, heard a metallic clunk from somewhere inside the works, pushed the door open and flipped on a light switch.

He was inside Le Val's armoury room. All around him were racks of weapons, stored in accordance with high-security regulations. He walked over to a steel safe and unlocked it with a long key from the ring he was carrying. The safe was filled with an assortment of pistols and revolvers. He reached inside and lifted one out, an old standard-issue military Browning Hi-Power 9mm. He laid it on a nearby table, reached back inside the safe and took out two magazines and a box of 9mm ammunition.

Even as he'd been talking to Kim Valentine, he'd decided that there was no way he was walking unarmed into a strange address in Paris to meet people he already knew weren't who they said they were. There'd been enough surprises.

He just couldn't figure it out. Ever since Valentine's call he'd been working through the pieces in his mind, and coming up with nothing but questions. Who was she? Were these people interested in Morgan Paxton's research? Connected with Kamal? Somehow, he didn't think so. This was something else.

He quickly loaded thirteen rounds into each mag. He slotted one into the butt of the pistol, the other he slipped into the left pocket of his jeans. Then he put the pistol in the other pocket, picked up the cartridge box and left the armoury.

Behind the farmhouse was the converted Dutch barn that was now the garage block. He pulled open the weathered wooden doors and sunlight sparkled off the striped green bodywork of the Mini Cooper inside. As he chucked the overnight bag onto the back seat, he felt a pang of loss for his old army bag. He'd had that for years. He got in the car, stuffed the pistol and ammunition into the glove compartment, fired up the engine and spun the wheels on the gravel as he drove out of the yard.

Twelve-forty. He'd be in Paris by four.

He was there by quarter to. As he cut and slashed his way through the heavy traffic on the city's Périphérique outer ring road, he called Valentine. She gave him an address in the suburbs. He knew the area.

'Be here at six,' she told him. 'We'll be waiting.'

Two hours to kill. That suited him. He headed east through the city. Hit Boulevard Haussmann, took a right onto Boulevard des Italiens and headed for his old flat. It had been a long time since he'd been there. The place was simple, functional to the kind of extreme only a soldier could tolerate, but it had served him very well in its day. At one time he'd seen it as his safe-house, his doorway to Europe. Now it was just a symbol of the life he'd left behind – or was trying to. He'd been meaning to come back to Paris anyway, whip the place into order and put it on the market.

He didn't even know if anyone would want it. Its location was ideal, tucked away down an alley close to the heart of the city, but the only way into the place was through an underground parking lot, up a murky back stairway, and through an armoured security door. Not exactly a cosy family home.

The flat felt cold and unlived-in when he got there, and everything was covered in a light coating of dust. He fired up the heating system and spent a few minutes cleaning the place up. He'd no intention of spending much time in Paris. This was going to be a flying visit – one night only, find out what Valentine had to say to him, and then straight back to Le Val in the morning. After that, he never wanted to think about any of this ever again.

Checking the kitchen cupboards, he found he still had a few tins of food and an unopened pack of Lavazza ground coffee. Better still, three bottles of the red table wine he used to buy from the grocery store down the street.

He drank three cups of strong black coffee and smoked a couple of Gauloises. Then it was time to make a move.

The address in the suburbs surprised him somewhat. It turned out to be a shabby little place in a shabby little street, the last in a row of terraced houses next to a disused filling station where a rusted Esso sign creaked in the breeze. The neighbouring house was obviously derelict, boards over the windows and the door nailed up. The sky was grey, and rain was threatening as Ben parked the car a little way up the street.

He flipped open the glove compartment and took out the Browning. Racked the slide of the pistol, chambering the top round, and clicked on the safety. Shifting forward in the driver's seat he slipped the gun into his belt, behind the right hip, where it was covered by his leather jacket. He stepped out of the car, feeling the light patter of raindrops on his face.

He walked up to the house and knocked on the door. After a few moments there was the sound of footsteps from inside, and the door creaked open.

Ben knew the guy standing in the doorway. He was the smaller of the two men who'd been on the beach in San Remo. The one who'd run away.

'Stolen any good handbags recently?' Ben asked him.

The guy didn't react. He shut the door and led Ben down a hallway. The inside of the house didn't look any better than the outside. Wallpaper was hanging in strips from the walls of the empty rooms and the carpets were threadbare.

'Cosy little place,' Ben said.

'This way,' the guy said. They came to a door and he pushed it open.

The other side of the door was the kind of operations room that a very small team running on a minuscule budget would set up. The three beaten-up armchairs and the old desk in the corner looked as though they'd been rescued from a skip. The desk was covered in clutter – papers, a collection of phones, a whirring notebook computer. A couple of cameras, one with a long lens. A couple of open aluminium cases on the floor contained an assortment of audio surveillance equipment. In the middle of the room, a Formica slab resting on two beer crates made a low table covered in plastic cups and the remnants of a fast-food meal. The place smelled of instant coffee and stale bodies and damp carpet. The blind was drawn down over the single window. The atmosphere reminded Ben of various police stakeouts he'd seen – only twice as depressing.

And he still didn't have a clue who these people were.

Seated in one of the armchairs was another man he'd seen before. A big guy, broad shoulders, heavy arms folded across his chest. His neck was enveloped in a foam brace and his posture was stiff and awkward, as though it still hurt to move. His eyes were rimmed with red from pain.

The smaller guy went and stood with his back to the window. Ben walked into the room and gazed from one man to the other. 'Where's Valentine?'

'She's here,' said a familiar voice. Ben turned.

'So we meet again,' she said.

She stood framed in the doorway of a small kitchen. Her hair was brushed down flat against her head and tied back tightly, the way it had been on the video call. The vulnerable feminine look he'd seen in San Remo had disappeared. Her face was drawn and pale, and the jeans and navy jumper looked slept in. 'Thanks for coming. Can I get you a coffee?'

'You can get me an explanation,' Ben said.

Valentine nodded. 'I owe you one. And I'll tell you everything. But first, let me introduce you to my colleagues.' She pointed to the big guy in the armchair. 'This is Udo Wolff.'

Wolff nodded stiffly to Ben.

'Don't get up,' Ben said.

'This is Jimmy Harrison,' Valentine said, pointing at the small guy who was standing by the window. 'And we need your help. I'm glad you came. You want to sit down? This is going to take a while.'

Ben moved over to one of the armchairs and sat down with his legs out in front of him and his arms folded. 'I'm listening,' he said. 'This had better be worth it.'

'It is,' Valentine replied. 'But you're not going to like it. Get ready for some big shocks.'

'I'm ready.'

She stepped across to the desk. On top of the pile of papers was a brown A4 envelope. She reached inside and took out a large photo print. She didn't look at it as she walked over to Ben and passed it to him.

He studied the glossy colour print carefully. It wasn't very nice to look at. The photo showed a woman, or what was left of a woman. It was worse than the pictures of Morgan Paxton's body – a lot worse. She was naked and looked as though she'd been passed through a combine harvester.

'You're looking at Linda Downey,' Valentine said. 'She was the fourth member of our team.' She paused, swallowed. 'And she was my friend.'

He handed the picture back to her. There was complete sincerity in her eyes. And other things, he thought. Anger, maybe fear, too.

'You might be wondering who did this to her,' Valentine said. 'And what this has to do with why you're here.'

'I'm wondering,' Ben said.

Valentine tapped the picture with her fingertips. 'The person who did this to Linda is called Berg. We don't even know if that's his real name. Whoever he is, he's totally off the grid and untraceable. But we do know the name of the man he works for. The man on whose orders he did this.'

Valentine laid the photo face-down on the desk, as though she couldn't stand looking at it any more. There was tension in her jawline.

'Berg's employer is Colonel Harry Paxton,' she said.

Chapter Thirty

Ben stared at Valentine for a long moment. 'I think you'd better explain yourself more clearly. Just exactly who are you, what do you want from me, and what are you trying to say?'

'All right,' she said. 'I just wanted you to see the picture. I wanted you to know the kind of man Harry Paxton really is. But let me back up a couple of steps and start at the beginning.'

Ben just watched her coldly. Harrison and Wolff were silent.

Valentine pointed at the two men. 'Until five weeks ago, the three of us were special agents with Interpol.'

Ben kept gazing at her steadily.

'You don't believe me?'

'That's something I can easily check. I know people in Interpol. I've got a few connections.'

'I'm sure you have,' Valentine said. 'Feel free to check up on us. I'll give you the exact details of people we worked with, section chiefs we were answerable to, names of departments, the colour of the wall tiles in the toilets at the General Secretariat in Lyon.'

'I'll be sure to make some calls,' Ben said. 'But let's just say for the moment that I believe you. I still don't understand why I'm here listening to this.'

'You're here because Harry Paxton's not who you think he is. Because it's time you knew the truth.' Valentine paused. 'Let me tell you about the real Harry Paxton. He's an arms dealer. He's been trading illegally in weapons for more than a decade. He sells to anyone. Terrorists, mass murderers. He's given power to despots across the world. Fuelled war crimes and genocide in just about every war zone going. Africa, South America, Asia, the Middle East, you name it. He's smart, ruthless and will kill anyone who stands in his way. The reason we're here in Paris is that he's due to arrive tomorrow afternoon for a meeting with one of his business associates at the Georges V hotel. It could be a break for us. We're going to follow the bastard everywhere he goes.'

There was a long silence. Anxious looks passed between Valentine, Wolff and Harrison.

Ben stood up. 'I don't have to listen to this. You're talking complete bullshit. There's no way Harry Paxton is an arms dealer. It's insane.'

'Sit down, Major Hope. Hear us out.'

But Ben was already walking to the door.

Then a voice made him stop dead in his tracks.

'Listen to her, Ben. She's telling the truth.'

He turned slowly, and for a moment he was speechless.

It was Zara. She stood in the doorway from which Valentine had emerged before. She looked anxious,

232

tense. The black T-shirt and jacket she was wearing made her face seem even paler than it was.

But she still looked beautiful. He took a step towards her. 'What are you doing here?' he asked, incredulous.

'I'm with them,' she said, motioning at the three agents. 'I've been helping them. Harry thinks I'm visiting a sick friend in Rome.'

As Ben gaped at her, his mind was sprinting backwards through all the things that had happened. The time in San Remo, when they'd been followed. Now he understood why Zara had seemed so unconcerned about it. 'You were in on this the whole time?'

She nodded. 'It's true about Harry. He isn't who you think he is.'

'And there's more,' Valentine said. 'A lot more. I really think you need to sit down and listen.'

Ben didn't know what to say. He felt dazed as he walked back to his chair and sat down.

'Thank you,' Valentine said. 'I mean it. I know this is hard for you.'

It was getting dark in the room as evening fell outside the window. Valentine walked over and flipped a light switch. A bare bulb in the middle of the ceiling lit up with a weak glow that made the room seem even gloomier.

'Let me get this right,' Ben said. 'You know all this about Harry, yet he's a free man. Why isn't he in jail now?'

'Like I said, he's smart,' Valentine answered. 'He always stays a step ahead of the game, and nobody's ever been able to catch him. He uses his yacht charter business as a front, shipping arms consignments all over the world. Any idea how much cargo one of those superyachts can hold?'

'A lot,' Harrison said.

'A fuck of a lot,' Wolff added.

'Interpol have been watching him for a long time,' Valentine went on. 'The bastard has been my whole life for two years. But we just couldn't get anything concrete, and our superiors pulled the plug on the investigation. They said if we pushed it any further, it was going to look like harassment. So, case closed. That was six weeks ago.' She smiled grimly. 'His SAS training came in handy, I imagine. He goes in, does the business, gets out and it's like he was never there. You must know all about that, Major.'

'First off,' he said, 'you can drop the Major bit. I'm Ben. Second, you don't seem to have a lot of proof. Third, why are three ex-agents pursuing a private investigation of a man with a record as clean as Harry's when their superiors have already dropped the case? It looks to me like a personal vendetta.'

Valentine nodded. 'It is.' Her fingers brushed the back of the photo on the desk. 'Let me tell you about Linda. She was only twenty-six. She'd been with us on the case just three months. I put her on the team because she was a star linguist, spoke perfect Russian, Spanish and any number of African languages. She was the perfect close surveillance operative. She could get in anywhere.' Valentine paused, and a look of sadness passed over her face. 'Algeria, seven weeks ago. I had a report from her. She said she'd finally got the evidence that was going to put Paxton away.'

'What evidence?' Ben asked.

'That's just it,' Valentine sighed. 'I never saw it. Linda didn't turn up at the RV. Three days later she was found ninety miles away up the coast. It looked like the sharks had got her. You've seen the picture.'

'How do you know the sharks didn't get her?'

Valentine shook her head vigorously. 'Because it doesn't add up. An eyewitness reported that she was dancing and flirting drunkenly with two guys in some strip joint the night before, a mile from where her body was found. The official story is she went off with them. But it's all wrong.'

'Maybe she did,' Ben said. 'Maybe you just want to believe there's more to it.'

'Linda wouldn't have gone off with two guys she met in a bar,' Valentine said. 'They wouldn't have been her type.'

'You know that for a fact?'

Valentine looked at him sharply. 'She was gay. I know *that* for a fact. A personal fact,' she added meaningfully. 'And I know she wasn't there. Paxton had her butchered and the whole story was concocted to cover his tracks. That's how he works. And we're going to get the fucker. For what his trade does to innocent victims everywhere, and for what he did to Linda.' Valentine's face was tight with rage. A tear rolled down her cheek, and she brushed it away. 'We're going to do whatever it takes to nail him.'

Ben didn't reply.

'That's where you come in,' Wolff said. 'We're on

our own here. We desperately need help from someone Paxton trusts.'

'And you were hoping that, based on no evidence at all, I was going to betray him.' Ben turned to Zara. 'How can you listen to these people?'

Zara came over to where he was sitting and crouched down on the floor next to him. She held his hand tightly. 'You've got to believe them, Ben. When I met Harry, I could only see his charm. But that's not who he is. He's a monster. A tyrant. He's the most evil, cruel, dominating man ever born.'

'We approached Zara four weeks ago,' Valentine said. 'We'd been watching them whenever they were on shore together. We could see they were arguing a lot. We took a chance.'

Zara looked deep into Ben's eyes. 'Do you remember that day we were together? When I told you I wanted to leave him but couldn't because of Morgan's death?'

'I remember,' Ben said.

'It wasn't because of Morgan. It was because of what Kim, Jimmy and Udo told me. They showed me terrible pictures, of African children whose arms and legs had been shot off with guns that had been bought from Harry. Little bodies covered in horrible burns, faces disfigured. Villages that had just been destroyed, along with everyone in them. That's what he does, Ben. That's where all the money comes from. How was I supposed to just walk away?'

'You're just taking their word for it.'

'No. After I agreed to help them, I started trying to look around the *Scimitar*. Down in one of the cargo holds, I found these crates. Big locked brown metal boxes with white stencilled writing on them. Then I heard voices. Harry and some others. I hid. I couldn't see them, but they were talking about a shipment. I heard the sound of them opening one of the crates, and a kind of gun sound.'

'A kind of gun sound?' Ben said sceptically.

'A sound like this,' Harrison said. He took a Colt .45 auto from under his jacket. With his left hand he racked back the slide on the large, stainless steel automatic and released it with a metallic *shlack-clack*.

'Just like that,' Zara said.

'I think that's called leading the witness,' Ben said.

'Let her speak,' Valentine cut in.

'When they left, I sneaked away. When it was safe, I went back down there with a camera. The crates had gone.'

'That's what I call real hard evidence,' Ben said.

Valentine looked uncomfortable. 'We know. We haven't got a shred. That's why we came up with the plan to get me onto the *Scimitar*. It's very rare for Paxton to let anyone on board. Zara told us about your meeting. We checked you out. Your military background, your wife's murder. I had a feeling you'd be the kind of man who would help out a lady in distress.'

'I was a fool to,' Ben said.

'I thought you were a hero,' Valentine replied. 'I was sorry we had to trick you. But there was really no other way.'

'Why trust me now? How do you know I'm not working with Harry?'

'We thought of that. It didn't figure.'

'Maybe I was just too clever for you, the way you claim Harry is.'

'We thought of that too. But thanks to Zara we have a recording of your talk with Paxton. It's pretty clear from the conversation that you're not involved with his business. You went to Cairo for him, but you didn't kill those men. We know about the citizen's arrest, too. As far as we're concerned, you're clean. Clean, but very interesting.'

Ben glared at Zara.

She squeezed his hand. 'I'm sorry I spied on you. We had to know.'

'And I take it you didn't find anything during your little snooping expedition,' Ben said, turning back to Valentine. 'Or you wouldn't be talking to me now.'

Valentine sighed. 'I was hoping I could find something on his personal computer. I sneaked into his study and fitted a miniature keystroker with a transmitting device. That way, we can intercept everything he writes. But guess what? He hasn't written a word.'

'And guess what? I've had enough of this conversation. It's a joke.'

'We can't let you go,' Wolff said.

Ben looked at him hard. 'If you try to stop me, everyone in this room except Zara is dead.'

'He doesn't mean it that way,' Valentine said. 'He means you can't leave without letting us tell you the truth about Harry Paxton.'

'Seems to me you just gave it your best shot,' Ben said. 'And failed.'

'There's more to tell. By the time I'm finished, I guarantee you'll see him in a whole new light. You'll realise you don't even know him.'

'I served with him. I fought alongside him. I think I know him a hell of a lot better than you do.'

'And he also saved your life,' Valentine said. 'Sierra Leone, May 14th, 1997. Right?'

'Right.'

'Wrong.'

He glowered at her. 'What did you say?'

'I told you you weren't going to like it. You're going to have to make some mental adjustments.'

'I know the truth.'

She shook her head. 'You believe in a lie. Harry Paxton, then a Lieutenant Colonel with the Special Air Service, did not save your life that day. You were just supposed to think he did.'

'I didn't see you there that day, Valentine. Where were you, hiding under a stone? I'm the only witness to the fact that Harry saved my life. He shot the Cross Bones captain who was just about to kill me. He was awarded decorations and promotion for it.'

'There was another witness,' Valentine said. 'One who saw the whole thing. Someone who wasn't shot to pieces and half unconscious when it all happened. Someone whose testimony holds up a lot better than yours.'

'Who?'

'His name is Tinashe. He was sixteen when your SAS squad attacked the Makapela Creek mission in Sierra Leone. He was a member of the Cross Bones

Boys militia. One of the many youngsters brainwashed by The Baron into killing.'

'A great witness. A brainwashed murderer, sixteen years old.'

'He's a different person now. In some ways, it's thanks to you. After that day, it was like the spell broke. He ran away from the Cross Bones militia and swore he'd never get sucked into anything like that again. That's why he was so hard to find. It took us a long time to track him down. Shall I tell you what he saw that day – what really happened?'

Ben tried to control the anger that made him want to tear the room apart. 'Let's have it,' he said coldly.

'Tinashe was frightened by the battle. He managed to crawl into the hollow of a dead tree. From there he had an open view of the ruined schoolhouse.'

Ben felt a stab of shock at the words. In any official archived report that Valentine might have been able to access, the scene of the battle was described as the mission complex at Makapela Creek. There'd never been any mention of the schoolhouse. He could feel his insides churning.

Valentine went on. 'According to my witness, most of the militia force fled when the air support arrived on the scene. Does that sound accurate?'

'It's perfectly accurate.'

'So far, so good,' Valentine replied. 'Now let me tell you the rest. It was at that moment, just after the helicopters came in, that the witness saw Lieutenant Colonel Paxton walk up behind you and your team-mate, later named in the official report as Sergeant

Gary Smith. But Paxton wasn't alone. He was with the Cross Bones second-in-command, Captain Kananga.'

Ben was too stunned and furious to do anything but listen.

'The witness then saw Paxton shoot you in the back, then shoot Smith. Smith went down. Then Paxton walked over to you as Kananga watched. You had gone down on your face, but you rolled over and were looking up at Paxton as he was about to kill you.' Valentine paused. 'Is this detailed enough for you? No way we could have known all this, correct?'

Ben didn't answer.

'Smith was almost dead from Paxton's bullet, but not quite. He still had enough reserves of energy to let off a burst of fire. It took down Kananga and it caught Paxton in the arm. Smith's the man who really saved your life that day, Major Hope. He's the one you should be honouring.'

Ben was silent.

'Paxton turned around and shot him in the head. That's the point where you passed out. Your colonel would have put one in your brain, but that's when the troops from 1 Para had touched down and were moving through the wreckage. Paxton had to let you live.'

Ben's heart was pounding. It was hard to breathe. 'Why?' was all he could say.

'Can't you guess what it's about? Paxton was supplying arms to the Cross Bones Boys. Among many other rebel groups he was trading with, using the army as his cover. While your unit was twiddling its thumbs in the Embassy in Freetown waiting for the green light, he was sneaking away and doing business with The Baron. Guns for conflict diamonds.'

'The Makapela Creek operation was a trap,' Wolff said from his armchair. 'We think that Paxton suspected someone from your unit was onto him. We think he deliberately engineered the intelligence leak that led to the assault, so that your team could be ambushed and wiped out. Paxton was meant to be the sole survivor. As it turned out, you managed to slip through the net.'

'Think about it,' Valentine said. 'It all makes perfect sense. There's nothing in the witness account that you can deny. And his testimony would have been enough to bring Paxton down.' She sighed. 'But the problem we have is that Tinashe's too scared to talk openly. Even now, the child soldiers who helped in the genocide of the Sierra Leone Civil War are hated by their own people – even though they were victims too. There have been reprisals, revenge killings. They've become like some kind of untouchable underclass. Tinashe is one of the lucky ones. He's managed to leave his past behind and he wants to keep it that way. Which leaves us with you. You're the only one left who can help us.' She looked at him earnestly, searchingly. 'So will you? Please?'

There was dead silence in the room as Ben sat and digested the whole thing. A whole minute went by. His mind was bursting.

He stood up. 'No. You're all lying.' He headed for the door.

Zara rushed after him, grabbing at his arm. 'Ben, wait—'

He brushed her away. 'Leave me alone.' He crashed through the door and walked out into the dingy hallway. She ran out after him, pleading and protesting. 'Please, Ben. I love you.'

He stopped. 'Do you?'

She looked as if she'd been slapped.

'You've done nothing but lie to me and use me,' he said. 'So that your little friends could spy on the man who saved my life.' He started back up the hallway, heading for the front door.

'What was I supposed to do?' she screamed.

He didn't reply. Reached the front door and tore it open.

'Where are you going?'

'As far away from you as I can possibly get,' he said. 'Go back to your cronies in there, Zara. They're waiting for you.' He stepped outside into the rainy night and slammed the door in her face.

Chapter Thirty-One

Ben drove the twenty minutes to the underground parking lot in a daze, and was barely conscious of parking the Mini and stumbling up the concrete steps to his safehouse. He managed to key in the code for the door, and staggered into the flat. The pistol was a hard lump against his hip. He tore it out of his belt and flung it away.

Heading straight for the kitchen, he tore open the cupboard door and snatched one of the bottles of table wine. He stood there balancing it in his hand, for a moment unable to decide whether to open it or hurl it through the window. He opened it. Filled a glass. Paced up and down, fists clenched, wanting to smash something. Wanting to punch the wall until his knuckles were a bleeding mess.

Then he slumped at the table and downed one glass after another. The bottle seemed to empty itself in seconds. He grabbed another and started on that one.

His head was spinning feverishly. It wasn't the wine or even the fact that he hadn't slept properly for days.

He felt completely overwhelmed by the things he'd just been told.

After a while, he walked in a stupor to the bedroom, fell back on the bed and closed his eyes. He lay there, trying to shut down his thoughts and relax the cramping tension in his muscles.

Slowly, he began to drift. Thoughts blurred. He slept, but it wasn't a restful sleep. He was back reliving the horror of Makapela Creek once again.

The nightmare unfolded in slow motion. Ben saw the figure walk out of the fire, gun in hand as he gazed down at the man he was about to kill.

But something had changed. Now there were two men standing over Ben and, instead of the faceless, nebulous forms that normally visited him in his dreams, now he could see them vividly. Two men, one African and one European. The black man was powerfully built, wearing khaki fatigues, and the ArmaLite rifle cradled in his arms looked shiny and new and glittered in the firelight.

It was Kananga. He was glancing nervously this way and that, up at the helicopters that were closing in on the mission complex, then across at the dark jungle as though anxious to follow his fleeing men. *Let's get this done*, his expression said.

Beside him stood a tall, thin white man in SAS tropical combat uniform. Paxton. Ben was suddenly seeing him for the first time – that face so familiar and yet so alien, half bathed in the red glow of the burning mission. The eyes filled with a strange and terrifying light. The pistol in his fist rose up to point at Ben.

Ben tried to say something, but his words were a muffled echo lost in the thump of the choppers. He saw Paxton smile.

And, behind Paxton, lying in the bloody dirt, propped up on one elbow, his face pale, shaking with the effort of raising his gun one last time, Ben saw Smith. Paxton spun as the dying soldier's bullet caught his arm, fired back and Smith crumpled into a lifeless heap.

Then Ben was awake, jolting upright on the bed, every nerve in his body jangling. He put his head in his hands and remembered what Brooke had said. *You should listen to your dreams.* She'd been right. And he was listening now, seeing it clearly for the first time.

It was as though a part of his brain had awoken after a long sleep, dormant memories suddenly leaping into focus. As if, somewhere deep inside, he'd always known the truth but just hadn't wanted to face it. Easier to repress it from his conscious mind. Easier just to stay in the comfort zone of self-deception.

The realisation left him breathless. He'd been fooling himself for years. He'd been on the verge of killing for this man, so close he could taste it. And Paxton had just been using him, exploiting a debt of honour that had never existed.

As he sat there, his mind spinning, Ben remembered what Wolff had said. *Paxton thought someone in your unit was onto him.*

His mind flew back, connections firing that had lain in hibernation for years, images flashing up that he'd completely wiped away. He remembered Smith. Saw the man's face as clearly as though it had happened yesterday.

They'd been in their quarters attached to the Embassy when the sergeant had come up to him. He seemed agitated about something.

'I need to talk to you,' he'd said. There'd been no *sirs* between them.

'Talk,' Ben had replied. 'What is it?'

'It's delicate,' Smith had said. 'I'm not even sure.'

Then Paxton had appeared in the doorway and suddenly Smith didn't want to talk any more; he just lowered his eyes and shuffled away. Strange behaviour from the normally confident soldier. Ben had meant to approach him about it later on – but then they'd had the green light for the assault, and everything had started rolling so fast there'd never been another chance. After what had happened next, Ben's memory had just blanked it out. Until now.

As he sat there on the bed, he thought back to the old Bible story of the conversion of St Paul in Damascus. Once blind, Paul had suddenly been able to see God when scales fell from his eyes. That was how Ben felt at this moment – except it wasn't God he could see but the face of Harry Paxton in his mind.

And Paxton was going to pay.

Ben's head was suddenly clear. He burst out of the flat, sprinted like an athlete to the Mini and took off through the night streets. The rain had stopped, and the stars were twinkling over the Parisian skyline.

He cut across the city, back to the house in the suburbs. Parked the car, ran to the door and banged on it loudly.

This time it was Valentine who answered it. She stared at him, bemused.

'I thought you weren't coming back,' she said. 'Why are you here?'

'To say I believe you now. And that I want to help, if I can.'

Valentine smiled. For the second time since he'd met her, she went up on tiptoe and kissed him lightly on the cheek. 'You'd better come inside.'

'Is she still here?' he asked her in the hallway.

Valentine nodded. 'She's staying the night here, and going back to San Remo tomorrow.'

Ben didn't reply. He followed her through to the makeshift operations room. Harrison and Wolff were sitting drinking coffee. They exchanged glances as Ben walked in, and grinned at one another and at Valentine.

'Glad to have you back,' Wolff said.

'Sorry about the neck,' Ben replied, pointing at the brace.

'Forget it. You did what you had to do.'

Valentine put her head around a doorway. 'Someone here to see you,' she said.

A moment later, Zara appeared. She saw Ben and rushed over to embrace him, eyes shining.

'I'm sorry I doubted you,' he said. 'Sorry I've been so blind for so long.' He turned to Valentine. 'You want me to work with you?'

'I was kind of hoping so,' she said.

248

'Then you've got your wish. But I have some conditions.'

She blinked. 'Such as?'

'I don't want Zara involved in this any longer. It's far too dangerous.'

'Hold on,' Zara protested. 'I *want* to be involved. Nobody's going to stop me. I'm going back to San Remo in the morning, and I'll be working from on board the yacht to find out everything I can while Harry's here on business.'

'These guys aren't an official team any more,' he told her. 'That means no backup for you if something goes wrong. No extraction plan. No witness programme to hide you. You'll be completely vulnerable and out in the open.'

'So will you.'

'It won't be the first time for me.'

Zara shook her head. 'I have to go back. Even if I were leaving him, I'd need to go back for my things.'

'I'll get you new things. Anything you want.'

'My documents.'

'Easily replaced.'

'And what about me? Where am I going?'

'My place.'

'In Normandy?'

He nodded. 'I'll drive you to Le Val in the morning.'

'But Harry knows where it is,' she said. 'You don't think he'll come looking for me? I know him.'

'Harry will have other things on his mind, once I get started on him. And you'll be safe there. It's like a military camp, and I have trained men, with guns and

dogs. Not even Harry can get in there. You'll be safe.'
Ben turned to Valentine. 'Then I'll come back here, and we'll make plans.'

'Wait a minute,' Valentine cut in. 'This isn't the deal. We need Zara on board. She's an integral part of this. You can't just take her out of the equation.'

'Negative,' Ben said. 'We do this my way, or you're on your own.'

Valentine sighed and glanced at Harrison and Wolff. Harrison shrugged. 'We can't afford to turn him away,' he said.

'OK,' Valentine said to Ben. 'It's a deal. So what happens next?'

Ben took Zara's hand, felt her warm fingers slip eagerly through his. 'Let's go.'

Chapter Thirty-Two

Claudel had been working on the encrypted file day and night for longer than his frazzled brain could recall, and was seriously worried for his own sanity.

He'd exhausted every possibility, explored every avenue until his eyes were burning, his fingers trembling. He'd scoured his brain for every name, place and any other kind of reference he could come up with that might somehow unlock this infernal thing. But it was simply not within the bounds of feasibility to hit on the correct password. It could be absolutely anything. It might have to do with the Pharaoh Akhenaten; or then again it could be the name of Morgan Paxton's great-grandfather's cat.

And the more Claudel racked his brains and sat there typing in random entries that never came to anything, the more bitterly he resented Kamal for making him do this.

Earlier that day, feeling on the brink of a nervous

breakdown, he'd driven back out to the Abusir pyramid site and just stood there under the hot sun. He wanted to weep as he scanned the ocean of rubble that was the four-thousand-year-old wreck of Sahure's necropolis. Prayed for a miracle that could make him see what it was that Paxton was into. None had come.

Then he'd had a thought. Something poor Aziz had said that day, minutes before his death. That when Morgan Paxton had come running from the ruins, he'd been covered in dust and cobwebs. *Cobwebs*, in a place like this. That could mean only one thing. Paxton had been inside something. And there was only one place you could actually be *inside* in this arid ruin. Sahure's pyramid.

Why didn't I think of that before? he'd thought. He knew the answer. With Kamal's brooding presence around, it was impossible to think clearly about anything.

So Claudel had dashed towards the crumbling old heap that was all that remained of the king's ancient tomb. He'd run around the edge of the monument to the dilapidated entrance. He'd crawled inside the claustrophobic passage, webs brushing his face. No archaeology excavation had ever managed to access the rubble-choked interior burial chamber – but maybe there was something in the shaft leading up to it. He'd shone his torch all over the inside, looking for markings, clues, anything.

Nothing. Just dust and spiders and crumbled rock.

He'd crawled out again, feeling utterly defeated. Dragged himself back to the villa and the hated computer. He'd been sitting staring at that password box ever since, deep into the night, too paralysed with fear and stress and rage and frustration to eat or drink or even take a piss.

A sudden surge of resentment made him kick his desk chair back and stand up. He paced the room. Sitting on another chair nearby was the well-worn military-type haversack Kamal had taken from the Englishman, Hope. Claudel lashed out with his foot and sent the chair clattering to the floor.

For a moment Claudel thought he'd broken his toe, and he cried out at the pain. He fell back on the floor and sat there for a minute, groaning and rubbing his foot and hating himself for smashing up his own beautiful possessions. It was the kind of thing Kamal did.

Then he noticed the fallen bag. Half spilled out of it was the crumpled blazer that had belonged to Morgan Paxton.

Claudel staggered up to his feet and hobbled over. Even in his seething rage he hated to see these nasty things trailing on his expensive carpet. He bent down and picked up the blazer between finger and thumb and inspected it in disgust, holding it up in front of him the way someone might hold up a dead rat by its tail. Only an Englishman could wear something this tasteless, he thought to himself.

He was just about to stuff it back into the bag, out of sight, when something fluttered down out of the breast pocket and landed on the floor. He picked it up. It was just litter, a faded receipt. He crunched it up in his hand.

He stopped. Looked down at his hand. Opened his

fist and gazed at the piece of paper. Straightened it out delicately with his fingers.

There was a phone number scribbled on there.

His mind suddenly went into overdrive, his anxiety forgotten.

It wasn't an Egyptian number. It was British. He stepped quickly over to the phone on the desk, punched in the international code for the UK followed by the number on the crumpled piece of paper.

After a few rings an answerphone cut in. It was a woman's voice, speaking English in a strange accent that Claudel couldn't immediately pinpoint. What was that? Irish?

'University of St Andrews. Faculty of History,' said the voice. 'If you know the extension number you require, please enter it now. Otherwise, please hold for an operator.'

Claudel's eyebrows rose, and his heart began to thump. Faculty of History. Interesting. He glanced back at the paper and dialled in what he now realised was the extension number underneath. 345.

After a few rings, an answerphone cut in. Claudel listened to the voicemail message and scribbled down a name.

Then he called Kamal.

Chapter Thirty-Three

Paris

It was after eleven by the time Ben and Zara found a quiet restaurant down a cobbled street in the Latin Quarter and were sipping iced Moël at an intimate candlelit table in the corner.

Watching Zara, Ben felt a surge of mixed emotions. He knew he should be consumed with rage, now that he knew the things Harry Paxton had done. But somewhere in the midst of all those feelings of anger and resentment and betrayal that had emerged from listening to Valentine's revelations, a strange new sensation had begun to glow inside him.

It was a feeling of freedom. Incredible, heady, intoxicating freedom. No longer bound by any moral obligations and the old debt of gratitude to Paxton that he'd been harbouring for far too long, it seemed as if a whole new future had opened up in front of him.

It made him think about something else Brooke had told him. *Go with your heart*. Now, at last, he could.

'Penny for them.' Zara reached across the table and took his hand.

'Sorry. I was miles away.'

'Tell me about your home,' she said.

'You'll be seeing it soon enough.'

'Describe it to me.'

He smiled. His thumb caressed the back of her hand as he spoke. 'It's beautiful there. This time of year, the woods are full of flowers. Everything's bursting into life. The air's rich with wild thyme and rosemary and lavender, and at night the stars are so bright you feel you can almost reach out and touch them.'

Her eyes sparkled in the candlelight. 'And the house?'

'It's a traditional eighteenth-century country house. Rambling old place, stone floors, wine cellar. That kind of thing. A pretty far cry from the *Scimitar*.'

'I can't wait to be there.'

'I hope you might want to stay there a while,' he ventured.

She squeezed his hand tighter. 'I know I'll want to stay there a long time, Ben. All I want is to be near you.'

After dinner they wandered out into the street, feeling close, holding hands. Ben hailed a taxi. 'The Ritz,' he said to the driver as they slid across the back seat together.

'The Ritz? We already had dinner,' she giggled.

'I meant, as in hotel. I was thinking you might want to stay somewhere nice tonight.'

'But don't you have a place here?'

256

He smiled awkwardly. 'I was also thinking the Ritz might be more what you were used to.'

She frowned a little. 'Is that how you see me? I didn't always live on fancy yachts. You should have seen the place I grew up.'

'Secondly—' he started,

'I know what you're going to say.'

'You do?'

'Yes. And the answer is that I do want to spend tonight with you.' She touched his hand. 'All night. At your place. I don't want a fancy hotel. I just want you.'

Ben gave the driver the address, and the car took off. The city lights zipped by, but they were more interested in each other, talking softly, laughing, touching. A few minutes later, the taxi was pulling up in the street near the entrance to the underground parking lot.

'Where is this place of yours?' Zara asked, looking around her as the taxi drove off.

'Follow me.' He led her down the cobbled alleyway, through a side door that led into the dark, echoey parking lot.

'Where are we going?' she giggled.

'You'll see.' He took her hand and she followed him to the concrete steps that led up to the security door. He entered the security code. 'Remember this number,' he told her as the door swung open.

'Wow. Talk about secure. A client gave you this? What was he, some kind of mobster?'

'Close. He was a government minister. Anyway, you'll be pretty safe here.'

'I'd feel safe anywhere with you.'

They walked inside, and he shut the heavy door behind them.

'Alone at last,' she said, taking his hands.

'Drink?'

'Later.' She kissed him. 'Is that the bedroom door?'

He nodded.

She started walking backwards, dragging him towards it. Pushed the door open with her back and led him inside. She lay back on the bed and pulled him down on top of her.

'I can't believe this is really happening,' she murmured in his ear.

Streaming sunlight woke him the next morning. He stirred and rolled on the rumpled sheets. Blinked a few times and smiled to himself as he remembered what had happened.

He stretched his arm out sleepily and his hand touched the pillow next to his. Zara wasn't there.

Hearing her pottering about the flat, he glanced at his watch. It was almost eight. Time to make a move, if they wanted to get to Le Val by lunchtime. He was just about to haul himself out of bed when the door opened and Zara walked into the bedroom. She was dressed, and pulling on her jacket. She bent over him and kissed him. 'You slept like a baby.'

'Going somewhere?' he asked.

'There's nothing for breakfast. I'm off to the pâtisserie down the street to get some croissants.'

'We can have something on the road.'

'Come on. Indulge me. I want to make you a nice breakfast before we leave.'

'But—'

'No buts. I'm making you breakfast, and that's official. You rest a while longer. I'll be back before you know it.' She turned to leave the room, but hesitated at the door. Stepped back to the bed and bent down over him again and kissed him long and tenderly. 'I love you,' she whispered in his ear.

When she was gone, Ben dozed. After a while, he opened his eyes and sat up. It was just gone eight-thirty. Feeling more relaxed than he had in a long time, he got out of bed and headed for the shower. He pulled on the spare jeans, a white T-shirt and grey V-neck jumper from his overnight bag.

He suddenly realised that Zara had been away a while. Was there a queue down at the pâtisserie? Or maybe she'd forgotten the combination for the security door. He went and checked, half expecting her to be standing there outside the door with an apologetic grin and a brown paper bag full of croissants. But the hallway was empty.

He came back inside, perplexed.

Then saw the folded note on the kitchen table. He snatched it up and read:

Ben,

I know you're going to be pissed off with me, but I had to go back to help Kim and the others. It's the right thing to do. I knew you wouldn't let me go unless I slipped away. Please don't be angry with me . . .

I love you. We'll be together soon, I promise. It'll all work out, and don't worry about me. I know how to take care of myself.

Kisses,

Z

He stamped about the flat, furious with himself for letting it happen. Even more furious with Kim Valentine for luring Zara into putting herself on the line. Valentine and her colleagues should have known better than this, after what had happened to Linda Downey. He thought of the photograph of the agent's mutilated body, and it made him shudder.

He snatched out his phone and was about to dial Valentine's number when he thought better of it. He'd go there instead, talk some sense into Zara and bring her away. Then off to Le Val as planned.

He quickly gathered up the few things he'd brought with him, and stuffed them into his overnight bag. The gun was still lying under a chair where he'd thrown it carelessly down the previous evening. He grabbed it and chucked it into the bag as well. Locked up the flat, ran back down to the Mini. The squeal of tyres echoed through the concrete cavern as he skidded out of the parking lot, hit the ramp and burst out into the street.

He sped through Paris until he got snarled up in a major traffic jam caused by an overturned delivery van that was blocking a main street. Ben drummed his fingers on the steering wheel and cursed under his breath as the angry Parisian drivers sounded a cacophony of horns. Then police cleared the road, the mayhem dissipated and fifteen minutes later he was on his way again.

It was almost ten by the time he skidded to a halt outside the house in the suburbs. He marched up to the entrance and thumped loudly to be let in.

The door swung open of its own accord. He stepped inside. They must have been expecting him, he thought. But it seemed strange to have left the door open like that. Careless. 'Zara?' he called down the hall. 'It's me.'

No reply. 'Valentine? Where are you? We have to talk.'

He reached the door at the bottom of the passage. It was ajar, maybe an inch. No sound from inside. That worried him. Had they already left? Was Zara on her way back to San Remo? Then he was too late. *That fucking traffic jam.*

He pressed his palm against the door and pushed it open. It creaked on its hinges and he stepped into the doorway.

The blinds were drawn, and the room was dark. There was a strange feeling underfoot. As though someone had spilled a lot of water, or there'd been a flood. He felt a squelch as he stepped into the room, groping on the wall for the light switch.

That smell. It was sharp and distinctive and triggered memories. Not good ones.

His fingers found the light switch and flicked it on.

What he saw in front of him made him stagger back towards the doorway.

Chapter Thirty-Four

Valentine, Harrison and Wolff were all staring at him from inside the room. Their mouths were gaping open, but they had nothing to say. Their three severed heads sat in a neat row on the makeshift coffee table. Blood was congealed thickly across the Formica slab, dripping down into the soaked carpet.

The rest of their bodies were scattered about the room. It was hard to tell which bits belonged to whom. An arm here, a leg there. The place resembled an abattoir. It was like the picture of Linda Downey. Even worse.

Ben fought back a gag reflex. 'Zara—' he said out loud.

That was when he heard quiet footsteps behind him, and turned. A figure was standing in the passage behind him, silhouetted against the pale square of light shining through the dappled glass of the front door window.

The figure stepped closer.

'Hello, Benedict,' Harry Paxton said. Only the blunt, black shape of the 9mm SIG Pro in his hand made him appear anything less than welcoming. It was trained on Ben's heart.

'What have you done with Zara?' Ben asked.

'You mean my dear, faithful wife?' Paxton replied.

'If you've hurt her—'

'What? You'll kill me? I really don't think so.'

'Believe it,' Ben said.

Paxton chuckled. 'She's alive. For the moment, at least.'

'I want to see her.'

'She's not far away,' Paxton said. He snapped his fingers. Ben heard a door click open behind him in the room, and wheeled around. Across the room, on the other side of the grisly row of heads, a man appeared in the doorway from which Zara had emerged the day before.

She was there with him. A fillet knife was pressed to her throat and there was a strip of silver packing tape across her mouth. Her eyes were huge with terror.

Ben stared at the man holding her. He'd seen him before.

'This is Berg,' Paxton said. 'He's an associate of mine.'

It was Thierry, the launch pilot who'd ferried Ben and Kim Valentine to and from Porto Vecchio in San Remo. Ben watched him, and all he could see in his face was that placid, stony blankness that comes with mindless cruelty.

'See?' Paxton said to Zara. 'I told you he'd come. He is in love with you, after all.' He turned back to Ben. 'You don't think I knew about agent Valentine and her friends from the beginning? And little Miss Loyalty here, arranging for them to spy on me? Oh, yes. I knew all about it. I only had to fit a GPS tracker to my intrepid wife, while she was off pretending to visit her sick friend. She led me straight to them.'

'You're dead,' Ben said. 'No question about it. You've just dug your own grave and you're standing right on the edge of it.'

'Don't overreach yourself, Major. Remember who you're dealing with. There isn't a single trick in your book that I didn't write there for you. And remember that it's thanks to me that you're still alive.'

'May 14th, 1997,' Ben said. 'Who are you kidding?'

'Sparing a life is as good as saving one, Benedict. Remember waking up in the hospital that time? Me sitting by your bedside? I was all ready to smother you with your pillow if you'd recalled anything that happened. So you really do owe me your life, whatever might have happened that day.'

Ben could hardly find the words. 'Why did you do it, Harry? How could you? They were your unit.'

Paxton shrugged. 'Smith had his suspicions about me. I did what I had to do, before he went and told anyone. I had to protect my business. You'd have done the same. It's called survival.'

'Your business. You mean selling death.'

'I cater to the demands of my clients, that's all. What they do with my products is what humans have been doing from the dawn of history. That's just the way things are, and always have been. "Only the dead have seen the end of war."'

'Plato,' Ben said. 'Don't try to glorify what you do by quoting classical philosophy. You're just a cheap gun runner.'

'Don't be naïve. If it's not my guns being used to kill people, it'll be someone else's.'

'There's a saying, Harry. *You are what you do.*'

'I'm a necessary evil.'

'But evil just the same.'

'You're the last man I'll take a lecture in morality from,' Paxton said. 'There's no blood on your hands? You think you were in a different business? And you were one of the best at it. But I think you know that.'

'I left, Harry. I don't fight dirty wars for corrupt men any more. I got out of it, but you went in even deeper. That's the difference between you and me.'

'We're not as different as you like to pretend,' Paxton said. 'That's why there isn't a man better suited to do a job for me.'

'I did the job. It's over.'

'It's not over. I have another for you, and this time you're going to do it exactly the way I want.'

Ben made no reply.

Paxton smiled. 'That's right. You're going back to Egypt. You're going to find Morgan's treasure for me.' He laughed at the look on Ben's face. 'Yes, of course I knew what he was into. Do you really think I sent you all the way to Cairo to avenge my dear son's death? Maybe I would have, if he'd been my own flesh and blood. But I'm afraid he was just one of Helen's little dalliances. I don't like people who betray me.'

The meaning of his words took a second or two to sink into Ben's mind. 'You killed her,' he said quietly. 'You killed your own wife.'

Paxton smiled a thin smile, and nodded. 'The same week I found out that all those years, she'd been cheating on me. I made it look like a heart attack. Massive adrenaline overdose. She went out like a light.' He grinned. 'And I was going to slaughter her bastard, too. I should have known he was no son of mine. I couldn't bear to be near him any more. I was just biding my time, waiting for the right moment to rid myself of him. He was all set to have one drink too many on board the yacht and fall into the sea. A tragic accident. But then he told me about this thing he'd stumbled on, something that could be worth a lot of money. That was the only thing that was keeping him alive. You think it hurt me when he was killed? I just didn't want to lose the treasure.'

'So you decided to set me up,' Ben said. 'If I'd killed those two junkies for you, you were going to try to blackmail me with it, get me to go after the money.'

'It wasn't a perfect plan, I admit,' Paxton replied. 'When you foiled it by doing things your own way, I quickly realised that I was going to have to find another way to persuade you to work for me. I'm not blind. I could see what was developing between you and my wife. So, thanks to your amorous impulses, you've provided me with a perfect solution.'

Ben glanced back at Zara, tried to put reassurance in his eyes. She returned his gaze, but he doubted that she could even see him. She was transfixed with shock and horror. They must have made her watch the slaughter of the three agents. She would have thought she was next.

'So now, Major, it's all up to you. You have a mission to complete. If you succeed, you can have her. If you fail, she dies in a very horrible way. You're on the clock.'

'You're making a huge mistake, Harry. There's still time to back out. Walk away and let her go now, and I won't come after you.'

'The mistake would be to underestimate me,' Paxton said. 'Any tricks from you, and Berg has a green light to do what he wants with her. Don't even think about trying to find her. You wouldn't. She could be on any one of a dozen vessels, anywhere in the world. You come within a mile of any of my fleet, and I'll know about it.'

Ben stayed silent.

Paxton reached into his jacket pocket and took out a small object. He tossed it in the air, and Ben caught it. He held it in the palm of his hand and examined it. An inch-and-a-half long, brand name embossed in white on pale blue plastic. It was a computer memory stick.

'Morgan's research,' Paxton said. 'The file you sent me. Still encrypted, of course, but that's your problem now.' He looked at his watch. 'Well, Major, I suggest you'd better get moving. You have seven days, starting now, to find Morgan's treasure.'

It seemed absurd. 'Seven days?'

'You heard me,' Paxton replied. 'One week. I'm not a patient man, Benedict. I've waited long enough for this. Call it a challenge. You've faced challenges before.'

Ben hung his head. 'You've got me. I'll do everything you want.' As he said it, he was thinking about the Browning in his overnight bag, just yards outside the front door in the Mini. It was a delicate matter of timing and luck – but if he could somehow get to it, he could end this quickly. Kill Berg first, then Paxton, then get Zara far away from here.

Paxton was watching him keenly. 'I know you so well, Benedict. You could be my son. I know the way you think. Everything that's going through your mind. You're already working out ways to get out of this. You think I'm just going to let you walk out of here now, while I'm still inside?' He shook his head, chuckling to himself. 'You must take me for such an idiot.' Still holding the SIG in his right hand, he reached inside his jacket with his left hand and came out holding a strange long-barrelled pistol.

Ben knew what it was. A CO_2-propelled tranquilliser dart gun. His heart sank. No way out.

'By the time you wake up, the three of us will be far away,' Paxton said. 'You'll find everything you need on the desk. I wish you a very pleasant journey back to Egypt, and all the best of British luck.' He smiled. 'I'll be keeping in touch for progress reports. *Bon voyage*, Benedict.'

He took his time aiming the dart gun. Ben tensed, waiting for it. He threw a last look at Zara, then the pistol coughed in Paxton's hand and there was a sharp pain as the dart pierced his neck.

The blackness came quickly. His last sensation was a strange feeling of weightlessness, and his face thudding into the blood-soaked carpet.

Chapter Thirty-Five

It could have been seconds later that he woke up, or it could have been years. He felt himself rise up from the black depths, break the surface and bob up towards consciousness, and flickered his eyes open to a world of blurs and echoes. Nausea hit him like a bad smell, and with it the sick memory of what had happened.

He was still lying on the floor, but somehow it felt different, harder, colder. His left arm was flung out in front of his face. His eyes fixed on the hands of his watch and for a few seconds they meant nothing to him. Then, as the synapses in his brain started firing again, he understood that it was almost midday and he'd been unconscious for nearly two hours.

That thought gave him the burst of energy to jerk himself upright. One elbow on the floor. Then one knee, and he was staggering to his feet, shaking his head to clear the grogginess. He pressed his hand to his neck, feeling the sharp pain where the dart had punctured him.

The room around him was the same, but it had

completely changed. He was standing on bare boards, just a few nails and bits of fluff around the edges of the walls to show where the carpet had been taken up. Of all the furniture, only the desk remained, and it had been stripped almost bare. The computer, cameras and surveillance equipment were gone. So was the makeshift table – and the dismembered bodies. There was no sign of what had happened there. Harry Paxton had covered his tracks one more time.

Ben could smell soap on his hands. They'd even sponged the blood from the carpet off him while he'd been unconscious.

The acrid stink of something burning outside drew him over to the window. The blind was drawn all the way down, and he yanked it open and looked out through the dusty glass at the back garden. It was over-grown and weedy, surrounded by a high wall. A big fire was burning itself out in the middle of the patchy grass, black smoke wisping upwards from the charred remnants of the rolled-up carpet and what was left of the furniture.

He turned away from the window and walked across to the desk. It wasn't quite empty. Lying on its surface were two items.

The first was the computer memory stick that had been in his hand when he'd been knocked out. The second was a drawstring bag, tied at the neck. Ben weighed the bag in his hand, undid the knot and looked inside. There were two stacks of money in there, one larger than the other. He brought each one out in turn. Euros and Egyptian pounds – about a thousand of one and ten thousand of the other. Paxton really had thought of everything.

As the seconds passed, Ben became acutely aware of his predicament. All he knew was that he had to do what Paxton wanted. There was no choice. Paxton was no ordinary kidnapper. He was an ex-SAS colonel, and he knew Ben's mind. He'd trained him, educated him, watched him grow into the soldier he'd become. There was no way to outwit him. The colonel had Ben sewn up tight.

Seven days to find something that had been lost for thousands of years, and he didn't even know where to start. He picked up the tiny memory stick, held it in the palm of his hand and slipped it into his pocket, feeling his car keys still in there. He hefted up the drawstring bag full of money, slung it over his shoulder and left the house.

The street was empty outside. Ben walked over to the Mini, bleeped the locks and dumped the money on the back seat next to his overnight bag. Right away, he could see that someone had gone through his things. He checked. The Browning was no longer there.

He drove slowly, mechanically, back to his flat, parked the car in his usual spot in the underground lot, killed the engine and sat there at the wheel for a long time, staring blankly through the windscreen at the bare concrete wall in front of him. He knew he couldn't bring himself to go up to the flat. Everything in there would remind him too much of Zara. The imprint of her head on the pillow. The rumpled sheets. Her damp towel in the bathroom. The lingering scent of her perfume. Her note, still lying there on the kitchen table.

He blamed himself. *Why did you let her go?*

He got out of the car and walked. He didn't know where he was going. Up the ramp to street level, and he took a right and wandered up the alley. In a few minutes he was ambling numbly along Boulevard Haussmann, only vaguely aware of the people around him and the traffic streaming by. He kept walking. Crossed the boulevard and almost got mown down by a bus. He barely noticed it as it lurched to a halt a metre from him, horn blaring. He made it to the other side of the street and kept putting one foot aimlessly in front of the other.

As he walked, he put his hand in his pocket and held the memory stick tight in his fist. Somewhere inside the tiny electronic device, locked away behind an impenetrable curtain of secret codes and passwords and God knew what kind of techno-gimmickry, might be everything he needed to know. But there was no way in, no way to access it. He'd already tried. It was a dead end.

Unless . . .

He suddenly remembered. The slip of paper he'd found in Morgan's blazer pocket. The grocery store receipt with the scribbled phone number. He'd completely forgotten about it, thinking it was unimportant. And maybe it was, but right now it seemed like the only scrap he had to go on.

But what had the number been? He struggled to bring it back. Forced his visual memory to cough it up. Nothing.

It was only when someone bumped into the back of him that he realised he'd stopped dead in the middle of the street. He stepped aside, muttering an apology.

He leaned against a railing. He felt sick, and it wasn't just the after-effects of the tranquilliser drug. He watched as some pigeons strutted about the pavement, pecking in the dirt around a roadside tree.

Damn, the number wouldn't come. It had been a British landline number – that much he could remember. But when he tried to focus on it, all he could see was Zara's face in his mind. The knife at her throat. Berg's impassive gaze. Paxton's little smile.

The roar of traffic seemed to fill his head, making it feel as though his thoughts were being dissolved in a swirling mess of confusion. He felt feverish with it. His mouth was dry, his heart rate was accelerated, his hands were shaking. He was falling apart.

Damn you, Hope. Get it together.

He walked on, eyes to the ground, fighting to bring the number back.

Nothing.

Then his feet reached the edge of the pavement. He looked up, and suddenly he knew where he was. He'd walked all the way up to the Place de la Trinité. Ahead of him across the busy square, nestling behind trees, was the dome of the Trinity church. It somehow seemed to beckon to him.

He crossed the square, walked up the steps to the entrance and went in. The inside of the church was cool and dark and rich with the pungent smell of incense. His footsteps echoed off the time-smoothed flagstones and carried up to the vaulted ceiling as he made his way up the aisle and settled in a pew. The traffic rumble was far away. Diaphanous light filtered in through the stained glass windows. He bowed his head, closed his eyes, felt the serene atmosphere penetrate his senses, purge away the confusion and shine clarity into his thoughts.

He visualised himself in that stinking tenement building back in Cairo.

Finding Morgan's blazer on the stoned-out girl with the angel tattoo.

Searching through the pockets back at Morgan's flat.

Finding the crumpled piece of paper.

Reading the number.

Come on.

Reading the number.

Suddenly, it came to him. His heart jumped. He opened his eyes, grabbed a pen from his pocket and scribbled the number on the back of his hand.

He stared at it. Yes, it was right. He was sure of it. The area code was 01334, but he'd no idea where in the UK that was. Then there was the main body of the number, and then the three-digit extension, 345. That part had been easy to remember.

He stood up. Stronger now, somehow. More focused. Clearer.

He walked out of the church, leaving its cool serenity behind. The building was surrounded by pretty, well-tended gardens railed off from the street. The trees rustled lightly in the breeze, and little sparrows hopped across the lawns. Ben headed for an old wooden bench under a gnarly oak. He sat down on the edge of it, took out his phone, glanced again at the number on his hand and punched it out on the keys.

After four rings his heart was already sinking. Maybe this wasn't going to lead anywhere. Maybe the number meant nothing. If the junkie girl had been wearing the blazer for a few days, the piece of paper might have been hers. Doubts gripped him.

On the sixth ring, an answerphone cut in.

'University of St Andrews. Faculty of History,' said the female voice on the recorded message. She spoke with a lilting Scottish accent. 'If you know the extension number you require, please enter it now. Otherwise, please hold for an operator.'

This didn't sound like a contact a Cairo dopehead would have. Ben entered the extension and waited. Then swore under his breath as another answerphone kicked in after a couple of rings.

'Hi, you've reached the voicemail of Dr Lawrence Kirby. I'm not around right now, so please leave your message—'

Ben killed the call before he got to the beep. So now he knew whose number he had. This was suddenly looking more promising. Maybe not much, but better than nothing.

Leaning back on the bench, he did an Internet search on 'Dr Lawrence Kirby, St Andrews University'. His phone's search engine took him straight to the Faculty of History website, where he found Kirby listed in the directory of staff members. He clicked on the name, and a thumbnail photo appeared with a two-line bio.

The picture showed a somewhat bemused-looking, pasty-faced individual who hadn't shaved that morning. He had a wild shock of black hair, a tuft of it hanging down across his brow.

Ben gazed at it. *Is this fucker going to be any use to me?* he wondered.

He laid the phone down next to him and took out his cigarettes and lighter. Lit up, watched the smoke curl away on the wind and tried hard not to think of Zara. It didn't work. He finished the cigarette and went straight into another. After a few minutes he snatched up the phone and dialled Kirby's number again.

This time, there was no answerphone, and it kept ringing and ringing. Just as he was about to hang up, a man's voice answered breathlessly, as though he'd been running to get the call.

'Dr Kirby?' Ben said.

'Speaking,' the voice panted.

'Dr Lawrence Kirby?'

'This is he,' the voice replied jovially. 'Who's this?'

'You don't know me. I'm calling about Morgan Paxton.'

The phone went dead.

Ben swore. He tried again. This time, Kirby answered on the second ring.

'We got cut off,' Ben said.

'No, we didn't.' Kirby didn't sound so jovial any more. 'I cut you off.'

'Why did you do that? I was just trying to talk to you.'

'I cut you off because I don't know any Morgan Paxton.'

'You remember his name pretty well, though.'

'Listen, I don't know who you are, or what you're talking about,' Kirby answered, sounding panicked. 'You must have the wrong number.'

'It's the right number and, if you let me explain, you'll understand why I need to talk to you. It's important.'

There was a pause on the other end. 'I've nothing to say to you. I don't know who Morgan Paxton is.' Kirby hung up again.

Ben turned off his phone. *OK, if that's the way you want to play it, Kirby*, he thought. St Andrews. East coast of Scotland, just north of Edinburgh.

Fuck it. He could be there in a few hours.

Chapter Thirty-Six

Ben hammered the Mini the fourteen miles northeast to Paris Roissy airport and got on the first plane bound for Edinburgh. After a short flight, he stepped down on Scottish soil. The air was colder and crisper than France, but he wasn't interested in taking in his surroundings. At the Avis car rental outlet he picked out a Mercedes SLK two-seater sports that seemed about right for someone in the kind of hurry he was. Settling into the snug black leather interior, he entered his destination into the sat nav and hit the road fast and hard. Edinburgh shrank away quickly to nothing in his mirrors. He blasted across the giant suspension bridge spanning the Firth of Forth and carved north-wards up the twisting A roads of the east coast until he reached St Andrews.

He vaguely remembered from his theology studies that the old university town had at one time been the religious capital of Scotland, steeped in the blood of butchered, tortured and burned martyrs. Its violent past was hard to imagine as he drove through the quiet streets, past ivied university buildings, cafés and hotels.

It didn't take him long to locate the Faculty of History. He left the car and walked along a path overlooking the sea, with the ruins of the medieval cathedral behind him and the craggy remains of St Andrews castle and the coastline stretching out in a wide curve ahead in the distance. He filled his lungs with the fresh, salty air and tried hard, for the millionth time, to keep Zara from the foreground of his thoughts but knew it was impossible.

Arriving at the fine stone building that housed the Faculty of History, he walked in the iron gates, crossed a small car park and shoved through the front entrance into a large reception area. There was nobody at the desk. He glanced around him. A row of chairs, some historical prints framed on the wall, a broad stair-case winding upwards. On a panel by the bottom of the stairs were the names of the academic staff with their room numbers and a little push-button LED that showed who was in. Ben ran his finger down the list until he found Kirby and a room number – 42. The little light next to it was on.

He headed up the stairs, two at a time. A bunch of students were heading down, clutching books and folders, chatting among themselves. They glanced at him as he went by, and he ignored them. At the top of the stairs, a sign pointed right for rooms 21 to 45. He batted through a fire door and strode quickly up the narrow, neon-lit corridor. When he got to room 42 he checked the name-plate on the door: 'DR LAWRENCE KIRBY'.

Ben pushed in without knocking, and found himself

in a large office. The place was a chaotic sprawl, books and papers and yellowing crumpled copies of the *Guardian* everywhere, piled high on the desk, stacked in heaps on the floor. At the back of the room was a dusty window, and between it and the cluttered desk stood the man Ben instantly recognised from the Internet page as Lawrence Kirby.

Kirby had been in the middle of stuffing a huge book into a crammed, battered leather briefcase on his desk when Ben burst in. 'Can't you kn—' he started. His voice trailed off, and he froze, staring at Ben. He was exactly like his photo, except maybe a little scruffier, and the unruly shock of black hair hung even lower over his brow.

Kirby dropped the book and walked out from behind the desk. He was wearing frayed cord trousers, his shirt was hanging out under his tweed sports jacket. He was a few pounds overweight and moved awkwardly. 'Who are you?' he demanded. His eyes darted up and down, as though he were nervously sizing Ben up.

'I'm the one you didn't want to talk to on the phone,' Ben said. 'Remember?' The draught from the opening of the door had blown some documents off the desk, and he stooped quickly to pick them up. The top one was a car insurance renewal form with Kirby's name and home address on it. 'You dropped these,' he said, trying to keep his tone more friendly. He could see Kirby was rattled, and he didn't want to seem a threat to the man. He laid the papers down on the desk and smiled.

'I was just leaving,' Kirby said abruptly.

'I need to talk to you.'

'I told you, I have nothing to say to you,' Kirby said, flushed. 'I'd like you to leave.'

'I came a very long way to talk to you, Dr Kirby. Just give me a few minutes. That's all I ask, then I'm gone and you won't see me again.'

'I'm calling security.' The historian made a grab for the phone that was half buried under the sea of paperwork on his desk.

'Please don't do that,' Ben said.

Kirby's hand stopped short of the phone. His eyes were round and staring. 'Are you threatening me?'

'I'm not threatening you,' Ben said. 'You don't have to be afraid. All I want is to ask you some questions about Morgan Paxton and the Akhenaten Project. I need to know what you know.'

'Morgan's dead,' Kirby said.

'I know that. And your number was in his pocket when he died. Were you and he working on the research together?'

Kirby swallowed. 'His father sent you here, didn't he?'

The mention of Harry Paxton brought a fresh image of Zara into Ben's mind. He felt his blood rise. 'No. I'm not working for Morgan's father. I was in the army with him. And until two days ago, I thought he was my friend. I was wrong. When this is over, I'm going after him. But right now I need your help. I need it badly, Dr Kirby.'

'Who the hell are you?'

'My name's Ben Hope. And I'm not here to hurt you. Trust me.'

Kirby hesitated, frozen by indecision and nerves.

'Please,' Ben said.

Kirby stared at him a second longer, then stabbed a button on the phone keypad. 'Security? This is Dr Lawrence Kirby. There's an intruder in my office.'

There was nothing Ben could do to stop him. He could have taken the phone off him, or ripped the wire from the wall. But strong-arm tactics weren't going to get him anywhere. He knew he had only seconds before security arrived and he needed to make the most of that time.

'I know that Morgan was looking for treasure. I need to know where it is.'

'That's a surprise.'

'I haven't time to explain,' Ben said. 'How much do you know?'

But before Kirby could answer, the door flew open and two security guards walked in. The older one was craggy, hardened-looking, the white hair contrasting with his red nose and the thread veins on his cheeks. Maybe a former boxer. His companion couldn't have been more than twenty. Not long in uniform, Ben thought. Itching for some action.

'This man burst into my office and has been threatening me,' Kirby said, pointing at Ben. 'I want him removed.'

'Let's go, son,' the older guard said, reaching for Ben's arm. 'We don't want any trouble.'

'I'm not bringing any,' Ben said. 'I just wanted to talk to him about something.'

Kirby grabbed his briefcase. 'Well, I'll leave it to you gentlemen to take care of.' He walked past Ben with his eyes on the floor, breezed through the doorway and was gone.

'You'll have to come with us,' the craggy guard said. 'We have to take details from you.'

'I don't think so,' Ben said. 'I didn't do anything.'

The younger guard folded his arms. 'That's not what Dr Kirby said.'

'I don't give a shit what Dr Kirby said. I'm leaving now, and you're going to let me.'

'No chance, pal. You're coming down to our office and we're calling the police.' He pronounced it 'polis'.

Ben made a step for the door. The younger guy grabbed his wrist. 'I have to warn you, I'm a black belt in Aikido. I don't want to have to hurt you.'

He was unconscious before he hit the carpet.

Ben turned to the older guy. 'I didn't come here looking for trouble. Best you don't give me any, OK?' He pointed to Kirby's chair, and the old guy went over and sat down, fuming but knowing better than to get up.

'Sensible,' Ben said. 'Give me your radio and mobile phone.'

The guard wordlessly slid them across the desk and Ben shoved them in his pockets. 'Now I'm leaving, and you're going to sit quietly until this prick comes round.' He ripped the phone wire out of the wall, and walked to the door. He threw a last warning look at the guard, left the room and locked the door behind him, leaving the key in the lock.

He looked at his watch as he walked down the corridor towards the exit. Time was ticking by too fast.

As he strode out of the entrance and headed for the car, he was already dialling up Google Maps on his phone and punching in the postcode that had been on the car insurance renewal form in Kirby's office. The address came up as Drummond Manor, eight miles west of St Andrews.

Ben slid inside the Mercedes and entered the details on his sat nav. Now to find Kirby and make him talk. Properly.

Chapter Thirty-Seven

Lawrence Kirby knew he was a terrible driver, but he didn't generally care and he cared even less today. As he sat peering over the wheel of his bright yellow Smart Car and lurched and stalled his way towards the old family home eight miles out in the countryside, he was thinking about this guy, Ben Hope, who'd accosted him in his office. And about Morgan, and about the treasure. He wondered how the hell Hope had managed to track him down so easily.

Whatever it all meant, it scared the shit out of him. As he pulled in off the road, passed under the archway of trees and into the gravelled forecourt of Drummond Manor, he was wondering whether it was time to pack some stuff and take a holiday. Maybe take the sabbatical leave he'd cancelled the day he'd heard about Morgan's death and bailed out of his Cairo trip.

He climbed the steps to the big stone manor house, fumbled for the key in his pocket and pushed open the heavy oak door. Every time he walked inside the huge stone-floored entrance hall, he had the same thought: how much he hated all the crap his father had insisted on displaying on the walls. The stuffed trophy deer heads always seemed to watch him wherever he went, and their antlers made spiky shadows at night that freaked him out. He couldn't stand the sight of the crossed sabres and muskets gathering dust on the carved wood panels, either. On a velvet panoply over the fireplace were two big ceremonial Kukhri knives, left over from His Lordship's days as an officer with the Gurkha regiment.

But the old man's will hadn't specified that his son, the new Laird of the manor, couldn't just bung the offensive lot in a skip. And Kirby planned to do exactly that. He just hadn't got around to it in the months since he'd inherited this rambling pile.

He dumped his briefcase in the passage, walked through to the kitchen and made himself a mug of instant decaf. Carrying the thin brown liquid through to the only one of the manor's many reception rooms that he ever used, he gazed out of the window across the overgrown lawns behind the house. Beyond a stone wall and a row of trees, he could see the derelict agricultural buildings in the background. The place had been a working farm once but, ever since the old man had got frail and sick, everything had fallen into decay. Abandoned stacks of hay bales were mouldering and turning black in the rusty barn. And the slurry pit was sure to be attracting rats. It was becoming a health hazard. He'd have to tear the whole lot down.

That was Kirby's last thought before he sensed a presence behind him and spun around in surprise to see two men striding fast towards him across the room.

Two guns in his face. He dropped his coffee and let out a short scream. Fell to his knees.

Neither man spoke a word as they grabbed his arms, hauled him roughly to his feet and marched him out of the room and down the passage. He struggled and pleaded. 'What do you want with me?' As they frog-marched him across the hall, he glanced up and saw with a shock of horror that there was an empty space where one of the Gurkha knives had hung.

Oh Christ, they're going to cut my head off.

'What are you going to do to me?' he screamed.

They ignored him and dragged him out of the front door. There was a white Suzuki mini-van sitting parked on the gravel outside. The back doors were open. The men shoved him towards it.

'Where are you taking me?'

No reply.

All the strength had left Kirby's legs and he was shaking with pure terror as they bundled him into the back. He slid across the bare metal floor, tried to scramble to his feet and whacked his head against the low roof. The doors slammed shut. There were no windows. Kirby was suddenly in darkness.

The kidnappers walked around the van's sides to the cab, pulled open their doors and climbed in. They spent a moment making their pistols safe and securing them inside the tactical concealment holsters they were both wearing under their jackets. They didn't speak, but shared the quiet satisfaction of a job cleanly and quickly executed. Now it was time to get out of here and deliver the package to the place outside

288

Glasgow that their cell used as a safehouse. Neither man had any clear idea of the purpose of this job – they only knew that a call had come in from overseas the night before, and it was from someone their bosses obeyed instantly. It had also been put in no uncertain terms to them that to mess this up would mean severe punishment.

The driver twisted the key.

Nothing happened. The van was stone dead.

'Fuck,' he said in Arabic.

'What's wrong with it? It was fine a minute ago,' said the man in the passenger seat.

The driver muttered another curse, reached down below the dash and yanked on the bonnet release mechanism. There was a dull clunk and the bonnet popped free of its catch and opened half an inch. He kicked open his door, jumped down from the van and walked around to the front.

The passenger watched through the windscreen as his colleague lifted the bonnet and disappeared behind it. He heard some noises, then nothing. He stuck his head out of the window. 'Hurry the fuck up,' he yelled in Arabic. 'We've got to get moving.'

The bonnet crashed down with a clang that shook the van. The passenger looked, expecting to see his colleague wiping his hands and giving the thumbs-up – *OK, sorted, let's roll.*

But there was nobody there.

He frowned, opened his door, climbed down. His footsteps crunched on the gravel as he walked around the front wing. He looked down and saw the driver's legs sticking out as though he were lying on his back to work on the underside of the van.

'Hey, what the fuck are you doing down there?'

But then he saw the legs give a violent, spasmodic twitch.

And he saw the blood that was pooling outwards from under the van and across the gravel.

After that, he saw nothing more.

Chapter Thirty-Eight

Ben cut the man's throat in a swift sawing motion, stepped aside to avoid the blood spray and let the body slump to the ground. He laid the long, curved knife on the gravel between the two dead men and quickly checked them for any kind of ID. As he'd expected, there was nothing – but the moment he'd seen the van arrive and the two Middle Eastern guys get out, he'd known who had sent them. Kamal must have found the phone number in the blazer pocket and followed the same trail he had.

There was a frenzied thumping and yelling coming from the back of the van. Ben walked around to the rear doors and opened them.

Kirby looked crazed and dishevelled. 'It's *you*. What are you doing here?'

'Just dropped by for a chat,' Ben said. 'I was about to talk to you, when I saw you had company. Decided to hang back and see what happened.'

'Who the hell are you?'

'Right now, under the circumstances, I'd say I'm the best friend you have in the world,' Ben said. 'Ready to trust me yet?'

Kirby lowered himself gingerly out of the back of the van and froze when he saw the two bodies. He put his hands to his face. 'Oh, my God. You *killed* them.'

'You're right. Maybe I should have just reasoned with them. I'm sure we could have worked something out.'

'What's going on here?' Kirby gasped.

'You know perfectly well what's going on,' Ben said. 'Your secret's out, and everybody wants a piece. What did you think was going to happen?'

'I'm calling the police.' Kirby started staggering towards the house.

Ben stopped him. 'Not if you want to stay alive.'

'What?'

'You call the police, I'm out of here. Then, when these guys don't phone in or turn up, more are going to come. Sooner or later, they'll get you, take you away, interrogate you and probably torture you to death. There's nothing the police can do to prevent it. If that's what you want, go and dial 999, and I'll say goodbye.'

Kirby's shoulders slumped helplessly. 'All right. Obviously I don't want that. So what am I going to do?'

'First you're going to tell me where there's a toolshed with a wheelbarrow in it. And then you're going to help me carry these bodies over to the slurry pit over there, where nobody's ever going to go looking for them.'

It took less than ten minutes to make the two kidnappers vanish. A concrete lane led from the side of the manor to the dilapidated farm buildings two hundred yards away beyond the trees, and Ben used the creaky old barrow that Kirby found for him to roll them one at a time to the edge of the slurry pit.

At twenty yards, the stink of putrescent liquid dung was noxious. At ten it was overwhelming, and very few people would have got closer than five. Ben held his breath as he kicked back the bolts on the hatches and opened them up to reveal the filth underneath. He rolled one corpse in with his foot, then the other. Two brown splashes, a stream of bubbles as the slurry filled their lungs, and they were gone. The next time anyone saw them, there would be nothing but bones left. Nature was efficient that way. Ben tossed the bloody Kukhri knife in after them, slammed the hatches shut, slid the bolts home and moved away quickly towards cleaner air.

Kirby was waiting for him beside the old hay barn, looking deeply perturbed and shaken. 'Now what?'

'Now let's get out of here,' Ben said. 'My car, not yours.'

He led Kirby to where he'd parked the SLK behind the trees, out of sight of the manor.

'I feel sick,' Kirby moaned as he settled into the car.

Ben fired up the engine and the acceleration pressed them hard back in their seats as the car sped up the road. The countryside was open and the roads were quiet. He didn't know where he was going – he just wanted to put distance between them and the house before finding somewhere they could talk. He drove fast along the winding coast road, between green fields dotted with sheep and spring lambs, drystone walls, little white cottages and farmhouses here and there in the distance. The sun was beginning to sink lower in the sky, casting a reddish glow over the sea.

'Do you have to drive so fast?' Kirby complained.

'We've got to talk, Kirby.'

'Stop the car,' Kirby muttered in a strangled voice. Ben snatched a glance away from the road ahead and saw that the historian was deathly pale, slumped over in his seat, both hands pressed against his sternum.

'I'm going to puke.'

Ben hit the brakes and pulled over onto a grassy verge. Kirby's door was swinging open as they rolled to a halt. He staggered out across the verge and leaned against a fencepost. Bent over double, he clutched his stomach and threw up violently.

Ben let him get on with it for a minute or two, then got out of the car and walked over to join him. 'It's just stress,' he said. 'You've had a shock. Can we talk now?'

'I need some air,' Kirby muttered. 'I'm going for a walk.'

On the other side of the road, a little rocky path led downwards towards the shoreline. Kirby set off down it, and Ben followed. Minutes were passing. Minutes he couldn't afford to lose. He was thousands of miles from where he needed to be, and getting nowhere. He could only hope this guy was worth the effort.

Kirby paused by a big rock and took several deep breaths. 'Oh, Christ.' He ran trembling fingers down his face. 'How did I get into this? Those people, back there. Did they kill Morgan?'

'It's complicated. I don't have time to go into every detail.'

'I need to know.'

Ben let out a sigh. 'I suppose you're entitled to an explanation.' He ran quickly through what had happened. About the robbery, about Kamal, about Harry Paxton. But it was a simplified version in one major respect. There was no reason why anyone needed to know about Zara.

'He's *blackmailing* you?' Kirby asked, amazed.

Ben nodded. 'Someone close to me stands to get hurt if I don't retrieve whatever it is you and Morgan found. I'm on the clock. Can you help me, or not?'

'It's unbelievable,' Kirby said. 'Morgan always regretted having let on to his father about the discovery. He knew the old bastard was too interested in it for comfort.'

'Now it's your turn to talk,' Ben said. 'What's the connection between you and Morgan? What's this about?'

'Morgan was my friend,' Kirby muttered. 'We were at university together. We went back a long way.'

'So this was a joint project. You were in it together.'

'It was Morgan's brainchild, but we were both working on it. I was going to join him in Cairo. But then I heard about what happened. I've been crapping myself ever since. Just waiting for them to come after me.' He looked up. 'How did you know where to find me?'

'I told you. Your number was scribbled on a piece of paper in Morgan's pocket.'

'Damn,' Kirby said. 'When Morgan went to Egypt, I was in the middle of moving here from Lancaster Uni.

This is a new job for me. I called him on his mobile to tell him about my new number. He must have jotted it down on the first thing that came to hand.'

'Fine. Now tell me what you know.'

'I need a drink,' Kirby said. 'There's a pub another mile up this road. Get me a drink, and I'll tell you everything.'

Chapter Thirty-Nine

The road twisted downwards until they came to a coastal village. A cobbled street led to a harbour where small fishing vessels drifted and bumped on the tide, flanked on three sides by an ancient stone dock and a rocky beach. Lobster creels and salt-crusted nets lay piled on the pier, and in the falling dusk the lights from the huddled cottages on the sea front threw a golden, shimmering glow out across the water.

Ben parked the car and he and Kirby walked down a cobbled slope to a long, low pub with a weathered sign that said 'The Whey Pat'. Inside, the décor looked as though it hadn't been touched in centuries. A pitted old bar, some spartan benches and a couple of bare tables. No paper napkins or place mats on the tables, no chalkboard menus on the wall, just a well used dartboard for the men who came in here to drink and nothing else. Ben wouldn't have been surprised to see sawdust on the floor.

There were a few locals at the bar. The hum of conversation paused a beat as Ben and Kirby walked in, and one or two stares landed on Kirby before people looked away and the chatter picked up again.

'Seems you're popular round here,' Ben said as he guided Kirby towards the empty far end of the pub. They grabbed a table near the fire, where a couple of logs were crackling and spitting. Ben went over to the bar and ordered two double Scotches. He didn't know if Kirby drank whisky normally, and he didn't care. If the guy wanted a drink, he was going to get him one that would loosen him up as fast as possible. There wasn't much time to mess about, and beer was just too slow. He took a fistful of change from his pocket and fed it into the CD jukebox in the corner, selecting a bunch of noisy rock tracks that would allow them to talk without being overheard.

Back at the table, he slid Kirby's glass over to him. He took out his Zippo and his last few Gauloises, and lit one up.

'You can't do that in here,' Kirby said. 'It's illegal.'

Ben glanced up towards the bar. It wasn't the kind of establishment where anyone seemed to give a damn, and he didn't care if they did. 'So is murder,' he said. 'And you've got two dead bodies at your place. Now drink that and start talking. The Akhenaten Project. Facts, figures, details, the works. Now.'

Kirby peered down at the glass, looked as if he were about to complain, then thought better of it. He picked it up, closed his eyes and knocked it back like medicine. When he put his glass down, his face had lost some of its pallor. He wiped his mouth with his sleeve.

'Backstory first,' he said. 'You need it, to understand the rest.'

'OK, but keep it short.'

'Akhenaten was a pharaoh,' Kirby said. 'He reigned during the Eighteenth Dynasty, 1353 to 1336 BC. His real name was—'

'Amenhotep IV,' Ben cut in.

Kirby stared, arching an eyebrow. 'I didn't take you for an Egyptologist.'

'I'm not. Theology at Oxford, years ago. But I still remember a few things.'

'You said you were a soldier.'

'I was. But we're not here to discuss the story of my life.'

'Army. Theology. Kind of a culture clash, wouldn't you say?'

Ben just stared at him.

Kirby shrugged. 'OK. Whatever. Where was I?'

'Akhenaten.'

'Right. So maybe you know that Akhenaten was a little unusual. In fact, he was totally unique in the whole history of ancient Egypt.'

'I know that he was the first king of Egypt to worship a single god.'

Kirby nodded. The whisky seemed to be relaxing him. 'Aten. Otherwise known as the sun god, symbolised by the sun disc that Akhenaten instituted as a national icon. That was the guy's whole crusade, to wipe out the old polytheistic religion, do away with all the traditional gods that Egyptians had venerated for thousands of years, and introduce this radical new thing that he called Atenism. It's the first time in recorded history that anyone tried to implement a monotheistic state religion. To some historians he's the precursor to Jesus Christ, to others he's just a radical crackpot.' Kirby finished his drink, gazed a little wistfully at the empty glass. 'Can I get another drink?'

'In a minute.' Ben slid his own glass under the historian's nose. 'Have this in the meantime.'

'Thanks. I need it.'

'Let's cut to the chase. I know about Atenism. And I know that Akhenaten was called a heretic for his religious reforms. But what's this got to do with Morgan Paxton? I'm not seeing the connection here.'

Kirby picked up Ben's glass. 'Let me go on. You wanted to hear this, didn't you? All the background stuff's really important. Otherwise you won't—'

'OK, go on then,' Ben snapped.

'This pharaoh was only a young man when he took over from his father Amenhotep III,' Kirby went on. 'But he'd always been a little weird. Even physically weird, misshapen. All kinds of peculiarities about him. And soon after he took power, he started implementing this incredible, unthinkable plan. In the fifth year of his reign he adopted the name Akhenaten, which means "glorious spirit of the Aten". That was the first sign of trouble. The crunch came when, in his ninth year, he basically abolished all of the old gods. We're talking about a gigantic revolution, a total reorganisation of the whole foundation of the society. Figures like Anubis, the jackal-headed god. Osiris, ruler of the Underworld. Amun, big cheese of the whole lot.

Akhenaten just swiped them away.' Kirby gestured with his arm. 'Just like that. All the people were left with was this very exclusive compulsory state religion, Atenism. Meanwhile, Akhenaten and his royal retinue abandoned the state capital of Thebes and went off to found a new city called Akhetaten, meaning "horizon of the Aten", better known as Amarna.' Kirby had finished Ben's glass. He looked at him expectantly.

'Same again?' Ben asked, pointing at the empty glasses.

'Why the hell not?' Kirby replied.

Ben got up, strode over to the bar and came back with two more doubles. He slammed them down on the table. 'Right. Keep talking.'

Kirby drank, seemed to lose his thread for a second, then continued. 'OK, this is coming up to the important bit. While this crazy pharaoh is living it up in his own private paradise, worshipping his god like some new-age California hippie, the whole country's going to the dogs. He basically didn't give a toss what happened to the economy, to state security, or to the people. It all started crumbling away to shit. He was bringing Egypt to its knees.' He paused for another long sip. His cheeks were rosy now, and his eyes were brightening steadily. 'So, as you can imagine, a lot of people were terribly unhappy with Akhenaten. The temples played a very important role in the economic and social life of the community, and he'd destroyed all that. Meanwhile, the level of state censorship was pretty much on a par with the Nazi book-burning frenzy in pre-war Germany. Akhenaten ordered the destruction of vast hoards of treasures that had been created in veneration of the old gods. Everything from the biggest statue to the smallest amulet – if it depicted the old polytheistic order in any way, he wanted it suppressed. The gold was to be melted down and turned into Aten idols. The temples were all closed up. A whole profession of craftsmen, masons, sculptors, scribes, were suddenly forbidden from carrying out the trade they'd been practising all their lives. And the high priests were basically redundant. In short, just about everyone was seriously upset with this crazy pharaoh they regarded as a troublemaker. Worse than that. A heretic.'

Kirby paused. 'And now we come to the legend. The old, old myth of the heretic's treasure, which tells that someone may or may not have managed to rescue a gigantic quantity of precious religious artefacts from destruction by Akhenaten's agents.'

'Who?'

'They don't call it a myth for nothing,' Kirby said. 'The fact is, nobody has ever known who, or how, or whether it even happened. It's just one of those camp-fire tales that have been rolling around for millennia, and which nobody has taken seriously for centuries.'

Ben could feel his muscles tightening. 'So this is all just hearsay. No substance to it whatsoever. This is what I'm wasting my time on.' He was on the brink of walking out of the pub. Despair was beginning to well up inside him again. Why was he here? Why hadn't he tried to follow Paxton's traces back in Paris?

Kirby seemed to sense his mood. 'Hold on.

I haven't finished. What I'm about to tell you changes everything.'

'It had better be extremely good,' Ben said.

'It is. Here's where the legend ends and reality begins. Morgan's and my involvement with this kicked off with a chance discovery in Antakya, Turkey. Which at one time was the site of the ancient Syrian city of Antioch.'

Ben knew the name from his theology studies. Antioch was where the followers of Jesus had been called Christians for the first time. A city ravaged by centuries of wars and sieges, crusades and earthquakes. It had passed through the hands of the Egyptians, the Greeks, the Romans. But that still didn't tell him much.

'A couple of years ago, Morgan was there on holiday,' Kirby explained. 'He always liked browsing around in little antique shops, street markets. Most of what you find in those places is fake trash. Ancient papyri that are really last year's banana leaves with a bit of paint on them. Any old bit of bone that's been carved, fed to turkeys so that the gastric juices make them look all ancient, then passed off as precious artefacts. But then, on his last day before he was due to fly back home, among all the crap Morgan found something special.'

'What was it?'

'A small casket,' Kirby said. 'All eaten away with age. The vendor said it had been dug up near the ruins of the Antioch ramparts. Must have thought it was just junk. Morgan snapped it up right away, took it home and spent half the night opening it up. Inside it was a papyrus.'

'Not last year's banana leaf?'

'No way. This was the real deal. It was written in authentic hieratic script, which was a simplified, abbreviated form of hieroglyphics used for writing letters.'

'I know what hieratic script was,' Ben said. 'Go on.'

'It was an unfinished letter, written by a resident of Antioch around 1335 BC, sometime after the death of the pharaoh Akhenaten. The author introduced himself as Diodore of Heraclea, a very sick old man with something important to say.'

'For God's sake, Kirby. I haven't got time for all this.'

Kirby held up a finger. 'Bear with me. This is where it gets exciting. Because the letter was addressed to Sanep, the High Priest of Thebes, and in it Diodore revealed an amazing secret. He was confessing, openly and willingly, to one of the biggest heists in the history of Egypt. But it wasn't a crime he was ashamed of, or that he'd be punished for. In fact, if the letter had ever been finished and reached its destination, he would have been brought back to Egypt and paraded through the streets as a hero. Let me tell you why.'

Ben didn't reply. Waited for the rest. Maybe, just maybe, this was getting interesting.

'You need to flash back a few years,' Kirby continued. 'To when Diodore wasn't Diodore at all. His real name was Wenkaura and he was Egyptian, born in Thebes. He'd been one of the city's most revered and influential High Priests, and in those days Sanep was his young novice. Now, in the letter Wenkaura describes how, back in the year 1344 BC, he and two of his fellow clergymen, Katep and Menamun, had all decided they had to do something to prevent the disaster that Akhenaten was bringing down on their country and their religion.'

Ben was listening now. 'Do what?'

'Well, imagine the situation. All this is happening around you. Everyone's convinced that the king is batshit-mad. He's threatening the very survival of the state with his cultural revolution and this nutcase sun cult. Destroying all these magnificent treasures, priceless even at the time, and everything you believe in. The situation isn't going to get better on its own. What would *you* do? What would you *have* to do? Think about it.'

Ben already knew the answer.

Kirby grinned at the look on his face. 'Right. One option they had was to conspire to have the bastard assassinated. I'm sure they must have thought about it. But a murder plot was too risky – he had agents and informants everywhere. Nobody could be trusted. So they decided to wait it out, in the hope that once this reign of madness was over, normality would be restored. It was only a question of time.'

'So they decided to hide the treasure for posterity,' Ben said. 'Hoping that one day, it could be returned to its rightful place.'

Kirby nodded enthusiastically as he took another gulp of whisky. 'Wenkaura, Katep and Menamun didn't want the treasure for themselves. They saw themselves as its stewards, its protectors. So they used their influence to salvage all they could over a period of several months, maybe a year, and stored it up in a secret location in Thebes. Bit by bit, they started stashing it away, somewhere it could never be found, using what power they still had to keep the operation secret. But it was a wildly risky thing to do. Suicidal. Sooner or later the pharaoh's agents were bound to get wise, and they did. Informants talked, people were tortured. Suddenly the priests were marked men, and it became impossible for them to keep shifting treasure the way they'd been doing. They stashed the last of it wherever they could, somewhere out in the desert. Wenkaura described how he was able to smuggle himself out of Thebes safely by stowing away on board a merchant vessel. He only heard later what became of Katep and Menamun. Rather than be captured and tortured, they'd committed suicide by drinking poison.'

'Wenkaura fled to Syria?'

'A resourceful guy, clearly. He got himself a job as a private tutor to a rich man's son, assumed his new identity and became Diodore. Years went by. Then one day he heard the news. Akhenaten had died. Maybe assassinated, nobody knows. Suddenly the old order was being restored, Akhenaten's reforms and his name were stamped in the dirt, and his successor, Tutankhamun, reinstated the old religion with Amun as head of the gods. It was Wenkaura's dream come true. He was old and sick by then, and scared that if he didn't act soon, the secret of the treasure would go to his grave with him. He sat down and started writing his letter. Sadly, or perhaps not so sadly, it was never sent. We never knew why. Maybe he died before he got the chance to finish it. Maybe he had second thoughts.

Who knows? Who cares? What matters is, we found it. And that treasure is still out there, just waiting.'

Ben was quiet for a few moments, taking it all in. 'Is this for real, Kirby? Because there's a hell of a lot riding on it.'

'Trust me, it's *very* for real. Morgan and I spent months deciphering the papyrus.'

'Where's the papyrus now?' Ben asked.

'In London,' Kirby said. 'Locked away in a safe deposit box and, now Morgan's dead, I'm the only person in the world who knows where.'

Ben frowned. 'How do we know it's genuine? How do we know that this Diodore really was Wenkaura?'

'Because by way of a letterhead, he marked it with the personal seal that only he would have used, during his tenure as High Priest. It would have been unique to him, and very few people would ever have seen it. It instantly identifies him as Wenkaura. I'll show you.' Kirby took a pen from the breast pocket of his jacket, grabbed a stained beer mat from the table and hunched over it, scribbling something. He slid it over to Ben. In a blank corner of the beer mat was a small, distinctive circular logo, bearing an image of what looked like a temple in the centre. It was flanked by palm trees, and a crowned bird sat over the top of it.

Ben looked at it for a moment, then slid the beer mat back towards Kirby. 'If this is so genuine, why aren't Egyptologists the world over talking about it?'

Kirby let out a derisive snort. 'Because our esteemed peers are a bunch of closed-minded arseholes. According to a panel of eminent professors, our research was speculative, unscholarly, nonsensical; and to resurrect the old myth of the heretic's lost treasure would have done our careers about as much good as writing papers on astrology.'

'Maybe they were right.'

Kirby took another slurp of Scotch. 'Oh, yeah? These are the same kind of pricks who said Imhotep was a myth, until 1926 when a chance discovery proved them wrong and caused a lot of red faces. So Morgan and I thought, stuff 'em. They deserve to be humiliated. And they will be. I guarantee it.'

'So you're saying the letter indicates where the treasure is?' Ben asked. 'Simple as that?'

Kirby shook his head. 'I'm afraid nothing's ever that simple. Morgan and I reckoned that the old man was concerned it might be too easily intercepted en route. If he'd just given a location – X marks the spot – anyone could have found it. Wenkaura was cautious. And very smart. He'd seen the whole thing coming years before, and in the letter he tells how, before he'd fled Egypt, he'd devised a series of clues, sitting right under the noses of Akhenaten's agents, that could point the way to where the vast bulk of the treasure was hidden.' Kirby leaned back in his chair and smiled.

'You know these clues?'

Kirby's smile dropped. 'Not quite. The way it works is that the first clue is in the papyrus. That leads you to a second clue, then the second leads to a third, and so on. All we had was a cryptic reference in Wenkaura's letter, giving the specific location of the second clue.'

'Which is what?'

'The tomb of "He who is close to Re"', Kirby said.

'That doesn't sound very specific at all,' Ben replied. 'Since Re was one of their chief gods, I imagine quite a few people would have thought themselves close to him. You could be working your way through half the tombs in Egypt before finding anything.'

'Exactly. And that's what Morgan was working on in Cairo.'

'And he found out what it meant?'

'He found out something, that's for sure.' Kirby paused, sighed. 'Problem is, I don't know what. While he was out there I came home one day to find a phone message from him. He sounded all excited, saying he'd figured out the first clue, that it had led him to the second clue like clockwork, and he was going somewhere the next day that he was sure was going to offer up the next. I was supposed to call him back, but his phone was switched off. And that was the last time I ever heard from him. Next thing I knew, he was dead, and all his research notes were stolen. If he got round to updating his notes, we'll never know. They're gone.'

'Maybe not.' Ben dug in his pocket, took out the little blue memory stick and laid it on the table. 'Morgan's notes, taken straight from his laptop.'

Kirby snatched it up. 'How the hell did you get hold of this? On second thoughts, don't tell me.' He held the memory stick in front of him, gazing at it. 'What I wouldn't give to see what's in here.'

'You're not the only one. The bad guys have it too.'

'But they'd never get into it,' Kirby smirked. 'Not a

chance in hell. The most fiendishly crack-proof encryption ever known. Morgan's and my secret.'

'We need computer access,' Ben said. 'We can't go back to the house.'

'But we could drive to my office.'

Ben looked at his watch. They'd been sitting in the pub for over an hour, and night had fallen. 'Then let's go. Right now.'

Chapter Forty

Back in St Andrews, Ben parked the Mercedes under the amber glow of a street lamp and followed Kirby to the iron gates of the Faculty of History building. They were locked.

'It's OK,' Kirby said. 'We all have a key, in case we need to come back to the office after hours.' He unlocked a creaky side gate and they walked across the dark, empty car park to the entrance. Ben glanced up and down the street as Kirby opened the door. There was nobody around. Inside, Kirby was about to turn on the lights when Ben stopped his hand. 'Keep the place dark,' he said.

They climbed the stairs by the moonlight that shone from the windows, and Ben led the way through the shadowy corridor to Kirby's room.

Ben drew down the blinds in the dark office as Kirby fired up the laptop on his desk and fumbled blindly to insert the memory stick. After a few moments the screen lit up, casting a bluish glow over his face in the darkness. 'Hardware recognised. OK, here we go.' He clicked the mouse, tapped a few keys. 'Now for the password. Calypso Jennings.'

'Calypso Jennings?'

Kirby glanced up. 'She was a junior lecturer in ancient Greek, when Morgan and I were undergrads together at Durham. Hottest academic you've ever seen. We were both nuts about her. She seemed the obvious choice of password. Like I said, the most crack-proof encryption known to man.'

Ben watched as Kirby's podgy fingers scuttled quickly over the keys, typing in the password. The file unlocked instantly, and they were in.

'Here we go, the Akhenaten Project research file,' Kirby said proudly. He held down a key and scrolled down through the document, text skimming across the screen faster than Ben could read it. 'Nothing new here so far,' Kirby muttered. 'This is all stuff we already know.' He took his finger off the key and an image froze on the screen. Ben peered at it. It looked like some ancient document, covered in old script that meant nothing to him.

'This is a high-resolution scan of the Wenkaura papyrus,' Kirby said. 'You can see how aged some of the inscriptions are. We had a hell of a time decipher-ing it.' He gazed at it for a moment longer, and went on scrolling down, staring hard at the screen.

Ben moved away from the desk, parted the blinds with his fingers and glanced cautiously out of the window. The street below was deserted.

Kirby clicked his tongue, shook his head. 'All this stuff is exactly what I already have. There's nothing new. What I want is to see if Morgan added anything at the bottom. That last entry could be—'

He broke off mid-sentence, craned his neck forward. 'Oh, shit.'

'What?' Ben asked, stepping back to the desk.

'I don't fucking believe it.'

'What?'

Kirby looked up from the screen. 'Sahure,' he breathed. 'Sahure. Of course. What an idiot I was, not to get that.'

'Sahure?' Ben echoed.

'So you didn't learn about *him* in Bible class?'

'Theology. And no, I didn't.'

Kirby was giggling to himself, clenching his fist in triumph. 'Morgan, you were a frigging genius.'

'Are you going to explain this to me, or do I have to beat it out of you?' Ben resisted the urge to grab Kirby's throat and drag him across the desk.

Kirby stopped giggling, and looked serious. He tapped the screen. 'Look here. The final entry, right at the bottom. Morgan worked it out. It's the first clue.' He smirked.

'Explain.'

'You remember that the clue was the tomb of "He who is close to Re"?' Kirby said. 'Well, get this. "He who is close to Re" is the literal meaning of the ancient Egyptian name, Sahure. And Sahure was the second ruler of Egypt's Fifth Dynasty. He reigned from 2487 to 2475 BC and is buried at the pyramid complex at Abusir, just south of Cairo on the edge of the desert. Which means we know for sure that's where Morgan found the second clue.'

'Do we?'

Kirby's eyes twinkled. 'Absolutely.' He prodded the screen enthusiastically. 'And it gets even better two lines lower down. Morgan's added to his notes that he also found out that Sahure was a distant ancestor of Wenkaura. And the High Priest Sanep, to whom the papyrus was intended to be delivered, would have known that about his former master. He would have picked up on the clue right away. See how perfect it is? There's no doubt whatsoever that we're on the right track.'

Ben nodded. 'OK. It sounds plausible.'

'Happy you met me?'

'I can barely contain my joy.'

Kirby's smirk widened into a grin. 'What a team. The brain and the brawn. An intellectual genius and a soldier boy. We're going to find the treasure in no time.'

Ben looked at him. 'Hold on. *We're* going to find the treasure?'

Kirby nodded. 'You and me. You don't think I'm not coming along, do you?'

'Not a chance,' Ben said.

Kirby looked crestfallen. 'Why?'

'Lots of reasons. The main one being that it's dangerous.'

'Seems to me it's pretty damned dangerous if I stay here,' Kirby protested, flushing bright red. 'Apparently my life just went up in smoke. I can't go home any more.'

'So you want to team up with me.'

'You're a soldier. I've seen what you can do. You're exactly the kind of person Morgan and I could have done with sooner. I need you, and you need me. It's perfect.'

Ben shook his head. 'I'm not going to nanny you all the way round Egypt. I'm going to do this my way. Alone.'

'Really? Can you read hieroglyphics? Decipher clues that are thousands of years old? Because if you can, I'll be impressed.'

Ben didn't reply.

'Here's the bottom line,' Kirby said. 'If you want to find the heretic's treasure, you bring me along. Let's face it. Alone, you've got no chance.'

'Say we find this thing together. I can't let you have it. I told you, I need it.'

'I'll settle for academic stardom,' Kirby said. 'And maybe a trinket or two, so I can prove to my esteemed cretinous peers that they were dead wrong and Morgan and I were the superior scholars. That's all I want. I'll tell the bottins that the tomb robbers got there first. That'll rub it in even more. Come on. You know it makes sense.'

'What about your passport? We're not going back to the house for your things.'

Kirby smiled. 'No need for that. I keep all my important personal documents right here in my office.' He jerked his thumb over his shoulder at a lockable steel filing cabinet behind the desk. 'Including my passport. It's the only place I wouldn't lose them. That big old house just swallows things up.'

Ben was quiet for a long moment. Thirty seconds went by, then a full minute. Then he made a decision. 'All right, Kirby. You can come with me to Egypt. We'll head back south to Edinburgh and see if we can catch a late flight that'll get us into Cairo by morning.'

'Now you're talking,' Kirby said.

'But when we get there, you'll do as I say. You'll give me no trouble, won't slow me down. I'm going to move hard and fast. One peep out of you, get under my feet just once, and you'll be on the first plane back.'

Kirby beamed. 'You won't even know I'm there.'

Chapter Forty-One

Dawn was breaking over the Mediterranean as Ben reclined in the business-class armchair, sipped on an espresso and watched the sunrise from above the clouds. They'd been lucky to grab the last-minute seats on the night flight. It would be early morning in Cairo when they landed.

He felt weak with fatigue. His eyes were burning, his head was throbbing with worry and lack of sleep, and his heart palpitated every time he thought of Zara and what was happening to her. But he knew he had to keep moving forwards, stay alert and see this thing through to the end. He couldn't even begin to contemplate what would happen if he failed.

At his left elbow, Kirby was awake, sitting with earphones on and watching the in-flight movie. Every so often his podgy hand would dip into the packet of potato crisps he was eating for breakfast, and he would jam a pile of them in his mouth and chew loudly.

Ben gazed back out of the window and took another sip of the hot coffee. He could only hope he was doing the right thing. He wondered again where Zara was, and how she was. He remembered their time together in Paris. Then his thoughts drifted off into darkness, and the nightmare image of the three severed heads of Valentine, Wolff and Harrison came flashing back to him. He thought for a long time about what he was going to do to Harry Paxton when this was over. So much had changed, so fast.

Finally his exhaustion caught up with him, and he gave in to sleep. His dreams were unsettled and frightening. He was roused from them by the sound of Kirby's voice asking him something.

'What?' he said sleepily.

'I said, how long were you a soldier?'

'You woke me up to ask me that? Long enough.'

'My dear departed father, the Laird, wanted me to join up. I wasn't having any of it. I think that's what Morgan and I had in common.'

'That you both hated your fathers?'

Kirby grunted.

'That's something I don't understand,' Ben said. 'If Morgan didn't get on with his father, why did he tell him so much about his project?'

'He had mixed feelings about his dad,' Kirby said. 'There was a part of him that resented him for all that macho-wacho military stuff he stood for. But there was another part of him that wanted to prove to his dad that he was really worth something, that he could make something of himself against his expectations. That's why, the last time he went to visit his dad and his trophy wife on board that silly yacht, he got pissed one night and said more than he should have. He told me after how much he regretted it, but it was almost a compulsion.'

Ben flinched at the mention of Zara, but kept quiet.

'After that he got really paranoid,' Kirby went on. 'He thought his father was after the treasure. That's when he made me promise that, if anything ever happened to him, I should never breathe a word to anyone, and especially not to his father, that I knew anything about this.'

'Probably wise.'

Kirby turned to him. 'So, did you like it?'

'Did I like what?'

'Being a soldier.'

Ben sighed. 'Yeah, I loved every minute of it, Kirby. We all had a terrific time. Now, if you don't mind, I was sleeping.'

'Oh.'

Ben fell back to sleep quickly, and the next thing he knew was Kirby shaking his arm and his voice saying, 'We're landing.' He stretched and looked out of the window. The morning sunlight hurt his eyes.

Cairo – again. His second mission for Harry Paxton in a matter of days. Whatever happened, this was going to be his last.

After clearing passport control and customs, Ben led Kirby to the airport's car hire centre and picked out a black four-wheel-drive Mitsubishi Shogun, did the paperwork and used some of Harry Paxton's expenses money to pay for it. They were about to get in and drive off when Ben's phone rang.

'I was just wondering how we were doing,' Paxton's voice said pleasantly. 'I hope for Zara's sake you're making good progress.'

Ben shut the car door and walked a few yards out of earshot. He waved at Kirby to get inside.

'I was hoping you were going to call, you piece of shit,' he said to Paxton.

'Now, now, Benedict. Let's be civil about this. Where are you?'

'I'm where you wanted me to be. Where's Zara?'

'With me,' Paxton said. 'Right close by, where I can keep an eye on her and where you'll never find her.'

'I want to talk to her.'

'You don't make the rules.'

'Proof of life,' Ben said. 'The number one principle of kidnap and ransom negotiation, and I didn't invent it. Let me talk to her. Otherwise it's a deal-breaker. Instead of going after the treasure, I'll just dedicate the rest of my life to coming after you.'

There was silence on the line for a few moments. Ben strained to make out the muffled background sound. Voices, footsteps. Then someone was picking up the phone.

'Ben?' Zara's voice. She sounded scared and anxious.

'Zara—' Ben started.

But Paxton had snatched the phone back from her. 'Happy now, Benedict? You have your proof of life. Get on with the job. You have six days left.'

'Hold on, Harry. Don't hang up. There's something more I want from you.'

* * *

At 9.28 a.m., Ben and Kirby were waiting at a prearranged spot on Sharia Talaat Harb, central Cairo's main street, a hubbub of roaring traffic and bustling crowds, cafés and shops. Ben was leaning against a signpost, smoking his last cigarette and watching the street as he waited for Paxton's contact to come and pick them up.

Kirby coughed and made a big show of wafting the smoke away. 'Do you have to do that?'

'Worried about passive smoking?'

'Of course I am,' Kirby said. 'Everyone should be.'

'Then you'd better get off this street, and out of Cairo. Just standing on this spot, the air pollution is equivalent to smoking thirty cigarettes a day. So I don't think my extra little contribution is going to accelerate your demise much, Kirby.'

'And I don't like this situation,' Kirby muttered. 'Who are these people, anyway? Where are they going to take us? I thought Harry Paxton was your enemy.'

'If you're having second thoughts about being involved, now's the time to tell me,' Ben said. 'You can still back out. Head back to the airport and go home to Drummond Manor.'

'You know I can't go back.'

'Then sit it out in a nice hotel somewhere, out of harm's way and out of mine.'

'Don't you worry about me,' Kirby said. 'I'll be OK.'

'Good. Because you said I wasn't even going to know you were there. And I do. It's annoying.'

Kirby shut up, and Ben went on smoking and watching the street.

A moment later, at exactly half past nine as arranged, a big SUV darted out of the traffic flow and pulled up alongside the kerb. Its bodywork glistened black, and the windows were tinted opaque. The rear door opened, and Ben saw three men inside, two black-haired, olive-skinned Egyptians and a white-haired Westerner sitting behind them. Nobody was smiling.

'Get in,' said the Westerner. His accent sounded German.

The SUV had three rows of seats. Ben and Kirby climbed inside and sat at the back. The German slammed the door shut and the vehicle took off and slipped back into the fast-moving traffic. He turned and handed Ben and Kirby each a black hood. 'Put these on.'

Kirby looked in horror. 'What the fuck? I'm not wearing this. It's what they put on people about to be executed.'

'Put it on,' Ben said quietly. 'And shut up. Or I'll execute you myself.'

The drive seemed to last a long time, and nobody spoke. Blind behind the hood, Ben tried for a while to keep track of the twists and turns, but after a few minutes he'd lost his bearings and had no idea where they were being taken. He rested back against the seat, feeling tension emanating from Kirby next to him. Then the car swerved right, bumped up a short ramp and rolled to a halt. He heard voices from outside. They echoed, as though the car had driven into a large empty space. There was the noisy clatter of a steel security shutter being pulled down. The doors of the SUV clunked open, and someone ripped off their cloth hoods.

Ben blinked and looked around him.

'Get out,' the German guy said, and Ben and Kirby stepped down from the vehicle, closely watched by their escorts.

They were inside an enormous empty building. The walls were bare block, and the floor concrete. Overhead were thick riveted steel girders and neon striplights suspended from chains. At the far end of the building were racks of empty industrial shelving.

He and Kirby were surrounded by a group of men, the three from the car ride plus another three. Two of them were cradling compact submachine pistols – not just for show, but in a way that showed they thought they might need them. Clearly, Paxton had given his associates an idea of who they were dealing with.

Five yards to Ben's right was a long industrial steel workbench. It was covered with firearms of all shapes and sizes. Scores of them.

Kirby glanced nervously at the men, then his gaze rested on the arsenal of weaponry. 'You've got to be kidding,' he whispered furiously.

Ben silenced him with a look, and walked over to the bench. The men stepped aside to let him pass, and the German smiled coldly and gestured as if to show off his wares.

Paxton's associates were only small fry in the great scheme of the illegal arms trade, but the display was impressive. There was everything from small handguns to submachine guns to full-size assault weapons to RPG launchers. Everything was new, oiled and shiny under the lights. On the far side of the bench, a row of crates were filled with ammunition of various types. The last in the row was stacked with 40mm grenades. On the concrete floor, a large canvas holdall was unzipped and waiting.

'You like what you see?' the German said.

Ben didn't reply. Conscious of the men's eyes on him, he ran his hand along a cluster of military handguns and picked up an Israeli-made Jericho. 15-round magazine, 9mm calibre. Simple, rugged and practical. He nodded to the men and the gun was placed in the open holdall.

But Ben knew he was going to need more than a pistol this time. His brush with Kamal had already shown him the kind of people competing to find the treasure. He walked slowly along the length of the bench, assessing each weapon in turn. He needed firepower, but he couldn't walk about Cairo with a full-size military rifle.

Then he saw exactly what he wanted, and picked it up.

'The FN F2000 assault rifle,' the German said. 'Good weapon. 5.56 NATO, high-capacity magazine. Ultra-compact bullpup design, inbuilt scope and on-board fire control system computer with laser rangefinder. Underbarrel 40mm grenade launcher.'

'I don't need a guided tour,' Ben said, and the German shut up. Ben turned the short, stubby weapon over in his hands. It was a wild, space-age design, plasticky, brutal and ugly. But it was perfect for what he needed. He nodded. One of the Egyptians took it from him and placed it in the holdall with the pistol.

'OK, that'll do. Can we go now?' Kirby said.

'Not yet,' Ben answered. He picked up a small, snubby .38-calibre revolver from the end of the table and handed it to Kirby. 'This is called a Ladysmith. It's yours.'

'I don't want a gun,' Kirby said, wide-eyed. 'I don't like it.'

'You're getting one. We're partners, remember. And with that, you won't blow your own foot off or put a bullet in me. Even a child could work it.'

Some of the arms dealers were sniggering quietly. Ben snatched the little pistol back out of Kirby's hands, tossed it to the guy with the holdall and it was added to the collection.

'Fifty rounds for each pistol,' Ben said to the German. 'Two hundred for the rifle. And ten of the 40mm grenades.'

'You are expecting a small war, it seems?'

'Possibly.'

'Will there be anything else?' the German asked mock-politely.

'That should do it,' Ben said. 'You know who to send the bill to. Our friend the colonel.'

Five minutes later, Ben and Kirby were hooded and riding back towards the city in the SUV with the holdall between them on the seat. The drive back didn't seem to take as long, and then their hoods were removed again and they were dropped at the pickup point on

Sharia Talaat Harb. The men didn't even glance at them as they got out. The car took off and disappeared into the traffic.

'Well, thank you for that experience,' Kirby muttered. 'It was perfectly charming. Hoods over our heads. Men with guns. And now we're going around Cairo with a veritable arsenal. Is all this really necessary?'

Ben hefted the heavy holdall over his shoulder and started heading towards the car. 'Welcome to my world,' he muttered, to nobody in particular.

Chapter Forty-Two

By midday they were blasting back out of the city, heading south down the west bank of the Nile. The Shogun was fast and powerful, and Ben nailed it for seventeen kilometres through the lush but narrow green belt that edged the great river and had sustained Egypt for thousands of years. Then, with Kirby navigating, he swung right, and, a little way further on, the tarmac ended abruptly at the edge of the desert. They rolled across the sand for a few hundred yards, and the ancient ruins came into view.

'This is it,' Kirby said. 'The pyramid complex and mortuary temple of Sahure, and where we find our second clue.'

Dust rose and drifted around the Shogun as they stepped down from the air-conditioned atmosphere of the car and into the vicious midday sun. Ben shielded his eyes from the white glare of the sand and surveyed the landscape around him.

The place was a field of rubble. The four clustered pyramids looked more like towering slag-heaps than the geometric perfection of those at Giza. It was hard to imagine that at one time, thousands of years ago, this must have been a magnificent and proud temple. Now it was nothing more than a sad, lonely ruin. Beyond it, heading west, there was nothing but arid wilderness all the way to Libya, then Algeria and the Western Sahara.

'No tourists, do you notice?' Kirby said. 'This place isn't popular with them. They're all too busy off gawking at the Sphinx. Which means we're free to poke around undisturbed for as long as we need to.'

'What are we looking for?' Ben asked.

'Fortune and glory,' Kirby answered. 'Your fortune, my glory.'

Ben opened up the back of the Shogun, unzipped the holdall and took out the Jericho and a box of 9mm rounds. He quickly loaded, cocked and locked it and slipped it into his jeans.

'Can't you keep that thing in the bag?' Kirby asked. 'It's making me nervous.'

'Lead the way,' Ben said.

They walked among the rubble. With their backs to the greenery of the Nile banks, and apart from the intense blue sky and the burning sun above them, it could almost have been a lunar landscape. Rocks and stones lay scattered for hundreds of yards all around them. Here and there, a solitary pillar stood forlornly, covered in heavily eroded carvings.

Kirby pointed at the pyramids. 'Each one houses a different tomb. That one is the pyramid of Nyuserre. That one was for Neferirkare, who died while it was still being built. And that one is Neferefre's. But the one we're interested in is that one there. The northernmost

328

of the four and the first to be built on this site, housing the tomb of Sahure – "He who is close to Re". That, I'm pretty sure, is where we're going to find what we're looking for today.'

Ben followed as Kirby led the way through the sea of sand and rubble towards the pyramid of Sahure. They passed through a ruined causeway and between a pair of desolate-looking stone columns that looked as if they had once formed part of some grand arch. The original layout of the buildings was barely discernible amid the wreckage.

The pyramid loomed up overhead as they approached. Up close, the stonework looked dangerously loose, as if it could just dissolve in a giant landslide that would bury them in thousands of tons of rock. Kirby trudged in the deep sand around the edge, looking thoughtful.

'There would have been a whole complex of rooms and chambers here,' he said, motioning with his hand. 'This area would have been a huge courtyard, decorated with reliefs showing scenes of Sahure hunting and fishing. And over here would have been a chapel.' He bent down and picked up a fragment of rock. 'Limestone. Probably from the ceiling.' He stepped a few yards to his left, gazing around his feet at smashed red granite floor stones. 'And that would have been an Offering Hall.' He pointed.

Ben followed the line of his finger, but all he saw was empty space.

'Over there would have been a huge false doorway,' Kirby went on unabated. 'Through which the ancient

Egyptians believed the spirit of the dead king would come to eat the meals left for him. Everything would have been lined with gold. All stolen by looters a long, long time ago.'

Ben could feel every second ticking by. 'But there's nothing here,' he said impatiently. 'It looks like a bomb hit it. It looks like Kuwait City after Saddam Hussein.'

Kirby didn't seem to hear. He was deep in thought, gazing around him. 'It has to be here,' he muttered. 'If Morgan found it, it has to be here.' He stopped and put a finger to his mouth. 'Maybe we need to go inside the pyramid. Sahure's is the only one it's still possible to enter.'

Ben followed at a distance as Kirby scooted along the pyramid wall and came to the crumbled entrance. The historian started down the steps, dropped to his knees and began scrambling in through the narrow space.

'Watch out for snakes,' Ben said.

'Give me a break,' Kirby snapped back.

'Scorpions too.'

'Don't be such a Cassandra.'

'Cassandra happened to be right about the Trojan horse.'

'Yeah, well, I happen to know there are no snakes here.'

Ben shrugged and said no more. Kirby wriggled away out of sight into the passage. Ben settled on a boulder and lit a cigarette. He filled his lungs with the smoke, let it trickle out of his lips and watched it tail away on the air.

Twenty minutes later, he heard wheezing and gasping

as the historian re-emerged, his face red and shiny, his clothes covered in dust and his hair full of cobwebs. Kirby stood up stiffly and leaned against the side of the pyramid, recovering his breath.

'Well?' Ben said.

'Zilch. There's nothing in there.'

Ben turned away and scanned the desolate landscape. His guts were churning. Somewhere out there, Zara was being held hostage. This couldn't go on. The days were going to tick by until the sands had run out of the hour-glass. And the rest was unimaginable.

He turned and walked away.

'Where are you going?' Kirby called after him.

'This isn't leading us anywhere,' Ben replied. 'I'm going back to the car.'

Kirby followed him along the causeway, protesting. 'You can't just walk away. It's here. I know it's here. Morgan found something and, if he could find it, I'm going to find it too.'

They'd reached the two pillars at the end of the causeway when Ben turned back to face him. 'You don't even know what you're looking for. Maybe Morgan *thought* he found something. How do you know he even did?'

Kirby leaned against one of the pillars, wiping sweat from his brow. 'Christ, it's hot out here.'

'Don't move,' Ben said.

Kirby looked up sharply. 'What?'

'Don't move a muscle.'

'Is this some kind of soldier-boy joke?' Kirby demanded, turning red.

Coiling around the base of one of the pillars, camou-flaged against the sand as it slithered towards Kirby's foot, was a large snake. Ben instantly knew what it was. The eyes in the broad, triangular head were black and beady. Above each eye was a horn. Horned viper. One of the deadliest snakes in Africa. Its six-foot length wound slowly around the base of the column. The black forked tongue flickered in and out. It glided over Kirby's foot.

Kirby felt the sensation, looked down and saw it. His eyes opened wide in horror, and his face turned from red to deathly white.

'Stay put,' Ben said quietly. 'It'll pass. It'll only attack if you provoke it.'

But Kirby was already stamping and dancing around in panic. The snake reared up aggressively. Rasped its coils with the threatening *ffffffff* sound that said it was about to attack. The triangular head drew back and the long fangs folded out as it prepared to lunge at Kirby's leg.

The strike never happened. Ben drew the Jericho from behind his hip and fired, all in one fluid move-ment. The snake's head exploded and its body flopped in the sand. Kirby was yelling and screaming as the gunshot echoed across the ruins.

'No snakes around here,' Ben said. 'Isn't that what you told me, Kirby?' He felt bad about having killed the creature. He stepped over to the limp body and bent down to pick it up and fling it away.

That was when he noticed that his bullet had chipped a piece out of the stone column behind Kirby, and removed some of the carved markings on it. Ben sighed. A few history books were out of date now.

He stood up, holding the dead snake in his hands.

Then he stopped. Let the snake drop, and crouched back down in the warm sand next to the pillar.

'My heart, my heart. Jesus.' Then Kirby looked down at Ben. 'What are you doing now?'

Ben didn't reply. He ran his fingers over the weathered stone, down from the bullet-chip to the strange carving he'd noticed near the column's base. It was a little distinct from the other markings on the column, and seemed to be done in a different style.

There was no doubt about it. 'I think you need to look at this, Kirby.'

'What?'

'Look.' Ben pointed at the markings on the stone.

'I see,' Kirby said, puzzled. 'But that's—'

'Not those, this one. The one lower down, away from the rest.'

Kirby stared.

'It's the seal you showed me,' Ben said. 'The temple, with the palm trees and the crowned bird.'

Kirby dropped to his knees next to him. 'Shit, yes, I see it.' He carefully brushed sand out of the markings with his finger. Studied them for a few seconds, and turned excitedly to Ben. The snake was forgotten now. 'You're right. It's the seal of Wenkaura. He was here. This is what Morgan must have found.'

'What's that marking underneath the seal?' Ben asked.

Kirby moved closer. 'It's pretty worn with age. Looks like a hieroglyph, though.' He flattened his portly shape out on the sand to inspect it, tracing his finger along the symbols. 'I'm pretty sure that's the glyph for a chair, or a seat.' He looked up. 'But what does it mean?'

'You tell me. You're the expert, apparently.'

'There has to be more,' Kirby said. 'We should scour the whole place.'

'I thought you'd already done that,' Ben said. 'Let's go. We've wasted enough time here.'

'But—'

'Move it, expert. You can figure it out.'

They climbed back in the Shogun. The seat was burning hot against Ben's back as he fired up the engine and spun the wheels in the sand, bumping away from the pyramid site. They hit the road, windows open, cool air blasting in, and soon the Shogun was speeding northwards between green fields.

'It's a metaphor,' Kirby said.

'A metaphor.'

'Got to be. Wenkaura is trying to communicate an idea through that symbol. Something that's going to lead us to a specific place. Chair. Seat.' He frowned, pressing his fingers to his temples. 'Got it. It's a symbol of authority. Position. You know, like our use of the expression "country seat". Obvious, really.'

'You're just grasping at straws, Kirby,' Ben said as he overtook a slow-moving truck and gunned the big car up the road.

'You have any better ideas?'

'Not yet. But you're not doing so great yourself. You're talking bullshit. And I don't think the ancient Egyptians went in for metaphors.'

'No, listen,' Kirby insisted. 'It makes complete sense. We know that Wenkaura, like all High Priests, was a man of very high position and privilege until Akhenaten started demolishing the religious order. He had an estate near Thebes, which is now the city of Luxor. Maybe that's what Morgan had sussed out. Perhaps he was heading for Luxor.'

'So what do you propose we do, professor?'

'I wish you wouldn't call me that,' Kirby said testily. 'I think we need to go to check out Wenkaura's estate, or what's left of it. Maybe we'll find something.'

'Like what?'

'I don't know until we get there, do I?' Kirby snapped.

Ben was clutching the wheel so tightly that he felt he could almost rip it off the steering column. 'Seat,' he muttered to himself. 'Chair.' He thought about it.

And stamped hard on the brake. The Shogun pitched on its suspension and Kirby flopped forwards against his safety belt. The car ground to a halt in the middle of the dusty, empty road.

'What the hell did you do that for?' Kirby yelled.

'It's not land or estate,' Ben said. 'It's not a place. It's not a metaphor.'

'What?'

'You're making this more complicated than it is. The answer is simple.'

'Then what is it?'

'A seat. An actual seat. As in a chair. As in a throne.'

Kirby stared for a moment, and burst out laughing. 'A throne? You mean the king's throne? You think Wenkaura left a clue on the throne of Akhenaten – his enemy, the heretic? Why would he do such a thing? It would be insane.'

'His own, you idiot. He was a High Priest. He was an important guy, and all through history it's been traditional that important guys have big chairs to sit in. Plus he would have had all the time in the world to have whatever inscriptions he wanted engraved on it. We need to look for the throne that sat in the temple where Wenkaura presided.'

Kirby scratched his chin and thought about it. 'Shit, you know what? You might even be right.'

'I might.'

'So where to now?'

'Somewhere they have a lot of old chairs,' Ben said.

Chapter Forty-Three

A short throw from the east bank of the Nile, right in the heart of the city, the grand museum housed Egypt's largest single collection of priceless artefacts. The sun was beating down on the lawns and palm trees and clipped hedges of Tahrir Square as Ben and Kirby approached the building's neo-classical façade and walked up the steps to the tall entrance. It was cool and quiet inside, with the hushed solemnity of a cathedral.

Their footsteps echoed as they walked across the atrium. Giant statues towered up to the high ceiling. All around them were stunning displays of Egypt's ancient heritage.

'I haven't been here for years,' Kirby whispered, gazing in awe around him. 'You forget just how mind-blowing it is.'

Under different circumstances, Ben might have agreed with him. But time was pressing. Leaving the historian to wander around, he walked up to the main desk. The attendant sitting behind it was a sombre-looking man in his late forties, balding and gaunt. 'Can I help you?' he asked softly in English as Ben approached.

'I hope so,' Ben said. 'I'm interested in ancient ceremonial chairs, thrones, things like that. Do you have a special exhibit for those?'

The desk attendant pursed his lips, considering the odd request. 'We house over one hundred and twenty thousand artefacts in the museum, including many thrones and ceremonial chairs. The Tutankhamun exhibit fills the upper floor, east and north wings. His throne is there. You may be interested to view it.'

'Thanks, but I'm not interested in Tutankhamun. I'm interested in a High Priest from a few years before that, called Wenkaura.'

The man thought for a moment. 'We have a chair and other furniture belonging to Queen Hetepheres.'

'I'm not interested in her either.'

'Then I'm afraid I can't be of much assistance,' the man replied, a little hotly. 'The item you wish to view must be elsewhere.'

Wonderful, Ben thought as he walked away from the desk. He could see Kirby at the far end of the room, hopping excitedly from display to display. He wanted to wring his neck.

He wandered around the lower floor of the museum, deep in thought, hardly noticing the archaeological treasures that he passed by. Where to now? It seemed like a complete dead end. They had a clue, but no way to follow it up.

At the back of the room, Ben suddenly stopped dead and realised that he'd wandered into the Amarna exhibit, the home of the relics dating from the brief, troubled reign of Akhenaten and the city in the sands that his successors had tried so hard to erase forever.

He'd found himself standing face to face with the heretic himself.

The stone bust seemed to gaze right back at him with slanted eyes, and he was struck by the strangeness of its features. The long, drooping face and grotesquely elongated cranium were eerily peculiar, almost disturbingly alien in appearance. He remembered what Kirby had said about the king having been regarded as odd, perhaps misshapen. So little was known about the man himself. Who had he really been, this heretical pharaoh who'd inspired so much hate and fear, to the point that his own people would have tried to write him out of the history books?

Ben was too absorbed by the strange relic to notice someone else walking up behind him. He sensed the presence and turned to see another museum attendant, a younger man with a friendly smile.

'Excuse me, sir, but I couldn't help overhearing your conversation with my colleague a minute ago. I might be able to help you.'

'I hope so,' Ben said. 'I was looking for the throne of the High Priest Wenkaura, from the time of Akhenaten.'

'And I'm afraid that particular piece doesn't belong to the museum's collection,' the attendant said. 'My colleague was right about that. But there are many private antiquities collections across Egypt, as well as Europe, the USA and elsewhere. One of them may very well have what you're looking for.'

'Is there a directory anywhere of these collectors, and maybe a list of the items they have?'

'I'd have to check that for you with the curator,' the attendant said. 'He's very busy, and it might take some time. But there's a way you could save a lot of trouble. I know a man who could have this kind of information. Frankly, what he doesn't know about the antiquities world isn't worth knowing. He might well know where your throne is.'

A ray of hope. Ben felt his pulse pick up a step. 'What's his name?'

'His name is Pierre Claudel,' the attendant said.

'Where can I find him? I'm extremely keen to speak to him.'

The attendant smiled. 'Step this way. I have the number in my office.'

Claudel was alone at the villa, sitting slumped at his desk with a long, strong drink and dwelling endlessly on morbid thoughts, when the phone rang at his elbow. He turned slowly and watched as the vibrations of the silent ringer propelled it towards the edge of the desk.

For a long moment, he resisted picking it up. Why not just let it creep to the edge of the polished wood, drop off and smash itself on the floor? It would only be Kamal. He was the only person who called any more. Claudel could barely remember the days when he'd been running a thriving business and his phone had never stopped. For that matter, he couldn't remember the last time he'd given a shit about blue skies and sunshine, or beautiful art and music, or beautiful women. When had he last woken up in the morning and not wanted to crawl deep under the covers and never come out again? Chronic fear was like a chilling, suffocating fog that had settled over his whole life.

But then Claudel remembered that the caller couldn't be Kamal. He'd said he was going to be away on business for a few days and wouldn't be in touch. Something to do with those plans he kept alluding to. That was a subject Claudel didn't want to dwell on, not for a moment. He wanted to blot it all from his mind forever – though how could he, when all he could think about was that, any day now, Kamal was going to take him out to the desert, put a bullet in his head and leave him for the vultures? He mused for a moment: would Kamal give him a quick death? Was being left out to rot in the desert a better end than a long, drawn-out suicide by booze and antidepressants?

The phone kept ringing insistently. Claudel felt a surge of curiosity that was just strong enough to overcome his despondency and reach out for the phone. He snatched it up and muttered a desultory 'Hello?'

'Is that Pierre Claudel?' said the voice on the line.

Claudel didn't recognise it. He narrowed his eyes. 'Speaking. Who is this?'

'You don't know me. My name's Ben Hope. Are you free to talk for a minute?'

Claudel jolted into life at the sound of the name. Ben Hope – of all the people who could have popped up. The man Kamal had encountered, and been raging about ever since. The mysterious foreigner who seemed to know an awful lot about Morgan Paxton's project.

Claudel's head was suddenly spinning with possibilities. He covered his surprise well, and summoned up all the polite charm he had left in him. 'Certainly. How may I help you, Mr Hope?'

'I'm a writer carrying out research for a book,' the voice said. 'I've been told you're the best person to approach regarding a query about Egyptian antiquities.'

For the first time in days, Claudel managed a smile as he listened to the lies. Why was this person interested in the throne of some obscure High Priest? His mind raced to connect the dots.

'Why, I would be delighted to help you. You must come over to my home to talk it over and see if I can be of any assistance. Yes, I'm free now. Let me give you the directions.'

The Shogun's fat tyres rasped on the gravel as Ben pulled up outside the grand villa. 'This place is incredible,' Kirby muttered as he scanned the classical façade of the house, the gardens, the ornamental fountain that tinkled and burbled in the courtyard, and the sleek red Ferrari gleaming in the hot sun. He turned to Ben. 'Who did you say this guy was?'

'I don't really know. An antiquities expert. Maybe a dealer.'

The front door of the villa opened, and a tall, elegant man in beige chinos and a dark blue silk shirt ambled easily down the steps to greet them. He smiled and extended his hand as Ben stepped out of the car. 'Mr Hope? Pierre Claudel. Delighted to make your acquaintance.'

They shook hands. 'This is my research assistant, Lawrence Kirby,' Ben said.

'That's, uh, *Dr* Lawrence Kirby,' Kirby shot sideways.

Genial and suave, the Frenchman led them inside to a plush reception room and offered drinks. Ben felt restless and jumpy as he sat back with a glass of excellent white wine and tried to look as though his interest in Egyptian antiquities was purely intellectual. Kirby was admiring the décor, open-mouthed.

'So, Mr Hope, tell me more about this book you're writing,' Claudel said with a smile.

Ben kept his composure as he rattled off what he hoped was a convincing stream of lies about his reasons for wanting to locate the throne of Wenkaura. 'It seems to be an area of that period's history that's little touched upon,' he finished. Inwardly, he was wincing at his performance. To him it reeked strongly of bullshit.

But Claudel seemed quite convinced. He topped up their glasses with more chilled wine, nodded thoughtfully, agreed unreservedly, and for a few minutes they chatted about the desirability among collectors of relics from the Akhenaten era.

'I don't want to take up too much of your time,' Ben said, fighting to keep the tension out of his voice. 'Would you happen to have any idea of where the Wenkaura throne could be?'

Claudel seemed about to reply, but then glanced at

Ben's empty glass and tutted. 'I seem to have run out of wine to offer you. Let me fetch some more from the cellar.'

'Please,' Ben said, biting his tongue. 'There's no need.'

'Really,' Claudel replied warmly. 'I insist. Excuse me for just one moment.'

When Claudel had left the room, Kirby leaned towards Ben and whispered, 'Seems like a decent bloke.'

Ben didn't reply.

A second later, Claudel reappeared in the doorway. He was holding something in his right hand, but it wasn't a bottle of wine. It was an AKS automatic weapon.

Chapter Forty-Four

At that moment, Kamal was in the middle of a business meeting. He knew little about the three men sitting facing him across the table in the stark white room. Just that they were Europeans, that they spoke English with an accent he'd never heard before, and that they were extremely dangerous people to deal with.

The senior member of the group was a large, broadshouldered man in a boxy suit – unquestionably the Boss. He looked about seventy, thick white hair and a complexion that had seen too many hard winters. His eyes were small and beady, so penetrating that even Kamal found himself breaking eye contact first, looking down at the closed folder that lay on the table in front of him.

He hated himself for doing it. On any other day, in any other situation, with anyone but these people, he would never have tolerated that kind of humiliation. But he knew he couldn't afford aggression here. He'd been waiting for this meeting for a long, long time, and he was going to get only one chance. It was a desperately important moment in his career. One that was going to make his name forever. It was going to change everything.

So Kamal bit his lip and paid the appropriate respect to these men who had come a long way to meet him. These kind of people didn't make themselves available to just anybody. Just meeting with them face to face was a privilege.

And a gigantic risk. He was committed now.

'The money,' said the Boss. He was a man of very few words, and when he spoke his voice was low and rumbling.

'I can make a downpayment of one million US dollars,' Kamal said. 'Cash or wire, whichever way you prefer.'

'The price is *twenty* million dollars,' the man on the right said, arching an eyebrow. He was thinner and younger than the leader. His hair was oiled and combed back slickly across his scalp. His left eye was surrounded by a mass of scars, as though someone had once tried to remove it with barbed wire. 'Cash only. I thought we had already made all of this clear to you.'

'I am concerned that you might be wasting our time here, Mr Kamal,' said the man on the left, fingering a briefcase on his knee.

The Boss kept his penetrating gaze locked on Kamal, saying nothing. His big, gnarled hands rested on the table.

Kamal glanced away. 'I will have the money.'

'When?'

That was the question that worried Kamal the most. After all these months, he was still no closer to the treasure. That dog Claudel was going to answer for it one day.

'Soon,' he said. 'I will have it very soon.'

'You realise this is highly irregular,' said the one on the right. 'There will be a penalty to pay for the delay. An extra five million. As well as a time limit for completion of payment. You understand these terms?'

Kamal understood them very well. No cash, and the men would show their lack of appreciation in their own particular way. But he was willing to take that risk for what was inside the folder in front of him.

He opened it and spread the documents out again to look at them. The photographs were black and white prints. The A4 sheets were the technical specifications of the five ex-Soviet warheads that had never made it back after the post-glasnost Russian recall of the nuclear stockpiles in Kazakhstan.

He ran his eye down the printouts and his heart quickened. Just looking at them brought it all so much closer. Now, at last, reality was dawning. All that he'd dreamed of looked possible. He, Kamal, was going to be the one.

'We would like to know your plans,' the Boss rumbled. 'You understand.' He gave a mirthless smile. 'We also live somewhere.'

'I understand,' Kamal replied. 'Please rest assured that my plans will not pose any risk to you personally.'

'Your proposed targets?'

Kamal couldn't hold back the grin that crept over

his face as he reached into his jacket and took out a single sheet of paper. He unfolded it and laid it flat on the table. Spun it around with his fingers, and slid it across to show the three men. The Boss drew a pair of thick glasses from his breast pocket and craned forwards to read what Kamal had written in bold black ink.

It was a simple list. Five names. Five cities.

'My targets in Western Europe and the USA,' Kamal said quietly. 'I will wipe them off the face of the planet.'

Chapter Forty-Five

Claudel walked slowly towards where Ben and Kirby sat. 'Stay in your seats, please. I'll shoot if you make me.'

The gun wavered slightly, and Ben could see the man wasn't used to handling one. But, looking down the barrel of a high-powered assault rifle from across a room with no chance of disarming his enemy, that knowledge was little comfort.

Beside him, Kirby was gripping the arms of his chair in desperate panic, his face tight and pale.

Claudel took another step forward and stopped and looked keenly at Ben. 'You see, Mr Hope, I know who you are.'

'Really.'

'My associate, Kamal, told me all about you.'

There was a long silence in the room. Ben was assessing his options. There wasn't much to choose from. If Claudel took five more steps in the right direction, there was an outside chance that Ben could launch himself out of the armchair with enough speed and force to take the weapon away from him, or at least deflect its fire until he'd subdued him and got him to the floor. The rest would be easy. But the problem was that Claudel wasn't coming any closer. At this range, any attempt at disarming him would be pure suicide. He'd be running headlong into a bullet.

'So what happens now?' he asked. 'If you wanted us dead, you'd have done something about it by now. That means you want something else.'

'Maybe I just don't want blood all over my furniture,' Claudel said.

'Then you wouldn't have brought us here. You'd have picked a better spot for it. Somewhere the neighbours wouldn't hear rifle shots going off. So, what do you want?'

Claudel paused for a few moments before replying, and Ben could see there was a lot of intense thinking going on behind the man's eyes. He looked as if he was under immense pressure, and just about ready to crack. The AKS muzzle was trembling now, and Ben guessed that it wasn't just because of the gun's weight in the man's hand.

Then Claudel did something very strange. Keeping the gun aimed straight at Ben, he took a deep breath and said, 'Please, I need your help.'

There was another silence. Kirby was glancing frantically from Ben to Claudel, gaping in confusion.

'You have a strange way of asking for it.' Ben pointed at the weapon.

'I'd put it down,' Claudel replied. 'But I'm rather concerned about what you might do next.'

'You think I'd kill you a second later.'

'It crossed my mind.'

'You're wrong. I'd be too curious to hear what you have to say.'

Claudel bit his lip and hesitated. 'I want you to get rid of Kamal for me.'

'Get rid of?'

'What's the preferred terminology in your profession? Eliminate. Take out. Or do you just say kill?'

'That's a very peculiar request.'

'This is a very peculiar situation. Will you let me tell you about it?'

'You're the one holding the gun,' Ben said. 'You have the floor.'

'If I put it down, will that make you feel better?'

'It usually does.'

'No tricks?'

'No tricks.'

Claudel went to lay the assault weapon down at his feet.

'I'd maybe apply the safety first,' Ben advised. 'That's the little pressed steel lever near your right thumb. Push it until it clicks.'

Claudel did it, then hesitantly put the gun down.

'Now let's hear it,' Ben said.

For the next few minutes, Claudel told his story. He described what he did for a living, and the day in the desert when Kamal had offered him the chance to make a lot of money fencing an incredible antiquities find.

'The smaller treasure,' Kirby breathed. 'The stash

that Wenkaura put away in a hurry when he was found out. Then we were right. It's all real.'

Claudel nodded sadly. 'Yes, it's all real. Kamal found it in the Western Desert, purely by chance. He was very quick to figure out that there was a great deal more, hidden elsewhere.' Claudel went on, explaining how he'd become so inexorably dragged into Kamal's affairs. 'He's a maniac. A reckless, brutal killer. I've never feared nor hated any man so much in all my life, and I bitterly rue the day I ever became involved with him.'

'Who is he?'

'I don't know for sure,' Claudel said. 'A professional criminal. A terrorist. He and his men have virtually taken over my life. He even keeps a store of firearms in my wine cellar, and ammunition, and boxes of something called PP-01.' He pointed in disgust at the gun on the floor. 'Where do you think I got this? I wouldn't have such things in the house. I also know he's working on some kind of plan. He talks about it all the time. It's what he wants the treasure for, to finance it.'

Ben's mind instantly shot back to the day in Morgan's old flat. *You'll find out soon enough,* Kamal had said. *You all will. The day is coming.*

'What kind of plan?' he asked.

Claudel shook his head. 'He's never discussed it with me. But I've heard him speak about it to his men. They're planning an attack. Something really terrible.'

'And this is why you want me involved.'

'That, but also because I have to be free of this man. He's like a cancer. I can't breathe any more. I'm desperate.'

Ben thought for a moment. 'I understand your predicament, Pierre. But you're not the only person under pressure. Why is this my concern?'

Claudel wiped sweat from his brow. 'Because Kamal is after the same thing as you, and that's a problem for you. And because I can help you find it. I know where Wenkaura's throne is.'

'That's great,' Kirby cut in.

Ben ignored him. 'Why would you want to help me find it? I'm a rival. You're hunting for the treasure, so am I.'

'I don't want anything more to do with the treasure. My life is in pieces. No amount of wealth is worth this. I had a perfectly good business before I got into this situation. Now all I want is for things to go back to the way they were. I want rid of this man. So my offer is this. You agree to free me from him, and I'll tell you where the throne is.' He looked levelly at Ben. 'So, can you help me? Are you capable of this task?'

'You mean, can I kill him?'

Claudel nodded uncomfortably.

Ben paused. 'Yes, I'll make your problem go away, if you help me find what I'm looking for.'

Claudel's face lit up. He suddenly looked five years younger. 'We have an arrangement?'

'Yes, we have an arrangement. Now, I don't have time to waste. Where's the throne?'

'In the private collection of a certain Sam Sheridan. Have you come across that name?'

'No, I haven't. Who is he, and where do I find him?'

'He's easy enough to find,' Claudel said. 'He's the

US Ambassador in Cairo. He's also a millionaire and a passionate collector of artefacts from all over the ancient world.'

'How can you be so certain he has the throne?'

'Because I've seen it there. His collection is housed within his private apartment at the Embassy. And I happen to know that he's throwing a big party tonight. It would be a perfect opportunity.'

'Sounds as if you know this Sheridan pretty well,' Ben said. 'I think you should pick up the phone right now and get us all invited over to the Embassy party.'

Claudel shook his head ruefully. 'I didn't say I knew him well. I knew his wife very well. A little too well, perhaps. That's why I could never go there to introduce you to Sheridan. He was the one who caught us. You might say I'm *persona non grata* in that household.'

'I don't care,' Ben said. 'I'm going to that party.'

'How?' Kirby asked, looking perturbed. 'Surely not even you would just walk into an Embassy party as an uninvited stranger and demand to inspect a priceless throne.'

'That's exactly what I'm going to do,' Ben said. 'I'm going to walk right in the front door. But I won't be asking anyone's permission for anything.'

'You're crazy,' Kirby said. 'Raving. Delusional. How the hell do you think you can get in there? There'll be massive security all over the place.'

'That's the whole idea.' Ben turned to Claudel. 'Can you provide me with a plan of the building?'

'I know exactly where you need to go,' Claudel replied. 'I've sneaked up the backstairs to visit Eloise

Sheridan often enough to know my way around the place.'

'Excellent. Now, here's what we're going to do. Kirby, you stay here with Claudel. I have a couple of things to take care of.'

'Things?' asked Kirby, cocking an eyebrow.

'Things you don't need to know about. But first, I want to visit the wine cellar.'

Claudel looked mystified. 'Why? You want some wine?'

'You have very good wine, Pierre,' Ben said. 'But I'm more interested in PP-01.'

Chapter Forty-Six

Garden City, Cairo
That evening

At one time in Cairo's not-so-distant past, the quiet, leafy district just south of the city centre had been the urban playground of the Egyptian social aristocracy; now it was the high-security home of the British and US Embassies, the American University and several luxury hotels. It was just after seven-thirty when Ben and Kirby walked out of the lobby of the Nile Hilton, both wearing black tuxedos. Ben's was an expensive item on loan from Claudel's own wardrobe, and it fitted perfectly. Kirby's had been a last-minute rental.

'I feel awkward in this thing,' he complained as they walked down the tree-lined street. 'My body's the wrong shape, or something. Do I look OK?'

'You look like a dosser who just broke into an Armani boutique. But don't worry about it. Nobody's going to care.'

'That's just great.'

A Rolls-Royce purred by, perhaps delivering guests to the Embassy party, quickly followed by a Bentley.

'Capitalist bastards,' Kirby muttered.

'Coming from a Laird's son hunting for a billion-dollar treasure.'

Kirby ignored that. 'And I'll tell you something else. The tux isn't all that's making me uncomfortable. This party thing is a really, really bad idea. You still haven't told me how the hell you plan to get us in there.'

Ben didn't reply. They were drawing closer to the US Embassy building. Floodlit against the darkening sky, it was a fine, imposing post-colonial mansion standing on the corner of two adjoining streets, surrounded by tall iron gates and overlooked by a mass of surveillance cameras. Palm trees threw long shadows in its elegant gardens, and the Stars and Stripes waved gently in the evening breeze.

Outside the grand entrance, US Marines stood to attention with rifles. At the front of the gated grounds, guests in evening wear were stepping out of their cars and limousines and showing their invitations to armed security personnel.

Ben and Kirby were just a few yards from the gates. 'Keep it natural,' Ben said. 'Calm down.'

'No way they're going to let us in,' Kirby mumbled. 'Not a chance in a million.'

Ben glanced up the street that flanked the side of the Embassy grounds. It was empty apart from a white Peugeot parked in the shade of a tree. A two-man security team were standing next to the car, looking through the windows, letting their sniffer dog wander around it to hunt out any suspicious scents.

'See how tight security is?' Kirby asked irritably as they joined the throng of people at the gates. A laughing woman in a low-cut evening dress brushed by him, and he followed her with his gaze.

Ben didn't reply. He watched as the dog returned to its handler and the security team gave up on the Peugeot and moved away. They started walking back towards the corner, into the glow of the floodlights. Ten yards, fifteen, twenty.

He took out his phone.

'Who are you calling?' Kirby asked. 'Why can't you talk to me? You know, I'm getting pretty tired of the whole Mr Mysterious routine.'

Ben scrolled down to a preset entry in the phone's address book and hit the speed dial.

A sequence of rapid beeps as the phone automatically dialled the number in its memory.

Then a deafening explosion from the perimeter of the Embassy grounds.

There was half a second's stunned silence as people recoiled and whipped around in horror at the blast, and then the screaming and panic and mayhem took over completely. The crowd broke into turmoil as security guards ran everywhere, yelling into radios, tearing out their guns as alarms shrilled. Smoke was pouring out of the white Peugeot and drifting up over the street. Almost instantly, a flood of US Marines poured out of the Embassy building, rifles poised. *This is not a drill*, their faces said.

Ben and Kirby were in a sea of chaos as the security staff fought to control the panicking crowd. Kirby's eyes were huge. 'What the hell was that?' he yelled.

'We're under attack,' Ben yelled back as a security guard shoved past with a squawking radio. Sirens were already wailing in the distance, and Marines were dousing the Peugeot with fire extinguishers. Ben grabbed Kirby's sleeve and led him quickly through the mayhem. 'Follow me and stay close,' he said in his ear. Kirby looked blank for a second, then understanding dawned. 'Oh, Christ. It was you.'

Ben dragged him through the gate. The security personnel and soldiers were all too preoccupied to notice them slip into the grounds, trot across the shadowy lawn to the building and sneak into a side entrance. They found themselves in a back kitchen. The place was empty. Alarms were still screaming all through the building. Ben could hear voices and running footsteps moving in all directions. He guessed that the Ambassador and his wife were already being whisked across town in a high-speed limo convoy, under heavy guard.

'Mind telling me what just happened?' Kirby rasped.

'Not much,' Ben said. 'Just over an ounce of PP-01. That's what the Serbs call C-4 plastic explosive. Enough to make a bit of a bang, not enough to do any serious damage.'

'You're insane.'

'Not really. Think of it as doing them a favour. It'll shake them up a bit, keep the CIA busy for a few weeks. Their security's not as tight as they think it is.'

'There was a sniffer dog. How did you do it?'

'Sniffer dogs can't smell through a sack of spices. Now let's get moving. Try not to get under my feet, OK?'

They made their way through the Embassy, following Claudel's layout plan and the directions to get to the Ambassador's private residence within the huge building. Nobody noticed them move quickly and quietly through the red-carpeted hallways and corridors full of gilt-framed paintings until they reached the backstairs Claudel had described. The scream of the alarms grew a little fainter as they climbed to the third floor. Kirby was red-faced, badly out of breath and gripping the banister rail as they reached the top landing. 'I'm going to have a heart attack.'

'Fourth door on the right,' Ben said. 'This way.'

There was no longer any point worrying about setting off alarms. When Ben found the door Claudel had told them about, he took a step back and lashed out his foot. The door ripped open, crashing off the wall inside. Ragged splinters hung from the shattered frame. Ben walked quickly into the room, dragging Kirby behind him. He flipped on the lights and took in the scene.

'Look at this place,' Kirby gasped, forgetting all about his heart attack.

The room was large and magnificent, the walls lined with crimson velvet. The light from the crystal chandeliers shone down on Ambassador Sam Sheridan's priceless collection of ancient Egyptian artefacts. Statues from five thousand years of history lined the walls. Glass-fronted display cabinets were filled with vases and pottery, alabaster jars and sculptures, scarab amulets, old papyri, fragments of tapestry. On a large marble pedestal sat a block of stone with painted reliefs showing images of Egyptian nobles.

'People shouldn't be allowed to have this stuff,' Kirby muttered under his breath. 'It belongs in a museum. There should be a law.'

But Ben wasn't listening. He moved through the room, interested in only one thing. He quickly saw that Sheridan's collection comprised about a dozen different chairs of various size and design. 'Kirby, come and help me.' He pointed at a large seat woven from rushes. It looked remarkably like modern bamboo furniture, staggeringly well preserved. 'Would this be it?'

'That's not it,' Kirby said. 'We're looking for something much grander.'

'What about that one?'

'That's more like it.'

Half hidden behind a tall painted urn was a sturdy-looking, imposing chair made of wood and leather. The stunningly modern frame was square in design, with criss-crossed struts in the lower section and a high back. The seat was a thick pad of decorated hide that hung between two parallel spars. The throne's condition was incredible, the woodwork gleaming and smooth, as though the finest craftsmen in the world had built it just yesterday.

Kirby fell on his knees in front of the artefact, eagerly inspecting the intricate carvings and painted symbols that covered it. 'This is it,' he said breathlessly. 'Look – the seal of Wenkaura. This was definitely his seat.'

'Can you see anything?'

'Give me a chance,' Kirby snapped. 'I need to examine it.'

'We don't have all night.' Ben was very conscious of the alarms still ringing through the building below them. It wouldn't be long before the security teams swept through the whole Embassy and locked down every room.

'I don't see anything,' Kirby said.

Ben grabbed the throne impatiently and started dragging it into the middle of the room. It was solid and heavy. 'Let me have a look at it.'

'Careful. That's three and a half thousand years old.'

'Don't worry. It's been a while since I smashed any museum exhibits.' Ben crouched down and inspected it from every angle, running his fingers over every surface and join. The leather seat was incredibly well preserved, only slightly hardened and cracked with age around the edges. In the middle it was still supple and pliable. He touched and pressed every square inch. Crouched back away from the throne and studied the designs on it thoughtfully.

'I don't see anything,' Kirby said again. 'Maybe it's the wrong chair.'

The alarms stopped abruptly, plunging the building into sudden silence. That meant the situation downstairs was under control. Ben's ear tuned in sharply. Voices in the distance, maybe two floors below, maybe one. A door slammed. A radio crackled. It wouldn't be long now. His heart beat a little faster.

'These designs painted on the leather,' he said. 'What do you make of them?'

'It's all Atenist symbolism,' Kirby replied in a flustered voice, pointing out the stylised images of Akhenaten's sacred sun disc.

Ben nodded. 'So what does that tell us?'

'It tells us that the original artwork has been removed or painted over.'

'So if Wenkaura had planned for the artwork on the throne to convey a message of some kind, you're saying it's been obliterated?'

Kirby sighed. 'Looks that way. Obviously the throne went the same way as so many other religious artefacts of the period. It's been hijacked by the sun-worshippers.' He glanced over his shoulder at the door. 'We'd better get out of here. It's all been for nothing.'

Ben didn't reply for a moment. He just sat there crouched in front of the throne, gazing at it thoughtfully.

'Didn't you hear me?' Kirby said. 'Let's go. We're going to get arrested. What are you thinking?'

'I'm thinking about winners and losers. About the spoils of war. The nature of revolutions.'

Kirby stared at him. 'Say what?'

'If the design was hijacked as you say, then why didn't they paint out the seal of Wenkaura on the back panel? Why leave the insignia of a traitor on display for posterity?'

Kirby swallowed, thinking fast, eyes bulging.

'It doesn't make sense,' Ben said. 'They just wouldn't have done that. Think about it. You're a historian. When the Moors took Jerusalem from the Christians, did they leave a single cross standing? No, they hacked

363

them all down and replaced them with their own crescent moon. And vice versa, when the crusaders came back to reclaim the city. That's how it works. It's the nature of war. The old order swept away by the new. Winner takes all. No compromises. What would be the point?'

The voices down below were getting a little closer.

'And Wenkaura would never have made such a compromise either,' Ben went on. 'He was as much at war with the new order as they were with the old religion he represented. It would be a sacrilege to him to have his seal on this piece of Atenist propaganda. It would be like finding Winston Churchill's signature on a swastika banner.'

Kirby frowned. 'So what are you saying?'

'I'm saying there's only one possible explanation for why we're seeing Wenkaura's seal on what looks for all the world like a trophy captured by the enemy. It's because these symbols weren't put there by the enemy. They were put there by Wenkaura himself.' Ben patted the leather seat. 'He fooled them. He had his own throne recovered with Atenist symbols, to protect it from being destroyed by the Pharaoh's agents. And there's only one reason he would do that. To preserve whatever it is he left inside. It's a trick. Another clue in itself, telling us that there's something hidden here waiting to be revealed.'

Kirby's face brightened. 'Shit, you could be right. Again.'

'Feel this leather,' Ben said. 'It's soft. Feels like sheep nappa, but it's thicker than cowhide. There must be half a dozen overlaid panels of it making up the seat. My guess is we'll find something under here.'

Kirby let out a gasp when he saw the small penknife in Ben's hand. 'You can't do that—'

'Yes, I can, and I'm going to.'

'But it's priceless.'

'I'll pay for it when we find the treasure.' Ben slashed the leather open and carefully peeled back the top layer, praying the layers weren't stuck together.

Underneath were colourful images of Thoth and Isis, Bastet and Anubis.

'The old gods,' Kirby said. 'Akhenaten definitely wouldn't have approved of that.'

But Ben still couldn't see anything that hinted at a clue. 'Fuck it,' he muttered. He slashed again. Under the painted layer was a piece of plain hide, only slightly cracked with age.

Nothing.

But then Ben noticed something sandwiched between that and the layer below. He could barely make it out, but it looked like the yellowed corner of a sheet of papyrus. 'Look at this,' he said, moving aside.

Kirby examined it excitedly. 'We have to be really careful. It could just crumble away in our fingers.'

Slowly, delicately, they separated the layers of ancient leatherwork until the papyrus could be removed intact. Kirby slid it out and balanced it on his palms as though it could disintegrate into dust at any moment.

The two of them peered down at the old document. In the upper corner was the seal of Wenkaura that was becoming familiar to Ben. Below that was a faded block of delicately painted hieroglyphs that meant nothing to him. But the design in the centre of the yellowed, time-frayed page was unmistakable.

'It's a map,' Kirby breathed. 'This is it, then. We've found it.'

Time was ticking away dangerously. Ben snatched out his phone and took a snap of the papyrus up close. The voices below were getting louder.

'This is just incredible,' Kirby muttered, already deciphering the glyphs, his head bent over in concentration.

'No time to hang around.' Ben grabbed the papyrus map from Kirby and started folding it up to put in his pocket.

'Don't—'

But it was too late. The ancient document was already breaking up into dusty shards that fell through Ben's fingers.

'That was probably the oldest map in the history of Egypt, and you've just destroyed it. Nice work.'

'The historians don't know about it, do they?'

'And now they never will.'

'So what they don't know won't hurt them.' Ben grabbed Kirby's arm and yanked him to his feet. 'Enough talk. Let's go.'

'Where? Security's all over the building.'

Ben walked over to the window, yanked aside the heavy drapes and threw it open. French doors led out onto a little stone balcony. He stepped out onto it and looked down. 'This way.'

'No way I'm climbing down there,' Kirby protested. 'We're three storeys up.'

'Then we'll have to go out the front door, same way we came in.'

'We'll be caught.'

Ben walked away from the window and up to Kirby. 'Hold still.'

The historian looked around him in panic. 'What now?'

'Just don't move. I don't want to hurt you more than I have to.'

Kirby opened his mouth to reply when Ben socked him on the chin. It was a good punch, not hard enough to cause any real damage, but it knocked Kirby out cold. Ben caught him before he could slump to the floor, flipped him up with a grunt of effort and carried him over his shoulder to the door. He threw a last look at Wenkaura's throne and stepped out into the corridor.

The coast was clear – for now. Ben carried Kirby's unconscious body down the winding backstairs. He used the historian's feet to shove open a fire door, then made his way down a corridor with offices on both sides and a door that said 'Gentlemen'.

Up ahead the corridor curved around to the left, and Ben could hear rapid footsteps coming his way. He eased Kirby's weight down off his shoulder and laid him down on the floor. Kicked open the toilet door, dragged him half inside and let him sprawl limply on the tiles. He quickly arranged Kirby's arms and legs to make it look as if he'd collapsed. Then he kneeled beside him, pressed his hands flat on the historian's chest and started pumping hard, up and down.

The footsteps in the corridor reached the door. Ben looked up. 'In here!' he yelled. 'Security!'

Two Embassy security guards in black suits appeared in the doorway. They both had radio earpieces and were holding pistols. 'What happened here?' one of them asked. 'The building's been evacuated.'

'I'm a doctor,' Ben said. 'This man's had a heart attack. Get an ambulance, right now.'

Less than fifteen minutes later, Kirby was waking up in the back of the lurching, swaying ambulance as it sped towards the hospital, siren wailing. His eyes fluttered open. 'Where the hell am I? What happened?'

'Be quiet, you're dying,' Ben said.

Kirby winced, put his hand to his face. 'You almost broke my jaw. Ouch. Jesus.'

'I needed you to be believable in your role. And you were.'

Kirby sat up. 'Where are the paramedics?'

'You're in luck. They don't seem to have them in Egypt.'

'You bastard. You stitched me up. They'll put those electric shock pads on me, won't they?'

Ben could feel the ambulance braking to a halt. Through the window he could see they were still somewhere in the city, and caught up in a gridlock of traffic. Horns were honking as the jam thickened up ahead.

'This is our stop.' He grabbed Kirby's wrist and

hauled him off the bed before he could say anything. Opening the back doors, they stepped out into a sea of traffic and lights. Motorists stared as the two guys in tuxedos walked calmly away from the ambulance, headed for the pavement and mingled with the crowds.

Chapter Forty-Seven

It was after ten by the time Ben and Kirby got back to Claudel's villa. The Frenchman greeted them at the door, peering nervously out into the night as if he expected Kamal to return at any instant. 'Did you get it?' he whispered.

'We got it,' Ben replied. 'Now let's figure it out.'

Claudel led the way to a large comfortable study with a broad desk, three chairs and a sofa. It took Ben a few moments to transfer the image of the throne papyrus to Claudel's laptop and set up a feed to the big TV screen on the wall. The map lit up the screen in bright high-definition detail.

'What happened to the original?' Claudel asked.

'Don't ask,' Kirby replied quietly, shaking his head.

The three men started studying the map in detail. 'That's the same hieroglyph text as was inscribed on the chamber containing the first treasure,' Claudel said, pointing to a block of symbols. 'This part is the glyph for Amenhotep's name.'

'Hold on,' Ben interrupted. 'Amenhotep was Akhenaten's name, before he changed it.'

Kirby shook his head. 'That's true, but it also means "Amun is at peace" or "Amun is content". The phrase and the name are interchangeable, depending on context.'

'The full meaning is "Amun is content; the Heretic of Amarna shall be denied, the treasures restored to their rightful place",' Claudel said. 'Which I don't think leaves any room for doubt. Congratulations, gentlemen.'

'Fine,' Ben said. 'Now let's figure out where this bloody treasure is.'

Over the next hour, as the two experts pored over the papyrus, scribbled notes and stopped occasionally to consult a thick dictionary of hieroglyphics, they gradually puzzled it out. Eventually, Kirby got up from the desk and sat heavily on the sofa with a sigh of relief. He wiped sweat off his brow and flapped the notebook in his hand. 'Let me read you what I've got. I'm paraphrasing, but here goes. "From the home of the Kingdom of Kush, follow the path of Sah as he sails to his rest. Twelve hours of march will lead you to the horizon. Pass through the teeth of Sobek, and you will discover. The Heretic shall be denied."'

Ben couldn't make sense of it.

Claudel smiled. 'It's quite a clear set of directions. Let's go through it. The Kingdom of Kush was an ancient civilisation dating back to 2000 BC, or even earlier, in what was then the land of Nubia, down the Nile to the south of Egypt. They lived in the shadow of the ancient Egyptians, and in many ways tried to emulate them. By Wenkaura's time the Kingdom was all but dead, but an educated man like him would have known that its capital was a once-great city called Kerma that lay close to the third cataract of the Nile. That's the first step.'

'From there you follow the path of Sah as he sails to his rest,' Kirby cut in. 'Not as obscure as it sounds, if you know what to look for. The ancient Egyptian god, Sah, was named "the glorious soul of Osiris". But he was also an astronomical symbol, the personification of the star constellation known today as Orion.'

'The ancient Egyptians always envisaged the motions of celestial bodies as boat journeys, sailing across the sky,' Claudel added. 'Thus the place of Sah's rest would be the point where Orion sets.'

'In the west,' Ben said.

'Correct.'

'So from the site of the ancient city of Kerma we need to head due west,' Ben said, frowning. 'But for how far? Twelve hours of march isn't exactly a precise distance. It could vary hugely.'

Kirby shook his head. 'Actually it's a fairly specific measurement. The ancient Egyptians used the term an hour of march to signify a distance of 21,000 royal cubits. One royal cubit is about twenty inches long. It was the standard measurement used for everything from laying out street plans to building pyramids.'

Ben did some quick sums in his head. 'Then an hour of march equals about eleven kilometres. Which means the papyrus is telling us to travel a hundred and thirty or so kilometres west from Kerma.' He reached for a heavy volume that lay on Claudel's desk, and flipped it open. It was a book of ancient maps. He leafed through the pages, stopped and studied it closely. Ran his finger down the path of the Nile, from Giza southwards to Thebes, and then further down past Aswan, deep into what had once been the land of Nubia. It was a long, long way downriver to the ancient city of Kerma. He ran his finger westward from that point, and imagined the kind of landscape there. Nothing much would have changed in thousands of years. It would be an arid wilderness of desert and rock, stretching over a vast area.

Claudel seemed to sense his thoughts. 'What perplexes me is the lack of a precise physical landmark or orientation. We're simply told "head for the horizon". That strikes me as very vague.'

'Show me the glyph for horizon,' Ben said.

Claudel pointed it out on the screen. 'Here. The word is denoted by the setting of the sun in a U-shaped cleft in the rock.'

Ben thought for a second. 'What if it had a double meaning? What if Wenkaura was describing an actual physical location?'

Claudel considered the idea. 'In what way?'

'Perhaps a rock or mountain, with a cleft formed like this.' Ben waved his hand in a U-shaped gesture. 'Into which the sun settles as it sinks in the evening sky.'

'It's possible,' Kirby said. 'Definitely possible.'

'Though you won't know until you get there,' Claudel added.

'Which leaves the teeth of Sobek,' Ben said. 'Who or what is Sobek?'

'Sobek was the Egyptian crocodile-headed god of

water,' Claudel replied. 'As to what the reference means—' He shrugged. 'It's obscure.'

'With my luck it probably means we've got to navigate a croc-infested river,' Kirby said, shuddering.

Claudel gave a grim little smile. 'There's only one way to find out the truth. You're just going to have to wait and see.'

Ben returned to his book of old maps. He tapped the page with his finger. 'Now, if I'm not mistaken, these directions are taking us smack bang into the middle of the Sudan.'

Claudel looked grave. 'It looks that way to me, unfortunately. One of the most unstable and dangerous places in the world. You'd be travelling into the Sahara desert, towards the Darfur region. The war there may be over for now, but there are still a great many rebel groups operating across the area, clashing with Sudanese military forces and posing a major threat to travellers.'

'Wonderful,' Kirby said. 'African war zone, man-eating crocodiles, certainty of death. Piece of cake.'

'How could Wenkaura have transported the treasure that far?' Ben asked Claudel, ignoring Kirby. 'It seems impossible.'

'The ancient Egyptians were able to cover huge distances,' Claudel explained. 'New discoveries have shown they ventured far deeper into the desert than previously thought. They were also extremely adept at river travel. It's quite feasible that Wenkaura and his helpers could have transported a large cargo that distance. Remember that as early as 3350 BC the Egyptians had mastered the art of sail.'

'See these two guys here?' Kirby said, pointing out two figures on the screen. 'These are the deities Osiris and Hapi. Wenkaura would have added them in as good luck charms to bless the journey of whoever went to reclaim the hidden treasure. Hapi was the river god, patron of the Nile. And Osiris was the god who ordained the river's annual inundation. It seems to me he's suggesting that the voyage be undertaken when the Nile is in flood, to allow swift navigation and the use of a vessel with a deep draught.'

'Like a cargo ship,' Ben said.

Claudel nodded. 'Which is a sign that they could have been carrying a very great deal of treasure.'

'Probably could have been done in just a few weeks, give or take,' Kirby said.

'We don't have that long,' Ben replied. 'So I need to get moving fast.'

'Sudan is extremely difficult,' Claudel warned. 'The country is a military regime, and the soldiers who patrol the border in heavily armed jeeps will tend to shoot first and ask questions later. Not to mention the risk from rebel groups running riot across northern Sudan. Westerners are major targets for robbery and kidnap. Even crossing the border legally can be a nightmare. Security's tight. You could take the train to Aswan and from there a twenty-four-hour ferry across Lake Nasser to Wadi Halfa. But the border is seething with police and you'd need to procure all the necessary papers to get in. As well as mandatory yellow fever, typhoid and cholera inoculations.'

Paxton's deadline was never far from Ben's mind,

and he thought about it again now. He couldn't afford the slightest delay. He shook his head. 'I'm not sitting it out in Cairo for five days waiting to get rubber-stamped by some petty bureaucrat. And I won't be going through any checkpoints.'

'Hey, what happened to "we"?' Kirby asked.

Ben turned to glare at him. 'You're not coming. I go it alone from here. You've done your bit.'

'You're kidding,' Kirby said, outraged. 'I have to go, too.'

'Think about what you're saying. You want to drive into hostile territory with me. A million acres of wilderness, armed border patrols chasing us, militant Bedouin groups everywhere, fresh from the Darfur conflict.'

Kirby swallowed. 'Yes.'

'Look at you. You couldn't even climb out of a window. You almost died climbing a few stairs.'

'What if you still need me? What if there are more things to decipher? How do you know this map isn't just going to lead to another clue?'

'He's right,' Claudel said. 'You just don't know what to expect.'

Ben sat in silence for a while, mulling it over. He sighed. 'Then I don't have much choice. We leave as soon as possible.'

'What about me?' Claudel asked.

'What, you want to tag along as well?'

'Certainly not,' the Frenchman said. 'I told you, all I want is out of this whole thing. I've had enough. But I don't want to be here when Kamal gets back. You said you were going to take care of him.'

'I will. But my business comes first. When it's done, I'll take care of yours. That was the deal.'

'So what am I to do in the meantime?' Claudel asked.

'Have you got a friend in Cairo whose wife you *haven't* slept with?' Ben asked him. 'That's where I'd be heading, if I were you. That, or leave the country. Take a long vacation. Anywhere but here.'

Claudel thought about it. 'Very well. I think it's time I paid a visit to France. I have a sister in Lyon. I'll leave early in the morning. You two are welcome to stay the night here.'

Ben shook his head. 'No stopping. We still have time to catch the night train to Aswan, and from there we'll drive south across the desert towards Abu Simbel and then the Sudanese border. Say a five-, six-hour drive if the roads are reasonable.'

'More running around?' Kirby moaned. 'Why can't we just fly to Abu Simbel in the morning? I'm knackered.'

Ben nudged the bulging holdall with his foot, and felt the weight of the weapons and ammunition inside. 'Because I think there could be an issue with taking this stuff through customs, and I have a feeling it's going to be needed.'

Chapter Forty-Eight

After the two Englishmen had left and he had watched the taillights of their car disappear down his driveway and into the night, Claudel poured himself a nice glass of champagne and leaned back on the chaise longue in his living room to listen to a Boccherini cello concerto and reflect on the sudden change in his fortunes.

It was almost one in the morning by the time he'd polished off the bottle, but he wasn't remotely sleepy. He wondered whether the two had managed to catch the night train to Aswan. If it was on time, they'd get there by about nine the next morning.

He couldn't believe the stroke of luck he'd had in meeting this Ben Hope, someone who wouldn't be afraid of a man like Kamal. If things went according to plan, he'd soon be free again. He could have his life back. Maybe one day he'd even be able to forget that this nightmare had ever happened to him. And perhaps it was time to get out of the whole antiquities game. It had turned sour for him now.

He paced up and down, feeling the tingle of

excitement growing inside him. Escape. It felt good. He couldn't wait to get out of here.

Then why wait at all?

He dashed upstairs, and hummed an air from Boccherini to himself as he grabbed two Louis Vuitton suitcases, laid them open on the antique four-poster bed in his room and started throwing clothes into them. Twenty minutes later he burst out of the bedroom with a case in each hand and the house and Ferrari keys in his suit pocket. Trotted down the stairs with jittery haste, crossed the marbled hallway between the busts of Roman emperors and headed briskly for the front door.

He was two feet away, and about to put down one of the cases to reach for the doorknob, when he saw it turn.

His blood froze. He stood there, paralysed, still clutching the cases.

The door swung open.

'Going somewhere?' Kamal asked with a smile. He was leaning casually against one of the pillars in the doorway, arms folded nonchalantly, his smile almost pleasant. The van was parked in the moonlight outside the villa. Claudel could see two of Kamal's men sitting in the front seat – Youssef and the one who never spoke, Emad.

Claudel struggled desperately to come up with a plausible excuse for the bags. 'I . . . I was just t-taking some suits and things for dry cleaning,' he stammered.

'The midnight laundry?'

Claudel was silent.

Kamal's smile never wavered. He pushed himself off the pillar, walked inside the house, clicked the door shut behind him. 'That can wait, can't it? Come and have a drink with me.' He slapped Claudel jovially on the arm. 'I have something to celebrate. I'll tell you all about it.'

Claudel sighed heavily and tried not to show his absolute despair and panic as he set down the cases and followed Kamal across the hallway and through the tall double doors into the living room.

Kamal was grinning as he flipped on the lights and padded over the cashmere carpet to the drinks cabinet. 'I see you've been having a private celebration of your own,' he said, noticing the empty champagne bottle and the single glass that Claudel had left sitting on the table. 'Wouldn't it be amazing if it turned out we were both celebrating the same thing?'

Claudel laughed nervously. 'I was just having a nightcap.'

Kamal threw open the drinks cabinet doors, grabbed two crystal brandy glasses, twisted the top off a crystal decanter, and poured out two enormous measures of vintage cognac. 'Sit down, Pierre. Drink with me.'

Claudel reluctantly accepted the glass Kamal handed him, lowered himself stiffly into a chair and sipped nervously at the brandy. He felt acidity rising in his guts, and it wasn't just because of mixing drinks. Suddenly the image of Aziz flashed up in his mind.

Aziz had died in this same chair. Just after Kamal had offered him a drink.

Claudel's glass trembled a little in his hand.

Kamal was leaning back against the wall, watching him closely. 'Why are you so nervous tonight, my friend?'

'I'm not nervous,' Claudel laughed shakily. 'Why would I be?'

'I thought perhaps you had something to tell me.'

Claudel swallowed. 'Like what?'

'Like you'd found some new lead,' Kamal said. 'You do still remember our project, don't you, Pierre? Our business partnership? The thing we were looking for?'

'I'm very confident we'll find it soon.'

'So am I,' Kamal smiled.

'That's good,' Claudel replied lamely. A trickle of sweat ran down his brow.

'Don't you want to know why I'm so confident?'

Claudel was silent.

'You haven't asked me what it is I'm celebrating.'

Claudel frowned. 'What are you celebrating?'

Kamal grinned. He wagged his finger reproachfully. 'Pierre, Pierre.'

Claudel's blood was quickly turning to ice.

Kamal walked up to the mantelpiece, and rested an elbow on it as he took another sip from his drink. He set down the glass and ran his hand down the side of the large antique glass-domed clock that ticked quietly over the fireplace. 'I've always admired this clock very much. What did you say it was?'

Claudel gulped. 'It's a rare chiming skeleton clock made in 1860 by James Condliff. Very valuable,' he added, watching Kamal stroke it.

Kamal met Claudel's eye. He gave another little

smile. Then his face contorted into fury as he shoved the clock off the mantelpiece and it smashed into a thousand pieces against the fire surround.

Claudel jumped to his feet. He gaped in disbelief at the fragments that littered the floor. 'Why did you do that?' he roared, beside himself.

Then his heart stopped. Somewhere among the wreckage of the clock was something that shouldn't have been there. Something that most certainly hadn't been put there by the clockmaker in 1860.

Kamal stooped down casually and picked it up. He tossed it through the air, and Claudel caught it. He stared at the miniature surveillance device in his palm and his legs almost gave way under him.

'There's what I was celebrating,' Kamal said. 'I wanted to drink a toast to the fact that we all know where the treasure is now. You, me, and your new friends.' He took a step forward. Glass crunched under his boot. 'Do you remember the deal we made, you and I, that day in the desert when we first met? I told you I was a man of my word. That if you helped me, I would repay you. But that if you betrayed me, it wouldn't work out so well for you. Do you remember?'

Claudel started backing away.

Kamal walked steadily towards him. 'So imagine my surprise when, on my way home from my business meeting, I discover that you've been conspiring against me. You've been useless to me from the start, and now this. I think the time has come for me to decide what to do with you. What do you think?'

'Listen, I can explain . . .' Claudel stammered, raising his hands in supplication. 'This Hope person came here with threats. I had no choice.'

'I heard every word of your conversation,' Kamal said. 'Here, in the wine cellar, in your study, everywhere. There were a dozen mini-webcams on you the whole time. You think I'm a fucking idiot? You think I've come this far by trusting shit like you?'

Claudel was backing away more quickly now. He glanced over his shoulder at the hallway behind him. Maybe he could make a run for it. If he could make it to the garden he could scream for help, and perhaps someone would hear.

'You're going to die now, Pierre,' Kamal said.

Claudel panicked and ran, his feet slithering on the marble hallway as he raced towards the front entrance. His hand closed on the heavy doorknob and he wrenched the door open.

Youssef and Emad were standing there in the moonlight, blocking the doorway. Youssef was holding a silenced pistol. Claudel let out a cry of fear, turned and dashed for the stairs.

Kamal bounded up the stairs after him. He lashed out a hand, caught Claudel by the collar and dragged him down to his knees. Claudel rolled on his back, struggling.

Kamal slapped him hard across the face, and again with the back of his hand. He kept slapping until his hand was red with blood.

'Please,' Claudel gurgled through burst lips. 'Please.'

Kamal's eyes were expressionless. He reached down

to his belt and Claudel screamed as his hand came up clutching the double-edged combat knife.

During the next fifty-five seconds, Pierre Claudel's worst nightmares were realised in a way that even he hadn't been able to imagine. He died horribly, bloodily and in extreme terror.

Kamal stood up and wiped blood off his face with his sleeve. His eyes were bright with the triumph of the kill as he turned to Youssef in the hallway below.

'Get everybody together. Get the vehicles and the weapons. We have a train to catch.'

Chapter Forty-Nine

The Cairo–Aswan night train

As the train rumbled through the darkness, carving its path between the Nile corridor and the desert, Ben sat pensively on the top bunk of the double sleeper compartment he was sharing with Kirby. He could hear the historian's soft, rhythmic snores coming from the lower bunk, mingling with the steady clatter of wheels on tracks. He was still fully dressed and, even though his body was crying out for sleep, he just couldn't turn off his restless mind.

It was less than an hour since the night express had departed from Cairo, but it felt like weeks. Time was dragging so slowly that it seemed to him almost as if it were being deliberately cruel. Seven days to complete his task, and the third day would soon be dawning. With nothing to do but sit and fret for the next few hours, the gnawing inactivity brought him face to face with his darkest thoughts and fears.

He reflected on the events of the last couple of days. He'd come a long way, but there was an even longer road ahead of him and no way of knowing what he was going to find at the end of it. Was he getting close now? The fact was, he just couldn't say. That was the worst thought of all.

Suddenly galvanised into action, he clambered down the bunk's ladder, grabbed his wallet and left the compartment. Out in the narrow, neon-lit corridor that ran along the right side of the sleeper car, he passed a uniformed guard and a guy in plain clothes who had the look of a policeman about him. Ben's eye picked out the shape of the concealed pistol on his hip. There was probably a separate security car at the front of the train with three or four more plainclothes detectives posted to protect the tourist passengers from terrorist attacks.

A few yards further down the corridor, Ben's phone vibrated in his pocket and he fished it out.

It was Paxton, and he got straight to the point. 'Have you found it?'

'I know where it is,' Ben replied, keeping his voice low.

'Well done. You're making good progress. I knew you wouldn't let me down.'

'If it's even there,' Ben added. 'If it really exists, and if it hasn't been looted away to nothing by Sudanese militia or Bedouins, or anyone else who might have stumbled on it any time during the last thirty-odd centuries. You're taking a big gamble on that.'

'You'd better hope you find it,' Paxton said. 'You know what'll happen if you come back empty-handed.'

'What if I do find it? How the hell do you expect me to transport it all by myself? I wouldn't get halfway back up the Nile.'

'You let me worry about the logistics. Your job is to locate the treasure, make sure it's safe and bring me proof and co-ordinates. I'll take care of the rest.'

'You don't think a truck convoy full of gold is going to draw attention?'

Paxton chuckled. 'I have ways of moving things around unnoticed, Benedict. It's what I do. Leave that part to me.'

'And when I bring you the proof, you'll release Zara?'

'I'm a man of my word. You honour your end, and I'll honour mine.'

'A man of scruple. A shining example to us all.'

The amicable tone dropped from Paxton's voice. 'Don't test me. I expect to hear from you soon, with the news I want. Remember you're on the clock, Benedict.' He ended the call.

Ben put his phone away and walked on down the length of the swaying, juddering train towards the restaurant car. It was closed, but he'd been more interested in the adjoining bar that he knew remained open through the night.

There had been just a thin smattering of passengers gathered on the station platform in Cairo to board the night train, and so Ben wasn't surprised to find the bar empty. The white-jacketed attendant had dark circles under his eyes, and served the double Scotch he asked for without a word. He sat there for a while, lost in thoughts that he hoped the drink would help to chase away. He wasn't sorry when he sensed a movement behind him and turned to see another passenger wander into the bar. He was about thirty-five, dressed in a denim shirt and pressed jeans. He perched himself on one of the fixed stools, glanced amicably at Ben and asked the barman for a beer. He sounded Canadian, maybe from Toronto. Ben remembered him from the railway station where he'd been boarding the train with his wife and young son.

It wasn't long before they were engaged in the kind of easy, loose, noncommittal dialogue fellow travellers fall into to pass the time. The man's name was Jerry Novak, and he was a computer salesman touring Egypt with his wife, Alice, and their boy, Mikey, who was seven. For the purposes of the conversation, Ben was a freelance travel journalist checking out the Cairo–Aswan rail route for a magazine.

Drinks finished, they bade each other goodnight, and Ben started making his way back to his sleeping compartment. As he walked from carriage to carriage, he sensed that the train had slowed right down to a crawl. Up the corridor from his compartment, he met the guard coming back, accompanied this time by two plainclothes cops.

'Is there a problem with the train?' Ben asked the guard as he passed them.

'Nothing to worry about, sir. We are experiencing minor engine trouble. Engineers are waiting at the next station, and we hope to be able to resume normal progress presently.'

Back in the compartment, Kirby was still fast asleep

on the bottom bunk. Ben clambered quietly up to the top and lay back on the narrow mattress, frustrated at the slow pace of the journey.

Time passed, the luminous hands of his watch ticking slowly around. The train seemed to take forever to crawl to the next station and it was a long time before they got moving again. He could hear the voices and clinking tools as workmen fixed the engine problem. Eventually the whine of the diesel started up again, and the carriages gave a jerk as the locomotive took up the slack and moved off. The rumbling clatter grew as the train picked up speed again and Ben lay staring up into the darkness, feeling the vibration of the wheels on the tracks pulsating through the bunks and the thin plywood partition wall next to him.

Sleep escaped him for a long, long time. Then, as the first fiery streaks of dawn began to light up the sky, he closed his eyes and felt himself drift. His body rocked gently with the motion of the train. His breathing was slow and shallow, his eyes closed. In his dreams, he was far away.

The air was cool and tangy and the sea sparkled under the sun. He was standing on the polished white wood deck of a yacht. Warmth on his face. The whisper of the blue-green waters lapping at the hull.

He heard a voice, and turned slowly to see where it was coming from.

Standing at the end of the deck, the endless expanse of water behind him, was Harry Paxton. He wore a friendly smile, and his old military battledress from Makapela Creek.

In front of him, her back clasped tightly to his body, was Zara. She was struggling against his grip, eyes full of fear. Against her right temple was the muzzle of the pistol Paxton was holding.

Ben started running towards them, shouting 'No! Let her go!' But his voice was weak and, the faster he ran, the further Paxton and Zara seemed to shrink away from him, until the deck stretched out between him and them for hundreds of yards.

Then it seemed to slope upwards more and more, so they appeared far above him. He clambered desperately up it, sliding back, struggling onwards, sliding back again, shouting 'No! No!' as he saw Paxton's finger tighten on the trigger.

The shattering gunshot made Ben jerk upright in his bunk and crack his head on the low ceiling of the sleeper compartment.

Only a dream.

But it wasn't a dream. Kirby was thrashing and yelling in a startled panic on the lower bunk as more shots rang out, followed by a burst of automatic fire. Suddenly a line of holes was punched across the bodywork of the carriage. Thin beams of sunlight streamed in.

Ben hurled himself down from his bunk. Still dazed from the nightmare, he staggered to the window and ripped up the blind. Out in the dawn light, about sixty yards away from the tracks where the scrub grass met the edge of the desert, four dusty 4x4 vehicles were bouncing and bucking at high speed over the sand, blowing up clouds of dust in their wakes and keeping pace with the train as it sailed along.

Eight men inside, and they weren't tourists. The lead vehicle was a black Nissan Patrol with spot lamps and bull bars. Behind it was a rusty Dodge SUV. The other two vehicles were what the army called 'technicals' – big open-backed off-road pickup trucks with .50-calibre heavy machine guns mounted behind their cabs. Both of the fearsome weapons were manned by gunners wearing masks and dark glasses. Both were swivelled towards the train.

Ben saw flame spit from their muzzles and threw himself to the floor as they strafed the carriages a second time and bullets punched through the flimsy bodywork, zinging everywhere. Broken glass blew inwards, and suddenly there was a stinging, sand-laden wind roaring through the compartment.

Kirby was gibbering in horror, pressed flat to the floor. Ben jumped up, grabbed his arm, tore open the sleeper door and hauled him roughly out into the corridor. They crawled rapidly on their bellies as more bullets chewed the carriage to pieces and debris and shards of metal flew around them.

Up the corridor and in the next carriage, Ben could see passengers screaming and running in panic. In the heaving, swaying space between carriages one of the plainclothes cops was clutching an MP5 and firing out of a window at the attackers.

As Ben watched, more gunfire blasted through the train and the cop was thrown back by multiple bullet strikes. Blood hit the wall behind him. His weapon went spinning to the floor as he collapsed.

Ben ran back inside the compartment to grab the

canvas holdall from the luggage rack. Glanced through the shattered window just in time to catch a glimpse of the front passenger inside the black Nissan. For one split second they locked eyes.

Kamal.

Then one of the pickups drew up level between Kamal's vehicle and the train, and Ben lost sight of him. But there was something else to worry about in the back of the wildly swinging, bouncing truck. Ben recognised the familiar shape of the weapon that was swinging around to bear on the train. A Soviet RPG-7 anti-tank weapon, its distinctive conical snout lining up on its target, ready to launch a high-explosive missile straight into its flank.

Ben ripped open the zipper of the holdall and wrenched out his FN rifle. He raced to load a 40mm grenade into the launcher tube under the stubby barrel, every muscle and nerve in his body screaming *move, move.* Ignoring the sixty-mile-an-hour sandstorm that was lashing through the broken window, he poked the rifle out through the jagged glass and quickly acquired the weaving, bouncing truck in his sights. Through the scope he could see the gunner's face screwed up in concentration as he readied himself to fire.

A broadside duel to the death. It was just a question of who could shoot first. Within a fraction of a second, the FN's laser rangefinder was sending data to the fire control system computer. Distance to target flickered up on the LCD display. The elevation diode in the sight reticule flashed red. Ben tilted the muzzle up a few degrees and the diode turned green and he fired.

The FN flashed and boomed. Before the RPG could let off its missile, the 40mm grenade blew the truck into a rolling fireball. It skidded, overturned. Bounced end-to-end across the sand, spewing wreckage and flames. Kamal's Nissan veered away sharply, and for a tiny second Ben thought he saw the terrorist's hate-filled face glaring at him through the dust and smoke.

He dashed out into the corridor. The train was slowing down again. Either the driver was dead or he was acting out of blind panic. In the next carriage, passengers were screaming and yelling, one of the guards trying and failing to control them. Ben caught a glimpse of another familiar face among the chaos. It was Jerry Novak. Beside him was his wife, looking almost catatonic with terror. Novak was clutching his little son to his chest, trying to shield him with his body. His horrified gaze landed on Ben standing there with the rifle. Ben shouted at them to stay down as he ran up the corridor to where the dead cop lay, hauling Kirby along with him.

He glanced out of the shattered window, too late to react to what he saw next.

Fifty metres from the train, the black Nissan was drawing level again. The rear passenger was aiming another RPG out of the window. There was a blast of smoke as the missile burst from the weapon. Ten metres into its parabola, the missile's rocket motor engaged. The high-explosive round snaked through the air leaving a white vapour trail, and Ben could only stare as it closed on the train.

Then it hit.

Chapter Fifty

The blast ripped through the train, obliterating everything in its path with fire and shrapnel.

The heat and noise were terrifying as Ben felt himself flying through the air. He cannoned backwards off something solid, collapsed to the floor as the fireball rolled over him. As if in slow motion, the train was knocked sideways with a sickening lurch by the impact and went careering off the rails. A screeching, juddering, bone-wrenching crash of buckling metal as it ploughed into the ground at forty miles an hour, kicking up a giant wave of sand and dirt and rocks as it twisted and broke apart. Ben was dimly aware of the carriage he'd just been standing in flipping upwards and crashing down with a deafening crunch.

Another impact tossed him violently sideways, and for a few moments he was aware only of the beating of his heart and the blood pounding in his ears.

Through the floating dust that choked the air came the screams and groans of the survivors. Ben struggled to his feet and saw that his carriage had stayed upright. Smoke was pouring from its far end, and through it he could see tongues of flame licking the roof and rapidly gaining ground.

Next to him, Kirby was stirring into consciousness. 'Are you OK?' Ben asked him, shaking his arm.

Kirby looked up. His face was pale and caked with dust and sand. 'I'm OK,' he croaked. 'I think.'

Ben glanced around him at the carnage. Not far away, the guard who'd been trying to control the passengers a moment earlier was lying dead. Jerry Novak lay sprawled unconscious beside him in the broken glass that littered the carriage floor, a trickle of blood on his brow, his clothes singed. Alice Novak was up shakily on her feet, wailing for help. There was a cut on her face. She was pointing wildly back at the smoke.

Ben suddenly understood what she was trying to communicate. In the impact she'd been separated from her son, Mikey, and he was somewhere at the back of the burning carriage.

Ben slung the rifle over his shoulder and ran into the fire, feeling the flames searing his legs. The far end of the sleeper car had crumpled into a concertina shape, plywood partitions and fittings and twisted bits of bunk all piled up and burning. He kicked away the wreckage, anxiously watching the blaze as it quickly spread across the width of the carriage. The smoke was thick and acrid, and it was hard to see. But, as he ripped away a section of crushed wall partition, he saw the huddled form of the child wedged in underneath. He was alive and moving.

Ben grasped hold of the coughing, wheezing boy and hauled him bodily out of the wreckage. His face was blackened, but there was no sign of burns on his skin or clothes. Ben carried him back to the other end of the carriage and passed him over to his mother. Alice Novak embraced her child, sobbing. Her husband was coming around, moaning in pain. They'd been lucky.

'We need to get out of here, now.' Ben pointed at the ragged exit hole the RPG round had made in the side of the train. Beyond it, the sun was shining through the smoke and he could make out the shapes of large boulders in the tufted grass and sand. Helping Jerry Novak to his feet, he guided the little group quickly out of the smashed carriage as the fire started gaining control of its mid-section, and directed them towards the rocks. 'Move, move.'

The train lay strewn across the ground like a broken necklace. Other passengers were emerging from points along its twisted length, staggering and dazed, some of them bleeding, supporting one another. Ben looked at the shattered ruins of the two carriages that had flipped over and virtually fused together with the impact. Flames were pouring like liquid from their windows. If anyone had been in there, they weren't coming out. His fists tightened with rage at what Kamal had done.

'They're coming back,' Kirby said in a shaky voice.

Across the tracks, a slanting column of black smoke was rising from the wreck of the terrorists' vehicle. The remaining pickup truck, the black Nissan and the Dodge had tracked around in a wide arc and now they were approaching fast for another pass, dust clouds billowing in their wake. Ben watched the black Nissan and instantly knew Kamal's intention. The terrorist was going to kill every single man, woman and child on board, just to get to him.

Except Ben wasn't going to let that happen. Not today. He dived back inside the burning train, battled through the smoke to what was left of his and Kirby's sleeper compartment, found the holdall among the wreckage, dragged it out and grabbed another grenade.

The three vehicles came roaring in across the sand. The black Nissan on the left, the Dodge on the right, the armed pickup in the middle. The .50-cal spurted flame. Bullets chewed through the smashed train.

'The rocks!' Ben yelled at the staggering survivors. 'Make for the rocks!'

People fled in panic as gunfire churned up the sand. A middle-aged man in a business suit was desperately running for cover, clutching an attaché case, when a long sustained chattering burst from the machine gun pitched him forward with his arms outflung. Papers from his ripped attaché case tumbled across the ground.

But he was the last victim that the gunner would ever claim. The fire control system diode turned green as Ben's sights locked onto the pickup. The FN blasted its grenade and the truck exploded violently. The other vehicle swerved out of its path as it flipped and rolled.

Ben loaded another grenade. Aimed at Kamal's Nissan and fired. But the driver somehow managed to swerve out of his line of fire. The grenade impacted on the rusty Dodge and kicked it away like a toy.

It blew apart into a million pieces as the fuel tank ruptured.

The Nissan was the only one left now. The driver banked sharply off course and the engine rasped as he accelerated away in the sand, wheels spinning. Ben chased the vehicle with a long burst of automatic fire, the FN bucking in his hands. Then his magazine was empty and the Nissan was disappearing fast into the morning heat haze.

He lowered the rifle. It was over for now. Kamal had taken a battering, down from eight men to three. But Ben knew he hadn't seen the last of him.

He ran back to the small crowd of survivors huddled among the rocks. Faces watched him, pale and frightened, streaked with dust and tears.

'Will they come back?' a woman asked.

'No,' Ben replied. 'They're gone.'

Suddenly the questions were firing from all sides.

'I can't find my wife.'

'What's going to happen to us?'

'How far are we from Aswan?'

Then a small Egyptian man in his late fifties stepped up. His suit was dusty and rumpled, and his long, thin face bore the melancholy look of someone who'd seen a lot of suffering in the past and was resigned to the knowledge that he'd see a lot more in the future. 'I am a doctor. Let me help you.'

Ten minutes later, the wounded were being attended to as well as the doctor could manage with the limited first-aid kit from the guard's van. All the water supplies they could find were gathered together in the shade of a rock. Ben used the radio from one of the dead cops to call the attack in to the Cairo police. Emergency teams would be on their way. He gave Kirby the rifle and the holdall to look after as he ran the length of the train, pulling open doors, searching through corridors and sleeper compartments, looking for more survivors. The first carriage he searched was sitting at a crazy angle, propped up against the one in front of it. Inside, he found a frail old man lying splayed out on the sloping floor. His neck was broken. It looked like he'd been sleeping when the crash happened, come flying off his bunk and hit the washbasin. Ben felt deeply saddened by the sight, and his hands were shaking with rage as he lifted the body out and laid it carefully on the ground outside.

In a short time, he found four more survivors in the wreck, three of them walking wounded and one with a concussion, and delivered them to safety among the rocks. But there were more dead than alive inside the train. The driver had taken a bullet as he sat at the controls. The guard nearest to the RPG strike had had his throat blown out by shrapnel, the other had been crushed in the impact of the derailment. All three plainclothes cops had been shot dead. One of them had caught a burst of machine-gun fire across the torso that had separated him into two pieces. The same string of bullets had killed a young couple as they sat together on their bunk.

Eleven bodies in all, not counting the charred remains that everyone knew were still trapped inside the smoking husks of the two badly burned-out and overturned carriages. Their recovery would be the terrible task facing the paramedic teams and fire crew, when they arrived.

Ben arranged the dead in a row on the ground a few yards from the train, and a woman passenger who turned out to be an ex-nurse helped him to cover them with sheets and blankets that they weighed down with rocks. Then he gathered up the weapons from the three dead cops, in case they fell into the wrong hands. Finding a fire extinguisher in the guard's van, he used it to douse the flames in the carriages that were still smouldering.

Once he was assured that the fires were all out and the survivors were safe, he returned to their sleeper compartment and muttered a quick thanks to God that the fire hadn't spread that far. Digging through broken glass and wreckage, he retrieved his phone, cash and the laminated photocopy of the Wenkaura map that Claudel had made for him.

As he worked, he wondered how Kamal had caught up with them. Had Claudel betrayed them? It was more likely that Kamal had pressed it out of him somehow. Which probably meant the Frenchman was dead as well – but it was too late to worry about that.

The real concern was that if Kamal had known to come after the train, it was certain he knew where the treasure was. In which case eliminating the opposition wasn't the terrorist's only goal. He wouldn't return to the scene of the crime. He and his remaining men were already heading for the Sudan. It was a race now.

The sun was rising, and it was getting hot. Walking

back to the rocks, Ben found the doctor and ex-nurse treating a woman with a lacerated arm. He kneeled down next to them and briefed them on the situation. 'The emergency teams won't be long,' he said. 'You're in charge now.'

'Where are you going?' the doctor asked.

'I'd rather not be around when the police get here,' Ben said.

The doctor's face creased into a sad, faint smile. 'I don't know who you are, or what you are. But you saved all these people. If you had not been here . . .'

'I wish I could have done more.' Ben stood up. He hated leaving the scene, but he trusted his improvised medical team to take care of things.

He scanned the horizon. The Nile was no more than a couple of kilometres away. And wherever in Egypt you could find greenery and water, you could find people and supplies. And motor vehicles ready and waiting to be bought, hired or stolen. There was always a way.

He turned to Kirby. 'We're moving on.'

Chapter Fifty-One

It was a long, sweltering walk. As Ben strode quickly along with the heavy holdall over his shoulder and Kirby stumbled sullenly in his wake, the sand underfoot became soil and the wispy tufts of yellowed grass became green and lush. Finally, as they topped a rise, they looked down and saw the roofs and winding streets of a small village below them. Beyond that, clusters of palm trees and the glittering blue waters of the Nile, dotted with boats and barges.

Ben was quietly thankful for Kirby's subdued mood as they headed down a grassy slope towards the first of the buildings. The task ahead of him now was a serious undertaking, and required careful planning. Driving hundreds of miles through the desert was no joke, even under favourable conditions. He'd been counting on picking up supplies at Aswan, and only hoped this village would be able to provide what he needed.

The dusty streets wound between traditional houses and buildings, some of them obviously dating back to medieval times at least. Ben and Kirby were the only

Westerners in the place, and drew a few curious glances from the garbed natives. Wandering into the centre of the settlement, they came across a wide open square filled with people and livestock and market stalls. Men in white, brown and lilac robes, swathed in desert headgear, standing alongside their camels and goats tethered up for sale. A small herd of mules stood placidly chomping on a pile of silage that was being forked down from an old trailer. The hazy air was filled with the animated chatter of traders and punters as they negotiated and bartered, the rasping croak of camels, the braying of donkeys. If it hadn't been for the occasional truck rumbling by, and the couple of dusty old motorbikes parked at the edge of the market-place, the scene could have belonged to any century stretching back to Biblical times and beyond.

Ben and Kirby wandered through the throng, eagerly followed by a stream of children all with something to sell and jubilant at finding strangers in their village. Kirby was staring around him in fascination, as though he'd landed on another planet. Walking up to a tethered camel and stroking its bony flank, he collected a generous jet of spit in the eye from the animal and a stream of abuse from its owner.

Ben grabbed his arm. 'You're embarrassing me.' Kirby pouted and wiped his face with his sleeve as Ben led him away to search for supplies. At a provisions stall, Ben bought a large jar of honey, some tea, a big bag of dried goat meat in strips, nuts and desiccated fruit. 'Fresh food spoils fast in the desert,' he explained to Kirby.

The historian frowned in puzzlement at the jar of honey and was about to ask what it was for, but Ben was already deep in discussion with the stall's owner. The trader smiled and pointed as he replied in quick-fire Arabic.

'What was that all about?' Kirby asked as Ben led him towards the edge of the market.

'I asked him if he knew where I could buy a vehicle good for the desert, and he told me that his cousin, Mohammed, runs a garage at the far side of the village.'

'Where the hell are we, anyway?'

'About three days' drive from where we need to be. So walk a little faster.'

An hour later, Ben was sitting in a shady back office over a tall glass of lime juice with his new friend, Mohammed, and shelling out Egyptian currency for what he hoped was their ideal ticket to the wilderness of the Sudan. Mohammed had three off-road vehicles for sale, and the one Ben had picked out was an ex-Libyan military Toyota. It was ancient and primitive, and large areas of its matt-green bodywork had been badly dented and restraightened with a hammer more than once; but it was all set up for desert driving with high-level suspension, new sand tyres, a spare wheel on the back and another on the bonnet, a full toolkit including a military folding shovel, and eight large metal jerrycans. You could never carry enough spare fuel in the desert, and Ben had Mohammed fill them to capacity as well as the tank.

It took another hour to gather together as many supplies as Ben could find – plastic litre bottles of

Baraka mineral water and two belt canteens, compass, firelighting kit, a compact solid fuel stove, two small aluminium pots and two tin mugs, and goatskins for the cold desert nights. A spice merchant sold him some small vials of geranium and lavender oils to deter mosquitoes and other insects – an old trick Ben had learned in the army, just as effective as any chemical repellent. Lastly he bought a pair of loose-fitting cotton tunics and two Bedouin headscarves for them to wear.

'I'll look like a tit in that,' Kirby complained.

'You already do. And you don't want to be in the desert sun with your head exposed.' Ben loaded the last of the stuff into the back of the truck and slammed the tailgate shut.

'I'd kill for a cold pint of beer,' Kirby said mournfully.

'This is a Muslim village. Try finding a bar. Also, you don't want to be drinking alcohol in the heat. You'll dehydrate in seconds. And watch your piss. If it starts to turn deep yellow, you're not drinking enough water. Remember, if you get sick, I'm not carting you back to civilisation. I'll leave you where you drop, and the sand spiders will have you.'

'Thanks a million, friend.'

'It was your decision to come along.' Ben climbed into the Toyota, slammed the door and fired up the engine. Kirby hauled himself up into the passenger seat.

It was midday – the worst time for setting off into the desert. In an ideal situation, Ben would have waited another four hours – but this wasn't an ideal situation. Kamal already had a long head start on them and there was no time to waste.

Ben pointed the Toyota southwest and they set off. It wasn't long before they left the verdant Nile corridor behind and were heading into the wilderness. They drove along with the windows wide open, but the air blasting in was impossibly hot. Kirby constantly fanned himself with the laminated map, slumped in his seat, his hair plastered and dripping with sweat. After a while he fell asleep, and Ben focused on driving.

For the first few hours, the road was metalled and quite busy in places with huge trucks that flew along, with scant regard for other traffic. Ben cautiously passed a couple of military patrols, but nobody stopped him.

Hours passed, Kirby slept on and Ben kept pushing the Toyota hard and fast. Later in the day, the road had thinned out to a track. An hour after that, Ben was driving on sand and forced to keep his speed down to reduce fuel consumption. Kirby drifted in and out of his doze, and they barely spoke. Only once every few hours did they see another vehicle passing the other way. The terrain was as flat as the sea, stretching out to infinity all around. It was more like navigating a ship than driving a car. With no visual references it was all too easy to drift off course, and Ben had to keep checking the compass to maintain their southwesterly bearing.

A tiny dot on the horizon. He watched as it grew larger, until the shape of the armed Land Rover was shimmering close in the heat haze. The vehicle flashed at them to halt. Soldiers climbed down, guns slung low.

'Who are they?' Kirby asked anxiously.

'Egyptian army.'

'What is this, a shakedown?'

'Maybe.'

'What'll we do?'

Ben said nothing to that.

The officer in charge swaggered casually up to them and leaned on the door sill. His eyes were hidden behind mirrored aviator sunglasses. 'Salaam Alaykum.'

'Alaykum Salaam,' Ben replied with a respectful bow of the head.

The officer smiled. 'Where are you from?'

'British nationals,' Ben said. 'Just touring.'

'There has been terrorist activity to the north. It is dangerous for foreigners to travel alone in the desert. Do you require an escort to the nearest town?'

Ben replied politely that they didn't. The officer shrugged, signalled to his men and they climbed back in their Land Rover and drove off. Ben let out a breath as he watched them go.

'That was close,' Kirby said, glancing behind him at the holdall full of weapons and ammunition.

'It'll get closer,' Ben replied.

They travelled on, always southwest. The sun bore murderously down, a stark white ball of molten steel in the sky. Its glare played endless tricks with depth perception. As they entered a zone of huge, undulating sand dunes, Ben almost drove straight into a near-vertical slope thinking it was flat. A few minutes later, Kirby was convinced he could see a village in the distance. It turned out to be a discarded jerrycan just eighty yards away.

The dunes became a miniature mountain range of soft, crumbly sand. Cresting a dune at any kind of speed was dangerous, as the weight of the vehicle could cause a slipaway that would risk their overturning. If that happened and they were lucky, they might be able to dig out a trench to roll the Toyota upright. If they were unlucky, it meant they would cook out here.

Slowly, the landscape began to grow rockier, until Ben found himself lurching over sandstone ridges and tracks so rutted that the suspension bottomed out with a jarring thump every few yards. He drove in silence while beside him Kirby gripped his seat, letting out a loud groan every time they hit a bad bump or crashed down into a ditch. But it was the kind of rough work that the Toyota was made for. Ben forced it on mercilessly, knowing it would take more than a few bumps to test the military vehicle to its limits.

With the cruelly slow passing of time, the sun faded from white to gold and sank back down in the sky as the temperature dwindled from that of a blistering furnace to merely insanely hot. Evening fell. Ben finally let the Toyota roll to a halt and got out, stretching his stiff limbs. He took a long, long drink of water from the canteen on his belt, feeling it soothe his parched mouth. 'We'll stop here tonight,' he said. He would have liked to keep going, but night driving in the desert wasn't advisable and he badly needed to rest.

'It gets cold so suddenly here,' Kirby said. 'It's like someone turned off the heater.'

They unpacked some of the dry meat and fruit, and sat on the sand a few yards from the car to eat, listening to the silence. Ben kept the FN rifle nearby. When night descended fully and the temperature plummeted further, he lit the solid fuel stove and brewed up some tea in their tin mugs. Kirby had little to say for himself, rocking slowly back and forth, huddling under his goatskin and sipping his drink.

Ben allowed himself a few hours' sleep. The first red and gold streaks of sunrise were in the sky when he awoke, long shadows cast over the dunes. It was cold, and he was shivering as he washed sparingly with their precious water supply. He nudged Kirby awake with a kick.

The historian stirred, grunted and squinted up at him.

'I want to show you something,' Ben said.

'What?'

Ben tossed the little .38 revolver down on Kirby's goatskin next to him. 'I'm going to teach you to use it.'

Kirby jumped up, scowling. 'I told you back in Cairo. I want nothing to do with it.'

'I need you to be armed, Kirby. We're not playing games here. So learn to shoot it, or I'll shoot you with it.'

Kirby hesitated, narrowing his eyes. 'You don't really mean that, do you?'

'Maybe. Maybe not.' Ben picked up an empty plastic water bottle and tossed it a few yards away across the sand. He pointed at it. 'Now shoot that.'

'I protest at this,' Kirby muttered as he picked up the little revolver. 'I really do.' He screwed up one eye as he raised the gun.

'The other eye,' Ben said.

Kirby corrected his aim. 'How do I know it's loaded?' he asked.

'See the edges of the brass cartridge rims there between the cylinder and the frame? That's how you know. Then just squeeze the trigger. There's no hammer, no safety. Just pull. Like I said, an idiot could use it. Which makes it perfect for you.'

Kirby glanced hotly at him, but kept his mouth shut. He aimed the revolver at the water bottle, his tongue protruding in concentration. Then he fired.

The snap of the low-powered .38 was lost in the flat air. The bottle spun as the bullet caught its neck. Kirby jumped back, the gun dangling loose in his hand as though it had stung him. 'Jesus.'

'Come on, Kirby. There's hardly any recoil from that. Four rounds left. Keep going.'

Kirby squeezed the trigger four more times with his finger in his ear. His second and third shots missed the bottle completely. The fourth one clipped it again, and the last one punched a hole right through the middle.

'Not bad,' Ben said. 'At least if Kamal is standing right in front of you and keeps still for long enough, you might get him worried.'

'I don't want to hear that,' Kirby said.

Ben took the revolver from him, flipped out the cylinder and ejected the five empty brass cases. He dropped them in his pocket and loaded five fresh cartridges, snapped it shut and handed it back to him. 'Keep it with you at all times.' He patted his right hip, where he had the Jericho hidden in his belt. 'I'm doing the same.'

410

'Kamal could be close, couldn't he?' Kirby asked nervously.

'He could be anywhere.' Ben turned and headed back towards the vehicle. 'Go and pick up the bottle,' he told Kirby. 'We're moving on again.'

Chapter Fifty-Two

The sun climbed, and the hellish heat returned. Neither of them had any appetite for food, but Ben made sure they kept themselves nourished with dried fruit and meat to keep up their energy levels. After a few more hours they stopped among the rocks and thorny shrubs to rest and drink in what little shade they could find. The bottled water was lukewarm, but nothing had ever tasted so good. Ben wrapped his Bedouin scarf around his head to keep the sun off, and Kirby imitated his example. Then Ben sat down and spent a few minutes studying the map and making his calculations from the GPS locator on his phone.

'So, where are we?' Kirby asked.

'Cutting southwest, past Lake Nasser and about level with Abu Simbel.'

'Abu Simbel,' Kirby echoed. 'The great temple of Ramses II.'

Ben nodded. 'More importantly, it means we're close to the Sudanese border. Things are going to become more interesting. If we don't get shot by border patrols, there'll be rebels out looking to kidnap us. Couple of juicy white men like us are worth a good ransom.'

Kirby paled, but didn't reply. Ben folded up the map and stood up. There was the faintest breeze, and he pulled back the hem of his headgear to let it ruffle his hair and cool his scalp. He clambered up a sloping flat rock and surveyed the landscape. It was almost Martian in its aridness, and completely empty. He wondered about Kamal. And about Zara. He'd never have let Kirby see it, but he was as close to despair as he'd felt for a long time.

A yell from the Toyota burst his thoughts and made him turn around suddenly. He looked down and saw Kirby bent over in pain with his hand clamped between his knees.

He ran over. 'What's wrong?'

Kirby's face was pale as he showed him his trembling hand. It was bloody.

'What happened?'

Kirby looked sheepish. 'I got a thorn.'

'For God's sake. Sit down.'

Kirby did as he was told, and Ben inspected his hand. 'OK, hold tight. This'll hurt.' He grasped the end of the thorn, and yanked it out sharply.

Kirby let out a yelp. Ben examined the inch-long thorn to make sure he'd got it all out, then tossed it away, grabbed Kirby's wrist and had a look at the bloody puncture wound.

Kirby yanked it away. 'It'll be fine. I'll wrap a bit of tissue round it.'

Ben shook his head. 'Even a trivial wound can get badly infected in this climate.'

'What are you going to do? I didn't see you buying any disinfectant.'

'Yes, you did.' Ben walked to the Toyota, spent a moment rummaging around in the back, then returned with the jar of honey.

'You see any hot buttered toast around here?' Kirby muttered. 'What use is honey to me?'

Ben unscrewed the lid, dipped a finger in the warm honey and started smearing it over Kirby's wound. 'So the professor finally admits that he doesn't know everything there is to know about ancient Egypt.'

'Give me a break.'

'Best antibacterial known to man,' Ben said. 'The Egyptians knew it thousands of years before we ever started fucking about with penicillin.' He screwed the lid back on. '*Now* you can wrap it up with a tissue. And try not to play with thorns again, all right?'

The long, weary trek continued. Sometime in the late afternoon they crossed over the unmarked border and became illegal immigrants into Sudan. No sign of army patrols. No sign of anything except sand and rock and the relentless sun. Another endless stretch of bumping, jolting, creaking drive as they slowly cooked inside the pizza oven of the Toyota. Another freezing night, as they lay listening to the howls of jackals across the rocky valleys.

Then it was another whole day of driving as Ben ploughed doggedly onwards. Whenever they stopped for rest and water he was sitting down with his phone and fine-tuning his calculations. Whereas Wenkaura's expedition had headed due south and then west, Ben

414

had cut from point A to B directly to form an isosceles triangle. The geometry was hard to pinpoint, but going by the fairly precise co-ordinates from the ancient map, he was sure he was close now. The treasure site was near. He could almost feel it.

But where could it be?

Late in the afternoon they hit a wadi, a dry river bed that had probably remained unchanged since prehistoric times. Its winding path snaked between increasingly high rocky banks that before long had grown up into the walls of a canyon either side of them. There was no turning off. Ben gritted his teeth and kept going.

Up ahead, the canyon path bore around to the right. Ben turned the bend, and braked to a halt.

Kirby had been dozing again. 'What's happening?' he slurred, sensing that they'd stopped.

Ben didn't reply.

Three hundred yards away up the canyon, a high rocky ridge dominated the skyline. Its top was flat and smooth and silhouetted black against the sky. Cut into the horizon, as symmetrical as the V-notch of a gun rearsight, was a perfect cleft. Ben studied it for a moment, shielded his eyes and looked up at the golden disc of the sun. It was dropping fast as evening drew on, and its line of arc was heading right for the cleft. In a few more minutes, it would be exactly positioned in the V-notch.

It was a stunning, perfect, completely accurate physical representation of the ancient Egyptian hieroglyph for the word 'horizon'. Now he knew he'd been right that day in Claudel's study. Wenkaura had meant to convey more than just an abstract symbol.

'Jesus, Kirby, I think we've found something.'

'What?'

'Look.'

Kirby looked, frowned, and understood. 'Holy crap. That's it. That's got to be it.' Not taking his eyes off it, he opened his door and stepped down from the car. 'That's our landmark. The heretic's treasure is right here in front of us. It's somewhere inside that ridge, or under it. There's got to be a cave or something.'

He started walking towards it, as if hypnotised by the spectacle.

'Stop,' Ben called after him. 'Wait.'

'What now?' Kirby said dreamily.

Ben pointed. 'Look there.'

Fifty feet away, directly between them and the ridge, was a crater hollowed in the sand. What had once been some kind of desert creature, maybe a fennec fox, lay ripped to pieces around the hole. The badly mutilated corpse was still fresh, a cloud of flies buzzing over it. Around the remains of the dead animal, scattered across the crater and for a wide radius around it, were fragmented shards of dark metal.

'Landmines,' Ben said.

'Landmines?'

'This place has been a war zone for years. They have a habit of getting left around.'

Kirby turned and scurried back to the car on the tips of his toes, clambered back inside and slammed his door, breathing hard. 'Shit. This is very, very bad.'

'This is Africa.'

'Where the hell could they be?'

'Anywhere,' Ben said. 'Everywhere. They could be all around us, and we'd never know until we step on one.'

'Then what?'

'You really need me to tell you that?'

'This is all we need,' Kirby groaned. 'After all this way. Can we get round the edge?'

Ben shook his head. 'The canyon walls are too steep. Perfect spot for a minefield. There's only one thing for it. We'll have to dig them out, one by one, and hope we don't hit any big ones.'

Kirby gulped. 'Big ones?'

'Twenty-five kilos of high explosive in a solid metal casing,' Ben said. 'Not the easiest things to handle in loose sand. And they become unstable after a few years. Nasty tendency to go off in your face.'

'This is just *intolerable*,' Kirby whined.

Suddenly the canyon was filled with the sound of engines and crackling gunfire. Ben and Kirby piled out of the Toyota and scrambled for cover.

Chapter Fifty-Three

Around the corner came two off-road trail motor-cycles, then a third, all speeding like lunatics, bucking wildly over the rough ground. The buzz of their two-stroke engines echoed off the canyon walls as they approached on full throttle. Two of the bikes had pillion passengers, dressed, like the riders, in Bedouin garb. The passengers were twisted backwards in the saddle, holding on tight and rattling off one-handed bursts of automatic fire from Uzi submachine guns at whatever it was that was following them.

Ben watched from the rocks, all senses on full alert and the Jericho ready in his hand as the bikes came screaming past. He could hear something else over the noise of their engines. Something unmistakeable. A steady, high-pitched whirring and creaking sound that he hadn't heard for years but wasn't ever going to forget. He tensed and watched the bend in the canyon, waiting for the inevitable.

The main battle tank came scuttling around the corner, an inhuman thing, like a grey-green steel dinosaur. The squealing clatter of its treads and roar of its engine reverberated through the canyon. Forty-six tons of pure brutal force, twelve feet wide and over twenty long, crushing stones into dust as it lurched forward. Its 105mm gun swept left and right, as if surveying the scene. Then fired.

The deafening boom was followed by a wail like an express train as its high-explosive shell hurtled through the canyon. It impacted against the rock wall in a gigantic blast of smoke and fire and tumbling rubble. The rear motorcycle was flung in the air by the blast, twisting and cartwheeling. Its rider and passenger were dashed against the rocks.

Kirby was pressed to the ground at Ben's feet, his face twisted in terror and his hands clapped over his ears. Stone chips, sand and dust showered down on them. Ben watched helplessly as the fallen motorcycle passenger jumped up and staggered away from his dead companion, firing his Uzi back at the tank. A long, deafening burst from the tank's heavy machine guns and the running man was cut down, his white robes spattered red.

Ben quickly realised what he was witnessing here. They'd stumbled into a running firefight between the Sudanese military and Bedouin militia rebels – only the balance of power was massively uneven as the army ruthlessly stamped out these last pockets of resistance in the wake of the Darfur war.

Up ahead the remaining bikes were tearing through the canyon. The one in front was suddenly blown in the air. Wreckage and body parts rained down on the canyon floor. It had hit a mine.

The big gun fired again. The screech of the shell

passing overhead, and a wall of the canyon disintegrated in a plume of dust and fire and smoke.

The last of the motorcycles was charging straight for the ridge, dead ahead. The sun was right in the cleft, exactly as the glyph on Wenkaura's map had predicted.

The tank lurched along the canyon in pursuit of its prey, its turret whirring from side to side as it tracked the target. Then it fired another deafening blast from its main gun. The shell slammed explosively into the ridge a few yards ahead of the machine. The bike wobbled, but somehow the rider kept going. The machine cannon blasted out another burst and he was blown off the bike and tumbled to the ground like a bloody rag doll. The bike slid down on its side with a shower of sparks, flipped and lay silent.

The tank came rumbling on, unstoppable. Now it was just yards from their Toyota and Ben realised it wasn't even going to slow down.

And it didn't. The tank's twelve-foot width kept on coming. The caterpillar tracks seemed just to engulf the parked vehicle. The tank's front lifted as it rode straight up on top of it, then sank down as the forty-six tons of steel and armour plate bore down, crushing it like an eggshell. The huge machine lumbered onwards as if it hadn't even noticed. In its wake, the Toyota was a flattened mess of twisted metal.

Kirby turned in horror to Ben. 'Now we're totally *fucked*,' he screamed over the roar.

Before Ben could stop him, the historian ripped the little .38 revolver from his pocket and aimed it at the tank.

Ben knew what would happen if he fired. It was like pitching a child's dart gun against a raging bull. The low-velocity round would whang harmlessly against the massive armour plate. It wouldn't even dent it, but the crew inside would hear. Then the tank would stop. The gun would swivel around towards them. It would locate them in an instant, and it would blow them to pieces. At this range, their bodies would be scattered over a circle of desert two hundred yards across.

Kirby squeezed the trigger. The .38 round kicked dust off the gun turret.

And at the exact same moment, the tank detonated with a gigantic fiery explosion and a screech of ripping armour plate.

Both of them ducked instinctively as the ground rocked under them. Shrapnel and pieces of caterpillar track and rocks and boulders blasted in all directions. The turret hatch burst open, and flames and black smoke poured from the hole. A burning man tried to scramble out, but fell back with his arms waving in agony. He disappeared as a secondary explosion tore the turret from its mountings. The armoured beast seemed to crumple and sink in death.

'Got the bastard!' Kirby yelled, waving his little revolver in glee.

Ben was stunned for a second before he realised what he'd just seen. 'Sorry to disappoint you, professor. That was a landmine.' And a big one, he thought. Maybe fifty kilos of high explosive. If they'd driven over it in the Toyota, they'd have been vaporised. He glanced skywards and said another quick thanks under his breath.

'Felt good anyway,' Kirby said. He was about to clamber over the rocks when Ben stopped him.

'Wait. And give me that before you do anything else stupid with it. You could have got us both killed.' He snatched the .38 from him.

They waited two minutes, then three, and Ben listened hard. But other than the crackle of the flames from the burning tank, the desert was silent. He guessed that wherever the rest of the Sudanese armoured division were, they weren't close enough by to worry about – at least, not yet.

After four minutes, Ben decided that he and Kirby were the only living human beings within a wide radius, and he stepped out from behind the rocks and surveyed the smoking battlefield.

He threw a long, regretful look at the ruin of the Toyota. There was nothing left there to salvage. No weapons, no equipment. And no water. The dark patch where their bottles had burst was quickly evaporating on the hot sand. With no vehicle, the only thing between them and a slow, baking death was what little water they carried in their belt canteens.

That was something else he could worry about later. Evening would soon be falling. Dying of thirst would be a more pressing issue in the morning. In the meantime, he had a treasure to find.

He wiped the dust and sweat off his face. 'Let's go,' he sighed to Kirby, and led the way through the canyon towards the ridge. Fifty yards further on, he stepped over the body of the motorcyclist who'd almost made it. The sling of the dead Bedouin's AK-47 had been snapped by a bullet and the weapon was lying a few feet away. Ben picked it up. The stock was decorated with metal studs and mother-of-pearl insets. The barrel was crushed and bent from a shrapnel impact.

He tossed the useless weapon back down. Walked grimly on.

The sun had sunk below the cleft now, just a shimmering golden rim of its disc visible over the rocks. Without the glare in his eyes, Ben could see the towering rock in more detail. He ran his eyes down its craggy face.

And stopped.

And stared at the cave entrance that hadn't been there before. The tank's final shell had carved away a section of the ridge, exposing a jagged black crevice a few metres up its face that before must have been covered with millennia of fallen rock and storm-blown sand.

Kirby had seen it, too. They glanced at one another, and ran. Sand and loose stone slithered underfoot as they clambered up the slope towards the cave entrance. Ben got there first, and peered cautiously into the dark space.

'We need a torch,' Kirby panted.

Ben ran back down the slope and trotted back to the motorcyclist's body. 'What are you doing?' Kirby called after him. Ben snatched up the ruined AK rifle and tore the dead man's robe away. He ripped it into ten long strips, stuffed nine of them in his pocket and wrapped the tenth around the end of the rifle. He ran back up to join Kirby at the cave entrance, took out his Zippo, flipped it open and lit the strip of material.

The improvised torch cast a dull, flickering glow on

the rock walls ahead as they moved deeper into the cave. The tunnel was long and winding.

'We're going downwards,' Kirby's voice echoed.

Ben nodded. The cave was leading them deep underground. The light began to burn out, and he quickly wrapped another strip of cloth around the rifle. They walked on.

From somewhere deep inside the rock came a long, low rumble. Dust and stones showered lightly down from the ceiling. Ben froze and tensed, waiting for a massive cave-in.

It didn't come. The dust shower stopped and he could breathe again. 'I don't think that tank shell did this place any favours,' he muttered.

The tunnel kept snaking downwards. It was a natural cave, but Ben could see from areas of smoothed wall that someone, somewhere in time, had been here before. Had that someone been Wenkaura, leading his expedition deep under the ridge, a procession of men carrying caskets of treasure to a place where the heretic pharaoh could never find it?

'It seems to go on forever,' Kirby whispered.

'There's a bend up ahead,' Ben said.

A few metres on, the claustrophobic atmosphere of the narrow tunnel suddenly seemed to lift, as though a bigger space had opened up around them. Ben wrapped more cloth around the dying torch and the flame burned brighter. He raised the flickering light over his head.

'Sweet Jesus, look at this,' Kirby murmured.

Chapter Fifty-Four

The scene ahead in the torchlight was breathtaking. They were standing at the opening of an underground cavern the size of the largest of cathedrals. The fire glittered off weird and wonderful rock formations.

'This is fantastic,' Kirby said, stepping forward.

'Careful,' Ben said, stopping him. He shone the torch downwards.

'Whoops,' Kirby breathed.

Below them was a deep abyss, falling away into blackness. Massive pointed stalagmites jutted up from the depths like huge stakes, waiting to impale anyone who fell into the chasm. Ben raised the torch higher, and the orange light flickered off great craggy stalactites that hung down from the cavern's ceiling a hundred feet above them.

'Looks like giant fangs,' Kirby whispered in awe. 'Like an enormous mouth. A shark's mouth.'

'Not a shark,' Ben said. 'A crocodile. You're looking at the teeth of Sobek, the crocodile god. "Pass through the teeth of Sobek, and you will discover."'

Kirby gasped at the realisation. 'But how the hell do we get across?'

Ben stepped towards the edge and the torchlight glinted off something in front of him. A rope bridge, spanning the void, stretched far into the darkness ahead. Ben put out his hand and his fingers closed around the thick, taut rope. It felt strong and dry in his fist.

'This way,' he said.

'No way,' Kirby protested. 'It's thousands of years old. It'll never take our weight.'

Ben stepped out onto the bridge. The wooden slats were cracked and grey with age, and the creak of the ancient ropes echoed through the cavern. But it held. He took another step. He was standing right over the abyss now. He turned to Kirby. 'Are you coming or what?'

Kirby hesitated.

'Fine.' Ben took another step. 'Then I'll find the treasure myself.'

'Not on your life,' Kirby said, following quickly behind. The bridge creaked and swayed as they made their way towards the darkness.

Another deep rumble echoed through the cavern. Stone grinding on stone. Millions of tons of pressure bearing down above them. Ben glanced up at the jagged ceiling and sucked his breath in between his teeth. Something was not right up there. Something fundamental within the structural integrity of the rock had been dislodged by the enormous impact of the tank shell. Maybe it was nothing. Or maybe it would all come crashing down at any moment and this place would be their tomb. There was only one way to find out, and only one way forwards.

'I feel like I'm walking into hell,' Kirby said shakily behind him.

'Maybe you are,' Ben said.

Another grinding rumble from above, and a shower of small rocks fell from the ceiling. One shattered off a stalagmite. The rest dropped away into nothing. It was a long, long way down.

From somewhere below in the abyss came another sound. The distant rush of fast-moving water. An underground river, an ancient relic from the days when the Sahara desert had been a lush, green paradise.

The crossing of the rope bridge seemed like an eternity, but eventually they reached the far side. Kirby took the last few steps at a run. The sweat was shining off his face in the torchlight. 'Thank Christ that's over.'

'Until you have to cross the other way,' Ben said.

'I really needed to be reminded of that.'

Ben didn't reply. He was already pushing on into the tunnel, wrapping another piece of cloth around the torch as he went.

This was no longer a natural cave. The shaft they were following now was man-made, dug with amazing precision out of the solid rock. The walls were covered in faded paintings, strange images that didn't look familiarly Egyptian to Ben.

'I don't know who carved this passage out,' Kirby said. 'But it wasn't Wenkaura.'

'You're sure?'

'Sure as I'll ever be. Look at these images. I've never seen anything like them before. These are nothing any scholar would recognise. Some Predynastic culture

427

built this place. Or Nubian, or some other civilisation we don't even know about. It's incredible. How Wenkaura found this place, we'll never know.'

A loud, echoing series of rumbling cracks made them spin around. Ben watched as a thin fissure slowly spread across the tunnel wall beside him and part of a painted image crumbled away.

'This can't be good,' Kirby murmured. 'The place is falling apart.'

Thirty yards further on through the dark, winding shaft they came to a dead end. The wall that blocked the tunnel was covered in ancient cobwebs and dust. 'Hold this.' Ben thrust the torch into Kirby's hands and brushed away the webs, revealing the cracks between stone blocks. 'There are more markings here. And these are definitely Egyptian.'

Kirby came up close. The firelight sent dark shadows into the carved hieroglyphs in front of them.

'Can you read it?'

Kirby's mouth dropped open. 'Oh, God.'

'Can you read it?' Ben repeated impatiently.

Kirby turned. 'It says, "Amun is content. The treasure is restored." This is it. We found it.'

'Then let's see what we've got.'

'Where are we going?'

'Straight through this wall,' Ben said. He took the blazing rifle from Kirby and swung the stock hard at the wall. The crash of solid wood on stone echoed through the tunnel. A block moved, maybe an eighth of an inch.

He swung the rifle again. The torch went out, and

they were in darkness. 'Stand back.' He hit it again, blind. There was a crash of something falling. He kept swinging and swinging until the rifle stock broke and clattered to the stone floor. He felt for another strip of cloth, wrapped it around the barrel, flicked open his lighter and relit it.

He smiled at what he saw. There was now a hole in the wall just about big enough to crawl through. He stooped down beside it, and felt a sigh of warm air escaping from the chamber inside. Dust particles hovered in the torchlight.

'Here we go,' Kirby said. 'Monte Carlo or bust.'

Ben took a deep breath and crawled through into the darkness. Shone the torch at a floating mist of dust.

Kirby struggled through the hole and jumped up to his feet. 'What do you see?' he whispered.

'Nothing,' Ben said.

But then, as the dust slowly settled, he *could* see.

Chapter Fifty-Five

The details of the room gradually emerged from the mist. Strange forms seemed to lurk in the shadows. Ben narrowed his eyes and raised the torch higher as he stepped carefully deeper into the chamber. He was suddenly aware that he'd stopped breathing for a few seconds. He blinked, caught his breath, blinked again.

Sitting like a silent council of elders presiding over the huge chamber were a circle of giant seated statues. The light of the flames rippled over their perfect contours and threw back the glint of gold. The faces of the golden statues seemed to peer curiously out of the darkness that had surrounded them for thousands of years. They weren't human, and they weren't animal. They were the animal gods: the falcon-beaked face of Ra. Bastet, the cat goddess. The fanged snout of Sobek, the Ibis head of Thoth. The refugees from the religious dictatorship of Akhenaten threw long, flickering shadows on the chamber walls.

The space at their feet was stacked ten-foot high with an endless profusion of objects. It was enough to fill a museum. A golden jackal lay watching them from a plinth. Gold caskets and vases and magnificent cups everywhere, stone urns decorated with polytheistic images and brimming with sparking gold coins, jewels, amulets, pendants and rings, bracelets and crowns. Gold falcons and ankhs, gold shields. There was gold everywhere, unseen and untouched for millennia, smooth and sparkling and beautiful.

Kirby let out a strangled cry. He ran forward and plunged his hands into one of the urns. Filled his fists with precious artefacts and rubbed them over his face. 'I found it,' he mumbled over and over again. 'I found it. I'm rich.' He slipped a gold bangle the size of a dumb-bell weight over one wrist, admired it with flashing eyes for a moment, grabbed a gold necklace and hung it around his neck. He cupped his hands and dipped them up to his elbows in glittering coins, brought out a piled handful and watched, mesmerised, as they slithered through his fingers. 'It's too much,' he whispered. 'It's unbelievable.'

Ben watched in the torchlight as Kirby danced from one corner of the chamber to the other, touching and caressing everything, wild with excitement. In his gold fever the historian seemed to have forgotten that they were stranded out here in the desert. They were virtually unarmed, they had no transport, and very little water. The mouth of the cave could be swarming with Sudanese soldiers by now, or rebel militiamen who might take a lot of persuading that these two white Europeans should be allowed to go on their way.

Ben propped the torch at the foot of a statue, took out his phone and used it to photograph everything.

Then he set it to video camera mode, walked to the middle of the chamber and filmed a slow, sweeping 360-degree panning shot.

'What's that for?' Kirby asked, looking up from a fistful of artefacts that he'd been gazing at lovingly.

'Evidence.' Ben snatched a foot-long, falcon-headed golden deity statuette from an urn and thrust the heavy object in his belt. 'Now let's get out of here before this place caves in on us.'

Kirby frowned. 'But the treasure—'

'We're not here to take the treasure,' Ben said. 'Just to find it. It's not ours.'

'You can't just let this slip through your fingers,' Kirby protested. 'You can't just walk away from it.'

'That's exactly what I'm going to do. Some things are worth more to me.'

'Like what?'

Another groaning tremor resonated through the rock, then stopped.

'Do you want to discuss this outside?' Ben asked. 'Or under a million tons of rubble?'

'That's what I'm saying. At least we can save some of this stuff, if the worst happens.'

'If the worst happens, it's someone else's problem,' Ben said. 'I didn't come here to fill my pockets with trinkets. Now move it.' He wrapped another strip of cloth around the torch, and saw Kirby's sullen expression in the dancing flames.

They crawled back out through the hole in the wall and made their way back along the tunnel. The historian was strangely quiet as they crossed the chasm and passed through the teeth of Sobek much faster than on their earlier journey, but Ben paid him little attention. All he cared about now was getting out of the desert and somehow contacting Harry Paxton to tell him the search was over.

Ben moved faster through the sloping tunnel. Behind him, he could hear Kirby's breath rasping as he fell further and further back in the shaft. At last, Ben found himself climbing the final stretch, towards the mouth of the cave. The air was fresh and cool. Night had fallen during their long exploration of the tunnels, and a pool of moonlight shone through the entrance.

When Kirby caught up with him a minute or two later, Ben took the .38 from his pocket and handed it to him. 'Take this back. No hard feelings, OK?' He walked on a few steps.

'Stop there, Ben,' Kirby said in a strange voice.

Ben walked on a couple more steps, then stopped and turned slowly.

Kirby was standing there with the gun raised in one fist, aimed right at Ben's head.

'What are you doing?' Ben asked.

'Put your pistol on the ground,' Kirby said. 'Nice and slow. No clever stuff.'

Ben hesitated, and eased the Jericho out from behind his hip. Dangling it on one finger from the trigger guard, he crouched down and laid it on the rock near his feet.

'Good. Now put your phone down next to it,' Kirby said. 'That'll come in handy for me.'

Ben took out the phone and placed it next to the gun.

'And now the idol,' Kirby said, with a glitter in his eyes as he glanced at the gold statuette in Ben's belt.

Ben tugged out the artefact and put it down with a heavy, solid clunk.

'Now step away from them.'

Ben stepped away. 'You don't want to be doing this.'

'Yes, I do. I'm sorry. I can't let you give away the treasure. It's mine.'

Ben said nothing.

'You think I'd have dragged myself after you and gone through all this just for glory?' Kirby asked. 'You think that's all I'm interested in? You think that's what Morgan and I were planning, just to get our names in some academic journal? Think again, soldier boy.'

'I can see I really misjudged you, Kirby.'

'You certainly did. And this is as far as you go. I'm sorry.'

'No, you're not. Why pretend?'

Kirby shrugged. 'Heck, you're right. I'm not really.'

'Just a couple of problems. One, you're stranded out here. You'll never get out alive.'

'I'll take my chances. There's always a way. I suppose you want to tell me the second problem?'

'I'll let you figure it out.'

'Fine. I will. Got any prayers to say before I kill you?'

'Not really,' Ben said.

Kirby nodded. 'OK. So it's goodbye, Ben. Thanks for making me rich.'

Then he squeezed the trigger. He didn't close his

434

eyes, or flinch. Instead, he took his time, and did it properly. At that short range, even with a snub-barrelled handgun, it was impossible to miss a man-sized target. Ben saw the cylinder turn as the internal hammer levered back, the mechanism aligning the round in the next chamber with the firing pin as it came down to punch the primer under spring tension.

The dry click of the empty chamber echoed in the cave entrance.

Kirby stared at the gun. He fired again. Another click.

Ben hadn't flinched either. 'I'm still alive,' he said. 'Want to know the second problem now?'

Kirby clicked again, and again, gaping in open-mouthed horror at the revolver.

'No use, Kirby.' Ben reached in his pocket and opened his fist to show the .38 lead roundnose cartridges that rolled clinking in his palm. 'Here's your second problem,' he said. 'I just emptied your gun.'

Kirby's eyes boggled.

'I lied about having misjudged you,' Ben said. 'I knew ages ago that you'd pull a stunt like this after we found the treasure. I saw the way you were eyeing up Claudel's mansion and his Ferrari, despite your whole hate-the-rich routine. I knew you weren't really the sort who'd take risks just for glory. So I took precautions. I taught you that if you could see the cartridge rims between the cylinder and frame, the gun was loaded. But what I didn't tell you was that it looks just the same loaded with spent shells. Why else would I have got you to fire off a few? For practice? I'm afraid not, Kirby. I just wanted some empty brass. So now you've gone and proved me right. And you're in the shit.'

Kirby's face was twisted and mottled as he searched for the right answer. 'I was just k-kidding,' he stammered. 'It was just a gag, that's all.'

'You mean you knew it wasn't loaded?'

'No. I mean yes. I mean—'

The crack of a gunshot blasted through the silence. The top of Kirby's head was blown away like a lid. Blood splattered on the cave wall. His knees crumpled and he collapsed straight down in a heap, like an empty suit of clothes. The revolver tumbled across the rock.

Ben whirled around.

Three men were standing in the moonlit cave entrance. One of them was holding an AKS with a wisp of smoke trickling from the muzzle.

But Ben hardly even registered him. He was looking at the man in the middle.

It was Kamal.

Chapter Fifty-Six

Kamal smiled. 'And here we are again.' His gaze landed on the gold statuette that was glimmering in the soft moonlight. He stepped over to it and snatched it up with a triumphant look. 'It seems you're always a step ahead of me,' he chuckled. 'And you have killed a lot of my men. A worthy adversary. There aren't enough of them in this world.' He motioned at Kirby's corpse. 'That's why I didn't want him killing you. I would like to reserve that pleasure for myself.'

'I'm deeply honoured,' Ben said.

Kamal gripped the statuette tight in his fist. 'But, before I do, you're going to show me where you found this.'

'Die if I do, die if I don't?' Ben said. 'You need to think that one through again, if you want my help.'

'There are different ways for a man to die,' Kamal said. 'Some merciful, some less so. I think we understand each other?'

Ben didn't answer. It was a straight choice. A slow, horrible death now, or a chance to buy some time and think about his next move. He didn't need long to decide.

'Fine, Kamal. I'll take you to the treasure.'

Kamal put out his hand, and one of the men passed him a pair of stubby black tubular Maglite torches. He tossed one to Ben. 'Lead the way. Emad, you go next and watch this son of a whore. Fekri, you follow me.'

Ben stepped over Kirby's body. The moon's reflection shimmered in the blood pooling on the cave floor. He walked back the way he'd come, down into the shaft, pointing the Maglite ahead of him. The terrorist called Emad followed with his AKS at Ben's back. He was about thirty, muscular and volatile-looking. Kamal followed behind him, and the smaller, darker one called Fekri brought up the rear.

They walked. The bright white beam of the torch picked out every crag and crevice. The hard muzzle of the assault rifle dug into the small of Ben's back.

Behind him, Kamal's cold voice echoed in the tunnel. 'Know that when I get the treasure, your Western world will change forever. My plans are complete.'

'So regular terrorism is just a little too warm and cosy for you. Murdering innocent train passengers getting a bit stale. You want to move on to something bigger.'

'You'll never live to witness what I can do,' Kamal replied. 'But many will, and soon.'

'It's a lot of money to blow on Kalashnikovs and Semtex,' Ben said. 'But do you really think that's going to change the world? You don't think they'll just hunt you down like all the rest?'

'Kalashnikovs and Semtex are for children to play with,' Kamal said. 'I have something else in mind.'

'And you're dying to tell me.'

Kamal gave a short, humourless laugh. 'How about the complete destruction of five major Western cities?'

He named them. And then he described how he was going to make it happen.

Ben's step faltered. He made no reply.

Kamal sounded pleased. 'At last. You begin to understand who you're dealing with.'

'You'll never succeed, Kamal.'

'No? And why not? You believe your Western security forces have any hope of preventing it?'

'No,' Ben replied. 'I don't believe they do. You'll never succeed, because I'm going to stop you. You'll be the baddest guy in the graveyard. That's as far as you're going to get. Believe me.'

'Fine speech,' Kamal said. 'Very patriotic.'

'I'm not interested in patriotism,' Ben told him. 'I don't fight under a flag. I don't care about oil or economics or politics, or any of the dirty double-dealing that gives elected gangsters the excuse to bomb someone else's country and call it justice. I was part of that hypocrisy once, and I walked away. But that doesn't mean I'm going to let a damaged little rat's arse like you murder millions of innocent people.'

'I could kill you now,' Kamal said. 'Just for talking to me like that.'

'Then you'd never find your way through the maze of tunnels down there,' Ben replied. 'There are a hundred hidden shafts, and as many false doorways.' It was a wild bluff, but he needed to buy all the time to could to think of a way out of this. 'You could spend years searching. Kill me, and you can kiss your private little jihad goodbye.'

Kamal's voice was tight with fury. 'Fuck you. Keep walking.'

'You're scared, aren't you, Kamal? Scared shitless you're not going to find anything down there. You know that the kind of people you're buying these nukes from aren't going to tolerate you not coming up with the cash. You thought you were the hardest, meanest guy in the world. But now you've done a deal with the devil, and you're pissing your pants.'

Kamal was about to reply when another rumble groaned through the rock around them. A ripping crack echoed through the shaft. In the white torch beam, Ben saw a fissure open up to the width of a man's thumb. Powder and dust cascaded from the ceiling, followed by a stream of small rocks that formed a pile up ahead.

'What was that?' Kamal asked, his fierce self-assurance slipping for an instant.

'Something I forgot to mention,' Ben said over his shoulder as he walked on, kicking rocks out of the way. 'The tunnels are becoming unstable. Your treasure just slipped a little further out of reach.' This time, it was no bluff.

Kamal quickly regained his composure, and laughed darkly. 'Then there's no time to lose. Move faster.'

Emad prodded the rifle hard into Ben's back, shoving him onwards. As they rounded the bend in the tunnel shaft, the giant cavern opened up ahead and the torch beams picked out the shape of the rope bridge.

'Keep moving,' Kamal said.

More dust and stones showered down around them. It was getting steadily worse. Cracks were forming everywhere, slowly widening. The ridge was crumbling, with them inside.

Another painful jab from the AKS behind him, and Ben stepped out onto the bridge. 'I don't know how safe it is for four men to cross,' he said truthfully.

'Walk.'

Ben stepped forwards. The bridge gave a long, juddering creak under the extra weight as Emad followed, then Kamal, then Fekri. Ben held his breath and kept moving. The torch beams bobbed and danced ahead of him, throwing long tubes of light into the dark.

Dangling over a bottomless, spike-filled chasm, outnumbered three to one, unarmed with a gun in his back, no possibility of escape and time fast running out. He was sure he'd been in tougher situations – but he really couldn't remember when.

Just then it got even worse. There was a grinding crack from somewhere high above them, and a huge dark shape hurtled through the beam of light ahead.

It was a falling stalactite, a solid rock spike, as thick as an oak tree, twice the height of a tall man. It narrowly missed the bridge. Seconds later it impacted on the stalagmites below with a roaring crash that shook the cavern and made the bridge sway alarmingly. Ben gripped the ropes at his sides and struggled to keep his footing. Fekri swore in Arabic. His voice was tense and frightened.

Then it happened again. A boulder as big as a large car plummeted not ten feet from where Ben was standing, and he felt the wind as it passed him. Another massive rumbling crash as it shattered into a million pieces on the spikes below. Smaller rocks rained down. A stone the size of a cannonball came crashing out of the darkness above and punched through the wooden slats of the bridge between Ben and Emad. Emad wobbled off balance, almost dropping his weapon as he grappled to stay upright.

Ben felt the impact's shudder running under his feet the whole length of the bridge. He looked down, and in the dim light he saw one of the ancient ropes beginning to unravel. The outer strands splitting, slowly rotating and peeling away; then the next layer, and the next.

That was when he knew they weren't going to make it across.

Crack.

They all looked up.

Fekri screamed.

Another giant stalactite had sheared off and it was plunging straight for them. Ben saw its craggy point looming up fast as it speared downwards. In the instant before it hit, he thrust the Maglite in his belt, looped his arm through the side of the rope bridge and held on tight.

Fekri was staring up, open-mouthed, as the massive spike caught him right in the face. It tore off his jawbone and kept going, lancing through his body, tearing him in two.

Then it crashed straight through the floor of the bridge and parted it like thread.

Ben fell through space. The wind roared in his ears

as he sailed downwards. He had the rope in a death-grip. There was no time to pray, or even to think. Then a stunning impact as the severed bridge came swinging down and hit the wall of the abyss. Ben was winded for a few seconds, and it was all he could do to hang on. He blinked to clear his head and the pain that shot through his whole body.

He slipped the torch out of his belt and shone it upwards, hanging by one hand. The broken bridge had become a wildly swinging rope ladder, and he was dangling from it like a fly caught on a web.

He shone the light downwards, and his heart jolted. Kamal's snarling face was staring up at him. The terrorist had managed to cling on, and he was scaling the rope ladder towards him. Between them, Emad hung limply from the ropes. The impact had smashed his skull. His weapon had dropped into the depths.

Kamal hung by one hand as he grabbed the dead man's belt and tore him forcefully from the ropes. The corpse somersaulted away into the darkness. A crunch as his fall was halted by the point of a stalagmite.

Kamal's teeth were bared in hatred as he kept climbing rapidly upwards, his hands shooting up like pistons, one after the other. He made a grab for Ben's ankle. Ben kicked out for his face, but Kamal dodged the blow. His hand went down to his belt and came up with a combat knife. He slashed at Ben's legs with it. Ben drew his knees up just in time to avoid the blade, lashed out again and caught Kamal's shoulder, driving him down several spars of the bridge. The terrorist screamed in anger and pain. The blade of the knife glinted as he flipped it over endwise in his hand, catching it by the tip between finger and thumb. He drew back his arm and hurled it straight at Ben.

The knife cartwheeled through the air. If it had been travelling horizontally it would have struck with lethal momentum, but the near-vertical trajectory robbed it of most of its kinetic energy and Ben just had time to twist out of its way. The sharp tip clanged and sparked against the rock an inch from his head and then spiralled away into the darkness. Kamal came on, punching and gouging. Ben swung down with the Maglite and caught him on the arm. Kamal cried out. Kept on fighting like a wild animal. The two of them swung crazily over the abyss.

At that moment the ropes gave way with a crack.

They hurtled down, locked together, the wind roaring in their ears.

Two seconds of freefall. Three. Four. Then another crashing impact as Ben felt himself hit a stalactite, narrowly avoiding being impaled by its point. He slid and bounced down its conical length. Rough stone tore at his flesh. Kamal's hands were still locked on to him, punching and gouging frenziedly even as they plummeted to their deaths.

They hit the bottom.

And went plunging underwater with a stunning splash. Dazed by the impact, Ben felt his body go limp. But with the first gulp of cold water he came to his senses and started swimming for his life. Bubbles erupted from his lungs as for an instant he was panicking in the murk, unable to tell which way was up and which was down. Then he realised he was still clutching the precious torch. The light beam sliced through the water and found the surface. He kicked out hard, and let out a wheezing gasp as his head and shoulders burst free of the water.

Kamal broke the surface a few feet away, saw him and swam towards him. His hands closed around Ben's throat. Kicking wildly in the water, Ben lashed out with the torch and felt it connect with something solid. Heard a grunt of pain. He clubbed him again, harder.

Now the current was carrying them along fast, breaking their hold on one another as each man struggled to stay afloat. Another falling rock splashed down violently nearby, sending up a choking wave of spray. Ben coughed and blinked and flailed desperately against the powerful tide. Felt the brutal scrape of rocks as the surging water carried him through a narrow opening and down another tunnel. He went under for a few seconds, and came spluttering back to the surface, shining the Maglite around him.

Then Kamal was splashing violently back towards him. Something glinted gold in the terrorist's hand, came lashing down and caught Ben across the shoulder. An inch to the right, and it would have shattered his collarbone. Kamal raised the weapon up again. It was the gold falcon statuette. Ben blocked the blow, twisted the precious artefact out of his hand and smashed it hard into his ribs. Kamal fell back, gasping.

The current was dangerously fast now, threatening to suck Ben under as swirling eddies grasped and tugged at his legs like the hands of water demons intent on drowning him. He kicked against them with all the strength he had left, but with both hands full it was nearly impossible to swim properly. He didn't dare lose the torch, and he couldn't let go of the gold statue. It was the evidence he needed to save Zara – it meant everything.

Just when he thought he was going under, he felt the hard surface of a rock under him. He clung on to it, dragging himself up out of the water, wheezing and coughing up water. Crouching on the rock with the underground rapids foaming all around him, he shone the light. Saw Kamal's thrashing body carried past the rock. The terrorist's eyes were round with horror as he tried to latch on to the slimy stone. But the water was too powerful. It carried him onwards.

Ben could see where he was heading. These were no ordinary rapids. The underground river was surging into a giant whirlpool, twenty-feet across – a vertical drop funnelling millions of tons of water crashing through its swirling vortex and straight downwards into the earth.

As he watched, Kamal hit the outer current of the vortex, a tiny bobbing figure against the dark water. Foam boiled around the rocks. Where the river had been rushing past them for eons, they were smooth and rounded. But the bits of rock that jutted above the waterline were jagged and sharp, like flint. Kamal's body was slammed into one of them by the furious current. His mouth opened in a scream that was drowned out by the roar of the water. He floated past it. Crashed into another one, and now there was blood on his face and his bared teeth were red. The current carried him on, around and around, faster and faster. Another rock sliced him, then another, and now Kamal wasn't screaming any more. His arms hung limp as the water tossed him and spun him and dashed him off another sharp rock. The foam boiled pink around him.

The terrorist's broken body hit the vortex. Ben caught a last glimpse of his face as the swirling water carried him down the sink-hole. Then he was gone.

It was a long, long time later when Ben finally staggered up the last few yards towards the mouth of the cave. Framed in its jagged arch were the moon and stars that he'd seriously never thought he was ever going to see again.

Exhausted, he collapsed on his hands and knees, leaving bloody prints on the rock from the hundred lacerations that criss-crossed his palms after the endless journey back along the river tunnel. He'd lost count of the number of times the surging current had almost pulled him back in. After that had been the crippling, killing climb back up the wall of the chamber of Sobek. Every muscle in his body screamed out for rest, but he had to keep going.

He struggled to his feet and hobbled out into the night. He let his gaze linger for a moment on Lawrence Kirby's body, then walked on. At the entrance to the cave, hidden in the shadows, he found his phone and pistol still lying where he'd laid them down earlier. He stuck the gun back in his waistband and pocketed the phone, thinking about the precious evidence stored inside it. He glanced down in the moonlight to the glinting statuette that was thrust diagonally in his belt. Ran his fingers along the smooth gold.

Now all he had to do was get out of this desert and back across the Egyptian border alive, then get to a place where he could phone Harry Paxton. He had two days to do it.

He made his weary way down the slope from the cave and walked up the moonlit canyon. He passed the dark shapes of the dead motorcyclists, and the smouldering hulk of the destroyed tank. With every step, he was flinching at the thought that there could be more unexploded mines buried just beneath the sand, waiting for him to tread on them.

A few metres further up the canyon, he paused to gaze regretfully at the flattened remains of the Toyota.

But just around the bend, he came across what he'd been hoping to find. Kamal's black Nissan Patrol glimmered dully under the stars. Ben trotted up to it, wrenched open the driver's door and almost laughed when he saw the key in the ignition. In the back of the vehicle were canteens of water, stores of provisions, tools and spare wheels. The steel jerrycans sloshed when he shook them. He reckoned there was just about enough fuel to get him where he needed to go.

He hauled himself up behind the wheel and drank thirstily from one of the canteens. Leaned back in the seat for a moment, shutting his eyes and letting his relief wash over him. Then he slowly turned and saw what was resting in the passenger footwell.

'My old bag,' he said aloud.

Chapter Fifty-Seven

Ben carved his way north through the night like a man possessed, stopping only to snatch a couple of hours' sleep when he could barely keep his eyes open any longer. The sun burned down viciously all of the next day as he crossed the Sudanese desert plains, and it was night again by the time he finally crossed over the Egyptian border. For a few tense hours he ducked and dodged the path of army border patrols. But even Special Forces would have been hard pressed to notice as he slipped by.

By next morning, the Nissan was overheating and running low on fuel – but it had done its job. He thrashed it mercilessly along proper metalled roads for as many miles as he could eke out of it. As the first signs of greenery in the distance signalled his approach to the Nile valley, the vehicle finally gave out. He abandoned it and started walking.

None of the lorry drivers or livestock transporters who blasted past on the highway would ever have guessed that the lone, dusty wanderer on the verge carried in his battered army haversack more gold than they would ever see in their lives, and the key to a billion-dollar treasure.

By the time Ben saw the first small town in the distance, he'd already got a signal on his phone and was calling Paxton's number.

It was the start of the seventh day.

Things happened quickly after that. Ben bought a cotton shirt and fresh jeans from a clothes stall, found a small hotel and checked into a room. He spent a long time under a cool shower, washing away the sand and sweat and blood. He changed and rested awhile, then wandered back outside with his bag on his shoulder, refreshed and hardly feeling the sun's heat any more. In the winding streets he discovered a little tobacconist and a grocer's stall selling fresh food out of palm-leaf baskets. He settled on a shady wall under a palm tree on the edge of town, and munched on aish bread filled with hummus and smoked a couple of the cigarettes he'd bought.

Not long afterwards, the black Lexus came for him. He offered up his Jericho to the two taciturn men in suits, and they ushered him into the back. After days of harsh desert driving, the smooth, air-conditioned Lexus felt like something out of a different world. Ben rested against the cool leather as the car whisked him the eighty miles north to the nearest airfield.

From there, a light Cessna Mustang jet flew him up the Nile, over Cairo and northwest towards the Mediterranean coast and the port city of Alexandria.

Ben had to admire Paxton's organisation. He'd barely stepped off the plane when another car sped him away across the city. They passed the new Bibliotheca Alexandria, rebuilt two thousand years after the greatest library of the ancient world had been burnt to the ground, and then followed the road up the long jetty of the Eastern Harbour. The car dropped Ben off, and he sat and watched the hundreds of boats passing by across the blue water.

Then, cutting through the busy port traffic, a white motor launch burbled to the pier and its pilot stepped out. He spotted Ben standing on the dock, spoke briefly on a phone, then started walking over.

It was Berg.

Ben's hands were shaking as he walked to meet him.

'Mr Paxton is anxious to meet you again,' Berg grinned.

Ben wanted to rip the look off the man's face. Instead he calmly walked past him up the jetty and stepped down into the launch. He sat in silence as Berg fired up the outboards and piloted the launch skilfully between the fishing boats and out of the harbour. The sea was flat and vivid blue, and the sky was cloudless.

After twenty minutes, a white dot appeared on the horizon and grew steadily larger. The twin-masted cruising yacht was resting serenely at anchor, her graceful ninety-foot hull swaying gently on the rise and fall of the sea. As they came nearer, Ben could make out the name *Eclipse* on the yacht's stern. The vessel was tiny compared to the *Scimitar*, and he couldn't see any crew on her deck as the launch drew up alongside. It looked as though it was just going to be him, Paxton and Berg, all alone.

He waited until the launch was a foot from the yacht's side, grabbed a rail and hauled himself on board. Berg tethered up the launch and followed him on deck, eyeing him coldly.

'So where is he?' Ben asked. 'Let's get this done.'

'Here I am, Benedict,' said a familiar voice, and Ben turned to see Paxton sauntering casually up the companionway from below, a long drink in his hand. He looked cool and relaxed. 'You look as though you've been in the wars.'

'I'm not here for conversation.' Ben reached into his bag, took out the wrapped statuette and tossed it down on the deck with a heavy thud.

Paxton stepped over to pick it up, and smiled when he felt the weight of it in his hand. He started unravelling the dirty cloth.

'It's not lead,' Ben said.

'I'm sure it isn't,' Paxton replied as he yanked away the cloth and the gold caught the sun. He looked up at Ben. 'Magnificent. So it was all true.'

'Yes, Harry, it was all true.'

'Then, for once in his miserable life, Helen's bastard son did something right. And what about the rest?'

'I don't think you'll be disappointed.' Ben took out the phone and tossed it to him. 'I took pictures.'

Paxton quickly found the photos and the video clip, and spent a few moments studying them keenly. Ben could see the same look in his eyes that he'd seen in Kirby's when the gold fever had taken hold of his mind.

Silence across the deck, just the whisper of the sea.

Berg walked around Ben and stood at Paxton's side, gazing impassively at him. Ben ignored him.

Paxton scrolled through the last of the pictures. 'What's this?'

'The map,' Ben replied quietly. 'Drawn thousands of years ago by the High Priest who hid the treasure. You don't want to know the details.'

Paxton frowned. 'This is gibberish. It's all hieroglyphics.'

'Don't get yourself all worked up, Harry.' Ben dipped into his pocket and took out the folded note that he'd written on the plane. Across the top of the headed paper was printed the banner 'Paxton Enterprises'. Underneath, in neat capitals, was Ben's translation of the clues. He handed it to Paxton. 'Now you have everything,' he said.

Paxton's frown melted away as he scanned the note, then folded it. Lying on one of the deck seats nearby was a little leather pouch. He picked it up, slipped the paper into it together with the phone, and closed the zipper. 'Thank you, Benedict. And well done. I knew you wouldn't let me down. I certainly chose the right man for the job.'

'Great. Now where is she?'

'You mean my wife?' Paxton replied with mock innocence.

'We had a deal,' Ben said. 'Remember?'

'I remember,' Paxton said. 'But there's no deal, Benedict.'

Ben shook his head. 'That's not how it works.'

'It works any way I say it does,' Paxton said. 'I'm in control here, not you.'

'Where is she?' Ben said again.

'Somewhere you won't find her,' Paxton said.

Berg grinned.

Ben tried not to look at him. His fists balled at his sides. 'You really are a piece of shit, aren't you, Harry?'

'I told you what I do to people who are disloyal to me,' Paxton said. 'I meant what I said.'

Berg grinned more broadly.

Ben's stomach churned. For a terrible moment the image of the three severed heads danced up in his mind's eye. Then the picture of the mutilated body of Linda Downey. Except he was seeing Zara's face on it. The glassy blue eyes, lifeless and unblinking. Blonde hair matted with dried blood. He tried to shake the image out of his mind, but it stayed there right in the foreground.

He suddenly wanted to vomit. *They'd killed her.* They'd kept her alive long enough to give proof of life, and then slaughtered her.

He closed his eyes and felt himself rocking on his feet. Reached out a hand to steady himself with the rail at his side.

When he opened his eyes, he found himself staring down the muzzles of two pistols. In his right hand Paxton was holding the same 9mm SIG Pro that he'd pointed at Ben in Paris, the leather pouch in his left. Berg was holding a massive Desert Eagle semi-auto with a barrel diameter half an inch across.

'We're going to shoot you,' Paxton said. 'Then we're going to feed your body to the sharks. But, before you die, Berg is going to tell you exactly what he did to my dear wife. In detail.'

Chapter Fifty-Eight

That was it, then. Paxton had beaten him. He should have known. Should never have gone looking for the damned treasure.

'Just shoot me,' he said. 'I don't want to hear.'

'Of course you don't,' Paxton replied with a smile. 'But you're going to nonetheless.' He turned to Berg. 'Come on. Tell our friend what you told me.'

Berg's eyes glittered. He opened his mouth to speak.

Then he stopped. His mouth opened wider, and he drew in a sharp breath. A tremor seemed to run through his body, making him sway on his feet. His eyeballs turned inwards as he tried to focus on the strange object that had suddenly appeared low down in the middle of his forehead.

It was the three-bladed steel triangular point of a hunting arrow, protruding four inches from his skull.

Berg dropped like a tree and landed with a crunch on his face. The Desert Eagle slid across the deck. The slim arrow shaft embedded in the back of his head was still quivering from the impact of the shot.

But Ben wasn't watching Berg any more. He was

staring as Zara emerged from the companionway hatch behind where the man had been standing. In a summery white cotton dress that emphasised her tan, her hair catching the sunlight, she looked even more beautiful than before. In her hand was the bow she'd been shooting the first time he'd ever seen her, and a quiver full of arrows hung at her side. Her eyes caught Ben's.

Ben couldn't speak, couldn't tear his gaze off her. His heart was thudding wildly in his throat. *Zara was alive.* Paxton had been enjoying a sick joke at his expense. He hadn't just wanted Ben to die – he'd wanted him to die in despair.

Paxton twisted around to stare at her, then gaped down at Berg's corpse, incredulous. 'You killed him,' he stammered.

She didn't reply. Instead she drew another arrow out of the quiver and fitted it expertly to the bow.

Ben saw the intent flicker through Paxton's face and the twitch in his muscles before the man even had time to swing his SIG around to aim at her. He dived for Berg's fallen pistol. Saw a clear line of fire and pulled the trigger. The Desert Eagle recoiled harshly. Paxton cried out as the large-calibre slug slammed into the side of his pistol and sent it spinning out of his grip. The leather pouch dropped to the deck as he staggered, clutching his injured hand. Fear in his eyes as Ben aimed the pistol steady at his head. The colonel suddenly looked much older, frail almost.

'Kick the pouch over,' Ben commanded him.

Paxton obeyed. Ben picked it up and stuffed it in

his jeans pocket. 'You're done, Harry. Interpol can have you now. I'm taking you ashore.'

Zara took a step closer, still holding the bow. She shook her head. 'No, Ben.'

He looked at her.

'You're not taking him anywhere,' she said.

Before Ben could react, she swung her bow towards Paxton, drew and shot him at point-blank range.

The arrow whipped across the short distance and caught Paxton in the right shoulder. He screamed in shock and agony. His left hand flew up, grasped the arrow shaft. Tried to pull it out, but the muscles around the wound had clamped it tight. Blood spilled down his silk shirt. He dropped to his knees. 'What are you doing?' he bellowed at her.

'Something I've been waiting to do a long, long time,' Zara replied softly. There was a cold look on her face that Ben had never seen before. Her hand moved quickly, expertly down to the quiver on her belt and she fitted another arrow to the bow. Drew and fired again.

The arrow stabbed into Paxton's left shoulder. Its bloody tip protruded five inches from his shoulder blade.

Ben suddenly understood. She wasn't hitting at random. As a champion archer engaging a large target at extreme close range, she could have hit any spot she wanted. She was deliberately drawing this out, by pure cruelty.

Paxton screamed again and fell back on the deck, writhing in blood, smearing it across the polished wood.

'Zara!' Ben yelled. 'Are you crazy?'

But she wasn't listening. She walked coolly around Paxton as he gaped up at her. The same swift, mechanical movement of hand to quiver to string. She fired again. The arrow lanced through Paxton's thigh and pinned him to the boards. Blood spurted in a fountain from a severed artery. Paxton was past screaming now. His mouth was opening and closing as he went into terminal shock.

'Stop!' Ben pointed the Desert Eagle at her, because he didn't know what else to do. 'That's enough!'

There was already a fresh arrow on Zara's bow. She turned nonchalantly to Ben. 'OK. You're right.'

And then she fired one last shot. The arrow took Paxton in the nostril and drove his head back and thunked into the wood. Paxton twitched as blood spewed from his nose and mouth. His muscles went limp, and he sank down against the deck and died.

The pistol in Ben's hand was shaking as he lowered it. 'What the fuck did you do that for?' he asked breathlessly.

Zara took a step towards him, and he realised there was another arrow fitted to her bow. The quiver was empty now. It was her last shot. And it was for him.

'The pouch,' she said. 'Hand it over.'

Ben was speechless for a moment. Nothing made sense to him any more.

And yet, in a horrible way it did. *What kind of hostage was free to walk about with a lethal weapon?*

'You and he were in it together,' he whispered. 'The whole time.'

Zara sighed. 'It's true, Ben. I'm sorry.'

Thoughts were flooding through his mind so fast that it was making him dizzy. 'But Valentine—'

'Harry knew she was after him,' Zara said. 'We came up with the plan. Or maybe I should say, *I* came up with it. To let them see us fighting in public. Harry slapping my face in the restaurant, me throwing my drink over him and walking out. All staged, to give the impression we were having problems. But they fell for it.' She smiled, shrugged. 'Soon afterwards, Valentine approached me and gave me the whole bit about her girlfriend, Downey, and the poor little Africans that Harry's guns were killing. The whole spiel. A real tear-jerker. So I played along, pretending to be all shocked and horrified.'

'When really you didn't give a shit.'

'I had to win their trust,' she said. 'It was the only way we could make sure we got them all in one place. We had to protect Harry's interests.'

'The man you just killed.'

'That's right. I hated Harry. He was a cruel bastard and a terrible husband. I hated him, but I'd have stayed with him for his money.'

'Wouldn't it have been simpler just to divorce him?'

'He'd have killed me for trying. And even if he hadn't, there was a prenuptial agreement. I would have ended up with nothing.'

'Nothing but your freedom.'

'You think I hadn't thought about it? But then you came along, Ben. You changed everything. When I met you, that's when I started looking for a way to ditch him. I was only sorry that I had to lie to you. I never wanted that to happen.'

Ben said nothing. There was nothing to say. A cold chill had settled in his stomach.

'I want the treasure, Ben. I've wanted it ever since Morgan got drunk that night aboard the *Scimitar*.' She snorted. 'Typical man, trying to show off to a woman he fancied and compete with his father at the same time. It was so easy to get him talking. I just kept pouring the drink down his stupid throat, and made sure he could see down my top. Works every time.'

'So you were just using everyone. Like you used me. Everything you told me was a lie. There was never anything between us.'

She shook her head. 'That's not true. When I told you I loved you, I meant it. I want us to be together.'

'You love me, but you'd let me believe you were a hostage? You'd knowingly put me through that?'

'What can I say? I had no choice. I had to find a way.'

'To get what you wanted.'

'For us.' Her eyes brightened with excitement. 'For you and me.'

'What if I'd been killed?'

'Not you. Not so easily. I knew you'd come back.'

'While you just spent the week relaxing, working on your tan with a cool drink at your elbow.'

She looked hurt. 'It hasn't been easy for me. Smiling at that bastard, keeping him happy, pretending everything was all right when I couldn't wait to see you again. We've done it. We're free now. We'll be rich.

What Harry had was peanuts compared to what we'll have. Think of all the things we can do. The life we'll be able to lead together.'

'So you and I run away into the sunset with the gold. Is that how you see it?'

She laughed. 'Why not? Why can't it be that simple? What's to stop us? I love you. And you love me.' Her smile wavered. 'You do love me, don't you?'

He let out a long sigh. 'Yes. I love you.'

'Then let's be together,' she said. 'Like we talked about that night in Paris.'

Ben was silent.

'Well? Aren't you going to answer me?'

'Forget it, Zara. It's over.'

'Please, Ben. I need you.'

'You're insane,' he said. 'I can't understand what kind of monster you are.' He pointed down at Paxton's body. 'You're worse than him. I love you, but I hate you.'

Her face seemed to twist. Her teeth bared a little, and the sparkle in her eye went dull. 'Fine. If that's the way you want it. I've always been alone. I'll survive.'

As she said it, she hooked three fingers onto the bowstring and the sinews in her forearm tightened as she drew her hand back to anchor against her cheek. The arrow shaft scraped softly back into firing position on its launcher. The thick glass fibre limbs of the bow tensed, cam wheels rotating, cables tightening, loading vast amounts of energy behind the razor-sharp arrowhead that was pointing right at his heart.

'You'd shoot me?' he said.

Her knuckles were white on the handle of the bow

as she held it at full draw. She nodded. 'I gave you the chance to share the treasure with me. To share a life with me. You didn't want it. Your choice. I'm sorry, but you're not giving me any other way out.'

'You could turn yourself in. Try and make some amends for what you've done.'

She laughed. 'Get real.'

He raised the heavy pistol and squared the sights right on her, centre of mass. Her laugh froze on her lips. Confusion flashed in her eyes.

'Now it gets more complicated,' he said. 'I've got two pounds of pressure on this trigger. You put that arrow in me, and all it takes is a tiny squeeze as my muscles go into a spasm. Just an ounce. And you'll be dead at the same instant as me. We both hit the floor at the same time. No more treasure for you.'

She didn't reply. They circled each other.

'Now you have a choice,' he said. 'Put the bow down, face the consequences. Or I'll shoot.'

'You wouldn't.'

He pulled the trigger. The Desert Eagle boomed and recoiled in his hand. The crack of the shot echoed out to sea.

Zara screamed and fell back. The arrow clattered harmlessly down, unfired. The string and cables hung loose from the bow, all the tension gone out of it. The cam wheel that Ben had shot off the end of its top limb bounced and rolled across the boards like a huge coin.

Zara lay on the deck, still clutching the shattered bow and weeping with shock and rage.

Ben let the pistol down at his side. Reached into his

pocket and took out the little leather pouch. Drew back his arm and hurled it far out to sea. It sailed up in the air, just a dark dot against the sun, and dropped down and hit the water with a splash.

Then he walked over to where Paxton had set down the gold statuette. He picked it up, walked to the rail and lobbed it over the side. A last glitter, and it was gone. Maybe in another few centuries, some lucky diver would find it on the sea bed.

'There goes your treasure,' he said to Zara. 'It's over. Finished. Was it worth it?' He reached out his hand, took her arm and pulled her gently to her feet.

Her tear-filled eyes searched his. Her hair was wild, jaw tight. 'Now I have nothing,' she said bitterly. 'You've ruined me. Left me without a penny.'

'I think you ruined things for yourself, Zara.'

She hung her head in despair. 'What are you going to do with me?'

He paused a long time before replying. Watched her face. The kind of feelings he had for her didn't just go away. They wouldn't go away for a long time.

'You know I could never harm you,' he said.

'Don't turn me in,' she pleaded. 'I'd die. I couldn't live in jail.'

'Who'd believe me?' he said. 'It would be your word against mine. You and Harry covered your tracks well. Now he's dead. You're free. And I'm gone.'

'No, Ben. Don't go.'

He turned his back on her and started walking towards the rail. Beyond it, the motor launch was bobbing gently on the swell.

He put a hand on the rail and was about to swing his leg over the side, when she ran after him and gripped his arm tightly. Her cheeks were streaked with tears. 'Stay with me,' she murmured. She came up close to him and stroked his face. The touch of her fingers was tender and warm, and for a moment he almost gave in to it. Emotion rose up in him.

Those kinds of feelings didn't just go away.

But they would, in time. He swallowed hard, and pulled away from her.

'Goodbye, Zara.'

'Ben—' Her voice cracked into a sob of pain.

He didn't reply. Zara watched forlornly as he climbed down into the launch and cast off.

Twenty yards from the yacht, he looked back and saw the lonely figure at the rail, staring after him, the breeze blowing in her hair. The sun was beginning to set behind her.

He didn't look back again.

Epilogue

The rain was lashing down out of a starless sky as Ben got out of the Mini and crossed the puddled yard to the house. The place seemed empty and desolate as he climbed the steps to the front door, opened it and went inside. He wearily hung up his jacket, and walked down the dark passage towards the kitchen door.

As he reached out his hand to turn the handle, he stopped and looked down, noticing the strip of light under the door. He walked in.

'Hello, Ben,' Brooke said. She was sitting reading in the soft glow of a lamp. She laid the novel face-down on the table and watched him for a moment. 'You're home.'

He pulled up a wooden chair and sat down in it with a sigh.

Brooke got up quietly. Fetched a glass from the cupboard and filled it with wine. Without a word, she brought it over to him and set it down in front of him.

'Yeah,' he said. 'I'm home.'

Author's Note

As a historical figure, the pharaoh Akhenaten may lack the glamour and romance of a Ramses or a Tutankhamun, but no other ancient Egyptian ruler is as bizarre or shrouded in mystery. The strange story of Akhenaten has been retold many times – the famous British crime novelist Agatha Christie wrote a play about him, modern composer Philip Glass has written an opera, and for fans of Death Metal there is even a song by the band Nile called 'Cast down the Heretic'.

There have been many weird and wonderful theories surrounding this enigmatic king: building on the hypothesis of the famous psychologist Sigmund Freud that Moses might have been a follower of Akhenaten, some historians have proposed that Moses and Akhenaten might actually be one and the same. Going still further into the realms of fantasy, there have even been suggestions that Akhenaten was *not of this earth*. Certainly, anyone who has seen his likeness will testify to the man's distinctly odd, alien appearance.

But whoever – or whatever – Akhenaten might have been, his claim to fame was his legendary attempt to replace the state religion of ancient Egypt with one of his own devising, the so-called Aten cult. This is the first monotheistic religion on record, and had Akhenaten succeeded in making it stick, he would have altered the face of his homeland forever. Unfortunately for him, his religious coup was destined to abject failure. Almost immediately after his death, Egypt reverted to the old polytheistic religion and no effort was spared to eradicate all trace of the despised heretic and pretend he never existed.

Most of the historical background in this novel is based firmly on actual facts. The three rebel priests who conspired to steal the condemned treasures from under Akhenaten's nose are entirely fictitious – though I believe that, given what the wayward pharaoh was up to and the degree of hatred and resentment he stirred up, it's not wildly beyond the mark to suggest that such a 'heist' might have been planned or even taken place. After all, so little is known about that time – scholars are even unable to agree on the exact dates of Akhenaten's reign. With amazing new discoveries being made each year, who knows what secrets the desert sands may yield up in the future?

I hope you enjoyed reading *The Heretic's Treasure*. Ben Hope will return again!

Scott Mariani

Read on for an exclusive extract from Scott Mariani's new novel, coming in 2010.

Chapter One

The Sonoran Desert
An hour's drive from Maricopa, Arizona
Early May

Rock and dust, scrub and cactus, and the blinding white sun beating down. Nobody ever came out here.

The dust from two offroad vehicles drifted upwards into the still air as they bounced and lurched across the arid wilderness. The big silver Subaru 4x4 in front crunched to a halt on the stones, the doors opened and three men got out.

One of them didn't want to be there. He stood out from the other two, and not just because he was the only Japanese guy and they were white Europeans. He was also the only one with a .45 auto to the back of his head and his wrists bound behind his back. Tape, not cord. Cord would leave a mark, and his captors didn't want that. A length of the same silver duct tape was pressed firmly to his face, muffling his protests. The T-shirt he was wearing was damp with sweat.

His captors knew his name was Michio Miyazaki,

and that he was a scientist. Beyond that, it wasn't their concern.

The bright red Jeep Cherokee following the Subaru pulled up alongside. Its driver was the only woman in the group. She killed the engine, stepped down, ran her fingers through her dark hair and wiped the sweat on her jeans. There was no sound in the stillness except the ticking of hot metal and the feeble protests of the prisoner as the two men started marching him away from the vehicles.

The woman walked around to the passenger side of the Jeep, opened the door and lifted out the small container she'd been uncomfortably riding beside through the desert. The Jeep was Miyazaki's, and it had a lot of his own equipment in the back; crates and cases filled with scientific gear.

The container wasn't his, though. It belonged to the group, and had its own reason for being there. It was a pale blue plastic lunch box, with tiny air holes pricked in the top. What was inside weighed almost nothing. The woman held it away from her body at arm's length. With her other hand she grabbed a shoulder bag from the footwell, then shut the Jeep door and trotted to catch up with the others. As she joined them she could hear the prisoner pleading with them incoherently through his gag.

They all ignored him.

'This'll be fine,' said the taller, leaner of the two white men, glancing around him. The stocky guy with the muscles under his cotton shirt kept the .45 aimed at Miyazaki's head.

The woman set the container down on the ground and stepped back, happy to get some distance from it. She reached into the shoulder bag and pulled out a pair of thick leather gauntlets. Tossed the right glove to her colleague, then the left. 'You do it,' she said. 'I'm not touching that thing.'

The tall, lean guy pulled on the gloves. The one with the gun swept his foot out and Miyazaki crumpled on his back into the dirt. He was crying now, tears streaking the dust on his face.

The tall man walked over to the container and squatted down beside it. The others watched as, very carefully, he unsnapped the lid, lifted a corner, peered inside, dipped his gloved hand into the container and stood up with the thing in his fist.

Miyazaki started struggling and protesting all over again when he saw the glistening brown scorpion trapped between the man's fingers. He'd spent his life deeply involved in one small specialised corner of science, but he had enough knowledge of other disciplines to know that these people had done their research well. This was an Arizona bark scorpion, one of the most lethal arachnids on the planet.

Miyazaki couldn't take his eyes off it as the tall man walked towards him with a smile. He struggled against his bonds as the scorpion came closer and closer. He could see it wriggling, the long tail lashing out, the stinger turgid with venom. Now it was right over him, six inches above his heaving chest. He could feel his heart pounding dangerously fast.

Then the man dropped it on him.

The scorpion landed on its feet and froze, as if cautiously assessing its new surroundings. Miyazaki began to gibber, chin on chest, every muscle in his body racked tight as he strained to see the thing that was perched on his body.

But the scorpion was more interested in flight. It scuttled away, slithered down his ribs and dropped down onto the sand.

'Shit.' The tall man stepped quickly over to where the creature was trying to dig itself in, and scooped it up. Sand ran out from between his fingers as he clenched the scorpion tightly in his palm.

Miyazaki was wild with terror, but nobody was listening to him.

'Try again,' the woman said.

The tall man nodded. He admired the creature. These things were tough. They'd been around for millions of years, unchanged, perfect. And they'd still be around long after humankind had been obliterated by nuclear war. He didn't want to harm it, just to stress it a little and activate its primal defence mechanisms. He squeezed hard and gave it a shake, feeling its hard carapace wriggle through the glove. Then he held it over Miyazaki's exposed neck, where sweat was pooling in the hollow at the base of his throat, and let it drop a second time.

This time the creature landed on Miyazaki's skin with its defences on full alert, poised to strike. The stinger lashed out, faster than a rattlesnake, and found its mark.

The scientist screamed behind the tape and thrashed on the sand as the creature scuttled away. His captors could see where the scorpion had got him, a livid pin-prick already swelling on his neck three-quarters of an inch from the main artery.

'That should do it,' the woman said over the muffled cries of terror.

'Gonna kill the fucking thing now,' said the stocky guy, watching the scorpion as it ran towards the cover of the rocks. He pointed the pistol.

The woman slapped his arm down. 'No shooting.'

'Yeah, leave it be,' the tall one said.

The stocky guy gave a shrug and put the pistol away. They looked down at the prisoner. His movements were already slowing, eyes rolling back in his head as the toxic shock started shutting down his weak heart. After another minute he wasn't convulsing or kicking any more. His arched back sank down against the sand, his head lolled to one side and stayed there.

The tall man kneeled down next to the body and used a clasp knife to cut the tape from the dead man's wrists, then ripped away the gag.

'Now let's dress this thing up how it's meant to look,' the woman said.

The Picos de Europa mountain range
Northern coast of Spain
Two days later

The killers set out early. Seven in the morning, the low sun glinting over the rocky peaks. They'd driven up the mountain until they ran out of track. It was a long way down to the tree line. The cold breeze buffeted the van and made it hard to open the door. The woman stepped down from the vehicle, and shivered. Reaching for the Minolta binoculars that hung from her neck, she scanned the mountainside, up, down, left and right. Saw nothing but rocks and shrubs.

Her two colleagues got out and walked around the van to join her. 'OK?' the tall man asked her without a smile.

'Let's get it done.' She stepped over to the back of the van and opened up the doors.

Julia Goodman blinked as the sunlight hit her eyes. Her heart was in her mouth and her hands wouldn't stop shaking. She knew what was coming. She'd known it for days. Just not how they'd do it.

'Let's go,' the woman said.

'Please.' Julia had repeated that word so often, it seemed to have lost all meaning. But all she could do was to keep saying it and hope. Her eyes brimmed with tears. '*Please.*'

The woman looked impassive.

'I'm so sorry.' Julia had been saying that a lot, too. 'I'm sorry I couldn't make it work. I—'

'Save your breath. We don't care.'

With a last glance around them, the two men dragged her out of the van. Julia struggled and kicked, but they held her tight and her cries vanished in the wind.

The woman walked around to the side door, slid it open and yanked out the quilted jacket, the hiking boots, the rucksack. Everything inside it had been checked and double-checked, right down to the keys to the blue Renault Espace that had been leased in the university lecturer's name two months earlier. The Renault had already been transported to a hidden storage nearby. By the time the accident was reported, the car would be up here waiting for the police to find it and trace the leaseholder.

Again, they'd thought of everything. They always did; every detail. It was what they were paid for.

The woman carried the gear over to Julia and dumped it all at her feet. 'Put it on.'

Julia obeyed, weeping uncontrollably and shaking so badly she could barely tie the bootlaces. 'Please,' she kept saying. 'Please.'

'You want to die some other way?'

'I don't want to die,' she sobbed. She collapsed to her knees, crying bitterly, and sank down to the stony ground. 'I don't.'

The men yanked her up by the arms and held her body steady as the woman grabbed the rucksack and looped the straps around her arms, then walked round to her front and did up the fastenings. Julia was sagging at the knees, too weak to fight them, making little whimpering sounds.

'See?' the woman told her. 'If you don't fight it, it'll be much easier.'

Twenty yards from where they were parked, the ground sloped sharply down to the edge of the precipice. The woman and the two men kept a tight hold of Julia as they walked her in that direction. With every step, they could feel her tensing.

'Please don't do this,' Julia said desperately. 'I'll keep

trying. I'll work harder. I can make it work. Give me another chance. Some more time. I—'

'Shut it,' the tall man commanded, and she did.

Then, with a sudden surge of energy, she ripped free of their grip. The stocky guy made a grab for her hair. She lashed out with a hiking boot, and he yelled in pain as the steel toecap caught his shin. Then she was dashing away from them, scrambling over the rocks.

She didn't get far before they caught up with her again and dragged her back. Ten yards to the edge. Five. Three. A sheer, vertiginous, thousand-foot drop below. The wind was whipping her hair across her face, where it was sticking to the stream of tears. She let out a cry when she looked down. Objects down below looked very small.

'Nice view from up here,' said the stocky guy, still grimacing with the pain in his shin. Then three strong pairs of hands shoved her hard down the slope towards the edge. She lost her footing and stumbled and rolled, grasping for stones and rocks, anything that would halt her momentum as she slithered towards the drop. Her fingertips found a crack, and suddenly she'd stopped sliding and was dangling with her legs in space. Her eyes were crazed, teeth bared, her breathing rapid.

'Damn,' the woman breathed. 'Why do they always make things difficult?'

'Don't let me fall,' Julia implored them. 'Help me. Please. Don't let me die.'

'Could just leave her,' the tall man said. 'She won't hang on forever.'

The woman shook her head. 'I want to see her go

over.' She thought about the options. Too risky to scramble down the slope towards the edge and kick her hands loose. A long stick would work, but there wasn't one around. She saw a jagged stone and picked it up. Hefted it in her hand. It was about the right size and weight.

'No,' Julia quavered in a high-pitched voice.

The woman lobbed the stone. It caught Julia on the cheekbone. She let go and went tumbling into empty space with a guttural shriek that died away as she spun and cartwheeled down to the rocks below.

Four long, drawn-out seconds later, the scream was cut short along with Julia Goodman's life.

Then the woman and the two men returned calmly, quietly, to the van, thinking about what to do with the rest of the day.

Chapter Two

Le Val Tactical Training Facility
Near Valognes, Normandy
Six weeks later

Ben Hope was sitting at his desk facing a mountain of papers, letters, contracts, insurance policies and bank statements, feeling impatience mounting up inside him after a long, boring afternoon and wanting to dash the whole lot to the floor when his radio beeped and the guy on the security gate informed him that the first of the new clients had arrived.

A few seconds later, a gleaming black Porsche Boxster drove fast into the yard. It circled between the buildings and let out two long blasts of its horn.

'Here comes Rollickin Holligan,' said Jeff Dekker from his desk on the opposite side of the office, looking at his watch. 'Right on time.' Jeff was a former officer with the British Army's Special Boat Service regiment, and Ben's right-hand man at the Le Val training school.

Ben threw a glance at his friend and felt like saying

something about respecting clients – but then he kept his mouth shut. The truth was, he didn't like Rupert Shannon any more than Jeff did, and had been glad that almost two whole months had passed without the guy turning up. But business was business, and the ex-Paras captain and his new six-man bodyguard team had booked Le Val for an intensive two-day refresher course in VIP close protection after landing some new contract in Switzerland. That was what Ben did, pass on his special skills to men like Shannon, so that vulnerable people would be kept safe and protected. It didn't matter what he thought about the guy.

Ben and Jeff got up from their desks and walked over to the window.

'I was getting bored of paperwork anyway,' Jeff said.

'Me too. Hate it.'

The two men stood shoulder to shoulder at the window and watched as the Porsche parked up forty yards away from the office building. The early evening sunlight glittered off its sleek bodywork and tinted windows. The driver's door swung open and Rupert Shannon climbed out wearing aviator shades, a shiny black leather jacket and a wide grin. The breeze ruffled his sandy hair and he quickly patted it back into place as he glanced around the yard.

Standing next to Ben at the window, Jeff shook his head. 'Will you take a look at this guy? If the fucker was made of chocolate, he'd eat himself.'

Ben was about to head for the door to go out and greet their arrival, when the Porsche's passenger door opened and Shannon's companion got out.

'Shit,' Jeff muttered. 'I had a feeling she'd be with him.'

Ben followed Jeff's gaze and saw Dr Brooke Marcel walk around the side of the car. Her thick auburn hair was tied loosely back from her face, and she was wearing jeans and a plain white T-shirt that hugged her slim figure. She looked as good as she always did, but today Ben thought he could see a frown on her face, a certain self-consciousness in her body language. She looked down at her feet a couple of times as she followed Shannon across the yard towards the office building. Seemed to be trailing behind, holding back. It wasn't like her.

'Why is Brooke here?' Ben asked. 'She's not needed for this course. This is purely practical. Shannon doesn't need lectures in hostage psychology.'

Jeff didn't say anything.

'And what's she doing with him?' Ben added.

Jeff snorted in disgust. 'Can't you tell?'

'They're –'

'Yup. Looks like it. They're an item.'

'Since when?'

'Not sure. Since the last course, I think. I'd noticed they were spending a lot of time together. I was going to tell you. Must have slipped my mind. Or maybe I just didn't want it to happen. Denial, or something.'

Ben watched her approach. Brooke Marcel. Expert in hostage psychology, with an alphabet of letters after her name. Based in London, she'd spent years consulting to specialised police and military units, but was recently spending more and more time lecturing at Le Val. She was thirty-four, maybe thirty-five. He suddenly realised that maybe he didn't know her as well as he'd thought.

'No reaction?' Jeff asked.

'Not my business.'

'Come on. There's always been something between you two. All those nights sitting together in the kitchen, drinking, listening to music. Going for walks. Don't act like you just don't care.'

'There's never been anything going on between me and Brooke. Only in your head.'

'I don't know what she sees in that pumped-up twit, anyway. You're more her type.'

Ben ignored that. 'He is what he is, but he's paying a lot of money for this course.'

'I get it. You want me to be nice to the bastard.'

'Too much to ask?'

Jeff kept his eyes on Shannon and thought about it. 'I think it might be, yeah.'

This time Ben said it. 'Remember what we agreed, Jeff. At Le Val we always respect our clients, no matter what. OK?' But he didn't like the lecturing way it came out.

'Even the arseholes.'

'Especially the arseholes.' Ben walked over to the door, opened it and stepped out just as Shannon reached the building. Jeff followed him outside, muttering something that Ben didn't catch.

Shannon's grin broadened as he greeted them. He was a big guy, four inches taller than Ben at six-three, probably fifty pounds heavier, about five years younger.

He raised his hand to his face and whipped off the aviator shades. 'Ciao Jeff, Ciao Benjamin,' he said loudly. 'How's it going, boys?'

'It's Benedict, not Benjamin. And you can call me Ben.' It wasn't a great start.

Shannon grunted. 'Whatever. Benedict, Benjamin, Ben, it's all the same to me.'

Ben could feel Jeff bristling beside him. He threw him a quick warning glance. *Respect the client, no matter what.*

Brooke came up behind Shannon. 'Hey, Ben,' she said softly, and smiled.

'Hi, Brooke.' Ben patted her arm affectionately, like he always did. Shannon noticed it, and cleared his throat. 'The rest of the guys should be arriving soon,' he said.

'Fine. The accommodation's ready for you all.' Ben pointed over at the low-slung trainees' block, across the yard from the main farmhouse.

'I won't be kipping here,' Shannon said. He put a big arm around Brooke's shoulders and pulled her tightly against his side. 'Us two are booked into the Cour Du Chateau. This little lady deserves a bit more luxury than this old place has to offer.'

'That's miles away,' Ben said.

Shannon grinned. 'I'll be here sharp and early in the morning. Always punctual.'

'Nice wheels, Rupert,' Jeff said dryly, motioning at the Porsche.

Shannon's eyes twinkled. 'Oh yes. I've hit the fucking jackpot this time.'

'So this would be the contract you were telling me about,' Ben said.

Shannon nodded. 'You don't know the half of it, Benjamin. Steiner Industries. Protecting the head honcho himself. Maximilian Steiner. The guy's a billionaire, for Christ's sakes. Seriously loaded. Have I hit paydirt, or what? He's paying one point two mill for this gig. And there's more to come. A shit load more. You should see the place we're going.'

'Congratulations, Rupert,' Ben said. 'Looks like this new business venture of yours is taking off already.'

'You bet your arse it is. And this is just the beginning, pal. I've been looking at new offices. Docklands, right on the river, three floors. PA, receptionists, you name it, the works.'

'Here's my advice, though,' Ben said. 'I know you're flush from getting this Steiner contract. That's great. I'm pleased for you. But take it easy. Don't go mad with it. This is a tough business, and you never know what's round the corner.'

Shannon reddened. 'Listen to this guy. Are you for real, Hope?'

'I just meant, be careful, that's all. Don't go spending it all at once, before you've even earned it.'

Shannon laughed and slapped him on the arm. 'You sound like my fucking nanny. You know what your problem is? You're getting old and slow.'

'Forty next birthday,' Ben said. 'Be dead soon. Can't remember the last time I went running.'

'Fucking forty,' Shannon guffawed. 'Five years from

now you'll be just another flabby-arsed, ulcer-ridden businessman sitting behind a desk.'

'You might be right,' Ben said. Now he could sense indignation radiating from Jeff Dekker in waves.

Shannon wrapped his arm around Brooke, squeezed her again and grinned down at her. 'Whatever. Now why don't we see about heading back to the hotel and grab some nosh?'

'Any plans for tomorrow?' Ben asked her.

She shrugged. 'Not really.'

'We'll be doing kidnap simulation exercises in the morning. How'd you feel about coming along and playing the principal?'

'That would be fun.' She smiled. 'Looking forward to it.'

THE DOOMSDAY PROPHECY

SCOTT MARIANI

A deadly conspiracy ... An ancient prophecy ... A race to prevent Armageddon ...

When ex-SAS operative Ben Hope decided to give up rescuing kidnap victims in favour of the Theology studies he abandoned years before, he should have known that fate would decide differently.

Searching for missing biblical archaeologist Zoë Bradbury, Ben finds himself embroiled in his riskiest mission yet. What is the ancient secret that Zoë uncovered? And just who is willing to do anything to protect it?

The investigation leads Ben from Greece to the American Deep South and the holy city of Jerusalem, and he soon discovers that it's not just his and Zoë's lives on the line, but those of millions, threatened by a fundamentalist plot to gain ultimate power. The stakes are terrifyingly high as Ben races to prevent a disaster that could kick-start apocalyptic events as foretold by the Book of Revelation ...

A thrilling, high-octane race to save civilisation that will engross fans of Dan Brown and Sam Bourne.

ISBN: 978-1-84756-080-3

Out now.

THE MOZART CONSPIRACY

SCOTT MARIANI

An ancient murder . . . A clandestine society . . . A conspiracy that will end in death . . .

Ben Hope is running for his life.

Enlisted by the beautiful Leigh Llewellyn – the beautiful opera star and Ben's first love - to investigate her brother's mysterious death, former SAS operative Ben finds himself caught up in a centuries-old puzzle.

Officially Oliver died in a tragic accident whilst investigating Mozart's death, but the facts don't add up. His research reveals that Mozart, a notable freemason, may have been killed by a shadowy splinter group of the cult. The only clues lie in an ancient letter, believed to have been written by the composer himself.

When Leigh and Ben receive video evidence of a ritual sacrifice being performed, they realise that the sect still exists – and will stop at nothing to keep its secrets.

From the dreaming spires of Oxford to Venice's labyrinthine canals, the majestic architecture of Vienna and Slovenia's snowy mountains, Ben and Leigh must forget the past and race across Europe to uncover the truth behind

THE MOZART CONSPIRACY . . .

An electrifying and utterly gripping must read for fans of Dan Brown, Sam Bourne and Ludlum's *Bourne* series.

ISBN: 978-1-84756-080-3

Out now.